LAST KISS
IN
TIANANMEN SQUARE

LISA ZHANG WHARTON

ISBN-13: 978-0615567624

(Fantasy Island Book Publishing)

ISBN-10: 0615567622

Credits

Front Cover © Lisa Zhang Wharton

Senior Editor: Pamela Brennan

Structural Editor: J. Darroll Hall

Front Cover Artist: Jake Riggle

Contact us at: www.fantasyislandbookpublishing.com

Dedicated to my husband, Eric Wharton, who has provided invaluable support.

To my son, William Wharton, who has provided constant amusement. His confidence in me has prompted me to finish this book.

To my parents, Kaiming Zhang and Meizhen Cheng, who have raised me in an unusual and story-worthy environment.

Dear Reader,

Please note that throughout this novel Peking University will often be referred to by its common name Beijing University and its colloquial name Beida

PROLOGUE

At dawn on April 22, 1989, Tiananmen Square awakened as the sun lit the sky.

Hundreds of students who had camped in the Square overnight came to life. They were waiting to pay their last respects to Hu Yaobang, a member of the political bureau, and former Secretary General of the Communist Party. The students wanted to voice their demands for a more free and open society. They wanted to continue what Hu Yaobang had started campaigning three years earlier: a free press and a multi-party system of government.

Police soon systematically cleared the vast space in front of the Great Hall of the People, where the memorial service was going to be held, but more and more citizens joined the peaceful demonstration as the rising sun shone in the eastern sky.

They remained silent and watched with some contempt as the police stopped traffic to let a dozen red-flagged passenger cars carrying the top communist leaders solemnly enter the Square.

The radios in some students' hands announced the start of the service, and the crowd began inching forward.

More police rushed out of the gate of the Great Hall of the People, brandishing clubs. The crowd shouted and cursed at the police, who linked their arms and barely managed to stop the sea of angry people.

"Wait. Be quiet. Please! We are sending our representatives in first," announced an apparent student leader through a megaphone.

Three student representatives, wearing white shirts and black armbands on their left arms (following the Chinese tradition: of a black armband on the left arm, indicating the deceased was a male. Wearing it on the right arm meant the deceased was a female) for the death of Hu Yaobang, appeared and knelt in the middle of the steps leading to the gate of the Great Hall of the People.

They waited to be led in. Each carried a piece of folded black cloth, which contained a list of their requests:

1. Authorities guarantee their safety
2. Let them enter the Great hall of the People to pay their last respects to Hu Yaobang.
3. Allow the Free Press
4. Install a multi-party system of government

Hours passed before the first representative, a young woman with short hair, fell down from heat and hunger. Then the tall and thin teenage girl collapsed. The last one, a short but muscular young man held up until the service finished.

The gate of the Great Hall of the People did not open. No one came out to take their requests. It was rumored that the officials had escaped through the back doors after the memorial service.

"If I had a cannon, I would have destroyed that Hall," one student said.

CHAPTER 1

The day Baiyun heard that Hu Yaobang was dead she knew a volcano would erupt.

It was Sunday afternoon. Baiyun's forty-six year old mother, Meiling, had shut herself in the bedroom with her boyfriend.

Baiyun was initially unaware of the activity in the next room when she came home, until she recognized their loud voices behind Meiling's bedroom door.

Meiling's voice penetrated through the door, "Am I right? Did that little bitch try to seduce you yesterday? Don't think I am blind!"

"Come on. That's absolutely not true. Don't be suspicious all the time." Baiyun recognized the deep voice as that of Meiling's new boyfriend, Lao Zheng.

Meiling and Lao Zheng purchased an industrial construction business last year and had been working together ever since.

"I just want to keep an eye on you," said Meiling.

Baiyun did not like Lao Zheng. Ever since Baiyun's mother broke up with her long-term boyfriend, a factory worker whom she used to call Uncle Weiming, Baiyun had had a hard time accepting anyone else. Baiyun had thought of Uncle Weiming as if he was her father.

Baiyun had a deep affection for Uncle Weiming ever since she met him when she was seven years old. It deepened as time went on. Just recently, it dawned on her that the affection she felt toward him might be more than the love between a father-and a daughter. She began to think of him as a lover. She actually managed to find his address and paid a visit to his apartment. However, she came back empty-handed because he was married with a young daughter.

So now, she was still nursing her broken heart, but she was too embarrassed to tell others.

This episode made Baiyun realize that she was too old to think of her mother's new boyfriends as uncles or stepfathers, especially since most of them were not much older than Baiyun.

To Meiling, Baiyun had become a rival.

Baiyun tried to deal with Meiling's new boyfriends diplomatically. After all, they had added some spice to the family's dull life after her real father's 'injury', when he returned from a labor camp, where he had to serve time during the Cultural Revolution.

Baiyun never spent enough time at home to fall in love with any of them anymore. At least, she hoped this was the case.

In order not to disturb Meiling, Baiyun tiptoed to the refrigerator and took out a Square of Spam, a dishful of stir-fried liver and a few steamed sesame buns.

While she was heating the food in the kitchen, Meiling stuck her head outside her bedroom door and yelled, "Hey, my college girl is home."

"Hi, Mother. Is it all right if I eat this food in the fridge?"

"Oh, yes. Your Uncle Lao Zheng made that especially for you. You should eat it up so you'll be big and strong."

"Mother. Stop! My classmates are calling me little fat girl. I need to lose weight."

"Nonsense. Who says fat is ugly? Look at those American movie stars." Meiling pointed to the movie star calendar on the wall, "They all have full bodies and beautiful big breasts. Skinny means sexless. Which of your classmates can afford such nice food at home? They are jealous of you!" Meiling disappeared behind the bedroom door.

Baiyun carried the heated food to the room that served as both her father's bedroom and the family living room.

It looked the same as when Baiyun left for college three years before. Her parents had added only one piece of furniture, a tall dresser with a full-sized mirror, which was in the corner. A heavy wooden desk was located by the window

4

in the other corner, and a round glass dining table dominated the center of the room.

On the far side of the room, an old man with a head of snowy hair lay on a single bed. A corner of a large dirty floral blanket covered his belly. His head tilted toward one side of the pillow where his dripping saliva created a dark water stain. His face was red and wrinkled and resembled a rotten apple. An arm hung loosely over the side of the bed. He wore a faded green sweat-stained shirt and gray cotton underwear. On the bed rail rested his two extraordinarily ugly feet, dry and covered with blisters.

Meow! Meow!" Father mumbled as though still enjoying the taste of wine in his dream.

Baiyun did not like her family much, especially after she found out that most of her classmates in college had far more normal family lives than she had.

Lately her father had started making cat noises, which felt like a knife cutting through her nerves every time she heard it. She often thought of running away, but how could she? The country was vast, but the people were mostly caged in like chickens.

Recently the government allowed people to leave the country and to go to America if they could pass the TOFEL exam, which allowed foreign students to gain admission into the American college system.

Baiyun had been studying English and getting ready to leave as soon as she could. America was definitely a place far enough to escape, she often told herself.

Baiyun ignored her father and sat down at the round dining table. First, she put two spoonfuls of tender and delicious fried liver into her bowl, followed by a thin piece of Spam. She spread out the 'China Daily', the only English language newspaper in Beijing, next to it. She indulged in her two biggest joys in life, eating and reading.

She read about Hu Yaobang's memorial service and the students' peaceful demonstration in Tiananmen Square. She remembered Hu Yaobang's resignation as the Communist Party General Secretary and the Chairman of China in 1987. Along with his friend and comrade Deng Xiaoping, he not only supported the free market reforms that Deng Xiaoping had initiated but also attempted to make China's government more transparent. The latter got him in trouble. He was blamed for a series of widespread student protests that occurred across China in 1987, and he was forced to resign. Twice purged in his life, Baiyun always believed that he would come back and rise to prominence again.

In the wake of his death, Baiyun lamented the idea that political reform in China might remain a dream forever, and then came the student demonstrations.

Even though Baiyun was away from her school, Beijing University, her heart was stirred. A desire was burning in her heart and she wanted to get back to school immediately to witness the movement first-hand.

After finishing the liver in the bowl, Baiyun cut a small corner of the Spam and added another spoonful of liver. She paused, deciding whether she should eat more or not. She patted her little round belly pushing up from her tight blue jeans and touched her puffy cheeks with her palms.

She pushed her bowl aside and stared at her dull reflection in the glass tabletop. She had an almond-shaped face, and behind her white-framed glasses, her eyes were large and brown. She also had a black spot on the right side of her nose. Some of her friends called it a beauty mark, but others said it was a misery spot. Sometimes she agreed with the second opinion.

She gulped down the last of the Spam in two bites and finished the fried liver.

"Hi, Baiyun. You're back." Lao Zheng startled her.

"Shh. Don't wake Father," said Baiyun, putting her index finger on her lips.

She turned around and saw her father still sound asleep. Sometimes she was not sure whether he was really sleeping.

She thought that maybe her father only pretended to be asleep all the time, since the reality was far too ugly to look at.

Baiyun ignored Lao Zheng and went back to reading the newspaper.

Lao Zheng edged himself into a chair next to Baiyun as if afraid of wrinkling his freshly ironed white shirt and brown pants.

He would have been attractive to Baiyun if only she did not find him to be so obnoxious. His body was tall and solidly built. His jaw Square and his face were ruggedly handsome. His eyes, though small, were full of charm.

"Just like your mother said, our great intellectual even makes use of her meal time to enrich her mind. I would say that's why you are ten times smarter than your mother."

"Yes, it's a big paper. I have to read fast," said Baiyun. She ignored him and kept her eyes on the paper.

"Your mother and I wondered where you were this morning."

"I went to a book discussion. We discussed Shakespeare's 'Romeo and Juliet'."

"Okay. I think your mother has told me about this play."

"Good."

"My mind is getting rusty. You can correct me if I'm wrong. Did they kill themselves in the end?"

"Ya. Only true lovers will die for each other."

"Oh. I see. I heard your mother say the same thing." He leaned forward, lowered his voice and pretended to be mysterious. "How about you?"

Baiyun turned around and stared at him. "Are you willing to die for love, or would you rather die for money?"

"A good question. I haven't decided yet. It depends on how much your mother loves me." He winked at her and asked, "Can you lend me a copy to read?"

"What are you two talking about? It sounds so interesting." Meiling strolled into the room wearing a red silk blouse and a pair of white pants. Her permed black hair was tied up behind her head with a tiger-eye barrette.

"Books," Baiyun murmured and dropped her head.

"Really? I didn't know he could carry on such a serious conversation." Meiling winked at Lao Zheng. She put her palms against her waist and tilted her upper body back a little.

"Hey, I only talk about intelligent things with an intelligent person." Lao Zheng sat back and scooted away from Baiyun.

"Mother, I'm going back to school." Baiyun jumped up and began collecting the dirty dishes on the table.

She could never bear to witness Meiling, Lao Zheng and her father in the same room. She heard stirring in her father's bed. She imagined her father standing up and finally confronting Meiling and Lao Zheng.

She sensed a volcano was about to erupt here in her own family. She would be safer back at school.

"You are leaving? Really? Why so soon? Why don't you stay? Your uncle and I are planning to take you out for dinner tonight."

"No, Mother. Please understand. My roommate Yumei is sick and I have to go back to take care of her. Besides, there must be a lot going on around the campus."

"Okay, I wouldn't hold you back. Be careful and keep in mind that you are going to America in three months. Don't get involved too much with those student activists, especially that Yumei. She is only interested in sleeping around. How awful."

"Yes, Mother," Baiyun said and pursed her lips. Still being a virgin, she was not envious of Yumei.

"Okay, you'd better get ready." Meiling and Lao Zheng went back to Meiling's room.

Baiyun took some clothes from the dresser drawer and a few tea eggs and apples from the refrigerator. Before she stepped out the door, she heard Meiling's voice. "Don't you want to say goodbye to your father and your Uncle Zheng?"

"Bye, Uncle Zheng." Baiyun mumbled.

She went to her father's bed and said "Goodbye, father." Her father opened his eyes. "Oh, you're leaving. See you." His lips trembled and then he closed his eyes as though nothing had happened.

Baiyun felt a stir in her heart, but she could do nothing except leave this mess behind her.

She walked to her bicycle, parked under the window in front of their apartment. She unlocked it and hung the bag of food on one side of the handlebars and the clothes on the other.

#

It was unusual weather for April; warm and humid. It was quite a change from the normal dry weather of spring in Beijing.

On the Beijing Industrial University campus, life was going on as usual. Baiyun rode her bike slowly among people who were just returning from work. Some of them rode with full loads, bags of groceries on each side of their handlebars plus wives with children on their laps, sitting together on the back fender seats.

No traffic police were on campus when Baiyun arrived. Drivers of cars did whatever they could to go by; bicycles swerved through the crowd; pedestrians wandered on both sides of the road; and children played in the middle of the street.

A bicycle bell rang behind Baiyun. A young woman, with a head full of hair curlers and a washbasin full of dirty clothes tied onto her bike seat swung by Baiyun like a gust of wind. She must have just come back from the community baths and gotten all her energy from the heat.

Ten minutes later when Baiyun arrived at the gate of the Beijing University campus, the guard hollered at her. "Your student I.D, please!"

She showed it to him and rode on. School officials enforced the gate only on special occasions, and she wondered what caused it today.

Although it was Sunday afternoon the streets were crowded with students coming back early from home, and Baiyun sensed tension in the air. People walked faster. Their faces were solemn, instead of happy and relaxed from a weekend's break. Some carried colored poster board under their arms.

Along the gray-brick dormitory buildings, huge computer printouts hung out of windows. They read 'Yaobang is gone, we mourn,' or 'Yaobang, we are never going to forget you,' or 'Yaobang, rest your soul, we will carry on your duty.' They flapped in the wind and made a crackling sound.

As she approached the 'triangle', a famous poster area and students' gathering place, she saw even more people. Layer upon layer of fresh new posters plastered the poster stand. Students were jammed in front of it on tiptoes.

As an experienced junior, she decided to go back to her dormitory first and join the crowd later. She knew this was likely the beginning of a new student movement.

She arrived at her dormitory, Building 27, and parked her bike. The long hallway spanning the ground floor was like a dark tunnel. Every time she walked into it, she felt like she was walking toward eternity.

She climbed the cement staircases to the fourth floor. She stopped for a while to catch her breath. She reached her dormitory room and found the door closed.

A pile of sunflower seed shells littered the hallway outside of the room.

She knocked and quickly went back to the hallway

"Who is it?" her roommate, Yumei, asked.

The door slid open. As soon as Yumei's face appeared, Baiyun jumped right in front of her.

"Ah," Yumei cried. "Baiyun, you've scared me." They hugged each other. "It's nice of you to come back early."

As usual, the room was in chaos. The dormitory room for six was just big enough for three double bunk beds on each side and a shared multi- purpose desk in the middle.

The desk was also used as a communal dining table and was now covered with dirty dishes and leftover food.

"Are you expecting Longfe?" Baiyun asked.

"Not really. I'm just bored. He was here Friday night and left for home on Saturday. Then Liu Ping came over for a while, but I kicked him out."

"Why?"

"He was so boring. I'm just bored. I want to cry, cry really loud." Yumei's face lengthened. Her almond eyes brimmed with tears.

"Then go and cry." Baiyun shrugged. Sometimes Yumei's theatrics went too far.

"No, I don't want to. People will think I'm crazy." Yumei dove back onto her bed and buried her head in the pillow.

"So what? So many people on campus want to cry out loud. If you do it, they will all follow you."

"Yes, and then I'll be the toast of the campus." She jumped up, waving her arms in the air as if she were dancing. "Let's take a bath. I haven't taken a bath in a week. I stink."

"Are you up to it?" Baiyen asked

"I feel fine now. Let's go." Yumei pulled a suitcase out from under her bed. She took out a red sweater and a pair of blue jeans and put them on. Then she threw her pajamas into the pile of blankets, wrinkled sheets and dirty clothes on her bed.

Baiyun also took out some clean clothes from the plastic bag she had brought from home. She wrapped them up with a towel, and put them into a washbasin along with soap, shampoo and a comb. Yumei followed suit.

"Let's go before I become the toast of the campus," said Yumei while rushing down the stairs, two steps at a time.

She is really charged up, Baiyun thought and she was always surprised by how fast Yumei's moods could change.

Although they were both about 5'4", Baiyun and Yumei were built quite differently.

Yumei was from a small town in southern China. She had a dancer's body with narrow shoulders, a tiny waist and a slim frame. Although her breasts were surprisingly large; they dominated her figure. Her outgoing personality made her even more beautiful. She was always proud of the interest shown in her by many of the male students. Study for her was a secondary matter, although she was a good student in spite of this.

Baiyun had grown up in Beijing. She was built like a typical northerner; her skin was darker and rougher than Yumei and in comparison, Baiyun had a thick waist and a plump body. Still, Baiyun was a beautiful woman with her dark eyes, thick eyebrows and exceptional red lips, though she often hid behind her glasses.

Unlike Yumei, Baiyun wanted to keep the boys away so that she could concentrate on her studies.

The cherry blossoms were out and crocuses were blooming all over the campus. The baths were located near their dormitory, just across a small brick road.

The streets were unusually quiet. A mourning atmosphere persisted. Even the sunset looked especially red.

"What did you do during the weekend?" Yumei asked, as she always did.

"I went to a book discussion and had an 'intellectual conversation with my mother's boyfriend."

"Oh, my great intellectual! You mean you spent the whole weekend studying. How boring!"

"Why not? I like it, especially when I'm reading a good book, I don't need to sleep."

"Amazing! How is your mother's new boyfriend?"

"I don't like him!"

"Why?"

"Because, he is such a stupid shit."

"Woo! Is he younger than your mother? That may explain your jealousy."

"Ten years younger. Come on, I'm not jealous. I just don't like the way he looks at me. It's full of lust."

"Ha-ha. You should like it when a man thinks you are attractive."

"I don't think so, especially when he is a stupid man. Besides, I don't want to fight with Mother over a man. Her life is hard enough."

"You're such a virgin, Baiyun."

"So, what." she replied, feeling somewhat embarrassed. "I know you are always secretly having sex with Longfe and whoever else. Everyone is talking about it. I would rather study. Youth is too precious to be wasted on anything else."

"Yes, exactly. Youth is too precious to waste. We should have as many experiences as possible before we finally have to get married."

"Why do you have to experience it all when you are young? My mother is forty-six-years old and she's dating a thirty-six-year old man."

"Your mother is incredible. I admire her. How about you?"

"Me? I don't know."

They arrived at the baths, threw their pre-purchased little white tickets into a hand-made wooden box by the door and walked right by the guard.

The guard, a little old lady, sat there motionless and did not even bother to lift her thin, rice-paper-like face away from her magazine to look at them.

A gust of cold wet wind hit them, because the baths were not very crowded, making the space colder than usual.

Not enough steam had been generated by the showers to warm the place. The ceiling window was cracked open as usual, which was necessary when the place was crowded and hot. Nobody ever bothered to close it when it was cold.

They walked through dressing rooms filled with white painted wooden lockers stacked together against both sides of the wall to the innermost room, hoping it was warmer there.

They set their washbasins on the bench.

"Wow, it's so cold here," said Yumei, shrinking her neck into her sweater collar.

"We have to strip down and run." Baiyun found a better-looking cabinet where the clasp of the lock was not broken and wiped the inside with her palm to see whether or not it was clean.

After they removed their clothing, they shivered and romped together toward the showers, carrying their soap, towels and basins.

"You stink, Baiyun." Yumei covered her nose with her towel.

"Really, how come I can't smell it?"

"Because, you are used to the smell of your stinky armpits."

"Why am I the only one who has stinky armpits? I bet you do, too. Let me smell yours." Baiyun pulled the towel away from Yumei and smelled it. "Mmm... Smells wonderful. It's the perfume. No wonder you smell so good."

"Stop." Yumei slapped Baiyun on the arm. "It's better than smelling like a wolf."

"Yes. We smell like wolves, we smell like wolves." They sang together as they ran toward the shower room.

The shower room was not as fogged by the hot steam as it usually was. It was clear and cold.

The noise of running water, bouncing against the cement floor told them that they were not alone.

They passed several rows of showers separated into stalls by concrete walls and found their favorite stalls. Since not every shower worked and not all of those worked well, it was very important to find a good one. Some were too weak; it took a long time to wet your body with a thin stream of water. Some were so powerful that the water peppered your body like bullets, giving you a headache. After three years of taking showers here, they knew the best showers, the second best ones and the ones to avoid. Usually they had to stand in line to get to the good ones. Today they were lucky.

They chose two showers next to each other, and started washing.

Yumei's hair was light and fluffy while Baiyun's dark and straight. They had to shampoo two or three times in order to get rid of a week's worth of hair grease. They only showered on a weekly basis.

"My head is so itchy," said Yumei.

"Me too. But, I have to be careful. I'm beginning to lose too much hair." Baiyun scratched her head under the shower.

"You have studied too hard."

"It's worth losing a few hairs to get more knowledge."

"You are kidding, right? If you lose any more, you'll look like a monk. You are so stubborn. Nowadays everyone cares only about making money, getting rich. No one cares about studying anymore." Yumei struggled to pull a comb through her long hair. Then suddenly she stepped back. "Oh, the water turned cold."

"That's why we have to go to the monastery to study. Only there can one find a peaceful environment."

"Baiyun, the water is cold." Yumei pulled Baiyun out.

"No wonder it feels a little cooler." Baiyun stared at Yumei and said.

"Oh, my great intellectual. Maybe we should wash our backs."

Baiyun helped Yumei tie her hair into a knot on the top of her head. Then she wet her towel under the cold water, squeezed it hard and rolled it into a spindle. "I'll help you first."

"Okay." Stretching her arms, Yumei bent forward and held herself against the stall with her palms.

Baiyun scraped Yumei's back hard. Soft, black gums of dirt rolled down on her back. Very soon, her back turned red.

"Ah! Ah!" Yumei whined.

"Am I hurting you?"

"No. Scrape it hard. Ah... I want it clean. Ah..."

Then Baiyun rubbed Yumei's shoulders, hips and circled around her breasts. Baiyun always envied Yumei's big breasts. She wondered what she did to deserve them.

She suspected that as a small town girl, Yumei probably grew up in a freer environment than she did. The wind of many political movements never blew that far. She was probably able to talk to those boys, play with them and even go out on dates with them during high school.

Unlike Yumei, Baiyun was reared in the political and cultural center of China, the capital and the second largest city in China, which was akin to being raised in a convent. She was so used to that kind of life; she even contemplated becoming a monk at one point in her life.

Her mother always told her that pretty women usually did not have good luck. Looking at her mother's life, she believed it.

Deep in her psyche, she wished that one day a prince riding a white horse would come to her, say he loved her and carry her away.

"Hey, are you daydreaming again?" Yumei asked.

"Oh! It's done. I was ruminating."

"Ruminating? I call it slow to react."

By the time both their backs were hot and burning, the water became warm again. They quickly soaped their bodies, rinsed themselves and were ready to dry off.

More students were coming into the bathhouse. Soon the baths became crowded. Steam and fog, like a thin veil, shrouded the small, thin college students. Some were too young yet to grow into full-sized adults, others were petite girls, simple yet elegant, from southern China.

Baiyun and Yumei wound their way through the now crowded sea of naked bathers, trying to avoid being splashed by soapy, brown water.

"Yes, I feel so clean - so good." Yumei leaped forward. She ran so fast that one of her slippers flew away and Baiyun had to pick it up for her.

It was dark outside. The spring blossoms filled the air with sweet fragrance. Baiyun was in high spirits. The earlier uneasiness caused by the strange encounter with her mother's boyfriend and compounded by the fantasy in the bathhouse had suddenly disappeared.

Spring always meant hope, didn't it? She asked herself. Maybe she should do something besides studying.

"What shall we do tonight?" Yumei asked.

Still indulging herself in the ecstasy of spring, Baiyun did not answer.

"I already know you're going to go to the library, study, and leave me alone in the dorm," Yumei sighed.

"You are the one who has a lot of friends, most of whom are boys. Why do you complain about being alone?"

"I'm tired of them."

"Perhaps we can stroll around the campus and read some big-letter posters."

"You're going to give up some of your precious study time?"

"You, rascal!"

On Sunday nights, the cafeteria was dim and the food supply scant with some leftover boiled bok choy, dry steam bread and cold pork sausage.

Behind the counter stood a tired young man, whose small slender body was a strong indication of his obvious lack of nutrition.

"I'm tired of this stupid steam bread and terrible vegetables," Yumei complained as she bought a strip of pork sausage and half of a steam bread to wrap it in.

Baiyun liked almost all the food at school. For her it was a change from the greasy food at home. She was not very choosy about her food and always looked forward to every meal. Yumei was different. Her small delicate stomach could handle only limited amounts and certain kinds of food and sometimes she could not stomach any food at all.

They decided to take their food back to their room.

Yumei swiveled her hips, walking like a dancer. A nice-looking, tall male student wearing blue jeans and a brown blazer approached Yumei.

"Hi, Yumei. How are you?" He asked.

"Hi. Hi." Yumei answered, a little startled.

"Don't you remember? We danced at a party last week?" The young man said tenderly. His small eyes formed a thin line, focusing on Yumei's breasts rather than her eyes.

"Oh... yes."

"I live in Dorm number 40. You can come and visit me tonight."

"Sure." Yumei nodded reluctantly while the young man walked away.

"I don't even know him. Don't you think it's strange?" Yumei asked. She was a little confused, and a little proud.

"You must have closed your eyes when he was dancing with you."

"You nasty woman!" Yumei hit Baiyun's back. The blow was so weak that Baiyun could barely feel it.

A few more young men waved at Yumei. Baiyun kept quiet, still feeling a little dreamy after remembering her fantasy of the white knight in the bathhouse.

When they reached the building entrance, a young man jumped in front of them. "Hi, girls," he said.

"Uh, Longfe, you jumped in front of us like a rapist. Take this food if you want," Yumei yelled to cover the excitement of seeing him.

"Ok, I'll bring it upstairs for you."

Longfe was a tall, slender, smooth-faced gentleman with a pair of dark-framed glasses.

"We were planning to visit you after dinner today," said Baiyun while they were walking up the stairs.

"Have you been waiting for us long?" asked Yumei. Sometimes she felt sorry for her cool response to Longfe's being overly nice to her.

"Not really. I just came five minutes ago and found the light in your room was off. So I decided to wait for a while, and here you are."

Baiyun unlocked and pushed open the squeaky, flimsy door to their room.

"Wow, the ladies' dorm is even dirtier than the men's!" Longfe shouted and covered his nose with one hand.

"Stop complaining! If you don't like it, you can help clean it up," said Yumei.

"What? What do you expect me to do? I'm not your husband." Longfe retorted.

"You sound like a mom," Baiyun joined in.

"Ha... Welcome back!" Longfe shook Baiyun's hands.

"I hope I'm not in your way," said Baiyun.

"Not at all. Actually I'm going to tell you both." He lowered his voice, "Have you heard about the march tomorrow?"

"No. We wanted to ask you," said Yumei, moving closer to him.

"Tomorrow morning at seven, we are going to meet at the triangle."

"What do we need to bring?" Yumei was getting excited.

"Bring some food and water. You should be prepared to spend the day in Tiananmen Square."

"Really? That sounds like fun." Yumei opened her eyes wide and her mouth dropped open.

"Don't think of it as having fun. I have something dangerous for you to do." Longfe took out a bundle of pink and yellow paper from his pocket. "These are pamphlets for you to distribute among the crowd. Try to avoid letting others see while you are doing it, because it could be considered a counter-revolutionary act."

Baiyun picked one, spread it out and read, "Those…"

Longfe touched his index finger on his lips.

Baiyun kept reading in a quieter voice. "Those who should die still live; those who should live have died."

CHAPTER 2

Meanwhile, one kilometer from the Tiananmen Square, life in the home of Dagong in downtown Beijing was going on as usual during the unusually hot and humid spring.

"Where have you been? Every day you come back so late. Have you lost your mind?" said Dagong's wife Zhang Ping.

She was a small, bony woman with protruding front-teeth. Her long pale face stretched longitudinally like a squash whenever she was angry. She stood up from her work at the sewing machine. "See, I'm working hard at home, making a shirt for you. You were out playing."

Dagong sat down on the bed and sighed. His white tank top was pasted to his back with sweat. The heat was already intolerable at the beginning of May.

He peeled off his blue jeans and put on a pair of shorts. "There is a revolution going on, Zhang Ping. Don't you know? Don't you care?"

"Of course, I care! I care whether we are going to have food on the table. I care whether our clothes will be washed. I care whether our cat is fed. What revolution? Haven't you had enough? If not for the Cultural Revolution , you wouldn't have to prepare for the graduate school exam right now. You're thirty-eight. You'd better go and get a real graduate degree or go to America so you can get a decent paying job. The phony college degree you got during the 'Cultural Revolution' is worthless."

"Shut up. I need quiet to study." Dagong walked out and sat on the cement steps leading to the corridor by his door.

Breezes were always welcome in early summer. They came at the right time, when Dagong was hot and sweaty.

The house where Dagong lived with his family used to be his Aunt Rose's home.

It was a six-room, one-story structure. It formed a closed rectangle with the yard in the center and rooms on all sides.

The style was known as a Hudong, which means 'Four Corners Courtyard,' and was a common home design in downtown Beijing.

The Hudong had fallen into disrepair. The red-tiled roof had turned dark grey. The golden paint that used to cover the walls was long gone and in some places, bare bricks were exposed. The paper windows with crisscross wooden frames, which used to be painted with flowers, lanterns and ancient beauties, were now covered with black and white newspapers, even blankets to keep out the cold wind in the winter. The wooden railing around the yard was fragile, and too weak to lean on. Children were taught not to touch it.

This had been a fancy house, but Dagong did not get a chance to enjoy it; he was born two years too late. In 1949, two years before he was born, the Communists took over Beijing and took the property from his Aunt Rose. They mercifully left one room for her and Dagong and invited five more workers' families in to enjoy the luxury.

Dagong grew up with the idea that he, a son of a 'capitalist's running dog,' was lucky just to have a place to stay.

Since his father owned a business and his grandparents were wealthy, he would forever be labeled as a 'capitalist's running dog'. In China, one does not inherit his parents' property. One is labeled with whatever bad titles the property could indicate.

He was also lucky that when Aunt Rose died twenty-one years ago, they allowed him to stay in the house.

It was ironic that he had wasted one-third of his life during the Cultural Revolution. Five years of hard labor in the countryside, two years as a factory assembly worker and four years as a college student.

He was, in turn, a representative to reform the universities for workers, peasants and soldiers. His experiences had done him no good, and so he became politically active again.

He now worked as an electrician in the same factory where he had worked after he got out of the phony college. Working conditions had not improved very much.

In 1977, the government decided to resume the college entrance exam to enroll college students directly from the high schools. Previously, students were enrolled from the countryside, the factories and the army according to one's political performance. Because of this, nobody took Dagong's degree seriously anymore. It was phony, and everyone knew that.

In the factory, he had a few years of easy time, playing cards and gossiping to kill time. The factory was over-staffed. They always could make up the quota just before the end of the year.

However, things had recently changed. Factories began to compete with each other. Workers had to work hard to get bonuses and the factory had hired some recent college graduates to do the managerial jobs.

Dagong felt insignificant and caught in-between where he could not move up and did not want to slide down. His brain was rusty and needed to be lubricated. It was not easy; because he had not touched a book for almost twenty years.

He promised Zhang Ping he would prepare for the Graduate School Entrance exam (GRE) and the TOEFL exam to study in America, but it seemed as remote as the North Pole.

Was going to graduate school the only way to get ahead?

He remembered what Aunt Rose told him before she died. She was lying on the bed, with her eyes closed. Lung cancer had taken away every bit of her flesh. "Do you remember your father?" she asked between constant coughs.

"Yes. He loved me, he loved me very much," Dagong said rather mechanically. He had never seen the man. How did he know?

"That's what I have been telling you? Okay. You know, there is something else I have to tell you. Before your father died, he said, 'Let Dagong be a businessman in the future.'"

"Yes." Dagong said. In his mind, he thought 'What a joke. I have suffered enough because he owned that damn shipping business. Now I'm about to go to the countryside to suffer more.'

"It may not make any sense to you. But that's what I have to tell you."

Aunt Rose died a few days later. Dagong never dreamed of being a businessman until recently. He knew it might be possible if the government loosened up a little. He had already resumed his connections with some of his relatives in Hong Kong and was waiting for the government to change their policies.

#

At 9:00pm, the yard was full of activity.

As summer approached, people went to bed at a later hour. Hot weather was always a bother. People had to bathe more often, they had to wash their clothes more frequently and they had to drink more water. They had to do all of this in a situation where no private baths, washing machines or fresh drinking water were available. Getting water required a lot of energy.

Pumpkin, a woman whose family shared the Hudong with Dagong's family, was one of those summer victims.

She was sitting in the yard in front of a washbasin, scrapping and rubbing the clothes on a washboard. Sweat appeared on her face as a fine layer of mist.

She had short, tousled, permed hair and a round face with fat cheeks. Her thick lips protruded from her face, and her two big eyes under thick eyebrows looked fierce.

Pumpkin yelled at her children, Broomstick and Potatofeet, as she washed their clothing and they sat in the yard, playing cards with their father, who was called Marshmallow. She yelled, "Where have you been? Your pants are full of mud.

Next time I should let you wash them yourself, so you'll know how to keep them clean."

Pumpkin pulled a pair of blue cotton pants out of the muddy, soapy water and turned the pockets inside out. She found a handful of toilet paper, some clay and a few stones. "Dirty boys," she grimaced.

As Pumpkin complained, Marshmallow, Broomstick and Potatofeet played cards under a dim light in the yard. They played 'Catch the black seven' and ignored their mother.

'Catch black seven' was an easy card game. The object of the game was simply to possess the Ace of Spades. The player who found the card was supposed to protect it by staying silent, since the person who had it at the end would win the game.

"I know Potatofeet has it. Father, don't protect him." Broomstick always tried to take advantage of his brother.

Potatofeet had been a handsome child before he contracted polio at the age of five. The disease left him permanently crippled, and he developed a stammer as well. His feet were shaped like two potatoes. His heels and toes could never touch the ground at the same time. He bounced instead of walking, with his toes usually turned inward. His knees were so weak that they seemed not to exist. He smiled most of the time. The constant dripping of saliva from his mouth made him look silly. "I am, am not..., going to... to tell you."

"I know either you or Father has it. Hey, Father, if you try to protect him, that's against the rules. We're supposed to play fair."

Broomstick was a handsome boy. His tall, slender body resembled a telephone pole.

"Hey, Son. Let me tell you, you're not very smart. You know from all the talking you did, how much shit you have given me?"

Although Broomstick and Potatofeet were slender boys, their parents were not slender people. Many would even call them fat.

Marshmallow was a sturdy man, with a bulging chest and a pockmarked face. His nose was small and pointy, his eyes round and benevolent. He was timid while his wife was loud.

Marshmallow and Pumpkin both worked in a government-owned restaurant as cooks, which was why they were fat.

They not only ate as much as they wanted to, but it seemed as though they also absorbed fat through their skin. They could not afford to buy good food for their kids with their small salaries.

In the yard, a few steps from the card table were two girls.

Little Pea, Broomstick's older sister, was sitting with Lili, the daughter of a policeman. They both graduated from the same high school. Little Pea worked in a grocery store downtown, while Lili waited at home for a government job.

"Have you been in the Square?" Lili asked Little Pea.

"No. There are too many people, and most of them are college students. They look so young. They are from all over the country, which I can tell because they speak funny dialects and look different. Some of them have silly crew cuts and wear hand-made clothes. They all wear glasses," said Lili while looking at her finger nails.

Little Pea sat quietly, working hard on her knitting. She was making a thick black sweater.

"How is your boyfriend?" Lili asked.

"He is fine," Little Pea kept knitting.

"I hear that you're going to get married."

"Maybe soon." Little Pea kept knitting as though they were talking about an upcoming dinner party.

"Are you ready for it?"

"I guess."

"It must be hard to prepare."

"Not really."

"Why?"

"I'm going to move into his parents' home since my parents don't have any room for us. That way we don't have to buy any furniture."

"Woo, I can't believe your parents can live without you."

"They can. My parents know how to cook." Little Pea finally raised her voice and showed some emotion.

"But I have never seen them cook at home."

"They will have to. Otherwise my brothers will have to cook for themselves."

"When are you leaving?"

"Next spring, when he saves enough money to buy himself a suit and have a tailor make a nice dress for me."

"That sounds exciting."

"I think so, too." Little Pea's voice tapered down and her small yellowish face cracked a smile. She soon resumed her sober expression. She wanted to keep her long-awaited happiness to herself. She was too shy to reveal it.

"Oh, it's already ten o'clock. I'd better go home. Otherwise my mother will complain again." Lili stood up and pushed back her long hair, which hung to her buttocks, and left.

The water faucet was dripping in the middle of the yard, making a splashing sound. A gust of wind blew through the yard. The weather was very pleasant at night. The heat soaked up the old laundry water and the dishwashing water on the ground. It smelled human.

At the same time, the policeman Lao Liu and Dagong were chatting. Dagong sat on the cement steps leading to the corridor by his door, and Lao Liu squatted next to him, smoking.

Lao Liu was a slender man. He wore a white T-shirt and a pair of police navy-blue polyester pants. A pair of black frame glasses sat on his pale, high cheek-boned face.

"I spotted you in Tiananmen Square today." Lao Liu said.

"You were there, too?" Dagong did not worry about Lao Liu because he was harmless, but Lao Liu's simple presence at the Square made him alert. Why did he need to go if there was no trouble? "What were you doing there?"

"We dressed up in civilian clothes and walked around."

"Do you have any dangerous news for the students?"

"Not really. We are not ordered to do anything yet. I have the feeling it's up to..." He pointed his cigarette up to the sky. He smoked continuously. His eyes were half-open and he rested his chin on his knees. He looked comfortable enough to fall asleep. "The top is fighting. The two sides couldn't agree with each other." He paused. "The situation is shaky."

"Obviously, the security has tightened up," said Dagong.

"That is true." Lao Liu suddenly looked around and leaned toward Dagong. "They have just installed a new video surveillance system around the Square."

Dagong nodded. They both sank into silence.

Lao Liu had a clear mind. During his more than twenty years in the security profession, he had been through many ups and downs.

The anti-rightist movement and the Cultural Revolution were labeled political movements. Actually, they were people-against-people movements.

He had seen many honest people get hurt. They were sent to jail or labor camps for crimes they had not committed. He tried to do his best to protect these people, but sometimes he just had to close his eyes to let things go by.

He had a wife, a daughter and a family to support. He was not in a position to make a real difference anyway.

He still vividly remembered a case he was assigned twelve years ago. The case was an extra-marital love affair involving a middle-aged woman and the head of the Beijing Automobile Parts Factory. They were both married. The woman, whose name he remembered as Meiling, the wife of a college professor, was notorious in the western district as a playgirl. The head of the factory was a political enemy of the judge. The case had obvious political motives. The judge, a fat woman with dark wicked eyes, wanted to use it against the head of the factory. In order to do so, they had to make Meiling confess to the relationship. Meiling denied the charge. The judge was enraged. She gave Meiling a five-year jail sentence with no appeals.

Lao Liu still remembered Meiling's daughter, a ten-year old girl and Meiling's husband, an old intellectual, as they were on the day of the ruling. They were not allowed to be present in the courtroom. They waited outside until the verdict was announced. The girl cried and her father lowered his head. He was too ashamed to react.

Lao Liu, then a young investigator, tried to persuade the girl. "Stop, stop crying. Your mother is a bad woman. Don't you understand?"

"I don't believe Mother is a bad woman. I don't believe it. I don't believe it."

"Let's go. You're going to cause me trouble." Her father tried to pull the girl out of there and said to Lao Liu and the judge, "Judge, we... Obey your order... We obey your order... She deserves it."

The girl kept turning her head back, staring as she walked away.

Lao Liu remembered the girl's red, earnest eyes. She was looking for some kind of message, or perhaps some sympathy. He tried his best to communicate his compassion to her with his eyes. He wanted to tell her that her mother was innocent, and her mother was a brave woman.

After that case, Lao Liu saw a lot worse. He dreamed he might be able to change the situation. Then he found out that the judge was one knot in a huge power net. They abused power together and they abused the law together. Then he started to close his eyes, letting things go by. He had never become a part of the power net. He managed to stay out. He just wanted to paddle through his old age peacefully.

Now the students stirred things up again. Lao Yu did not believe they would make any difference. China was too old and too big. He thought that if anything did happen, it would have to come from the top.

Recently, through reading the newspaper, he realized the whole world was changing. He held out hope that maybe the breeze of democracy and freedom would finally sweep through old China.

Lao Liu looked at Dagong, who was staring into the darkness. He had been surprised to see Dagong in the Square, among the students, listening to their debate.

He would be surprised to see Dagong simply ride through the Square given the present situation. He could not believe he was the same Dagong he used to know.

In his mind, Dagong had been dead for the last twenty years. Waves of political movements had whipped Dagong into a tame animal, tamer than a sheep. He never argued with anyone in the yard, did not even speak loudly to anyone. Dagong, the quiet, self-contained person he used to know, was now becoming an activist. God must be insane.

"Hey, do you know what time it is?" Dagong's wife, Zhang Ping, came out of the door. "Every night, you sit here, smoking. What are you thinking of? You'd better come back and study!"

Dagong stood up, sighed and trudged to the kitchen.

He found some hot water in the kettle on the stove. He poured it into a washbasin, mixed it with some cold water from the water tap in the yard and washed his face. He rinsed his feet and slippers with the leftover brown soapy water, and then returned to his room.

They had one room with a narrow storage room in the back. It had a double wooden bed, a desk and several suitcases stacked together. Rings of yellow stains covered walls with no wallpaper. A fluorescent light hanging from the ceiling bathed the small room.

As usual, when he came home, there was chaos.

"Let your father see what you have done in kindergarten!" Zhang Ping stood behind the door, red-faced, pointing her finger toward their five-year old son, Little Turnip.

He stared at the floor. An adult size T-shirt draped down on his shoulders like a nightgown. He held a small electronic toy in his shaking hands.

"He took the kindergarten's toy without telling his teacher." Zhang Ping said.

"You told me to do it," mumbled Little Turnip.

"I didn't tell you to do it in front of your teacher. Your teacher stopped by here earlier and asked me to tighten up the rules at home. I was so embarrassed. How can I hold my head up in front of other people?" She turned to Dagong, "You'd better study hard, and pass the test so we can go to America. Then we can afford to buy fancy toys like that ourselves."

Dagong did not react. He felt hundreds of bugs creeping along his back. He was hot. He was tired of Zhang Ping's usual complaints about money. He wanted to throw them both out of the house, but what could he do.

Who let him stay in this house? Who had assigned him his current job? Who had provided him with his wife? He should thank Zhang Ping's father for these things. He did not have many choices.

He was lucky enough to have it at all. Of course, he was concerned about his son. Little Turnip should get a good education and become a decent person. Even this was beyond his control. Zhang Ping was too possessive of their son. She was too possessive about everything.

He lifted Little Turnip up and held him to his chest, so he could talk to him face to face. "Little Turnip, did you hear what your mother said. Don't do that anymore - okay? Never bring a school toy home without asking your teacher."

"Yes." Little Turnip nodded. Tears ran down his face.

Then Dagong turned toward Zhang Ping. "Zhang Ping, I think you and Little Turnip had better go to bed. If you keep yelling, you might wake up the whole neighborhood."

Zhang Ping suddenly became very docile. She took Little Turnip. "Okay, Okay. We'll go to bed. So you can study."

In a while, the fluorescent light was turned off. Zhang Ping and Little Turnip fell asleep on the double bed.

Dagong was left in the corner, sitting in front of a wooden desk with a dim table lamp.

He opened the book and started preparing for the TOEFL Exam, which was the requirement for getting into an American university.

He glanced through a few lines and marked down the new words he did not know. Then he looked up the new words in the dictionary one by one and scribbled them down on a notebook almost as thick as the dictionary.

At thirty-eight, he could feel his age. Recently, he even found it hard to sit still. He was too agitated. A volcano was growing in his chest, getting ready to erupt. This was not like him, not him at all.

Twenty-one years ago, when his aunt had died and left him alone in the world, he thought he would never smile again.

During the five years of 're-education' in the countryside, he worked hard. He wanted the sweat to wash away his sorrow, and the soil to bury his grief.

He did such a good job, that a miracle happened. He was assigned to a job in the city and he worked as a janitor in a park. That was when Zhang Ping's father Lao Zhang discovered him and transferred him to the Beijing Radio Parts factory where Lao Zhang was the president.

Lao Zhang liked Dagong. They liked each other. Lao Zhang liked Dagong so much that he constantly acted as his protector.

Whenever a political movement waged in or when the capitalist's son was bashed, Lao Zhang would stand up to defend him. Then he followed Lao Zhang's suggestion and married his only daughter, Zhang Ping, who worked at the factory's food service.

Dagong never liked Zhang Ping. She was not his choice. He had not had any choice. No young woman at the time would want to marry someone like him with a dead capitalist father and several relatives overseas.

He married Zhang Ping out of gratitude to Lao Zhang. He married her out of desperation. When Lao Zhang sent him to the university during the Cultural Revolution in 1972, he was excited for a while.

As a straight-A student in high school, he always dreamt of going to the university. However, life turned out differently from what he expected. He had been deprived of the opportunity to go to the university because of his dead parents.

The university he attended turned out to be phony. During those years, the communist leaders did not appreciate intellectuals. They like to install social changes. Political movements were their games. They reformed the college, changed the curriculum, and educated professors with Chairman Mao's writing to make them humble.

He wasted his college years going to political discussion groups, self-criticizing meetings and writing politically correct poetry and posters. Although he also learned some high school algebra and contemporary Chinese history on the side, he knew that was not enough.

During those days he was extremely cautious, knowing if he did anything out of the ordinary, he would immediately become a target for people to spit on, to shit on, all because he was a capitalist's son. He worked to stay invisible, which was hard because of his height, and he sailed through four years safely.

Dagong and Zhang Ping's marriage was a peaceful comradeship, but he did not love her. Without Dagong having even a desire to kiss Zhang Ping, they somehow had a son. Zhang Ping did not like sex. A son was what she wanted, and once she had a son, there was no further need for sex.

For a while, Dagong was content with his life. He let the days slip away one by one and prayed for peace and stability. He thought he was lucky. He had a job in a big city like Beijing. The nine hundred and ninety nine million people in the other parts of the country envied him. He had a wife and a son and lived in the center of Beijing, one kilometer from the Tiananmen Square. What else would he want?

The book became blurry in front of him. The dark lines on the white paper turned into many beautiful faces; some with long straight hair, some with permed hair, all with big bright eyes and joyful smiles. He loved those college girls.

The sky suddenly turned colorful, not a dull grey color anymore. He felt energetic. He wanted to join the students to disperse his energy. Life is going to be interesting, he said to himself.

Then he got up and joined Zhang Ping and little Turnip in their bed.

CHAPTER 3

Several hundred people assembled in front of the men's dormitory, number 41, near one of the campus gates.

The red Beijing University flag was billowing in the wind.

Some windows of the dorms were open and the students who had overslept yelled; "Wait for me. I will be down in a second."

Some came down with a piece of bread in their hands.

When Baiyun, Yumei and her roommate Li Yan arrived at 7:00am, each girl had a different feeling about being there.

Baiyun wore blue pants and a faded jacket, hoping her appearance would attract no attention. Yumei's bright orange sweater indicated that she wanted to be noticed immediately. Li Yan wore a neutral white top and black pants, as though she was still in mourning for the death of Hu Yaobang, which was absolutely adequate. Her approach to life was more realistic. She was a stout girl with two bushy pigtails and she loved sports and politics, so she was just happy to be a part of it.

Their decision to skip class on Monday was a big one. The liberal arts students organized the march. Since the girls were Chemistry majors, Baiyun, Yumei and Li Yan would probably be the only people there from their class. Besides, most Chemistry majors would not have a friend like Longfe, an economics major, to inform them about the march.

Math class was important, but easy to skip. Physical education was not as important, however it was much harder to skip because as soon as they lined up, the instructor would notice who was missing immediately. The physical education teacher was reasonable though. Everyone loved to skip the Political Science class. No one listened during those lectures anyway. Everyone read either their math textbook or a novel right under the instructor's nose as he tried to politically indoctrinate his students by swinging his arms and spraying saliva through spaces between his teeth.

The sky looked gray on that spring morning, for the sun hid behind thick layers of clouds and seemed far, far away.

Occasional gusts of wind blew the dust into the air, a familiar scene in Beijing.

Yumei was a girl from Shaanxi, an ancient province southeast of Beijing. She began to sing loudly, even though they hardly knew anyone around them.

"Beijing, our great capital,
Beijing, a beautiful city.
But in the spring,
Ladies cover their faces with gray scarves."

Li Yan was a news addict, and she kept informed on everything through her radio. She was carrying a Walkman." On the broadcast they said it might rain today," Li Yan informed them.

"Come on, I never believe the weather forecast. They are rarely correct," said Yumei, absent-mindedly.

"But it rained yesterday," said Baiyun, pushing her glasses up a bit on her straight nose.

"Maybe God is weeping for Hu Yaobang's death," said Yumei, looking around to see if anyone had noticed her.

"Have you heard anything interesting on the BBC?" asked Baiyun. She knew Li Yan listened to the BBC short wave broadcasts every day.

"Yes. They're making all kinds of strange predictions about China's future. Some say Hu Yaobang's death is a sign that the conservatives will come back. Some say his death could stir up a full-scale student movement, which would begin to turn China into a more democratic society."

Longfe approached the girls. "Hi, Yumei! It's nice that you are here already." He wore a tan blazer and a pair of blue jeans. His big eyes were beaming behind his Square-rimmed glasses.

Baiyun felt ignored after Li Yan left to join students from other departments. She found Longfe very attractive. She liked his big tall body, the deep set of his eyes and his smooth round face. Although, every time he was around, she was too nervous to open her mouth.

She felt embarrassed just standing there, and an idea dawned on her. "Yumei... I'm going back to pick up our raincoats or an umbrella." Baiyun interrupted Yumei and Longfe's conversation. Longfe stared at her and frowned. Baiyun turned and ran away.

On her way out, she saw Li Yan along with Xia Nan, a communist party member and the head of the student association in the economic department, talking to a group of students with a megaphone.

Baiyun quickly got back to the dorm, and after looking through the suitcases, drawers, and under the beds, could not find any raincoats or umbrellas. Then suddenly she realized that she had left hers at home and Yumei had probably lost hers as usual.

She decided to go to the campus grocery store to buy an umbrella.

If she was late, she could always ride her bicycle to catch up with everyone. In any case, she wanted to be truly part of the march this time instead of being just a bystander as she had been on previous occasions. She was famous for always missing exciting events by staying in the library and studying.

As she walked toward the store, she heard a voice accompanied by the noise of a motorcycle behind her.

"Baiyun. What's the rush? Let me give you a ride."

Lao Zheng, fully equipped with a helmet, leather jacket and goggles, stopped his motorcycle behind Baiyun. He had a big grin on his face. Yuck, what is he doing here? Baiyun wondered. She quickly composed herself and faked a smile. "You've come to the wrong place to find Mother."

"Well." He set his left foot on the ground. "Are you going to Tiananmen Square? I can give you a ride. It's such a long way to walk."

"How did you know about the march?"

"I saw a group of students marching out of the gate when I came in. I asked them where they were going."

"Have they already gone?" Baiyun felt bad. What would her friends think of her if she were not there? They would think she had missed another important event again. Baiyun could just imagine how the others would talk about her: 'How clever, that Baiyun. Going back to get an umbrella is just her excuse. Do you remember how she got out of the march last time? She stayed in the library overnight and came out once everyone was gone.'

"Ha... You really need a ride now." Lao Zheng smiled like a victor.

"Would you?"

"Let's go"

Baiyun jumped onto the back seat of the motorcycle.

Although she hated the cigarette smell on his jacket, she had to hold onto it tightly and bury her head in it, because she did not want others on campus to see her riding on a motorcycle with such a man.

The streets were full of busy people going to work on bicycles, buses or occasionally on motorcycles. The ringing of bicycle bells and honking of bus horns awakened the city like a rooster's crowing at dawn.

At every street corner, there was a little yellow cylindrical station painted with red stripes. Policemen wearing white summer uniforms and sunglasses either sat in the station looking out, or stood in the center of the intersection of two streets, directing the busy traffic with a little blue and white stick.

Sometimes a policeman would stop an unfortunate bicyclist because he was carrying his son or both his son and his wife on the bike fender seat. They would usually get a warning from the policeman and were told to walk to the bus station so that the wife and son could take the bus, but as soon as they were out of the policeman's sight, they would get back on the bike and fly. Violating traffic laws was not considered a crime in China.

Lao Zheng and Baiyun found the marchers stopped in front of a big farmer's market, two kilometers from the campus.

"Hey, Baiyun, we caught up with them in no time at all. Let's ride along with them. What do you think?"

"Would you let me get off?" She pointed toward the market. "So I can buy an umbrella and find my roommate."

"Don't you want to march with me? We have a motorcycle, the modern transportation." Lao Zheng stood by his motorcycle proudly. With his sunglasses and shining new leather jacket, he almost looked like a movie star.

Baiyun was not impressed. "Please let me off!" She screamed.

"Actually your mother asked me to come here and pick you up. She worries about you," Lao Zheng's tone changed.

"I don't believe you. Mother never bothers me at school. She trusts me."

"Okay. I came here to find you myself. I think you'd enjoy going out with me. We'll spend some money and have a good time. This demonstration is boring. What do you think?" Lao Zheng put on his charming mask again.

Baiyun jumped off the slowly moving motorcycle and ran to the other side of the street where the students were, trying to hold back her tears.

"Baiyun! Baiyun!" Lao Zheng shouted dumbfounded.

"Baiyun, why are you so late?" Baiyun could hear someone in the crowd yelled at her.

As Baiyun crossed the street, she saw Yumei, Longfe, Li Yan and the other students staring at her. She blushed.

How shameful! She said to herself, but to the others, she was speechless. There was a lump in her throat.

"How do you know someone who owns a motorcycle? How exciting!" said Yumei. Then she took Baiyun's hands and smiled charmingly, which cheered Baiyun.

"According to the BBC, motorcycles are the practical modern transportation for the future in China. I'm proud of you, Baiyun. You'll be a pioneer motorcycle rider on campus," said Li Yan.

"I didn't know there is another side of you, Baiyun. Your hidden side is really exciting," said Longfe, looking impressed.

Yumei hit Longfe on the shoulder. "Stop!"

She took Baiyun to the side. "What's the matter with you?"

"I feel awful." Tears streamed down Baiyun's face.

"So that's your mother's boyfriend? What does he want?"

"He wants me to spend the day with him." Baiyun stared down on the ground as though this was the most embarrassing moment in her life.

"Oh, my God. He's really interested in you," said Yumei, half teasingly.

"Yes, is that awful?"

"I don't know. If you don't like him - yes."

"I'm not going to go back home anymore."

"Okay, stick with us."

"Sure," said Baiyun. She could not think of a better way to spend the day.

The wheat field around the Qinhua University, a top engineering school in Beijing located about 3 kilometers from Beijing University, soon appeared.

Behind the field was a huge broad gray concrete building, the main building of the University. In front of it, there was a statue of Chairman Mao, his body erect, his right hand waving as though he was inspecting the sea of worshippers.

A voice from a loudspeaker reached them. "Students of Beijing University, the Qinhua students are not participating in your march. Go back to your school and to class. Do not create chaos on our campus."

The gate of Qinhua University was locked and a truck equipped with a loudspeaker followed them from gate to gate, repeating the message.

The heavens gave them an additional warning. Thunder clapped. Lightning almost broke the sky in half and waves of dark clouds rolled toward them like a flock of sheep running madly. The gusty winds blew dust into the air, darkening the sky even more.

Baiyun covered her face with her hands to prevent dust from getting into her eyes. Yumei ran toward Longfe to seek refuge behind his thin and tall body.

Then the rain started pouring down from the sky.

There was a voice in the crowd. "If the Qinhua University student can't go, we'll go ourselves!"

Baiyun saw a figure wearing a green Mao jacket and a green hat tightly to his skull. He was a prominent person on campus, a graduate student in political science and a veteran activist.

Tears began to swell up in Baiyun's eyes. She suddenly felt as if she was becoming a part of a powerful force.

By the time they reached the University of Political Science and Law, the rain stopped and the sun peeked out again. The students there applauded, cheered through their dorm windows and banged on their tin plates and washbasins. They invited the students from Beida to their auditorium for bread and hot water.

"We are really a group of crazy people," said Yumei as she sat down on the concrete floor in the crowded auditorium with Baiyun, Longfe and Li Yan. "Look at my shoes, my pants. They are all soaking wet." She moved her feet inside her wet athletic shoes, which were half-full of water, generating a squeaky sound.

Everyone laughed.

"Yumei, you should dance in these shoes," suggested Li Yan.

Yumei stood up and started dancing. She bounced around, snapping her fingers. Her freckled face was radiant; her long wet stringy hair swayed back and forth.

"Longfe, join me!"

"No, I don't dare dance without music." He held his knees against his chest, watching her.

"We can create our own music," said Yumei.

"Okay. How about we sing, and you dance?"

Baiyun hummed along with the others. A feeling swelled up in her chest, almost suffocating her. She wanted to join Yumei in the dance, but no matter how hard the desire filled in her chest, she could not move her legs. Her face was red, and she could feel hot steam coming up from her wet clothes.

A tall handsome young man from the Philosophy Department joined Yumei. They danced a waltz. Students surrounded them, some dancing, some humming the song.

"What a wonderful way to dry out," someone commented.

The sun had come out of the thick layer of clouds as they left the auditorium and started marching again. The air was fresh and damp. It was noon.

The streets were busy again. People came out for lunch, to go home for a nap or to start a second work-shift.

The march was going at a normal pace. People on the street started cheering; "Hey, Beida!" or "Hey, that's great!" and "Keep going, we support you."

Baiyun was surprised to see so many people were brave enough to support them openly, especially when they approached the downtown area, where policemen were posted at every street corner.

Since 1978, when the Cultural Revolution had come to the end, no one believed another political movement would come along because people had lost faith in the Communist Party. They felt cheated by Chairman Mao. They turned from fully supporting the Communist Party to simply disbelieving.

Most people nowadays were interested in getting higher pay, larger bonuses and sending their children to the best universities. Even Baiyun's romantic mother had started her own business. It was so strange that people could still be excited by a political demonstration.

"No more corruption!" "Patriotism is no crime!" "Long live the people!" Baiyun chanted slogans along with others, lifting her right arm up and down.

It reminded her of her primary and high school days when chanting slogans were a part of daily life. They had to do it every morning before class. "Long live Chairman Mao!"

They chanted, "Down with the rich landlords!" and "Down with the capitalist's running dog!"

She even had to say, "Down with Yang Kaiming!" when her intellectual father, Yang Kaiming, was demonized on a stage along with other intellectuals. The demonized victims on the stage wore black pointy hats with their arms tied behind their backs and backs bending forward, which was called 'Riding the airplane'.

It all sounded so familiar, yet so foreign. A feeling of uneasiness bothered her. She wanted to stop chanting.

"Don't you think it's awful that we have to chant slogans again?" Baiyun asked Yumei, who was absorbed in the chanting.

"Why ?" Yumei seemed not to be bothered at all. She used all her strength, jumping and shouting in beautiful gestures as if she was dancing. She always did well in front of others.

Baiyun thought of a way to contribute to the movement other than chanting. "Yumei, don't you think we should distribute the pamphlets from Longfe?"

"Yes. How do you think we should do it?" asked Yumei.

"How about you climb a tree, pretending to observe the demonstration? Then you quickly tie the pamphlets to a branch." Baiyun paused for Yumei's reaction.

"And then..." said Yumei.

"And then you quickly come down the tree so I can shake it. The pamphlets will fly all over the Square like peace doves," said Baiyun proudly.

"You really think this will work with me going up to the tree?" Yumei was a little skeptical.

"You are lighter. You know me. Since I'm so clumsy, I may fall off the tree and cause a big stir."

"I think this sounds good in theory but I don't think it will work in reality."

"Okay. I have another idea. How about, I pretend to be sick? We can stay behind the demonstrators. The police only watch the students and they will not notice us if we stay behind. Then we can mingle with the civilians and spread the pamphlets. Don't you think this will work?"

"Yes. I think this might work," said Yumei.

Baiyun ran to the side of the road and began vomiting. She squatted and pressed against her belly, vestiges of the bread she ate earlier at University of Political Science and Law running out of her mouth.

"Baiyun, what's wrong with you?" Yumei and Longfe came over.

Baiyun shook her head.

"Longfe, how about you keep going? Baiyun and I will find you later," said Yumei. Then she pulled Longfe aside and whispered into his ears.

Longfe nodded happily while walking away.

Baiyun and Yumei stopped at the corner of Xidan market, about a half mile away from the center of the Tiananmen Square. The streets were crowded with demonstrators and shoppers.

They went into the crowd and threw bundles of pamphlets as far as they could. With the help of the wind, the pink and yellow pamphlets flew up to the sky like kites, landing on the demonstrators and the civilian crowd.

Baiyun and Yumei stood on the sidewalk, looking into the sky. They felt enormously proud and relieved. They hugged each other.

"I can't believe that your plan worked," said Yumei.

"You see I don't just make up theories," said Baiyun, feeling really smart.

By the time Baiyun and Yumei finally reached Tiananmen Square in front of the Monument of the People's Hero, the sky had turned dark again. Lightening broke above the Monument, from which hung a huge portrait of Hu Yaobang. Illuminated by the lightening, his solemn face seemed to come alive.

Baiyun stared at the ten-story high Monument of the People's Hero and realized something important. She was twenty-one years old and did not remember how many times she had been in front of the Monument. Every time she was here, no matter the circumstances, she felt the Monument was a symbol of people who had sacrificed their lives for something they had believed in.

As depicted along the two-meter high marble reliefs, in the last hundred years several important uprisings had changed the course of Chinese history. The Wuchang Uprising, a key event leading up to the Revolution of 1911, inflicted a deadly blow to the feudal dynasty in Chinese history.

She wished this democratic movement would eventually lay a corner stone to establish a democratic China. Along with the decline of the legacy of Chairman Mao and the Communist Party, Tiananmen Square and the Monument of the People's Hero also became a less meaningful symbol in the mind of the people.

Baiyun could not believe she was having her same old reaction to the Monument. Her blood rushed through her body and a sense of duty hit her. Yes, that was why she was here, to help her country to solve its problems.

Baiyun could hear her mother's voice, 'Don't get involved too much. Think about yourself. It is very hard for China to get over its problems. Go to America - that's the way to go. Don't you understand me?'

She knew what her mother was talking about. Nowadays all the smart people who had the connections had gone abroad, and very few came back. She wanted to leave, because increasingly her mother's lifestyle bothered her. She was afraid that one day the volcano in her house would erupt and it would be very hard for her to get out unscathed, but at this moment, all that had disappeared. She felt lucky to be here, to be involved in such an exciting event for a change.

"Baiyun, where is my raincoat?" said Yumei, taking her out of her reminiscence.

Both girls were soaked. They pulled at each other's drenched clothes and laughed.

"Look. I can see your bra." Baiyun pointed at Yumei. "Woo. There are your tits. How embarrassing!"

"What are you laughing about?" Longfe suddenly appeared.

"Girl problems. It's not your business!" said Yumei.

Longfe laughed as he put his arm around Yumei and squeezed her, which caused water to drip down from her like a sponge.

"You're soaked. How about wearing my raincoat?" He draped his long thick raincoat around Yumei's shoulders and asked. "How are you?"

"I'm fine," said Yumei. She seemed comfortable under Longfe's arms.

"You look wonderful. Your face is radiant and your lips are red as though you have put on makeup," said Longfe, looking at Yumei even more intensely.

"Ha... You know I don't use makeup," said Yumei proudly.

"Of course. You don't need it."

Baiyun decided to leave them alone.

As she turned toward the crowd, several student leaders had gathered on the top steps of the Monument.

"Attention, please! Attention, please! Sit down, everyone," said a young man, who wore an army green uniform. He had long hair, a wide square face and a protruding jaw.

"That's Wuer Kaixi. He is one of the student leaders." Baiyun heard a student say.

Thunder rolled and dark clouds re-invaded the sky dumping another ocean of cold rain down onto the Square.

Everyone sat on the cold and wet concrete without complaining. No one was holding an umbrella.

Yumei was leaning against Longfe. Baiyun felt cold and lonely.

The first speaker, Professor Chen Mingyuan, was about to speak. He was a noted professor and poet who had edited and published a famous collection of poetry from the 1976 Tiananmen Square movement. "Today's scene reminds me of 1976. It has also reminds many people in the crowd of those memorable, exciting days, of the bloodshed and our final victory!" His passionate and provocative voice drew Baiyun completely in. "I come here first as a citizen, then as your teacher, also as your friend, and finally as an old tired warrior in the struggle for democracy, "he continued." I want to be the first of your professors to come here and say that I support you."

Deafening cheers and applause followed this speech.

Baiyun remembered the 1976 Tiananmen Movement. She had been here with her friends just after Primer Zhou had died.

The Square was packed with people. Hundreds of poems were posted on the Monument of the People's Hero, and white flowers covered the evergreen shrubs around it like snowflakes.

That demonstration brought down 'The Gang of Four', a power-corrupted group led by Mao Zedong's widow, Jiang Qing, and started a new era in Chinese history.

That had been her first taste of the power of the people.

"Baiyun."

Baiyun was startled and looked back to see Longfe and Yumei standing behind her. Yumei was leaning against Longfe with her eyes closed. Her wet face was pale. Longfe was the one who had called her.

"Yes," Baiyun said nervously.

"Yumei doesn't feel very good. Do you know what we should do?" asked Longfe.

"She must be getting too cold and hungry. We have to get her out of here and find a warm place for her." Baiyun's heart went out to Yumei. She wished she could carry her out of there immediately and tend to her in bed.

"It's impossible to get out of here." Longfe said hopelessly.

"We have done enough. Those leaders should not let us suffer any further." Li Yan sounded very logical.

Baiyun agreed, but did not say anything more. Like being at a splendid party, she did not want the demonstration to end. Going home sounded like hell, and going back to school and sitting in the library forever seemed boring.

"Baiyun," said Xia Nan, who was the head of the student association. He carried a video camera and a megaphone. "You girls have done a good job of keeping everyone in good spirits. Why don't you say something?" He handed over the megaphone.

Naturally, Baiyun thought of Yumei first, "Yumei should do that."

"Baiyun, Yumei is in pain. Why don't you do it? I think you can," said Longfe.

Baiyun was glad that Longfe was so encouraging. In a fraction of a second, many thoughts swept through her head. She was pleased, of course, to be asked to stand up in front such a big audience to say something. On the other hand, she was also aware that there were most likely plainclothes policemen watching her, and she could jeopardize her chances of going abroad by speaking.

She stared at her wet, out-of-shape leather shoes and could not make up her mind. She thought of her plan to study abroad, her mother's advice, her father's encouragement and her eagerness to leave her family. She could feel many pairs of eyes staring at her, which generated enough heat to make her sweat. She hated these occasional moments in life when she had a hard time making up her mind.

She still remembered what her father told her when she informed him about her plan to take TOEFL. "It always has been one of my dreams to go and study abroad." He sounded rather clear-headed considering how much wine he had just drunk. "My family was poor and could not afford to send me. I worked as a tutor during college in order to earn some money for me to travel to the place where the exams were being held, but by the time I was ready, the opportunity was gone." Baiyun could see his old eyes glistening.

"Baiyun, stand up and tell everyone that we have a student sick here. We need help." Li Yan was the practical one.

"Baiyun, do it. Don't be afraid." Longfe stared at her with his passionate eyes.

Baiyun liked it. How could she refuse Longfe's request and how could she delay Yumei's chance in getting help?

"Hi, everybody." Her first sentence was so quiet that no one could hear it.

"Louder. Louder." Li Yan coached her from below.

"The rain has finally stopped. I guess our tough spirit has defeated the bad weather," she continued. Her jaw shivered, yet she was in a good spirits as she continued, "I'm glad that I have skipped classes to take part in this historical event, which was always what I wanted to do." Everyone laughed. "I'm a Chemistry major." Her voice was drowned in the loud cheering.

"Baiyun, you have never skipped one single class," said Li Yan.

"Hey, Chemistry doesn't just produce nerds!" shouted someone.

"The Police are coming! The Police are coming!" A voice in the distance stirred up the crowd. The sea of people started rippling, moving like waves.

Taking the microphone from Baiyun, Wuer Kaxi exhorted the crowd: "Don't panic! We aren't doing anything wrong! We have completely achieved our goal today." Waving his arms, he said, "Being here itself is a victory! We came here in a very orderly way; let's leave peacefully the same way. I'd like to have the brigade of marshal come to me and we could use some volunteers, too. We'll rent buses and send everyone home." His pockmarked face was gleaming in the dusk.

"Longfe, Li Yan, would you come and help me?" Xia Nan jumped into the action immediately.

"Who is going to take care of Yumei?" Longfe was still holding Yumei to his chest.

"Let Baiyun take over."

Longfe handed Yumei to Baiyun and shook her hands. "Baiyun. Take care."

"No problem." Baiyun's heart was dancing with joy because she and Yumei were left alone again.

The newfound closeness she felt for Yumei brought her joy, even though she suspected that Yumei did not share the affection in the same way.

The situation was rather chaotic in the Square. More people flowed in after dusk. They were citizens who had just come back from work. The Square was dark, without official lights. Many of the curious people just wandered around, and then gathered in circles, and talked quietly, as they listened to the reciting of passionate poetry. There was no sign of a police crackdown.

Because they walked slowly, Baiyun and Yumei soon fell behind the crowd. The rain stopped, but the wind was chilly. They found a stone bench in front of Zhongshen Park, which was a little further down from the Forbidden City, and sat down.

"How are you, Yumei?" asked Baiyun.

"I can't walk anymore," moaned Yumei. Baiyun held Yumei tightly to keep her warm.

"Okay, maybe I can find someone with a bike to take you home."

Yumei rested her head on Baiyun's lap and drew her legs up on the bench. It looked like the cold wind had caused another cycle of devastating cramps. Baiyun could tell because Yumei's moaning was getting louder. Her wet clothes became icy cold. Even Baiyun was shivering.

"Hi, girls. Do you need any help?" A tall middle-aged man stopped his bike in front of them.

He wore a pair of tight blue jeans, a white polyester shirt and a tan windbreaker. He sat erect on his very high bike seat. His eyes were deep and bright. His face was chiseled and sun-tanned. He had a head full of thick black hair. His long and straight nose made him look noble.

This nice man startled Baiyun. He was like a knight appearing in front of her. She blinked her eyes to make sure he was really there.

"Yes," said Baiyun. "She is cold and exhausted. We need to take her home immediately. We are from Beida, a long way from here."

The man swung his leg across the bike and got off.

He sat next to Yumei and felt her head softly. "She has a fever," he said. He turned to Baiyun. "My name is Dagong. I work in the Beijing Electronics Parts Factory. I think we should try to take her to Fuwai Hospital Emergency Room, which is not too far from here. Would you help me move her onto the bike?"

They lifted Yumei up and let her hold on to both of their shoulders.

"Where are we going?" Yumei slowly opened her eyes.

"We are going to take you to the hospital."

Then Baiyun asked Dagong, "Front seat or back?"

"Let's put her in the front," said Dagong matter of factly.

"Why not in the back?"

"Because you are going to sit in the back," commanded Dagong.

"Me? I can take the bus. Don't bother." Baiyun's heart leapt.

Yes, of course, she wanted to go with them but she was also realistic.

"You don't believe I can take both of you on my bike?" Dagong beamed at her and looked more attractive.

"I... do. But...it's hard. A lot of traffic police are here, you know?"

"Trust me. I know the area."

Baiyun did not respond. Staring at Tiananmen Square in the dark, people scurrying around, she suddenly felt tired.

"Come on. I can carry five or six people on a bike, no problem," said Dagong firmly.

He started to sound like a knight with magic power.

"Really?"

"Yes. I used to work for the Beijing Acrobatic Company," boasted Dagong.

Dagong sat on the bike first. Baiyun jumped onto the rear fender seat, which was a little too high for her. Dagong kicked the ground, and they were off.

"Hold on to me, if you have trouble staying on," said Dagong.

She wrapped her arms tightly around him.

Baiyun could feel heat radiating from his body. She knew he was riding hard. She gradually leaned closer until finally she was resting her head against his back.

"So, you are from Beida?"

"Yes. Have you heard of it?" Baiyun teased him. She could not believe that she was in such a happy mood.

"Are you kidding? Of course, it's the most famous university in the country. What do you study?"

"Chemistry."

"I have a degree in Physics."

"You have been in college too?"

"Yes. That was ten years ago. You see, I'm very old."

"No, I don't think so."

Dagong would be at least ten years older than she was, thought Baiyun. She could not believe her luck that she had run into such an attractive older man.

"What you are doing here in Tiananmen Square is great. Now I'm always looking forward to the evenings. I could just walk out of my alley, and see what's going on. It has become a habit."

"Do you live close by?" Baiyun realized it was very useful to know someone in the neighborhood, if they were going to come here more often.

"Yes, I have no excuses for not getting involved. Although I'm just a technician, I support you students whole-heartily. I believe you are going to make a difference."

"I hope so. I'm just a follower."

"You are telling me I'm just helping two followers?"

"But that's worthwhile," said Baiyun.

"Yes. Why?"

"Don't you think so?"

"I guess you are right, college student."

"How is Yumei?" asked Baiyun.

She just remembered her friend Yumei, who was still sitting on the front handlebar and she had not heard from her for a while.

"She is sleeping, I think," said Dagong while pedaling faster.

They rode through many small streets and alleys, and stayed away from the traffic police successfully.

It was a pleasant journey for both Baiyun and Dagong. Dagong had never ridden a bike that ran so fast and smoothly. Baiyun had never found a place so comfortable and so like home.

CHAPTER 4

Baiyun was riding her bicycle home while still indulging in the sweet dream of the exhilarating episode in Tiananmen Square the night before.

As the last ray of sunlight disappeared behind the horizon and the sky turned gray, reality hit her. Meiling called her dormitory that morning and the building manager woke her up from her dream. Meiling told Baiyun that she was sick and she needed her to go home to take care of her. How sick could her mother be? Would she not rather see her boyfriend Lao Zheng instead of her? Baiyun did not leave until she was done with her classes for the day.

The weather was windy and gloomy. A few people walked on the street alone and swayed with the wind. Women covered their faces with thin transparent nylon scarves; while men pulled down their hats' brims to hide their identities. They clutched their food baskets as though they might be snatched away at any moment.

The loudspeakers on campus kept telling people not to go to Tiananmen Square in order to avoid dire consequences.

Baiyun parked her bicycle outside and walked into the main entrance of the apartment building and then her own home on the first floor.

Right away, she noticed Meiling was lying in bed moaning in her bedroom with the door open, for once.

"Mom, what can I do for you?" asked Baiyun.

"Nothing. I should... be better tomorrow. You should bring some food for your father. I don't know what he is doing in the other room."

Baiyun was not used to take care of Meiling because she rarely asked her for help.

She would rather deal with her father. She was curious about what her father was doing because she smelled something funny.

It was a small, odd-shaped hallway, with the kitchen and a room on the left. An entrance led into two rooms on the right. The white wall in the hallway was cold and smooth like porcelain under the late afternoon sun.

Dried-up bok choy, muddy turnips and tall spinach lay, looking tired, against the wall.

In the middle of the hallway, to one side, stood a refrigerator and an old bamboo dish cabinet set on top of a wet-looking wooden rack.

Baiyun walked into her father's bedroom, which was also the dining room.

Her father was sunk down into a cushioned wooden chair trimming the end of a twig. A pot of sand sat next to the twig. In the dim light of a desk lamp, he examined the twig to make sure the cut was perfect. After several tries, he buried the end of the twig in the sand and set it next to a row of pots on the windowsill. With the help of the magnifying glass, he examined them one by one.

"Meow. Meow!" He yowled, and Baiyun took it as a sign of pleasure.

"Father," said Baiyun, which startled him.

"Oh. What are you doing here?" He looked at Baiyun with his old eyes and went right back to his trimming task.

After taking care of the plants, Father returned to his desk. He began scribbling on scraps of paper. Occasionally, he would crumple the paper and throw it into the wastebasket. Then he took a new piece and scribbled some more. Finally, he held a sheet of paper in front of his nose and laughed loudly.

"One and a half rats per flower pot, my honored citizens. That's right. Ha, ha..."

He spun around on his chair and picked up a white plastic pail from underneath the desk, which was full of dead rats. He took out the rats one by one and laid them on the dirt in flowerpots. Returning to his desk, he began cutting the rest of rats in half with a huge pair of rusty scissors, one after another. Blood spilled on the floor, and sprayed onto his clothes and face.

"Meow. Meow!" He seemed to enjoy the taste of blood in his mouth.

Watching this, Baiyun could not stand it anymore. She ran out of the room and thought about leaving that disgusting place.

Then she remembered her duty to bring food to father. She opened the refrigerator and found some cold stir-fry.

She heated it up on the gas stove in the small kitchen and walked back to the dining room with one hand on her nose.

Father was writing comments between the lines of a textbook using a magnifying glass. The book itself revealed why he had to use the magnifying glass. It was a textbook of advanced mathematics called, 'Special Function' that had equations and words. However, a handwritten version was superimposed on top of the print. In fact, most of the printed version had been either crossed out or pasted over with handwritten text.

Baiyun left the food on his desk. Underneath the glass on the table, Baiyun noticed many new pictures of red and purple roses.

Father wolfed down his food and continued writing in the textbook. After a few minutes, his head nodded. His hand dropped with the weight of the magnifying glass. The pen stopped; blue ink soaked through the page and created a large stain on the page. In a minute, loud snoring sullied the silence. Under the dim lamplight, the flushing of his face made him look like a roasted animal.

Baiyun looked away only to set her eyes on pots of roses in full bloom. Their color ranged from yellow to pink and from red to black. Most were bloody red like a girl's lipstick, ready to be kissed.

Baiyun realized her parents were in no mood or shape to talk to her, but before she decided to leave, she heard a motorcycle approaching. She sat down at the desk in the middle of the room.

Lao Zheng rushed into the apartment without knocking. He nodded to Baiyun, winked at her, and then went straight to Meiling's bedroom after letting the curtain down.

The curtain on Meiling's bedroom door was like a woman's summer dress—just long enough to hide the mid-parts of the body.

Meiling asked him "How much do we have now?"

"Oh, about twenty thousand," Lao Zheng answered.

"No. I don't believe you. You must have put away some for yourself."

"Come on, woman. You can't be serious. Have I ever cheated you?"

"Stop!" There was the sound of Meiling slapping Lao Zheng. "Don't think you can lay me as soon as you get here. Get serious for a minute. If a civil war started, we wouldn't have anything left. We'd better find a way to save our hard earned money."

"Okay, but let's talk about that later."

"Oh! What do you want? What do you want? Ha-ha..." Meiling's hysterical laugh indicated she was no longer ill. The handsome tiger embroidered on the dark brown knitted curtain suddenly came alive. His widely open mouth and pointed teeth revealed his great hunger.

"Don't be too rough with me! I'm sick."

"Come on, I'm the cure for your illness."

Two pairs of feet in slippers appeared in the space beneath the curtain. One was big and strong with bulging veins under rough dark skin, the other tiny and elegant as marble. They moved closer, separated and rose up onto the bed. The door was closed shut.

The tiger on the curtain seemed to roar. The curtain was thick and impenetrable. Peering through the tiger's eyes, Baiyun could see Meiling's and her boyfriend's ecstatic faces, which made her look away immediately.

Just before she was about to leave, she saw her father go into the kitchen.

Father lit a burner, took a fire poker and laid it on the fire. When the tip was red hot, he picked it up and marched toward Meiling's bedroom.

Without hesitation, he jabbed the fire poker directly through the eye of the tiger on the curtain. A hissing sound told her Meiling's bedroom door was closed and Father had also burned a hole through the wood.

Then he burned another and another. Finally, he threw down the poker, jumped at the door and, like a lizard crawling on a wall, spied into Meiling's room through the holes he had made.

He leaned against the door, making it squeak, and then he turned toward one side and slid down.

Something was growing in the front of his pants. He put his hand in, rubbing and squeezing. His face was scarlet and twisted.

"Aaeh! Aaeh!" This time his moaning became harsher and more intense.

"What's going on?" The door cracked open. Meiling poked her head out.

Their meeting in this situation scared Baiyun. Her heart came up in my throat. In order to distract them, she pointed to a bee on the bamboo cabinet, "Look, there's a bee!"

"What?" Father stared into the dark hallway with his two hollow eyes.

"Wow. What a beautiful bug!" Meiling leaned forward and took a closer look at the bee as Father retreated. "Look at the pretty black and yellow stripes. How beautiful." Meiling turned around her fulsome body, which was covered by an almost transparent nylon slip. She smiled with her perfect white teeth exposed and her big dark eyes full of charm.

"Yes. Yes." Father suddenly chuckled humbly. His shy eyes were cast down, and dimples showed on both cheeks.

He pulled his hands out of his pants and folded them obediently on top of his Buddha's belly.

"What are you staring at? Why don't you find a flyswatter and kill the bee?" Meiling commended.

"Kill it. No. I'm...I'm allergic to bees," mumbled Father. His tongue was always in the way when he talked to Meiling.

The bee flew away.

"My god, if it messes up my flowers, I'll kill it." Father gathered his strength and started chasing it.

"Okay. Let's catch it." Meiling shut her bedroom door behind her and followed father into his room. Baiyun found a flyswatter and joined them.

Father, whom Baiyun had never seen run so fast, used all his energy and jumped in front of the flowerpots scattered around the far end of the dining room.

"Don't touch my flowers or I'll kill you!" He threatened - his arms akimbo like a warrior.

Meiling, meanwhile, scampered after the bee from one side of the room to the other.

Baiyun followed her, waving the flyswatter.

"It's here, Baiyun! Here. Oh, you missed it. A little toward the right. Here. Here. Oh, shit!"

Stroke by stroke, Baiyun's technique was getting better. Then all of sudden, the bee landed on the windowsill.

"Baiyun, stop waving the net." Baiyun knew Father would intervene.

"Father, I'll be careful. I promise, I promise."

"Baiyun, aren't you going to listen to me?" He stared at her with two fierce eyes. His hands were clenched.

"Oh, Baiyun. Let your father take care of it. He may have the magic hands." Meiling turned around to her bedroom.

Silence returned to the house. The excitement the bee had generated disappeared.

Baiyun and Father gazed at the windowsill, which was occupied mostly by small flowerpots.

With one smack, Father killed the bee stupid enough to show up on the windowsill.

Silence this time came with the darkness. The place was as dark and cold as a grave.

Father strolled back to his faded brown, old heavy wooden desk.

Baiyun slipped out the door without saying another word. She got on her bicycle and started riding in the pitch-dark night. Hardly any stars showed in the sky.

She could feel the darkness weigh down on her, her city and the whole country.

The fresh air cheered her up and the paddling of the bicycle made her feel powerful. I will never come back here again, she was telling herself.

CHAPTER 5

At 9:00pm, Baiyun got back to her dorm but was too excited to sleep.

Meeting Dagong was a pleasant experience for her. Although she knew very little about him besides the fact that he was a nice, handsome young man. She felt he had the depth to understand her, her eccentric mother and her strange family. She found him easy to talk to and she could open her heart. She had not known him very well yet, she was telling herself. She decided that the next day she would go back to the triangle to try to find out more about the pro-democracy movement. She felt an obligation now. She had found many more interesting things to do; besides studying Chemistry.

It was as if a new chapter in her life suddenly opened up. She knew the situation would change as soon as she talked to her mother. Meiling would force her to study TOEFL again, but this was her life. Meiling could not control it anymore.

The sound of loud radio woke Baiyun up the next morning.

From the content, she soon realized that it was a new student-run campus news broadcasting station. "When the student marched to the Tiananmen Square last night, all along the road Beijing citizens came out to support them," said the Broadcaster. "People gave out cases of soda, juice, bread and eggs. The Square was full of people sitting vigil. At dawn, police started to appear. The students demanded that the authorities guarantee their safety and let them enter the Great Hall of the People to pay their last respects to Hu Yaobang. The government only granted the first request."

"Oh, my God. It's so early. Demonstration is a good thing, but they shouldn't disturb our rest." Li Yan went back to sleep.

Too tired to say anything, Baiyun went back to sleep as well.

When she woke up again, everyone had gone.

She looked up at her watch and it read 11:00 am. She knew she missed her 10:00 am Mathematics class.

Then she found a message on a piece of torn notebook paper.

"Baiyun,
I'm going to the class. I'll lend you my notes. You'd better sleep. Hope to see you in the next class.
Yumei"

An egg-bread was on the table as well as a bowl of porridge. Yumei must have gotten it for her from the cafeteria that morning.

She quickly washed her face and brushed her teeth at the concrete sink in one of the two large washrooms on the fourth floor. She ate the breakfast, made her bed and walked out of the dormitory. She decided to attend the rest of her classes, just to be good.

At 4:30 pm, Baiyun rode slowly back toward her dormitory. When Baiyun passed by the Triangle, she ran into Li Yan, who was rushing.

"Where are you going?" Baiyun asked as she balanced her bicycle between her legs.

"The News Center, the new campus radio station," said Li Yan. "You should stop by sometimes between your studies and social life."

"What social life are you talking about?" Baiyun sensed something new in her tone. Was she making fun of her for not having a social life?

"A worker named Dagong has been hanging around the campus and would like to meet up with you," said Li Yan and waved goodbye without noticing Baiyun was a little embarrassed.

Dagong was here! What was he doing here? Baiyun thought as she pushed her bicycle in the slow traffic.

She noticed some people on the street didn't all look like students. Some men were older, more muscular and had swarthy faces. Older women also ran around the campus, carrying blankets and tin containers under their arms.

The streets inside Beijing University were almost like any other street in downtown Beijing. What a change! The Pro-Democracy movement made Beijing University, normally an intellectual's paradise, into a community theatre. She could see clusters of students and workers on street corners, talking to each other like a family.

Wherever she went, everyone smiled at her in a friendly manner. Through this atmosphere, she could see changes that had already happened in people's hearts and souls.

As soon as Baiyun arrived at her dorm, she saw Dagong waiting for her by the door.

He wore a pair of dark green sunglasses. His starched white shirt and khaki pants made him look like a professor instead of a technician.

"Baiyun." He approached her enthusiastically.

"Hi, Dagong. What bought you here?" Leaning her bike against her waist, she shook hands with him.

"I'm here for a meeting with the Beijing Student Federation. We are planning a rally on May 4th to commensurate the seventieth anniversary of the May 4th student movement. We want to be part of it too. Also; I thought I might see you here."

"It's nice to see you." Baiyun let her bicycle go, which almost fell before it was rescued by Dagong, who moved quickly to catch it.

Seeing Dagong made Baiyun feel much better. The horror she experienced at home the day before was long gone from her mind.

"I'd like to show you the campus," said Baiyun.

"I would like to take you for dinner," said Dagong with a big smile. "Let's go. Do you want me to take you on my bicycle again? This time you can sit on the front handlebar and lean against my chest. I could hold you with one arm and hold on to the bicycle with the other," said Dagong.

"So people would think we are...a pair of sweethearts? No, I don't think so," said Baiyun shyly with her eyes looking down and her cheeks red. She soon recovered. She raised her head and said, "It is impossible to ride on campus now, especially near the Triangle. Have you been to the Triangle?"

"Not yet."

"Let's go then. Students always give speeches there." Baiyun felt uplifted.

They both parked their bicycles and locked them to the rack. They walked toward the Triangle.

By 5:00 pm, the sun had gradually disappeared behind the trees and buildings. The air turned a little cooler, but the amount of activities on campus had not decreased at all. It would go on until midnight. Nothing normal was happening on campus anymore.

As they approached the Triangle, they could hear someone speaking. "Our country has many problems that need reform. We have to start the change. Let's begin by overthrowing the official student association and establishing one that really represents us."

Baiyun didn't recognize the speaker, but she was eager to find out who it was.

"Anyone who has the courage to get up, give his name, his major and what class he is in, is automatically a member of the Beida Solidarity Student Federation." A different speaker announced to the crowd.

Several students started fighting their way toward the center of the crowd. They pushed and pulled with full strength. People cursed and yelled at them.

One of them jumped to the center of the stage. "My name is Li Ming and people call me Big Li. I am a junior in the Chemistry Department. I support the movement wholeheartedly," he said proudly. People cheered for him.

"I can't believe this nerd stood out," said Baiyun to Dagong.

"All kinds of people show up unexpectedly; even a dead man like me can come back to life," said Dagong.

Baiyun stared at him and then punched him lightly on the belly. "You are funny."

"I'm not entirely joking. I will tell you later. Let's see what they have to say."

"Comrade, it is so nice to have you." A medium sized young man came over and shook hands with Big Li.

Longfe stood up and started speaking. Baiyun whispered into Dagong's ears that Longfe was Yumei's boyfriend.

"Beida is a school with an honorable tradition, a tradition of leading true democratic movements. Recently Beida has fallen behind other universities. Hu Yaobang's death gives us the perfect moment. We should seize this opportunity to re-enact our tradition of democracy and science, but we must proceed with reason and planning."

Then many more students came out and gave short speeches.

Yumei walked out. After giving Longfe a hug, she started speaking. Her face was radiant. "Like most of people, I was drawn into the movement by emotion and excitement. I thought it was fun. Now I realize how important it could be. Our Beida is always ahead, like during the famous May 4th student movement seventy years ago. Our burden is heavy. Other schools are looking up to us. It is our responsibility to lead our country." She paused and threw her fist into the air. "Like many other movements, victory will not come easily. It may cost blood and even lives, but I am ready. I am ready to sacrifice my youth and my body to this honorable cause."

The crowd applauded her when she moved to the side.

"Wow. She is ready to sacrifice her beautiful body," said Baiyun to Dagong.

Dagong rolled his eyes and nodded. Then he started moving forward.

"Where are you going?" Baiyun whispered.

Dagong put his fingers across his lips to indicate that she should be silent.

Dagong stepped on a wooden stool, speaking. "I am not a student. I'm a technician from Beijing Automobile Parts Factory."

The crowd cheered.

"Unlike you, I suffered during the Cultural Revolution. Unlike you, I was not allowed to go to college due to my family background. Now, I'm proud to be part of this movement. You will need our help to move tanks." He raised his big fist.

With her mouth half open, Baiyun stared at Dagong. She could not believe her eyes, and she wondered how such a soft-spoken man could be such a confident speaker.

She jumped up and down cheering for him. Among this excited crowd of students, she found friends, solidarity, and she felt at home.

At this moment, her mother's warning, her eagerness to go abroad and leaving home had all disappeared. She felt that she was so proud to be here, to be part of this exciting movement.

Longfe stood up on a wooden stool and continued, "In the last few years, the corrupted officials robbed our people and created disturbances in our society. Isn't it the time to change our country and its leadership?"

"Yes!" The crowded shouted.

"Do you think the officials who benefit from the corruption, and all others who take the advantage of lawlessness, will be qualified to lead us to a better society?"

"No."

"So we as students have responsibilities. Hu Yaobang is dead, and we have begun a student movement. Are we trying to create turmoil and chaos in society, as the government always accuses us of doing?"

"No."

"But whenever we march, we stop the buses and disturb the pedestrians on the streets. Should we change the way we protest?" asked Longfe.

"We should."

A new world appeared in front of Baiyun. She did not know what it was yet, but it was becoming clearer and clearer.

"Should we go and have some dinner?" Dagong awakened Baiyun from her ruminating.

"Sure. Let's go to the cafeteria." Baiyun led the way.

They walked toward the cafeteria among many students on bicycles and foot.

As they walked, they ran into some of Baiyun's friends. She briefly introduced Dagong and said he was a friend she met in the last march. Her friends smiled and did not ask any questions, although rumors had already flown around the campus.

In the cafeteria, Baiyun bought a stirred-fried bok choy with tofu while Dagong purchased two boiled eggs in soy sauce.

They found a table and sat on benches across from each other.

The cafeteria was noisy with many people coming in and going. Students rushed into the cafeteria with a bundle of big-letter posters under their arms. Some Beijing citizens walked into the cafeteria to enjoy a slice of college life. It was like a county fair without animals.

Baiyun decided to ask Dagong about his speech to the students. "I thought you went to college. Didn't you say that you had a degree in Physics when you took Yumei and I home from Tiananmen Square?"

"Yes, but that was in 1975, which was in the middle of the Cultural Revolution, and it is not a real college education. You know that. We went to college to re-educate professors, not to gain knowledge, which is why I'm still a technician."

Dagong talked while chewing because he could not wait to answer Baiyun.

"So you had a chance to go to a real college but got turned down due to your family background?"

"Yes. In 1965, I was 18 years old and a straight A student. Every college in the country had rejected my application, including Beijing University." Dagong's voice was getting hoarse.

Baiyun could feel his sorrow even though it had happened many years ago.

"What is your bad family background?" Baiyun became very curious now.

"My father was a dead capitalist businessman and my mother died right after I was born. My aunt raised me and she passed away twenty-two years ago, right after the beginning of the Cultural Revolution. Afterwards, I was sent to Inner Mongolia for re-education."

She realized that Dagong was as old as Meiling's former boyfriend Weiming. Baiyun was deeply in love with her Uncle Weiming all throughout her childhood, but he disappeared forever. His absence left a void in her heart ever since.

As Baiyun stared at Dagong, her eyes grew moist. She was out of words.

"What's the matter? Too sad?"

"I too have suffered as a result of the Cultural Revolution. My father died in the labor camp during the Cultural Revolution." Baiyun lied.

Baiyun could not believe she lied about her father being dead, but who would believe her if she told the truth to anyone, especially Dagong, a fresh new friend. If she told him the truth, he would think she was crazy to put up with that family. He would not want to speak to her after that.

It was essential that she lie to him. He would not learn the truth as long as she did not invite him to her apartment. If the situation lent itself, she would deal with it then.

"My mother had many boyfriends living with us. My classmates used to treat me badly because my father was a professor and my mother had a taste for younger men."

"What? Younger men? Wow. It must be very hard to live with them."

"Not really. Sometimes it could be fun, especially when they had parties. It wasn't bad, except when one of them fell in love with me."

"Really? Did your mother break up with him? Why didn't you elope with him? It sounds like something I would read in fiction." Dagong stared at Baiyun in utter astonishment.

"Of course, I never told him I loved him, too. He could be thrown in jail for courting a minor, and he had enough trouble himself already."

"What trouble?"

"His father was a dead businessman."

"Just like me. I know what it is like being a dead businessman's son. It means you can't have the life you want to live and the girl you want to love."

"Exactly. Mother broke up with him and kicked him out of our apartment. I never saw him again." Tears slowly rolled down on Baiyun's oval face. Her tears, while telling Dagong this ancient story, surprised her. She wiped them off with her shirtsleeves and forced herself to smile for Dagong.

"Let's take a walk in campus, it might cheer you up. I hear music outside, it must be a concert." Dagong stood up and offered his hand to Baiyun.

"Sure. Let's go." Baiyun wiped her face quickly and followed Dagong.

People rushed by them as they were walking toward the music. Some of them even carried their own wooden chairs or stools.

"A concert by Cui Jian!" People yelled while running. "It is in front of the Library."

"Cui Jian? Who is he?" Dagong was interested.

"He's a famous rock & roll singer. At least, he is very famous here. He plays here on campus every week," said Baiyun proudly.

"If he is famous here, he will be famous all over China soon."

"As usual, Beida is the center of the rebellion."

"Or the center of the renovation."

"It is the same whichever way you put it," said Baiyun. She felt so much happier now. A good piece of music has the ability to make people cry or cheer them up. "If you keep coming here, who knows what will become of you."

"You are right," said Dagong looking into the crowd. "Let's hurry so we can get good seats."

He took Baiyun's hand and they started rushing.

As they approached the library where the concert was, it was harder to walk. They could see people standing and waving their arms.

"I guess it's standing room only," said Dagong.

"We'll be lucky if we can see anything at all. But you could see, since you are tall." Baiyun was a little disappointed.

"Finally, being tall is useful. I'm not just a Big Dumb Guy. I can carry you on my shoulders if you want."

"No. I would tip and fall into the sea of people since I'm so clumsy," said Baiyun, even though she wondered what it would be like if Dagong carried her on his shoulders. "Can you see anything?" Baiyun asked.

"Yes. He is blind-folded with a piece of red cloth."

"I hear people humming, 'A Piece of Red Cloth'. It must be the song," said Baiyun.

"The lights are blinding, maybe that's why he is blind-folded. I worry about him. I hope he doesn't fall off the stage." Dagong narrated. "He is playing a trumpet now. He is like Mozart and can play an instrument blindfolded. He has dancers on stage dressed in tiger skin suits doing a tiger walk."

"I'm envious you can see everything and I can't." No matter how hard Baiyun tried to tiptoe, she still could not see. All she could see was tips of people's arms stretching to the sky and the hair on their wobbling heads.

"Can you carry me?"

Dagong did not answer. He was too engrossed in the concert.

"Can you carry me?" Baiyun poked Dagong in the ribs.

"Oh. Sure." He squatted down and let Baiyun climb onto his shoulders.

With some effort, he stood up. Baiyun screamed. Her body wobbled and she discovered that she was afraid of heights. She held Dagong's neck tightly in order not to fall into the sea of people. What was going on stage transfixed her. The red cloth on Cui Jian's face was gone. Wearing a white baseball hat, a plaid shirt and a pair of khakis, he looked as if he were in a dream on stage among the artificial clouds and the tiger-skinned dancers.

At the end of the song, Baiyun cheered, as did everyone around her.

She stared into the distance and could almost see her voice traveling over many black-haired heads bouncing back and forth. She felt as if the people around her were staring at her in admiration. She had never felt so tall and so confidant. Her shyness totally disappeared, as though an alien had inhabited her and taken control of her brain.

After the concert, Baiyun climbed down from Dagong's shoulders with the help of those around them.

Dagong and Baiyun held hands and walked back toward Baiyun's dormitory, where Dagong's bicycle was parked.

"It was so much fun that I don't feel guilty for not studying TOFEL tonight," said Baiyun.

She could not stop smiling while skipping forward. Dagong had to walk fast to catch up with her.

"Like an old Chinese saying, there is no never-ending party. I will go back to my apartment and study TOFEL," said Dagong. His face was rather solemn.

"You are right. We should go back to study TOFEL instead of partying all night," agreed Baiyun, as a good and responsible student.

"Even though partying all night would be great!" said Dagong.

"You are too old to party all night," said Baiyun teasingly.

"Hey. You never know what an old guy like me can do."

Dagong stopped when they reached Baiyun's dormitory.

On the side of the building beside the entrance, Dagong held Baiyun by the waist and pulled her toward him. Baiyun's heart was beating faster. What was he going to do? For some reason she knew. She moved her head closer staring at him with her two innocent brown eyes waiting for his lips to reach hers.

A sound startled her.

"Hi, guys." It was Yumei's voice.

"Hi, Yumei."

Baiyun quickly moved away from Dagong.

"Oh, sorry. Have fun."

Yumei quickly walked into the dormitory door.

"Well, she stole our kiss," said Dagong. "I need to go now. It will take me a while to get home."

He held Baiyun's hands, staring into her eyes. He gave her a quick kiss on the cheek, and then turned away.

Baiyun was standing in the dark feeling lost. She wished he would give her a long kiss, although she knew it might be too fast and too rushed.

She needed to go to bed.

CHAPTER 6

At 2:00 am, on April 25th, Dagong arrived home after riding his bicycle for an hour and a half.

He pushed the squeaky gate to the four-corner yard open and saw someone sitting there smoking. As he walked closer, he realized it was Lao Liu with a cat lying next to him.

Oh my God, Dagong thought and wished that not a single soul in this yard had witnessed his coming home this late or this early. He did not want to explain himself to his neighbors.

He knew that some day he would have to explain to Baiyun that he had a wife and a child, so he couldn't marry her even though he was already deeply in love with her after only knowing her for a couple of days.

Of course, he could not tell Lao Liu about this.

"Lao Liu, why are you still awake? Are you day dreaming?" Dagong tried to be humorous.

"Dagong? You are late, wild man," said Lao Liu, as though he were waking up from a nap.

"Why are you still awake, dead man?"

"Wow. You are getting naughty, too. I guess it's good for you. You used to be the dead man in this yard. Now I'm it. At least my flowers are alive."

Lao Liu stroked the cat. The cat turned around and seemed to enjoy it.

Dagong sat down next to Lao Liu and lit a cigarette.

"Zhang Ping has been looking for you this evening. She wanted to go and find you in Tiananmen Square. I told her that it was impossible to find someone there. After the memorial service of Hu Yaobang, so many people were hanging around Tiananmen Square. It was like a county fair in giant scale. She didn't believe me. Then I told her I had seen you talking to the students. She screamed and ran into your apartment sobbing. So be careful. If I were you, I would spend the night here in the yard," Lao Liu said as he lit another cigarette.

"What happened to you? Have you been kicked out of your apartment, too? For falling in love with your roses?" Dagong made a face.

Lao Liu did not answer for a while, yet it was not quiet. The sound of water dripping off the laundry hanging from the ropes in front of every apartment could be heard. The crickets and cicadas were chirping, celebrating the late spring night. Even some loud snoring could be heard through the paper-thin windows.

Loud shouting suddenly drowned out the quiet sounds as a door flew open.

Mrs. Wang chased Mr. Wang out of the house. "Where did you go today after work?" Mrs. Wang shouted. She wore a torn T-shirt and a ragged pair of shorts. Her long hair was disheveled. She waved a shoe in her right hand.

"I went to Tiananmen Square to see what was going on." Mr. Wang said as he tried to run from his angry wife."Be quiet, or you will wake everyone up"

"I don't care. Do you know it is dangerous there?"

"Dangerous? I think it is safer there than at home with you."

He opened the gate and wandered out.

Mrs. Wang followed him to the gate and yelled into the darkness. "Okay. I don't care where you go now. But tomorrow I want you to come home after work before going off to some crazy political demonstration."

Dagong stared at Lao Liu and shook his head. He then waved at Mrs. Wang who was still breathing heavily from anger.

"Come and have a cigarette," said Dagong.

"Sure. I need one." Mrs. Wang sat down and started crying. "What am I going to do? We have four kids."

Her cigarette went out right away and she had to have Dagong light it again for her.

"Don't worry. He will come home. Where would he go otherwise? He loves the boys. When did he come home today?" asked Dagong.

In his mind, he could see Zhang Ping's anxious face as she was asking about his whereabouts.

"Eleven! What do you think he was doing?" Mrs. Wang calmed down a little.

"He might have been walking around at Tiananmen Square watching Poetry reading or a Rock & Roll concert, or maybe he went over to the college to work with students." Dagong was getting self-conscious.

"Whom are you talking about? Do you think that sounds like my husband? He goes to work and he comes home. He has never been interested in anything else. All of sudden, you think he has joined the pro-democracy movement? Is that absurd? I think he is seeing a woman." Mrs. Wang whipped her long hair to her back and took a deep drag on her cigarette.

"I don't know. The country is changing and people are changing." Dagong turned to Lao Liu. "Hey. Why are you so quiet? Sleeping? Where do you think Mr. Wang has been going after work?"

Silence.

Dagong tried to push him. "Hey, if you don't answer, I will push you into the fish pond."

"Ha…." Mrs. Wang started laughing hysterically while pounding the bare brick she was sitting on. "A dead cop in the fish pond. What a lovely sight! The government will have to send a new policeman to watch us here."

"Stop. You will wake everyone up." Lao Liu suddenly opened his eyes.

"Okay. You don't want me here. I'm leaving. I hear one of my boys crying." Mrs. Wang got up, tripped on a gap between bricks in the yard, steadied herself and walked quickly into her apartment.

Dagong could imagine Zhang Ping pushing down the door and charging toward him with a knife in her hand, her face red with fangs. He knew that he was in hot water or would be in deep trouble if he kept going to Beijing University and 'running' into Baiyun. He could not imagine not seeing her now though. Life is short. If he is ready to take risks in his life, now is the time, he told himself. If Zhang Ping kicked him out, he would just pitch a tent in the Square.

Lao Liu lit a new cigarette. "That was a nice nap."

"Are you awake? Where do you think Mr. Wang has been hanging out in the last few days?"

"The reason I didn't say anything was because I knew where he has been going," said Lao Liu rather seriously.

"Where?" Dagong was getting very curious.

"He has been taking pictures of the protestors for the police. I saw him in the official video. You see, that's why I didn't say anything. We have a spy here. We have a spy in our yard." Lao Liu was angry. He stood up and started pacing the yard."You have to go to Beijing University tomorrow and tell them to be careful, okay. I would like to get him arrested but you know I can't. He is on the government's side. Maybe I will have a chance in the future."

"Okay. I will go to Beijing University tomorrow and tell them this. I don't think they would stop doing what they are doing. I hear they are planning a march to Tiananmen Square to commemorate the May 4th student movement in two weeks. They are still trying to have a dialogue with the government and so far, the government refuses their demands. They may have a protest march in a couple of days. I'm a worker's representative for the Beijing Student Solitary Federation and I have to go back there tomorrow to organize that," said Dagong rather enthusiastically.

"You really like this movement, I can tell." Then Lao Liu turned toward Dagong and looked him in the eye. "Why? Why are you so brave this time? Who woke you up? Who brought you to life?"

"The students, I like them and I like freedom. Have you been to Tiananmen Square recently and looked around? I see them having poetry recitals, Rock & Roll concerts, acrobat performances and tarot card readings. People are enjoying themselves. Democracy has been around the west for several centuries and more than two hundred years in the United States. Don't you think it is about time for it to shine its light here? It's definitely not traveling at the speed of light. If so, it would have been here a long time ago." Dagong stood up as though he was practicing a speech.

Lao Liu cut in. "China tried that once before. It didn't work." Dagong knew Lao Liu was referring to the brief democracy that took place at the turn of the century under the Sun Yat-sen government.

It was after the toppling of the last imperial dynasty of China, the Qing Dynasty. China had its first democratic election in 1913. It was short-lived, and it only lasted for three months before Sun Yat-sen relinquished his power to General Yuan Shih-kai, who in turn declared himself as the emperor of a new dynasty. He ruled until his death in 1916. The warlords and Chiang Kai Shek ruled for the next 33 years without success, and they lost their power to the Communist Party in 1949. The Chinese people were used to a central government, as shown by more than 2000 years of civilized history. Lao Liu and Dagong both knew that.

Lao Liu took a deep drag from his cigarette and looked Squarely at Dagong." People in power don't like to give it up. It's so nice to be the 'Emperor of China'. So why do you think this time it's different? I can't believe how crazy you have gotten."

Dagong sighed, "Yes. I can't believe it myself. I suppose my rising from the dead after so many years has made me believe in miracles."

Lao Liu continued, "Don't you remember in 1957 when everyone was encouraged to speak up and to criticize the Communist government? In the end, the government came in, purged the most brilliant and most talented individuals and sent them to labor camps. Have you forgotten that? Have you forgotten the Cultural Revolution? Have you forgotten the labor camp yourself?" Lao Liu stood up, grabbed Dagong's shoulder and shook him. "Wake up!"

Dagong broke free from Lao Liu and he sat down again. He lit another cigarette and inhaled deeply, filling his lungs with smoke.

He exhaled, taking his time to answer Lao Liu. "I have not forgotten. But what is the meaning of life if we keep being passive and dead?"

"Who tells you to question that? You know many of these young people didn't even know what the Cultural Revolution was like. They were born after that. There is a sucker born every minute."

"That's the beauty of it - their naivety. That is why they will rise up and overthrow the government," said Dagong. He was surprised how forceful he had become.

"Then why do you think they would be interested in having a democratic government? What makes you think they are not interested in having the power all to themselves?"

"One can always hope. I don't know. I just don't want to be negative." Dagong looked up to the late spring night.

The moon came out from behind the clouds, looking huge and pale, emitting its cold light. He thought of Baiyun, her angelic face, her beautiful voice and her troubled family background. She, too, suffered in the Cultural Revolution. Why were they stupid enough to join the movement? He should find her and ask her that question. How much he wished he could see her now.

Lao Liu stretched. His bones creaked loudly; the sound echoed in Dagong's ears. "Oh. My old legs. I'm going inside, but you, Dagong, I think it is safer for you here. Zhang Ping is mad at you and she may strangle you as you sleep in your bed. Take a nap here by the fish pond instead."

Lao Liu slowly walked away.

He turned back to Dagong." Oh, I forgot to tell you that the police have been ordered to line up near the Beijing University and QingHua University so that when the students are ready to march again, they can be stopped in their infancy. Of course, the police will wait for orders. If there is no order, they will just stay there and watch. Tell the students to be careful. The police are armed. Good night."

"Okay. I will," said Dagong. He smiled at Lao Liu."Good morning."

Lao Liu chuckled and sauntered away.

Dagong tried to sleep on the brick wall by the fishpond. Fortunately, Lao Liu left a blanket behind for Dagong to cover himself with. He could not fall asleep. He thought about what was going to happen if he continued to ignore his TOFEL studies, joined the student movement and pursued Baiyun. Regardless of whether the students should succeed or not, he would have to change his life. He had woken up. He realized that he had lived in a self-imposed prison for too long. The wind of democracy finally broke the window of his cell so that he could also escape. It was up to him to decide whether he should get out or not. It is time, he was telling himself. He would at least set up a camp for himself tomorrow in Tiananmen Square, just like all the people from the other provinces.

As he thought about his escape, he heard the gate creaking. He could hear Little Pea's giggles, and her boyfriend Yu Gang's voice. As soon as they came in, they stopped whispering.

Dagong sat up, which startled Little Pea. She touched her lips trying to muffle her scream.

"Uncle Dagong, what are you doing here? Has Zhang Ping kicked you out? I don't understand. She adores you." Little Pea looked puzzled and sympathetic.

"Not really. I think I deserve a timeout myself for coming home late," said Dagong mater-of-fact. "Just like you, except your parents will understand and let you in. Zhang Ping still thinks I shouldn't get involved."

"She is still living in the past, I think. I understand you. It is hard not to get involved. Nobody is working or going to classes. Everyone feels that this time, change is inevitable. They don't want to miss it. This is a momentous event, and they want to be involved." Little Pea had really become an articulate girl.

"Did you have fun tonight?"

"Yes. We watched a poetry reading and an acrobat performance."

"Acrobat performance? What does that have to do with the pro-democracy movement?"

"They are patriotic acrobat performers. They are raising money to buy tents for people from out of town." Little Pea spoke rapidly; she was out of breath.

"Are you going to spend the night here?" Dagong asked Yu Gang.

"I think so. Little Pea, do you think your mother will approve of this?" gesturing at the two of them. Yu Gang sounded unsure.

"Of course. We are getting married, aren't we?" Little Pea gave Yu Gang a hug.

"Good night, Uncle Dagong." Yu Gang wrapped his arm around Little Pea's waist and pulled her toward Pumpkin's apartment while kissing her.

"Good night." Dagong watched them going away into the darkness and felt a tinge of jealousy. Right now, he could use a kiss from Baiyun or, rather, many kisses from Baiyun.

All of a sudden, he felt very tired. Nothing could stop him from sleeping. His eyelids were fighting to stay open, but it was a losing battle.

He decided to take a chance and go inside to sleep. Zhang Ping could not still be awake.

He tiptoed and tried not to make any noise as he approached the door. He opened the door slowly.

As he opened it, a shadow jumped on him.

"Dagong, where were you? Why haven't you come home?" Zhang Ping fell into his chest sobbing. "I have been waiting for you all evening and then dozed off for a while. I heard your voice in the yard. I was too embarrassed to join you. I heard that you were with the students. How brave and how stupid! Why have you given up your dream of going to America? Do you know how many days I have prayed for us to go to America? Do you think I'm just a stupid woman with no dreams? I do have dreams. I want to go to America, and you are my only hope."

She slipped down and fell to the floor since Dagong was not holding her tightly. She started pounding the floor and screaming.

Little Turnip woke up and ran towards his mother. They cried together. "Why are you so involved in this movement? There is no future in that. I know it. There never was and there will never be. Haven't you forgotten the labor camp?"

Dagong sat on the bed, numb. He was stunned to see Zhang Ping's reaction and to witness her desire to get out of China. She might be smarter than he thought, he told himself. He was too tired to think. He just stared into the darkness, listening and weeping silently.

"Okay. I will study TOFEL tomorrow." He uttered, to his own surprise.

Zhang Ping stopped crying immediately and stared into Dagong's eyes. "Really?"

She smiled through her tears. She told him she loved him, and she kissed him.

CHAPTER 7

At midnight, Baiyun was back in her dormitory room. By then Yumei and their other four roommates were fast asleep. Not wanting to disturb them, Baiyun went to bed quietly, without washing.

She had a dream that night. She dreamt that two people were pulling a rope to see who was stronger. They asked her to be the judge. After they had pulled for a long time, she could not declare a winner. Exhausted by watching every step they took and looking for evidence of cheating, she ended up calling it a tie.

Baiyun heard knocking on the door while still in a deep sleep.

The knocking persisted until it woke her up. She had a hard time opening her eyes due to the bright sunshine through the window.

By the time she opened her eyes, she noticed that all of her roommates had gone.

She was the only one in the room. They must have gone home for the weekend, Baiyun thought.

"Who is it?" She asked.

"Your Mother."

Baiyun thought 'Oh, my God, what is SHE doing here?' as she jumped off the top-bunk and opened the door.

Her mother was wearing a tan silk shirt and a pair of blue jeans with her hair tied up into a ponytail, looking much younger than her actual age of forty-six. Her plump figure was unusually full of energy.

After putting down two plastic bags full of food on the only table in the room, she wiped her face with her handkerchief.

"Oh, it's hot in here. Baiyun, are you alright?" She said to her still half-asleep daughter, who had crawled back into the bed.

Touching Baiyun's forehead, she said, "Aach. Are you having a fever?"

"No, Mother. I feel fine."

"You should be careful. Mother can't stay here and take care of you all the time. Last time, when I heard you marched to the Square, I was so worried." She sat down at the table across from the bunk bed.

"Mother, I am twenty years old and I can take care of myself!"

Baiyun just stared at the ceiling. She knew a long lecture from Meiling was coming.

"I don't know whether it is Mother's business to tell you or not. You are old enough to know how to deal with boys, but please stay away from those crazy students! And keep up your studies." Meiling was getting more emotional as she spoke.

"He is not a student, Mother," said Baiyun calmly. She knew that eventually she had to tell Meiling about Dagong.

"What? You have a boyfriend and he is not a student from Beida?" Meiling's mouth dropped and her two big long-lashed eyes looked huge behind her glasses.

"Yes. But… I'm just getting to know him. It feels good and I really would like to see more of him," said Baiyun while playing with her fingers. She was a little embarrassed.

"Okay, I don't care who he is. Mother is just concerned about your future, like always." Then she stood up, "Get up. Mother will take you to lunch."

"Where are we going?" Baiyun sat up.

"The Russian Tavern."

"Woo." Baiyun was excited.

She decided that it was worthwhile to sit through another one of Meiling's long lectures in order to have a nice meal.

After Baiyun finished cleaning herself in the common washroom and putting on a floral silk dress, she left for the restaurant with Meiling.

Unavoidably, Meiling's presence had attracted some attention on campus.

At the time, the other students were not so surprised, since it was just another example of a parent coming to take a student home. Many parents worried about their children's future during that chaotic time. Many parents decided to take their children home to keep them out of trouble. Nevertheless, plenty of students were still hanging out on the street. Besides, Beijing University had become the focal point for students from other universities, reporters from all over the country and small business people from all around town.

Baiyun's mother couldn't help to stop at a student fund-raising table, manned by a bald but well-groomed student. As a successful small businesswoman, Meiling enjoyed showing off her new wealth. She opened her purse and gave the student twenty yen.

"Thank you, Auntie," said the student with a big grin. He tucked the coins neatly into a metal box on the table.

"No problem. This is my daughter's school. I should support the students."

Baiyun was embarrassed, yet happy to see her mother supporting the movement.

A second young man with long hair and scruffy beard stood by the table. He was holding a flag with the Beijing University emblem on it. He picked up a small model of the flag from a box and gave it to Meiling. She proudly placed the flag in the buttonhole of her tan blouse.

After that, they passed a few impassioned street orators and the now common T-shirt vendors.

The restaurant was located across the street from one of the campus gates. It was a small, elegant restaurant specializing in Eastern European cooking.

Baiyun's mother often brought her there to treat her, although the meal did not always end happily. Still, Baiyun kept going back with Meiling. The food was too good to refuse, and the portions were large.

The restaurant was usually very busy, due to its location. It was not so today since the lunch crowd had not arrived yet.

A hostess, in a traditional Russian costume showed them to a small table for two covered with a green tablecloth.

A beautiful flower vase in the center of the table held a few freshly cut flowers.

"Oh, my God, it is so hot," said Meiling while sitting down. Her ample body always made her more sensitive to heat than others. "Baiyun, I think you are too skinny now. You see, Mother can't stop you from attending extracurricular activities, but we should set limits. It is not worthwhile to damage your health. My God, look at my tan and slender girl." She stared at her and frowned.

"Okay, Mother." Baiyun was so amazed to see how Meiling always worried about her being too skinny while her own concern was to lose some weight. Even by Western standards, she was not a skinny girl. It was not obvious to Meiling, however.

In fifteen minutes, the first course had arrived. Baiyun's was a bowl of mushroom soup while Meiling's was chicken soup. The soup looked white and creamy.

"Baiyun, listen to me. Please don't get involved in this protest business too much." Meiling lit a cigarette and started smoking. "You should think about yourself more and try harder to go to America."

Baiyun swallowed several spoonful of soup. Creamy soup was her favorite.

She finished it in just a few minutes. Then she raised her head and stared at Meiling. She did not answer her, but inside, she was asking, why wasn't she interested in going to America anymore?

In the last five years, she constantly dreamt of going to the western world because she wanted to escape the craziness of her family. Life had not been easy for her.

This noisy, strange family full of dark secrets had never felt like home for her.

While Baiyun was growing up, Meiling never had much time left to spend with her after working long hours and going out with her boyfriends.

Her betrayed, powerless father had enclosed himself inside a private greenhouse after work or played violin late into the night.

She always imagined a place far away where everyone loved her and adored her. America was a place distant enough for her to imagine.

Baiyun was not chosen to go to Europe to study during her freshman year at Beijing University, and she cried for a week. She experienced deep depression for the first time in her life.

That previous summer, she spent the weeks reading the English language newspaper. At the end of the summer, she found out that she needed to get glasses, and now all the eagerness to get out of the country had evaporated.

A powerful force had pulled her heart away from that dream. It was so strange that for the first time in her life she felt she was not in control of her life.

Through this movement, she found friends, community and most importantly, excitement. Could it be true that she always wanted to be a leader?

"Why don't you answer me?" asked Meiling.

"Mother, I don't know." At this moment, her heavy, inflated head thought of nothing but food. She felt like she could eat a horse.

"Don't mumble! Where is my hard working, determined daughter? I haven't talked to you for a couple of weeks; you seemed to have really changed. Okay. As I have always said, it is your life, not mine. You have to decide what to do with it."

She knew this was Meiling's old trick, transferring the responsibility to her, although Baiyun preferred it that way. It would help her to think more seriously about herself.

"Actually, it is to my advantage if you decide to stay here rather than going abroad. Why do I want you to leave, to go to a place so far away and not knowing when I would see you again? It is just for you and for your future that Mother encourages you to go to America," said Meiling earnestly.

Yes, Baiyun said to herself, she was very useful for Meiling at home. As the main cook and household chore person, Baiyun's leaving would be a major loss for her family, although Meiling had turned her boyfriends into cooks after Baiyun had left for college. Yet her going to America was an important decision for both her and Meiling.

Their main course had arrived. Meiling grinned happily at the waitress.

Baiyun had a cream-baked fish while Meiling had Russian-style beef, which was also full of cream and butter.

The waitress placed a hot iron plate in the middle of the table. It was full of seafood, eggs, sausages, onions and mushrooms. A propane burner was lit under it.

"What wonderful food! Thank you," said Meiling to the waitress.

"Do you need anything else?" asked the waitress coldly.

It was impossible to get a smile out of any of those state-employed waitresses.

"Not for a while," said Meiling through a mouthful of food.

By now, Baiyun was immersed in her food. Heavy cream was her favorite. Soon her mouth, inside and out, was coated with a layer of pink cream.

"Eat. Eat." Meiling kept putting food into her dish. "Baiyun, listen to me. Think about going to America soon. The situation here is very unstable now. The students may be right, but you never know what is going to happen next. The government keeps broadcasting threatening messages. Police are posted everywhere. Don't get confident too early. The situation could change overnight. By that time, it might be too late to go to America. They may shut China's door completely."

Baiyun nodded while putting a squid into her mouth. Her cheeks expanded. She was struggling to chew and swallow. The juice contained in the hollows of the squid oozed out from corners of her lips. She struggled to wipe it off before it dripped down to her dress.

"Baiyun, don't eat so fast. Otherwise you will have a stomach ache." Then her eyes gleamed and her face turned pale. "Baiyun, do you know how hard is has been for Mother to raise you? If not for you, I would have left this family a long time ago. Your father never loved me. He only loved his roses, you know. He is inhuman. Mother has sacrificed everything in order for you to become a useful and decent person...." Weeping now, she took out a handkerchief from her pocket and blew her long, delicate nose.

Baiyun was wondering how much Meiling had really sacrificed for her. She had not seen a lot of evidence, but she just kept listening. She knew the storm would be over soon.

"It is too late for me to become somebody," continued Meiling, "You are mother's hope, don't you know that?"

Baiyun moved her eyes to the dish where Meiling's entrée, the Russian beef was before. The dish was completely empty. She knew where Meiling's entrée had ended up; it was in her own stomach. Her lips were virtually glued together by the heavy cream. Her body was so clotted with fat that even her neck was stiff.

In an hour and a half, Baiyun and Meiling finished working through all the dishes and Meiling had finished pouring out all her thoughts.

They walked out of the restaurant after paying the bill at the counter.

Like usual, Baiyun did not feel good after that heavy meal. Her belly was so inflated, she felt her pants were going to burst open

She ran to the bathroom to loosen her belt one more notch.

With her eyes still moist, Baiyun's mother stared at the elegant Beijing University gate across the street. Baiyun's return did not disturb her.

"Baiyun, do you remember how hard you studied in order to get into the famous Beijing University? Both your father and I are proud of you very much. You should appreciate this opportunity."

"Yes. I do, Mother." She understood Meiling's wish.

Every mother wanted her daughter to be a good student, and it bothered her that Meiling mentioned her father. She worried about him and wished she could go home and pay a visit soon. She did not think she was up to it since the last experience.

She hoped Meiling would understand what being a good Beijing University student truly meant, which was to carry Beijing University's traditions and fight for equality, freedom and democracy in China.

When they were just about to cross the street, a group of forty to fifty bicyclers rushed out of the Beijing University gate. They immediately blocked the street.

Baiyun and Meiling had to wait for them to pass. Baiyun wondered where they were going.

She was sure that they were not going for an outing, because some of them wore armbands bearing slogans like 'Free Press' and 'Equal Dialogue'.

Then she recognized some of her friends and she ran towards them.

"Where were you today, Baiyun?" Her roommate Li Yan asked her while holding onto her bicycle under her armpit, which was a little too tall for her short body.

"I'm with my mother." Baiyun pointed her chin toward Meiling.

"Your mother, is she going to take you home?" Li Yan's eyes widened.

"No. She just lectured me for three hours," whispered Baiyun.

"Everybody. Let's go." Someone in the bicycle group announced.

"I have to go." Li Yan turned around and climbed back onto her bicycle.

"Where are you going?" asked Baiyun.

"This is a bicycle rally to support Beijing's journalists, who were meeting this morning with Hu Qili, a member of the Communist Central Politburo standing committee in charge of the press."

After the bicyclists left, Baiyun's mother came over and asked, "Who are those students?"

"They are friends at the News Center. I'm going to volunteer to be a reporter today," said Baiyun proudly. "Mother, during this great event, I would like to make significant contribution. I thought…my writing skill might be of use."

Baiyun felt a little embarrassed when mentioning writing to Meiling, because it had always been her secret passion. Even Meiling did not know that.

"A reporter? Baiyun, you always liked to lick on eight piles of shit at the same time when you couldn't finish even one. You should concentrate on your studies," said Meiling.

"Mother, you don't know how important this has become to me."

Baiyun and Meiling walked silently toward her dormitory where Meiling's bicycle was parked.

Still feeling full, Baiyun felt like jumping. She ran a few feet, stopped and waited for Meiling to catch up. Meiling's high heel shoes prevented her from walking too fast.

It was a sunny spring day, and there was a breeze. The cherry blossoms and the yellow forsythia flowers were everywhere along the road.

They were walking toward the campus lake, the 'Nameless' lake. The road zigzagged along the small artificial hills.

Hard-working students occupied most of the green park benches. These were often the only quiet places they could find on campus to study, but even here was no safe haven. Several student discussion groups occupied a few benches.

Baiyun found one of her classmates sitting on a bench by a tree, hard at work. Baiyun called to her. "Wenjing! Wenjing!"

A pair of thick-white-framed glasses sat on top of her delicate, cream-colored face, which resembled delicious steamed-bread just coming out of the steamer.

Had Wenjing been a piece of bread, Baiyun would not have been able to stop herself from taking a bite out of her.

Her short, straight black hair covered most of her face. She was reading intensely.

"What?" She raised her head from her thick GRE book and stared at Baiyun.

"Hey, Ms. Book, are you hiding here?"

"Hi, Baiyun. I thought you were in Tiananmen Square." Puzzled, Wenjing gazed at Baiyun as if she was not sure whether the sudden appearance of Baiyun was real or not.

"Almost all the time, but today I am with my mother."

"Your mother, is she going to take you home?"

"No. She doesn't have that much control over me," Baiyun said quietly, right before she smiled up at her mother, who was slowly approaching them from a distance.

Wenjing moved closer to Baiyun and whispered into her ear. "I have heard that you have fallen in love with a factory worker. Is that true?"

"Ha...." Baiyun laughed aloud, "Almost true, except that he is a technician, not a worker."

"Woo. I couldn't believe it. Is that because your romantic juice finally leaks out?"

The girls laughed loudly as Meiling finally caught up with Baiyun.

"Wenjing, this is my mother."

"Hi, Auntie," answered Wenjing shyly.

"Okay. We'd better go and leave you alone with your books."

Baiyun and Meiling left.

Before they reached Baiyun's dormitory, Meiling said, "Baiyun, you'd better tell me something about your new boyfriend before the rumor runs too far."

"He is a nice man. But it seemed that his charm got me right away." Baiyun did not feel like hiding anything from Meiling.

Although Meiling had never openly encouraged Baiyun to find a boyfriend and she always said that study should be her first priority, Baiyun knew that Meiling understood men better than most of her classmates' mothers would.

Even so, it seemed that her daughter's new behavior had given Meiling a great deal of worry. Meiling's face reddened as her voice rose. "He is a common worker, Baiyun!"

"He's a technician, Mother." Baiyun corrected her. "I think he really loves me. What can I do?"

"Baiyun, listen to your mother." Meiling stared at Baiyun and spoke earnestly. "That kind of love will not last."

"But I will enjoy it as long as it lasts," said Baiyun, and the sound of her voice carried a sense of mockery.

Baiyun was using the opportunity to tease Meiling, because Meiling's boyfriend, Lao Zheng was uneducated.

They were standing in front of Baiyun's dormitory, staring at each other across the bicycle.

"Baiyun, can you be more practical? Can you learn something from your mother?" Under the sun, Meiling's eyelids were glistening.

"Yes, Mother." Baiyun finally gave in.

She understood Meiling very well. Meiling's constant warnings and the example of her chaotic love life was part of the reason Baiyun stayed away from boys during her teenage years.

"Okay, then. You've made your mother feel better." Meiling wiped the corners of her eyes and rode away.

At lunchtime, the campus was busy.

Students riding on bikes rushed toward the cafeteria on narrow cement streets crowded by people and street vendors. Bicycle bells rang loudly.

These highly skilled bicyclists did not want to get off their bicycles, no matter how slow the traffic was. They could stay stationary and balanced for a long time until they found the tiny space between two pedestrians to sneak through.

Baiyun went into the campus convenience store near the 'Triangle' and bought a notebook.

The Triangle was extremely crowded. Big-letter posters written in Chinese calligraphy covered the poster racks like snowflakes.

Layers upon layers of student spectators filled up the rest of the Triangle.

Baiyun always enjoyed walking by the Triangle every day after lunch to see what was going on.

Today, among so many people, she had a hard time focusing.

She had felt like an organizer, a planner and an insider. Suddenly, in her new role as a reporter, she felt a need to become detached. As an outsider would be, in order to impartially observe the students' reaction toward the new movement.

It was impossible for Baiyun to observe anything from inside the massive crowd at the Triangle, and it was even harder for her to free herself from it.

As she was pushing her way through the crowd, someone touched her breasts. Her reaction was mute. She was too ashamed to yell.

She looked around and saw a few southerners nearby. She could not tell which one was guilty. Then she spotted a dark head fleeing in the opposite direction.

"Pervert!" she mumbled, which was her usual reaction.

Her stomach still felt inflated from the big meal and she had a lot to think about.

She thought about her plan to go to America next fall. She had to study hard to pass the exam. She really had an incentive to leave, because she could not imagine going to live back at home after the recent episode.

Baiyun had become a woman; she could no longer stand to be a 'cute little girl' for the men in Meiling's life to coo over, and she refused to be used as bait to get the men to visit her mother.

Baiyun felt her world disintegrating. She knew that she needed to leave Meiling's world completely in order to build one for herself. Even Meiling wanted her to leave for America, but did she really want to go?

Baiyun was flowing in the crowd aimlessly, like a leaf in the ocean.

The students' radio station was broadcasting. The reporter said that the students had waited patiently as the official memorial service for Hu Yaobang took place in the Great Hall of the People three days before. They prepared a petition that listed seven demands to deliver to the communist officials. They sent three representatives to the Great Hall but no one had come out to receive them. The representatives had knelt on the steps of the Great Hall, imploring Premier Li Peng to come out and accept their demands.

"Kneeling on the steps!" She was shocked and moved by students' sincerity.

She thought of Longfe and Big Li. They might be there, standing in front of the Great Hall of the People.

They might have gone without eating; perhaps they skipped several meals. They might even have camped overnight at Tiananmen Square.

She also thought of Dagong. He might have been in the Square at that very moment, organizing the workers and waiting for her.

Baiyun's head was spinning. The voice that came from the loudspeaker grew in volume and intensity. "The Beida Student Federation declares a Class Boycott that goes in effect immediately."

Baiyun was happy to hear the announcement. The old Baiyun would have reasoned that if there were no more classes, she could study for the TOFEL all day long. The new Baiyun walked toward the radio broadcasting station.

It was located on the second floor of Dorm number 28, which was adjacent to the Triangle.

She followed the announcer's voice to the radio station. She was eager to find out what was going on. She was determined to help.

She knocked at the door and was surprised to see her roommate Li Yan open the door. Then two male students welcomed her with big grins.

"Hi, Baiyun. Welcome to Beida Radio Station FM 101," said Li Yan. She shook Baiyun's hand, pretending to be formal. Then she turned to other two students. "This is Wan Gang and Zhang Jun. They are both students in the Electrical Engineering department. We found two used speakers and an old army radio transmitter, so we have a homemade radio broadcasting station."

"That sounds great. Li Yan will be the leading activist in our class," said Baiyun teasingly.

"Not really. I'm just doing some behind the scenes work. Electronics has always been my passion. I have dreamed of operating a real radio broadcasting station. So my dream has come true," said Li Yan proudly.

"Baiyun, do you want to help us? We have a lot to do. And you can do an awful lot without being too visible, if that's what you want," said Wan Gang.

"Actually, Baiyun should be a writer. She can help with the reporting," suggested Li Yan.

"Okay. I always thought I would do better with journalism than with Chemistry."

Although Baiyun had not yet made up her mind to get deeply involved, she accepted the offer.

"See, our Chemistry department is full of talent," said Li Yan.

Baiyun was appointed as the first correspondent in the news center.

They set up a reception area for the visitors. Soon, several students from the journalism department came to work as well. They helped to write the radio scripts, gather reports and announce the news.

Baiyun became immersed in the news broadcasts. She always liked writing. Writing was like bread and butter to her during her difficult childhood. She dreamed of becoming a writer someday, but she never thought that dream would become a reality for her.

She was glad that she had an opportunity to realize her dream, even during the busy school year. She also thought she would enjoy interviewing people. It seemed like such a fun job to be able to get the first-hand news directly from the people.

In the next week, Baiyun spent her mornings in the library studying for the TOFEL exam and she spent her afternoons working at the radio broadcasting station, staying until late at night.

Often as she studied in the morning, she wondered where Dagong was and she wished that he could join her so that they could study together.

Then she would remember Meiling's warning and her assertion that Baiyun should not have a boyfriend to distract her from her studies and she would put him out of her mind.

Still, Baiyun could not help but wonder why Dagong had disappeared. She found herself wondering what happened to him. She thought of looking for him, but she had no idea where to start or what to do when she found him. She decided to wait patiently.

The broadcasting station was very busy.

Each day, the Universities in Beijing, Tianjin and Shanghai sent representatives to the station with the daily news about their campus activities.

Baiyun enjoyed meeting all of the representatives. Unlike the often-pedantic students from Beijing University, she found that students from smaller universities were easier to talk to.

Talking to her own classmates sometimes made her feel inferior, but this rarely happened to Baiyun as a reporter. She was growing in confidence.

She had never found her life so occupied and interesting as it was, when she was working at the radio station.

She interviewed people, wrote scripts and did some announcing. She liked to be an announcer. It made her feel like an actress.

One day, when Baiyun was discussing a radio script with a journalist, two students with heavy accents from southern China rushed into the station.

They were tired and dirty. They eyes were red, their faces and clothes gray and covered with coal dust. They obviously had been on the train for several days and they were near hysterical. Judging by their appearance.

Baiyun knew immediately that something serious had happened.

"We've come from Xian. Please help us," said the tall slender student.

"It's terrible! It's terrible." The smaller student began to cry.

"Please sit down." Baiyun made two cups of hot tea for the students and started interviewing them without a notepad, since she did not want to make them nervous.

The tall student regained his strength after drinking the hot tea. He wiped his face quickly with a towel and he began telling Baiyun their story. "On the day of Hu Yaobang's memorial service, we planned a peaceful demonstration. We gathered quietly in the athletic field in our university and presented our hand-made wreath in order to pay our last respects to him. We were praising Hu Yaobang's past, we talked about our country's reform and the police interrupted our meeting. They declared that some of our participants were unemployed workers who looted stores during the course of the peaceful demonstration. Then the police rushed into the crowd and opened fire. They killed many innocent people. In response, we burned police vehicles. The Public Security Bureau people dragged many students away to the yard of the city government building..." the tall student started weeping uncontrollably.

"What happened then?" Baiyun, along with many of the other volunteers in the station, listened sympathetically to the student.

Their encouragement helped him to continue. "They beat them to death or threw them against the wall."

"Please help us to fight those wild animals." The small boyish looking student stared at Baiyun and the others as he earnestly pleaded for help.

Baiyun asked someone to lead the two students to a dormitory to rest.

After they were gone, many people asked each other in unison, "Do you believe it? Could it be true?"

Baiyun did not say anything. She knew that she had no way to verify the story. They had no fax machines or long-distance phones. It would take many weeks for them to find the right person and communicate through the mail. By then, the news would be too old.

In her mind, these two students' eyewitness accounts were more real than any other rumors she encountered recently.

She heard the police were surrounding Tiananmen Square. Troops were moving in from other provinces.

She suddenly felt a chill passing through her body. There might be blood involved. She was both excited and afraid. She was excited because it could be a golden opportunity for heroic acts to be performed. During her schoolgirl's

Communist education, she learned that becoming a hero should be every citizen's dream. She was also afraid because she knew there could be bloodshed.

She closed her eyes and imagined Dagong. She pictured his lanky body standing before her. She desperately wanted to see him. His embrace would make her brave again.

CHAPTER 8

Dagong worked during the day and studied for the TOFEL exam at night. He tried to forget about Baiyun, but the harder he tried, the stronger her memory became.

She was sometimes so real that he could sense her presence. When he could not stand it anymore, he went to Tiananmen Square to look for her among the students.

He walked to the Beijing University students stationed at Tiananmen Square and asked them about her. No one had seen her.

He told them of Lao Liu's warning, that the police would be moving in, but then he realized that they were already posted everywhere around the Square.

"What do you think the police are doing here?" Dagong asked a student at the Beida station.

"I don't know. I think they are targeting us so we have something to demonstrate about." The student laughed at his own joke before he answered Dagong truthfully." I think the government is just trying to scare us by sending the police and troops here so we will give up. It is not that easy. Reporters from all over the world are here, so the government has to consider their reputation. They don't want to lose face. They don't want to be the first ones to open fire."

"Have you achieved your goal of having a dialogue with the government?" Dagong asked the student.

"No. The government still refuses to talk to the United Student Federation. We are waiting patiently. If they still don't agree to meet with us, we are planning to have another rally in a week to coincide with the seventieth anniversary of the May 4th student movement."

On May 4th, 1919, students from Beijing University played a crucial role in the movement against the Versailles Treaty that awarded the German rights of Shandong province to Japan.

The student spoke boldly to Dagong. He said, "We can do it again, seventy years later."

Dagong waved his fist in the air in encouragement. He asked, "Do you need protection from our workers? I can find a group of strong workers to meet with you at Beida. We can serve as a human shield for you students." Dagong was becoming excited again for the first time since he pledged to Zhang Ping that he would forget about the movement and focus on his studies.

He knew he would be able to see Baiyun again and he would march with her. He suddenly could not stop thinking of her. Whatever it took, he would pursue her.

Dagong and the student shook hands and he turned to leave. Just as he was about to walk away, he heard a familiar voice.

"Dagong."

He turned around. It was Baiyun. She was wearing a blue and white floral long sleeve shirt and blue jeans. On her head sat a broad-brimmed hat. She beamed at him with her innocent eyes.

To Dagong, she looked like a flower in full bloom under the bright sunshine.

She extended her hand toward him. He took it, pulled her into his embrace and held her in his arms.

Baiyun rested her head against his warm chest. They held each other as they lost track of the time.

Dagong nearly forgot about the others around them; he had to stop himself from kissing her in plain view of everyone in the Square.

At last, he spoke to her. "I've finally found you. What brought you here?"

"I'm a reporter now, for the Beida News Center. I have to come here once in a while to report on what's going on. The rest of the time, I have been studying TOFEL because Mother asked me to promise that I would. I keep thinking it would be nice if I could study with you." She looked longingly at his radiant face.

"I have been thinking the same thing. Let's take a stroll, since we have been so good... too good, I mean." He wrapped his arm around her waist and guided her away from the crowd. "Let me show you downtown Beijing."

"Sure. What are you going to show me?" Baiyun looked at him sweetly. Her heart was beating fast.

"It's a secret," said Dagong. He was looking forward to being alone with Baiyun.

As they walked across Tiananmen Square hand-in-hand, they heard loud cheering coming from one of many circles of the crowd.

"Lets go and see." Baiyun pulled Dagong towards the crowd.

"I thought I was showing you around...," murmured Dagong.

He followed her. What else could he do?

Baiyun reached the crowd but she could see nothing. She pushed, shoved and ducked under people's arms. Dagong followed her with difficulty, because people cursed after Baiyun as she moved forward.

Finally, they arrived at the front row. Suddenly, Baiyun was not sure she wanted to see.

Many bald men were piled on top of a small bald man wearing a white cotton robe. His neck was resting on an edge of a knife. His face was red and his blood vessels bulged, yet his neck was intact. His eyes were closed and he looked serene and peaceful.

"Is this Qigong?" asked Baiyun.

"Ya. This must be a top Qigong performing troupe," said Dagong while watching intensively.

The crowd cheered louder as more bald men climbed on top of the pile. The man on the bottom was holding tight.

Baiyun could almost see the edge of the knife making a grove in his neck, but no blood streamed out.

"Let's go. I can't stand it." Baiyun pulled Dagong out of the crowd.

"Wow. That's impressive... Are you a little scared, Baiyun?" Dagong put his arm around Baiyun and looked into her face as he smiled.

"Not really. You don't know how brave I am. It just reminds me of something scary," said Baiyun, sinking deep into her thoughts.

She looked around to escape what was on her mind. She saw a crowd surrounding a poet nearby. "Let's go and see the poetry reading over there. It's not so crowded."

"Sure. I love poetry."

"You too?"

"Yes. It is the language of your soul, isn't it?"

"I agree." Baiyun nodded.

"Do you have any poems that I can read to see your soul?" asked Dagong.

"Yes. I'm not sure I want you to read them. It's too revealing." Baiyun made a face to him. "You?"

"No. But I can write some for you."

"Sweet." Baiyun smiled.

They arrived at the poetry reading at the edge of the Tiananmen Square where the Great Hall of the People was.

A very young looking man stood in the center on a makeshift stage that was put together with boxes piled up in a pyramid shape. He wore a wrinkled white shirt and a white headband with 'fight' in Chinese, printed on it.

He waved his hands as he spoke while trying to balance himself on the shaky stage:

In my grief, I hear demons shriek
I weep while wolves and jackals laugh.
Though tears I shed to mourn a hero,
With head raised high, I draw my sword.

"Good job, young man! Do another one!" Someone in the crowd shouted.

A young lady with short hair and a red string headband on her head jumped up in the front row and rushed to the stage.

She pushed the young man off the boxes after getting on. The stage wobbled and she, too, fell off.

The crowd laughed.

The young lady stood on the ground and started reading:

As I look into the sea of people
I see anger
As I look into the sea of people
I see courage
As I look into the sea of people
I see victory

"Let's go," said Dagong. "We can pick up something to eat."

They walked to a vendor with a cart full of steamed buns.

Behind it was a plump lady in a green polyester shirt and a ponytail tied up with a red ribbon.

Dagong ordered ten pork steamed buns and two bottles of orange soda.

When he handed the money to her, she asked, "Are you with the students?"

"She is from Beida." Dagong pointed at Baiyun

"Okay. It is free then," said the lady with a big smile.

"Thanks." Dagong shook her hand.

Then he turned to Baiyun and said, "Now let me take you to Wangfujing shopping mall to get some deep-friend cream puffs."

"Sure. I haven't been there for a long time," said Baiyun. She was getting very excited.

"Sounds like you are a country girl," said Dagong teasingly.

"Bad." Baiyun jabbed him on the ribs.

They had to fight their way through the crowd with a mixture of students, citizens from many parts of China and police in green uniforms.

As they approached Wangfujing Street, the famous shopping center, many shops with neon lights and signs and with merchandise inside and outside appeared.

The signs said, 'Olympus', 'KFC', 'Rolex', 'Gourmet Street', 'Calvin Klein', 'Nina Ricce', 'Gucci' and 'Prada' and so on in both Chinese and English. It was noisy. The voices of people bargaining and merchants yelling could be heard.

Then Dagong spotted a vendor with a table full of fried crickets, scorpions and grasshoppers on sticks.

"Baiyun, want one? I bet you have never had one of these."

"Fried bugs. Yuck. When I was in high school, my classmates used to eat fried cicadas and frogs. I had never been popular enough to have a friend who ate them. It is too bad. Otherwise, I would have developed a taste for them at an early age." She looked at the stiff crickets on their sticks and frowned.

"That's okay. It is for kids and the Westerners who think these are our delicacy," said the little man behind the table.

Sure enough, two tall and red-faced Westerners came and each bought two.

"One is too small. They usually buy two to three," said the little man.

"Let's go," said Dagong and walked toward the big tan brick building, the 'Xidan Shopping Center.'

As soon as they walked into the newly renovated building, Baiyun got lost.

She could not believe her eyes. Everything had changed. She was so amazed to see the freshly painted balconies inside with elevators that had glass walls. Many colorful banners were hanging down from the third floor. The old wooden escalators had been replaced with shining new ones with lights all round them. The atrium was full of well-dressed merchants with shining new products like Rolex watches,

Gucci purses and Sony cameras. In the center, a giant chandelier emitted soft white light. Spotlights on the vast ceiling shone down like many stars. TV screens along the walls of the balconies flashed ads constantly. The whole place made Baiyun dizzy, but she was in high spirits.

"I'm totally lost now. Where is the restaurant that has the deep-fried cream puffs?" Baiyun was really excited to be out with Dagong.

Before Dagong, the only person who took her to restaurants was Meiling. Even though the food was always good, Meiling was often in a bad mood. It was so refreshing that she could dine with such handsome and fun company.

"It's a surprise!" Dagong grabbed her hand pulled her toward an elevator. "Let's try this brand new elevator."

"Okay. I'm afraid of elevators," confessed Baiyun. "But I'm sure you would be able to protect me if I get sick. I'm afraid of getting stuck in the elevator. Now I'm looking forward to it as long as you are with me." Baiyun looked in Dagong's eyes and smiled.

Dagong pulled her toward him and gave her a squeeze, just short of kissing.

At that moment, the elevator stopped and they had to get on with a few others.

Baiyun was a little disappointed. Fortunately, they got pushed together closer in the elevator. Baiyun rest her head on his chest.

"Don't just stare at me. Are you surprised by how handsome I am?" Dagong teased her. "Look outside the glass wall. You are missing all the fun."

Baiyun gazed out as all the colorful banners, merchandise and the chandelier became a blur while the elevator travelled. She could feel her stomach churn. She quickly looked away.

"Are you sick?" Dagong asked, concerned.

Just at that moment, the elevator stopped and everyone swarmed out.

"No. I just need some food." Baiyun was so relieved that they were out of the fancy glass elevator.

As they walked to the restaurant together hand in hand, Baiyun could see some people watching them in admiration. A sense of pride hit her.

She tried to remember when the last time she had felt proud was. Growing up in shame and humiliation due to her father's troubles from being a professor and Meiling's many liaisons, she couldn't remember an instance when she felt proud except for the time when she got an 'A' at school, which had not happened for a while. It was a good feeling, and Baiyun loved it.

As they entered the brand new restaurant, Baiyun was surprised to see it empty as a group of waitresses stood in the corner chatting.

When they noticed Baiyun and Dagong, one of them scurried over. She wore a red embroidered traditional Chinese top and a black mini skirt matched with a pair of red patent spiky high heels.

She asked them where they wanted to sit among many polished and ornamentally carved tables. They chose a table for two by the wall that was decorated with a red rose in a vase.

After ordering some watermelon juice, they looked at the menu.

"What do you think? Should we sample some seafood dishes here before having their famous desert, the deep-fried cream puffs?" Dagong asked Baiyun. "I don't make a lot of money, but what the heck! Life is too short."

"I have some money. Mother always makes sure that I have some money with me. I agree. Life is too short," smiled Baiyun. "Let's have our last meal before we die for the good cause."

"Wow. I can't believe you are ready to die already. Don't you think you are too young to die? Would you have any regrets?" Dagong winked.

"I don't know. Because of my harsh childhood, I felt like an old woman by the time I was fifteen. Now I feel so happy, I'm actually getting younger. Maybe I'm too young to die. I want to experience true love." Baiyun stared at Dagong and her eyes were brimming with tears. "I can't think of anyone I'd rather share my last meal with."

"So, you picked me." Dagong beamed at Baiyun.

"I think you have picked me. Remember, it was your idea to come here?" Baiyun sounded a little happier. She was smiling.

"I think we have chosen each other." Dagong reached across the table and took Baiyun's hands in his.

"Are you ready to order?" The waitress showed up all of sudden.

"Sure," Baiyun was skilled at switching her moods as needed. She had plenty of training in hiding her emotions during her complicated childhood. "I would like to order a plate of sliced beef tongue and a plate of pig ears."

"I would like to have some crispy shrimp. That's it," said Dagong.

He handed the menu back to the waitress, who walked away, wiggling her hips as she went.

"I hate that she interrupted our nice conversation about the life, death and love, especially the last one," said Dagong. "I'm still curious about why the Qigong knife feat disturbed you so much. Do you care to tell me?"

"Why not, even though it will give me nightmares tonight," said Baiyun in a matter-of-fact way, as though she was commenting on the furniture.

"You don't have to, if you don't want to. I don't want to wreck your mood."

"No. Everyone knows that I'm different and strange sometimes… It is because of this… It's about time for me to tell everyone, so let me begin with you." She looked boldly at Dagong. "It is time for me to come out as a young woman instead of staying an old one." It felt good for Baiyun to say it aloud.

"Great. I'm glad that I helped you to come out," said Dagong.

"One day, I arrived at my apartment after school. After walking through the dark hallway, I opened the door. I saw my mother sitting, smoking a cigarette and on her right, standing by the bed was a slender young man with mustache."

The north-facing one-room apartment was dark in the late afternoon. A double bed and a single-bed filled up the far side of the room. On the left stood a dresser with a big vacuum radio on top and a big wooden desk. In the center, a Square wooden table. Initially it was so quiet that Baiyun could make out the clock ticking.

Then she saw the young man with the knife in his hand and the world no longer stood still.

Baiyun heard thunder in her head; her mind was racing. She remembered the young man coming to her apartment once before and she thought he was friendly.

She quickly realized that she was mistaken and the young man was obviously mad. He was mumbling chants and waving a knife as he slowly approached Meiling. Then with swing of his long arm, he grabbed Meiling's head and held the knife to her throat. Baiyun was ready to leap forward to punch him, or bite and kick him.

Baiyun heard Meiling's steady voice. "Take the knife away. Have you heard me? Take the knife away," said Meiling.

Her voice was so firm that it made Baiyun think it might be a joke that the young man was playing against Meiling.

All those years later, as Baiyun told Dagong about the incident, her voice was not nearly as steady as Meiling's was that afternoon. Baiyun stopped speaking to take a breath as Dagong listened.

"What happened next?"

"Nothing. Mother is still alive. He didn't even break the skin. He packed his things and left, as she finished her cigarette."

Nothing happened. Yet it was the most intense moment in Baiyun's young life.

Dagong was engrossed in Baiyun's story. He did not even notice the food they ordered had been set on the table before them.

Baiyun began eating.

"Does it give you nightmares?" he asked her.

She did not answer, but not because she did not have nightmares. She did not answer because her mouth was full.

Dagong did not yet understand; he assumed the best and joined in the feast.

"As long as you are eating, you are doing fine. Otherwise, you wouldn't have grown to be a college student. You would have perished a long time ago."

"You are right. I'm doing fine. Don't worry about me… it only showed me that my mother is invincible." As Baiyun said it, she realized that she could be invincible as well.

Baiyun looked at Dagong carefully, trying to gauge whether his attitude toward her had changed. She nearly regretted telling him so much, but whom else could she speak to?

Dagong touched Baiyun's hand. "If you ever need to talk about it, talk to me."

Baiyun smiled at Dagong through a mouthful of beef tongue. She swallowed before she spoke. "Am I full of surprises?"

"I love the fact that you are full of surprises."

Dagong held Baiyun's hand, and she knew he understood her.

"How about you, Dagong? Do you have any secrets?"

"Of course. I think we have revealed enough secrets for now. Maybe if you're lucky I'll tell you one of mine over the cream puffs."

Together they laughed over their past tragedies.

As they walked out of the Xidan Shopping Center, Baiyun was surprised and more than a little embarrassed to see Meiling riding on Lao Zheng's motorcycle. Although her helmet obscured half of her face, Baiyun could clearly see it was her mother.

A group of young men followed her on motorcycles and scooters. She was wearing a new shinning leather jacket and a pair of leather pants, which briefly made Baiyun think of Marlon Brando in drag. It could have been 'The Wild Ones' China-Style.

Baiyun tried to avoid being spotted because she didn't want her mother to see her with Dagong, but it was too late.

Meiling greeted her before she could hide from her mother's eye. "Hello, Baiyun! Baiyun, my daughter!" Meiling's loud yelling could be heard a thousand meters away.

"Mother... what are you doing here? It looks like you are leading a motorcycle gang."

"Yes. What an observant daughter! We are called, 'The Flying Tiger Brigade.' We ride our motorcycles and scooters around to pass information to people in Tiananmen Square," said Meiling proudly.

"I told you motorcycles would become a popular transportation in Beijing," Lao Zheng said smugly. He gave Baiyun a wink. "Do you want one? I can buy you a new BMW motorcycle."

Baiyun shook her head. The last thing she needed was to accept an expensive gift from Lao Zheng.

She quickly made up an excuse. "No. I don't need one. I'm a reporter now. If I travel too fast, I will miss crucial details."

"He looks familiar to me...," said Meiling.

Baiyun was surprised by the sensation of jealousy, as Meiling looked Dagong over.

"He's no one you know! He's a friend I met around here. Not in Beida." Baiyun decided it was better to lie.

"Hey, Dagong!" shouted one of the boys who were following Meiling.

Dagong couldn't see the boy's face, so he excused himself from Baiyun and Meiling. He walked toward the boy.

Once Dagong was out of earshot, Lao Zheng grinned wickedly. "A handsome boyfriend! Good for you, Baiyun!"

"Stop, Lao Zheng!" Meiling slapped him on his arm and turned to Baiyun. "How many times do I have to tell you? You should study for the TOFEL and go to America!" Then she pointed to the crowd of students in the distance. "Do you think this will turn into something? What will it accomplish? Nothing."

"Well, if it will accomplish nothing why are you so active in it? It is so unlike you," whispered Baiyun.

Meiling smiled in spite of herself. "It's an adventure. Besides, how many years do I have left to have fun and excitement? I'm getting old,"

A crowd formed around them. People were curious about what was happening with the pack of motorcyclists.

At the back of the pack, Dagong met the boy. His heart sunk when he realized the boy was Broomstick, the son of Marshmallow and Pumpkin.

Dagong thought he might be in trouble; a neighbor saw him walking with a beautiful young stranger.

He tried his best to look innocent. "Broomstick! You look good on a motorcycle. I bet your mom would be proud of you... I'm just here to grab something to eat...Um, later we will go and organize the workers to help the students..."

Broomstick said nothing; he nodded with a smirk.

"Well... it was nice to see you, Broomstick! Keep up the good work. Uh... see you later..." Dagong started to walk away, embarrassed.

Meanwhile, Baiyun found that her voice had a will of its own. She heard herself asking Meiling "Could 'The Flying Tiger Brigade' join our 'Spirit of May 4th' march'? It would be a great if you'd ride along with us."

Baiyun could not believe the words came out of her own mouth, yet she was powerless to stop them.

Meiling thought about it for a minute. "Sure. We'd love to support the students." Then she lowered her voice." Baiyun, after this march, promise me you will return to your studies. Don't give up your dream of going to America."

Baiyun nodded. "Okay, Mother."

She saw Dagong. He was trying to subtly wave her over from a distance. "Bye. Mother. We have to run!"

Baiyun quickly ran after Dagong.

"Come home sometime!" yelled Meiling.

"Yes," said Baiyun, although she was quite sure she was never going home again.

Baiyun gave a thumb up to Dagong as they disappeared in the crowd. "Good job for getting us out of here."

"Anytime." Dagong squeezed Baiyun's hand. "I hear that you students will have a 'Spirit of May 4th' demonstration in three days. I will try to organize a group of workers to protect you."

"Okay. That would be great."

They quickly swam through a sea of people and arrived at the Beida station.

"I have to go," said Dagong. "I will see you soon."

"When?"

"In three days, during the 'Spirit of May 4th' march."

Dagong quickly disappeared.

Baiyun watched him leave, disappointed.

She could not believe he was just going to leave her alone like that.

She tried to put Dagong out of her mind; there was much work to be done. She knew she needed to write a story about 'The Flying Tiger Brigade' right away, and of course, there were still many people to interview at the Beida station.

Baiyun tried to look at the afternoon with a practical mind; she had a business lunch with a workers' representative. He guaranteed to provide a protection squad to keep the students safe during their May 4th march. In addition to that, she picked up an important news item, and there was still plenty of time to conduct interviews.

It was an afternoon well spent; she congratulated herself for her accomplishments with only a hint of sarcasm.

Baiyun found a quiet corner, sat on a bench and started writing.

CHAPTER 9

Late that afternoon, Dagong's wife Zhang Ping walked through the rickety gate of their house. It let out a squeak, shook and soon balanced itself.

"Where is everybody?" The yard was quiet and her voice echoed.

"Mom, look!" Her son Little Turnip, pointed at the white cat who was comfortably nestling himself in a tray of rice on the porch.

"Go. Go away!" Zhang Ping woke the cat and chased him away. "I don't need fleas in my rice."

Zhang Ping opened the door of her apartment.

"What a mess! It looks like your father has been home and left. God knows where he is now. He must be in Tiananmen Square again. He doesn't even care about his family anymore."

She put away some clothes and went back to the yard again. She took the mop that leaned against the kitchen wall, rinsed it and went back to her room.

Little Turnip flew a paper airplane while Zhang Ping mopped the floor.

When she was finished, Zhang Ping wiped her face with a towel and poured herself a cup of hot water.

She walked back and forth in the room, making a trail of footprints on the wet floor. She sipped the hot water carefully, and then she walked to the radio on top of the dresser and turned it on. "Mourning activities for Hu Yaobang are officially over. Anyone who continues demonstrating will regret the consequences. Workers, please go back to your work unit. Students, please go back to school. Do not be fooled into a conspiracy. A handful of individuals with ulterior motives have used the grief of the students to create turmoil. They have set up illegal organizations. They have printed counter-revolutionary leaflets to instigate dissention, create national disorder and sabotage the stable unit in politics. This is an upheaval to negate the leadership of the Chinese Communist party and the socialist system..."

Zhang Ping turned off the radio. She grabbed the mop and rushed out of the door.

"Little Turnip!" Zhang Ping yelled. "Don't step on Uncle Lao Liu's flower beds!"

Little Turnip made his way through Lao Liu's small rose garden searching for his paper airplane. Then he spotted a worm and observed it.

"Little Turnip, let's go," said Zhang Ping, while washing the mop in the sink.

"Where are we going, Mother?"

"We're going to find your father."

"Why?"

"Do you want your father to get killed?"

"No"

"So, let's go then." She went over and grabbed Little Turnip's arm.

"My airplane. My airplane!"

"Forget about that fucking airplane! Do you understand? Let's go!"

Pumpkin's daughter, Little Pea and her boyfriend Yu Gang stepped in as Zhang Ping dragged Little Turnip out of the gate. "Hey, Auntie Zhang, where are you going?"

Little Pea wore a red knitted jacket and a pair of blue jeans. Her yellowish, dry face was radiant and cheerful, which was so rare for her. Yu Gang was a tall, skinny polite young man with Square shoulders.

"Hi, Auntie," said Yu Gang. He grinned and his small round eyes cast down.

"Oh, hi!" Zhang Ping nodded. "We're going to Tiananmen Square. I'm going to find Dagong and drag him home."

"I'm not sure you can find him. It's very crowded there. But you'll have a good time," said Little Pea.

Zhang Ping was not amused by Little Pea's idea of 'a good time.' "Woo. Even Little Pea talks about having fun nowadays... If I can't find Dagong, I'm going to ask the police to catch him."

Zhang Ping left, dragging Little Turnip behind her as he struggled to match her furious pace.

Little Pea and Yu Gang closed the door behind them and hugged.

"It's so nice. Nobody is here," said Little Pea.

Yu Gang lifted Little Pea's small body and kissed her. He carried her toward Little Pea's apartment in the far side of the yard with a big colorful movie star's portrait on the door.

They unlocked the door and went in. Little Pea's apartment had two big inter-connected rooms.

Besides the dining table, a dish cabinet and several bamboo chairs were in the living room. Three single beds lined up against the wall for the three grown-up children.

Yu Gang and Little Pea kissed and caressed for a while.

Then Little Pea lifted a corner of the window curtain and looked out. "It's almost 6:30 pm. Still no one has come back yet."

"They are either stuck at the Tiananmen Square or they're out having fun. Why do you worry about them? Are you afraid of being alone with me?" Yu Gang held Little Pea against his chest.

"No," said Little Pea. Her face blushed.

"So, do you think we should go back to the Tiananmen Square or not?" Yu Gang stared at Little Pea intensely.

"I don't know. What do you think?" She sounded uncertain, yet could not resist gazing back at Yu Gang.

"Don't you think it's exciting in the Square? People are so happy and talkative. I don't think we should miss it... Then again, it's nice to be here alone with you."

Little Pea rolled her eyes. She was skeptical of Yu Gang's sweet talk. "Men are always very sweet before the marriage.

After they get married and have what they want, that changes."

"Come on. That's old garbage and no longer true. One should be romantic forever." Yu Gang kissed Little Pea passionately.

Little Pea thought the line sounded familiar. "Who said that?" She snapped.

Yu Gang smiled at her serious mood. "Monica in 'Once in life'."

"But that's the movies. Real life is much tougher than that." She turned and buried her face again in Yu Gang's chest.

"So we have to try to make it better." Yu Gang kissed her once more.

"That's not what us common folks should worry about," mumbled Little Pea between kisses.

"Come on. That is exactly what students in the Tiananmen Square are trying to achieve. We want to be in charge. Maybe we should go back to the Square again and support them. And very soon we'll have a new government..." As he spoke, he kissed her again and again. "Our own business... Our own home... Our own car...."

"It sounds like heaven. Do you think that could come true?" Little Pea was intrigued.

"Sure. Let's go!" Yu Gang kissed Little Pea again and helped her to stand up.

Before they stepped through the door, they heard Pumpkin enter the house.

"Ah ya! I have never worked so hard in my life before." Pumpkin waddled in, followed by Broomstick and Potatofeet.

"Hi, Mother." Little Pea and Yu Gang called in unison.

"Woo. You two are smart, enjoying the silence and cool air here." She wore a yellowish short-sleeved shirt and a pair of black pants. Her shirt was soaked with sweat to the point of transparency. Sweat rolled down from her forehead and her fat, slightly sunburned cheeks, the red tip of her flat nose, her short chin and her thick eyebrows.

"I have never made so many steam buns in my whole life!" She continued, "We made five hundred pork steam-buns and handed them out free to the students and the common folks from the provinces."

"We did that earlier. We handed out free bottled water to the students." Little Pea wanted to assure her mother they did not just stay at home loitering the entire day.

"Did you see students run through the police line?" asked Pumpkin.

"No. We were at a corner near a truck-load of soldiers," said Little Pea.

"We kept feeding them soda so they could forget about fighting," said Yu Gang.

Potatofeet tried to get everybody's attention. "It was s-s-so easy to p-p-p-pass through th-the p-p-p-police line. Th-they just s-s-s-sur... They let 'em in. It's...it's like the g-games we puh-puh-play at...at sch-ool."

"Come on. You didn't see that. I was in a tree and I told you what was going on." Broomstick wanted to be the ultimate source of information.

"Who says the police surrendered?" Lao Liu, the policeman, came back from work.

Broomstick laughed, "Hey, the bad policeman is back. Let's beat him!"

Broomstick jumped at Lao Liu, followed by Potatofeet. They each took one of Lao Liu's arms and twisted them to his back. Lao Liu laughed at their horseplay as Little Pea giggled.

"Okay. Okay! Beat me, kill me! I'm a bad policeman. I'm a government's running dog." Lao Liu bent forward, pretending to be captured.

"Don't be too mean to Lao Liu. We know he can't hurt anyone." Pumpkin pulled them apart.

"Thank you. Thank you all. I know my dear neighbors will trust me. It's really no fun to be a policeman today. I took an easy job over Xianmen. Not much was going on until 3:00 pm, because students didn't come in from that direction. Then people swarmed in. We resisted a little at first. Then it became impossible, and our commander told us to give up completely. The worst of all was that people constantly cursed us, and threw stones and bottles at us. We were treated like shit. This is the worst day of my career. Look at my uniform."

Lao Liu took off his white summer uniform shirt and showed it to everyone. It was no longer white; it was covered in dirt and sweat, and large spots of it were dyed pink and yellow from soda stains. "Tomorrow, I'm calling in sick."

"I think you should have joined the students a long time ago," said Pumpkin.

"No, I can't in my profession."

"You coward!"

"Hey, that's enough, old woman!" Lao Liu snapped at her.

He walked away to his own home.

After a while, he came out with a bottle of beer. He sat on the steps in front of his apartment, drinking. In a while, he fell into a meditative state, as if he were a working-class monk.

Pumpkin played her radio in the yard.

The national radio broadcast was still playing the Beijing Opera. Nothing was said about the events in Tiananmen Square and across the city.

Little Pea and Yu Gang left for the Square.

Pumpkin began washing clothes in the yard.

After a while, she spoke to Lao Liu, rousing him from his trance. "Lao Liu, what do you think of this student movement?"

"I don't know," he answered. He sunk back into a meditative state; eyes closed, body frozen, elbows resting on stretched legs.

It was hard to say by looking at him whether he was listening to Pumpkin or not.

"I think our country needs a change," said Pumpkin.

"That's not easy. It's not up to us."

"You really sound like an old-dude. What is happening now has shown our people's power."

Lao Liu did not answer. The number of people who turned out in the Square today amazed him. He also knew they were ordered not to fight because the central government was split on the decision about how to deal with the students. They hoped to scare students by threatening them through the radio warnings. Obviously it did not work. He could not predict what would happen next. He knew the situation was dire. After being through so many ups and downs, he hoped he would survive once again.

Pumpkin had a lovely naivety. As merely a cook, she was not sophisticated enough to understand the danger or consider the consequences.

He wished he could warn them, but at that moment, he did not have the will to say anything more. He had enough of it for one day.

Lao Liu's daughter Lili came back with a college student. He was a stout young man, about twenty years old, with a round, swarthy face and a solid upper body. His short-sleeved shirt and blue jeans were stained and creased.

"Hi, Father. I'm glad you're home. This is Xiao Dong. He's a student from Nankai University. He's been in Tiananmen Square since last night. So I invited him home so he could have dinner with us and wash himself."

As Lili introduced the young man, Lao Liu noticed a red flush swept over her face.

He realized it was the first time she had ever brought a young man home. She was too shy to do so before now.

Lao Liu cared deeply about the students. He only wished they understood the seriousness of the situation.

In the face of Lili and Xiao Dong's youthful idealism, Lao Liu felt old and weary.

As he rose, his tired legs ached. "I'm going to take a nap. You can wait for your mother to come back and cook something for you." Lao Liu went inside.

"Lili, why don't the two of you have dinner with us?" Pumpkin said loudly, so Lao Liu could hear her.

"Thank you, Auntie."

"No problem. I always like to help students."

"Are you going to cook again tonight?"

"Yes. Little Pea is busy nowadays. It's nice to see her so happy. She's really excited about what is going on in the Square. So it doesn't matter if I end up doing a little more work at home."

Pumpkin finished putting soap on the clothes. She took out the garments one by one, squeezed out the water and threw them into another washbasin. Then she carried the heavy wooden basin full of soapy water toward the sink and poured the water out.

Turning on the tap, she began rinsing the clothes. She worked hard. A mist of sweat covered her forehead. The faded shirt and black pants she wore were soaking wet.

Because of the crowds of people in the nearby Square, the temperature in the area had risen dramatically.

The usual blessing of a breeze had been held off.

Summer came early that year. The air was humid and still. Pumpkin felt like she was in an overcrowded bathhouse; it made even the simplest activities difficult. She sighed and wiped her forehead with her soapy elbow.

"Goddamn, it's hot!" Mrs. Wang declared as she arrived with her four sons.

It looked as if she had to catch them one by one; their faces were stretched tight and they were being extremely quiet. Mrs. Wang had a habit of locking her family up in the house whenever there was chaotic activity in the Square to save herself from worrying about them. She was obviously unhappy because Mr. Wang had not come home yet.

"Come here!" Mrs. Wang yelled at the four boys, ranging in ages from seven to fifteen-year. They were dressed in identical white shirts and blue pants. Mrs. Wang poured some heated water into a basin in order to wash their hair. The boys were nervously waiting in line. After the powdered shampoo dissolved in the water, Mrs. Wang pushed the youngest boy's head into the basin.

"Don't move!" She jerked his body. "Lower your head!" The boy obeyed. "Relax!" She yelled to the boy, who could not hear her with his head underwater. "Why are you so stiff?"

After two minutes of rubbing and scratching, Mrs. Wang pushed him away and pushed another boy's head into the same soapy water, and then another and another, until each of them were soapy.

She poured the soapy water out and poured some fresh hot water into the basin.

The boys lined up in the same order and she rinsed their hair several times.

Before they were finished, Mr. Wang walked in slowly. His square-face and gray-haired head was drooping; his expression was one of guilt.

"Ha-ha… You're back. Where have you been?" said Mrs. Wang.

"I stopped by Tiananmen Square and helped the police to direct traffic. I could not stand the chaos. Chaos always makes me nervous. Why can't they find a better way to solve their problems?" said Mr. Wang quietly, a little ashamed of what he had done.

"Good Lord. When did you become such a nice person?"

"I don't think the police are bad. I can't bear to see people throw stones at them."

"You shouldn't be there in the first place." Mrs. Wang pulled a boy's wet hair to release her anger.

"Ow...." The boy cried.

"Be quiet!" She pushed the boy's head back to the basin, practically drowning him.

Mr. Wang sighed, went inside of their apartment and came out with a tobacco pipe in his hand.

He sat down on a stool and started smoking.

Mrs. Wang continued to lecture him. "You're too nice... You like to wipe other people's asses! And you don't realize you're the one who eventually gets hurt."

It seemed that Mr. and Mrs. Wang were perfectly matched in their marriage. Their life together consisted of Mrs. Wang's endless lecturing and Mr. Wang's chain smoking.

All of a sudden, the balance was tipped. Mr. Wang stood up. "Stop, would you?" He went over and grabbed Mrs. Wang's shoulder, shaking her. "I have had enough of this! I have had enough!"

"What? You want to beat me?" Mrs. Wang shook water off her hands and sat down on the ground, crying and hitting the ground repeatedly with her fists. "You want to get rid of me, eh... You want to get rid of me. Okay, I'm leaving. I'm leaving. You can cook for yourself. You can clean the room yourself. And you can take care of your sons."

"Get up, bitch!" Mr. Wang tried to drag her up by pulling her shirt collar.

Mrs. Wang hit his chest repeatedly with her small, bony fists, while Mr. Wang slapped her face repeatedly, shouting, "You get out of here, bitch!"

Pumpkin rushed over to separate them. Instead, she was the one who was hit the most. The fat on her body helped to absorb the blows.

Marshmallow stepped in and finally, with his help, the fight stopped.

The four boys had long since disappeared from the courtyard.

Mrs. Wang went inside their apartment as Mr. Wang started smoking again.

In the opposite corner of the courtyard, Lili's mother Wu Zheng was talking with Lili and Xiao Dong, her new college friend. As an administrator in the local government, Wu Zheng was a serious woman with short hair and a kind face.

"We understand how the students feel. We in the Government would like to work with you to achieve your goals," said Wu Zheng earnestly.

"I know. We like to work with our government too. That's why we're trying to keep our movement peaceful and we try not to disturb the traffic. We also made an effort to communicate with the government by sending our representatives to deliver our requests."

His eyes behind the white-framed glasses were bright and alert.

"That sounds reasonable."

"But it's been two weeks and we haven't gotten any reply yet. The government seems to think we are too insignificant to talk with. That's making the protesters restless; and because of this, things have become chaotic."

"Our leaders are very busy and the process is time-consuming. It will take time for them to decide on anything regarding your demands, and will take even longer for them to reply to you. Two weeks to you is a day to them."

"It has been two weeks since we made our demands but it's been a long time coming. Our country has waited for thirty years!" said Xiao Dong passionately.

"Yes, you are right. We need to be more efficient. But how can they hope to gain back the lost time?"

Lili rested her head on her right hand, listening attentively.

Little Pea and Yu Gang returned to the courtyard and found Pumpkin hard at work.

"Hi, Mother. I hope I'm not too late to cook dinner."

"No, I'm going to cook today," said Pumpkin while hanging clothes on the clothesline in the yard.

"Why?"

"Because I want you young people to do something more important."

"Mother, we're back. It's too crowded over there." Little Pea picked up a bok choy and went over to the sink to wash.

"Okay, you prepare it and I'll cook it."

Pumpkin went inside and Marshmallow sat in front of their apartment reading the newspaper.

He frowned and said, "Why would I expect the newspaper to tell the truth?"

"Mmm hmm." Little Pea agreed. She was occupied with finely chopping the pork loin.

Yu Gang strolled behind Marshmallow and glanced over his shoulder to read the newspaper.

"Ha-ha!" He laughed. "Nothing on the demonstration. They are still talking about how everyone is working hard for the socialist system."

When Little Pea finished chopping the ground pork she formed it into balls, cleaned the green beans and chopped the bok choy. Yu Gang helped her light the coal stove, and Pumpkin cooked.

In a while, the yard was full of the smell of meatball soup, stir-fried vegetables and steamed rice.

The radio was playing an Opera, as usual. The smoke from the stir-fry mixed with the melody of the Peking Opera. It lingered over the yard like an invisible roof.

Putting a small dining table and a few stools in the yard, Little Pea realized her brothers were not there. "I'm going to look for Broomstick and Potatofeet."

Just outside the yard, Little Pea found Potatofeet sitting against the wall. He was crying. His clubfeet twisted outward, laying flat on the dirt. Tears streamed out of his puffy eyes and rolled down his swollen cheeks. Saliva leaked out of corners of his mouth.

"Broomstick. Broomstick is g-g-gone, "he whimpered.

"Where did he go?"

"H-h-he...He left with a much-motorcycle g-g-gang. They-c-call themselves 'The Flying T-t-tiger Brigade'."

"I see. We'll find him later. Let's go in and eat." Little Pea pulled Potatofeet's arm, trying to help him get up.

She succeeded on the second try.

Dragging his clubfeet on the gravel, Potatofeet followed Little Pea into the gate.

People already sat around the table on little stools. Pumpkin was serving beer from a tall brown bottle into small tin cups.

"Woo. It feels like ice. I just took it out of the refrigerator," said Pumpkin. She already acted drunk without taking a sip of beer.

Lili, her mother and Xiao Dong sat among Pumpkin's family as if they were guests.

She introduced him as a student from Nankai University. "This is his first time in Beijing."

"How do you like it here?"

"I'm impressed by the size and of course, I'm overwhelmed by the hospitality. Thank you." Xiao Dong nodded.

Earlier, Pumpkin washed Xiao Dong's filthy clothes for him as he bathed. Once Xiao Dong was clean, Lili lent him one of Lao Liu's uniforms to wear while his clothes dried and they ate dinner.

Lao Liu's police summer uniform did not fit Xiao Dong. It was a little too big for him, yet his swarthy face and big dark eyes behind his white-framed glasses made him a handsome police officer.

Lili put some food on Xiao Dong's plate and she smiled sweetly at him. Her face was radiant, in part due to the beer but mostly because of her feelings for her new friend.

Wu Zheng watched them as they ate. She smiled in amusement.

Yu Gang made a toast. "Let's cheer for everyone's happiness, health and prosperity."

Everyone clinked their cups together.

"Let's cheer for our students' victory in Tiananmen Square!" Pumpkin raised up her beer cup once more.

"Let's cheer for our country's bright future!" Wu Zheng cheered. She grinned, took off her glasses and wiped her eyes.

Working as an administrator in the city government in charge of Propaganda, she rarely showed her emotions. It was not an easy job, especially during a time of confusion. It was hard to comply with the official policy and satisfy people's demands for reform at the same time.

Secondly, she had Lao Liu's depression to deal with. She knew that her husband's problem came from his many years of working in the legal system.

Many times, he told her "I have to play my role every day, and I'm tired of it."

He was working on some difficult cases. The Government was coming to the realization that they made some wrong judgments during the Cultural Revolution. They wanted to reverse some of the cases where they had wrongly prosecuted innocent people during that period. It was too late in most cases, where the victims had since died or had been driven mad.

Dealing with those tragic cases daily had turned Lao Liu into a moody person, and it had taken its' toll on Wu Zheng.

She had to go to work tomorrow, and only God knew what was waiting for her. She hoped it was not something too difficult. Although her boss was a nice person, they never could predict or change the official policy.

In the current uncertainty, she knew she had to capture each moment to be happy.

She swallowed her beer, which made her more talkative.

Wu Zheng poured herself more beer and spoke affectionately about Lao Liu. "My husband is a softy. He has never hurt anybody. He has secretly helped many people in his life. He just doesn't boast about it. Whenever some tragedy happens, he suffers. And he has told me that no matter what happens, he would never kill a student."

The beer had loosened her lips, and she failed to realize that she revealed a secret that had the potential to cause her husband trouble.

"Really?" said Pumpkin loudly. "I should go and offer my apologies to him. We scorned him when he came back from work. I should have known he wasn't one of those goddamn cowardly policemen."

The sun dropped below the roofline and the night reached every corner of the yard. Under the dim overhead light that hung from the porch ceiling, there was a party-like atmosphere. Everyone was in high spirits; they buzzed as if they were bugs circulating around the light.

The festivities continued when Broomstick arrived. He told everyone about his adventure with 'The Flying Tiger Brigade'.

"Exciting! They are really exciting guys! Wild! Gee. They're wild, too. " He was speaking as if he was in too much of a hurry to form complete sentences.

"What did you do with them today?" Little Pea asked.

"Em... Let's see... We transported sick students home. We do that, and we're messengers for the headquarters of different universities, and we're always on the lookout to warn the students if the police come." Broomstick was excited, as though he was living in a dream world. "It's just like the chase games we played when we were young, except this time it's for real!"

In contrast to the others, the Wang family ate in darkness.

They were very quiet, and no one bothered to turn on the overhead porch light in front of their apartment door.

Whenever the boys began to bicker, their angry mother quickly put a stop to it.

A cat had been sleeping on the porch railing. She awakened to find the Wang family sitting in the dark, as if they were dead.

She sauntered up to the table and jumped, landing in front of the soup bowl. Before dipping her head into the soup, she felt a blow to her head. The cat fell forward and tipped over the soup bowl. The soup flooded the table and dripped onto the youngest boy's pants.

"Ah. Ah." He cried.

"You damn cat!" Mrs. Wang chased the cat away into the yard.

The boys disappeared into the apartment, while Mr. Wang stayed at the table for a moment to light his pipe.

The party in front of Pumpkin's apartment was not disturbed until Zhang Ping came back.

Rushing in from outside with her son, she was furious. "This is crazy! Oh. It's crazy! Do you believe it? The Police put me in detention in a hot van for five hours."

"Why?" asked Pumpkin. "I can't believe they did that to you. People shouldn't let them. The students shouldn't let them,"

"But they did it to me. They did it to me!" Zhang Ping screamed. "They told everyone I was crazy. How could I behave normally when I was desperately looking for my husband?"

They were not surprised that the police thought Zhang Ping was insane; the way she wildly waved her arms in the air, did make her look crazy.

"Did you find Dagong?"

"No. I haven't seen a trace of him since this morning. How can I find him among thousands of people in the Square? I'm sure he knows some Beijing University students, so I looked for him among them. The police said that they didn't believe me to have a young student for a husband. I told them my husband was not a student, but he was with them. They thought I was lying. They thought I was following the students... What a shame! I quarreled with them, and they put me in detention. "

Zhang Ping sat on the porch steps by her door, sighing like a dog. Her permed hair was wild, the tiny pigtail hardly visible in the mess.

She was depressed, yet her long, bony face and protruding front teeth made her appear more vicious than sad.

Pumpkin tried to comfort Zhang Ping. "Don't worry. Such a big man, he wouldn't get lost. He's probably like you, he got stuck somewhere for some crazy reason. It's strange though. I have never known him to be interested in this sort of thing."

While trying to comfort Zhang Ping, Pumpkin found herself questioning the reason behind Dagong's absence.

"He often talks about politics with my husband." Wu Zheng said.

"But he is always very reserved," argued Pumpkin.

Then the porch lights went off and the party was over.

Zhang Ping was the last person left sitting in the yard. She stayed in the dark for a while, watching the sky, which was very clear.

Occasionally, she could hear the noise of the city and the rattling sound of leaves waving in the wind. The crickets' buzzing added a soprano part to the huge orchestra.

Looking at the bright stars in the sky, she thought of an ancient myth - the love story between a cowboy and a weaver. They were so far apart that they could only see each other once a year, but they loved each other and kept staring in each other's direction every day.

Zhang Ping never missed her husband so badly before. They had never been apart. Dagong was such a stable person that she never had to worry about his whereabouts. He came back home from work every day at about the same time. Then she would cook the dinner with his help. Sometimes he cooked and she assisted. After dinner, he would talk with neighbors in the yard while she did some sewing. She was aware that he might be too good for her. He was so handsome and so educated. Unfortunately, such a good man grew up in a capitalist's family, which was considered the worst kind of family background.

As a man of power in the Beijing Automobile Parts factory, Zhang Ping's father had discovered Dagong in a park where he was working as a janitor, and gave him a job. Zhang Ping married him because she adored him; it did not matter what kind of family he came from. She considered their life together to be a good life.

Just like her parents, their domestic life had been peaceful. They seldom quarreled with each other and their partnership was better than her parents was, because she and Dagong shared the household chores together. During the weekend, she and Dagong would go shopping together, or spend the day in the park taking pictures and rowing.

Maybe they did not openly show their affection to each other by kissing and hugging in public like some of those people in foreign movies. Behavior like that was for young people. That was for people who were dating, not for old married couples. To Zhang Ping, that was not what a marriage was about. Marriage was about dealing with daily life.

Maybe that was not what it was like for foreigners, but they were different.

Dagong seemed satisfied with her until recently, and he had become so short-tempered in the past couple of weeks. Zhang Ping wondered what she had done to upset him; maybe she pushed him too hard to study for the TOEFL exam.

However, she could not be blamed. Like everyone else, she wanted more out of her life now than before. There was a chance to have a better life. She wanted to see Dagong go abroad, to make a lot of money, and take her and Little Turnip to see the world.

Sometimes Zhang Ping wished she could go to college; perhaps if she were more intelligent, she would understand Dagong better.

It was too late, she had no chance to get an education when she was younger; so why worry about it at her age?

God knows where my husband is now, she thought to herself. She suddenly felt so cold. She began to shivering, and goose bumps appeared on her skin.

The moon hid behind the clouds. It was dark, and she was frightened. Evil thoughts came at her from all directions, trying to swallow her.

Holding Little Turnip in her arms, she went inside. She sat on the bed, frozen.

"Where is Father?" asked Little Turnip, as if he was still asleep and dreaming.

Zhang Ping did not answer.

"Is he in America?" asked Little Turnip again.

"No, he is farther than that," said Zhang Ping.

CHAPTER 10

As Baiyun walked toward the News Center on the morning of May 3rd, she heard an announcement over the loud speaker. "The government has rejected the United Student Federation's request to open a dialogue. Instead, they put together a group of students who were selected by state officials because they are complacent and they do not criticize state policy. This is unacceptable. We will go forward with our march tomorrow to protest government's insincerity and to commemorate May the 4th."

Baiyun opened the door and saw Li Yan talking on the phone while two student reporters sat at a table busily typing.

Many layers of loose papers were strewn about the table. Dishes with half-eaten food were piled up on the corner of the table and the windowsill along with many soiled cups that once held coffee and tea.

"Hello, busy reporters!" Baiyun called out loudly and stamped her foot, since nobody bothered to look up when she opened the door.

Li Yan put the phone call on hold. "Quickly, Baiyun, what news do you have? I'm taking donations from people from all over the world."

"Great! I've secured support from the workers for our May 4th March. My friend Dagong is organizing the workers to be our 'bodyguards.' I also have an item on 'The Flying Tiger Brigade'. Have you heard of them?"

"Yes! They transmit the news at lightning speed," said Li Yan with her eyebrows rose in excitement. "You got their support, too?"

"Of course." Baiyun was proud in spite of her slight embarrassment.

"Wow! Any details?"

"Yes. The workers will meet us here outside the Beida and march along with us. 'The Flying Tiger Brigade' will join us at the Three Ring Road near the Friendship Hotel."

"I will announce this to the public and it will be a huge boost to their moral! Thank you for the good work." Li Yan returned to her phone conversation.

Baiyun handed one of the writers the article she had written the night before.

The writer thanked her and made a Victory sign with his index finger and middle finger. She returned the gesture.

When she stepped outside, she found reporters from ABC, CNN, the BBC, The New York Times, the Chinese Daily, the Oriental Daily and the Hong Kong Daily News surrounding a few student leaders, including Longfe and Yumei.

As Baiyun watched, the reporter from The New York Times came over and put the microphone in front of her mouth. "Do you want to say something to the world?"

The reporter, a Chinese American with sleek black hair and square glasses spoke to Baiyun in Chinese with an American accent.

At that moment, Longfe's voice overpowered the others, silencing them. "I have an announcement to make. The government refuses to talk to us in spite of our efforts. Instead, they are calling us unlawful individuals with ulterior motives. They accuse us of using the grief of the students to create turmoil. So, the Beida Student Federation has decided that we will march to the Tiananmen Square tomorrow to celebrate the anniversary of the May 4th movement. Seventy years ago, students from Beijing University led the historical event that made it possible for our country to take back the Shandong province from the hands of the German and Japanese occupiers. Today, we need that spirit more than ever. Using this occasion, we will communicate our sincere hope for dialogue and we will prove to the world that we are not just 'a handful of unlawful individuals to create turmoil'.

We are an organization of students and citizens wanting to have a peaceful talk with the government."

The crowd cheered. Someone shouted out "Yes! The government is by the people and for the people!"

A short man, whom Baiyun recognized as Xia Nan, the head of the communist party at the Economics Department, stepped in. "The school officials have asked me to convey this message to you. If the class boycott continues, it will be very hard for them to continue in their support of you. If another demonstration takes place tomorrow, you will certainly lose your chance to have a dialogue with the government and you will have to bear the consequences." His voice was calm but chilling.

The crowd went silent.

Baiyun tried to move forward to speak; however, Big Li beat her to the front of the crowd. "Let's not give into government's pressure. In a democratic society, demonstration is a right. This is our first step toward having a democratic society. It is our condition for a dialogue with the government. Long live democracy! Long live freedom!"

The crowd cheered for him and soon scattered.

Longfe stepped over. He gathered up Big Li, Yumei and a few other student leaders. "Let's have a meeting to decide about the demonstration tomorrow. Baiyun, you should come to this meeting as a reporter for the News Center."

Longfe led them into the dormitory building. As they walked in the corridor toward the News Center, Baiyun noticed a few students shaving each other's heads and writing out their wills.

She nudged Yumei. "See. How do you think we could stop the rally?"

Baiyun dragged Yumei to the room where these students were. One of them was half-finished shaving is head, and he showed them his will, which he'd written on the back of a T-shirt in red ink. It said, "I join the student movement because

I love my country. I'm not a counter-revolutionary and a lawless agitator. Please understand my actions."

"Do you really think that you might die?" Baiyun asked him.

She was a little shaken by his zeal. All that time, she was immersed in the class boycott and excitement of being with Dagong. She asked herself if it was possible that the blood of innocent students would be shed.

"Let's go," said Yumei, as if she had thought through all of the potential perils.

"Wait. Let me write this down in my notebook so we can broadcast it from our radio station."

Baiyun wrote down the message written on the T-shirt and left with Yumei.

They entered a room next to the News Center. The room had four bunk beds, with two on each side.

As Baiyun entered, the smell of food and dirty laundry welcomed her.

They managed to squeeze in between Longfe and Big Li in one of the lower bunks. Several had to climb up to upper bunks since the lower bunks had been taken.

"What do you all think? Should we offer a compromise?" asked Longfe.

Yumei punched him on the arm. "Are you crazy? Did you see the students next door? They are shaving their heads. They're ready to die."

"It's too late to inform the Beijing Workers' Union not to join us," said Baiyun.

She was looking forward to marching alongside Dagong. She could not imagine going back to class, at least not for a while.

"We can show the government that we are serious about the dialogue," said Longfe calmly. "I mean, we can offer our compromise by only marching to the Third Ring Road and then turn back, only a third of the way to Tiananmen Square."

"But the genie is out of the bottle. Who can stop it?" Baiyun blurted out with a voice that was still unfamiliar to her.

She could not believe that she was the one who was willing to break the school's regulations.

Big Li nodded. "Yes. I support Baiyun. She is right. At this point, there is no way we could stop the rally tomorrow." He raised his voice. "Let's fight fire with fire!" His shaved head shone under the sunlight that crept through the window.

Longfe nodded. "Okay. I will tell the school officials that the rally is on, and we will try to turn back at the Third Ring Road, but we make no guarantees."

He stood up and went to the center of the room. "The rally is on!" He extended his hand and the others joined in. One after another, their hands piled up one by one in agreement.

As Baiyun put her hand in, her heart beat fast. She envisioned a new China and a different kind of life ahead of her.

She knew that many stood with her, and they were willing to sacrifice their lives. She closed her eyes and wondered if she had gone mad.

#

Early the next morning, Baiyun was awakened by the noise of people whispering in the room.

"Yumei and Li Yan. Why didn't you wake me up sooner?" She asked. She did not want to be late for the rally.

"You are awake. Shuuu." Li Yan put her fingers on her lips. "Be quiet. Wenjing is still sleeping."

"Is she going?" asked Baiyun.

"No. She is sick."

"Ya. I'm not surprised," whispered Baiyun.

"That's the official answer," said Wenjing, sticking out her head from under the blanket. She had short bobbed hair and her smooth round face looked pale. "I seriously think you guys are crazy. You'll be crushed by tanks and forgotten." She put her head back under the blanket and started snoring.

"Wow. What an inspirational speech!" said Yumei and then looked at Baiyun and Li Yan whispering, "She's a coward. Let's leave her rotting in bed."

After brushing their teeth and packing some water and snacks, they raced to the men's dormitory, number 28.

Of course, they could not move very fast. Several thousand students were lined up in the space between women's dormitory, number 31 and men's dormitory, number 28 by the north gate.

They could see Longfe and Big Li in the front holding flags but it was impossible to get to them.

Baiyun was on her tiptoes looking for Dagong, but to no avail.

They followed the sea of people after a student with a loudspeaker announced, "Let's march."

As soon as they marched out of the Beida gate, international journalists, photographers and camera crews followed them.

Then Baiyun's eyes lit up. She saw the sign saying 'Beijing Workers' Union'.

"There's Dagong!" She yelled and then turned to Yumei and Li Yan, "Bye. I have to run because I told Dagong I would march with him."

"No wonder you've been so happy lately. You have a boyfriend, don't you?" Yumei teased her.

"Of course. That's always the reason," said Li Yan mater-of-fact.

Baiyun waved at them, pretending not hearing what they said.

Her anticipation of seeing Dagong overwhelmed her while fighting her way toward the Beijing Workers' Union. They were easy to identify because they were a small group of muscular workers wearing black T-shirts, black workpants and white headbands stating 'Democracy'.

They did look like a group of intimidating bodyguards. Baiyun spotted six-foot tall Dagong right away. He was carrying a red flag, 'Democracy in China Now' printed in white across it.

In order not to disturb him, Baiyun decided to sneak in and follow Dagong secretly. A few workers asked her why she was there. She put her fingers across her mouth to indicate that they should be quiet. Of course, that did not last long. A few workers started chuckling quietly.

Dagong turned around and saw Baiyun. He halted and called out, "Baiyun."

Then he embraced her, which interrupted the whole flow of the Workers' Union group.

He pulled Baiyun to the side after giving his flag to a worker and telling them that they would catch up.

They stood under a tree holding each other's hands, gazing at each other. Although it had been three days since they saw each other, they still remembered where they had left off. Dagong had left her alone that day in the middle of Tiananmen Square without a proper kiss goodbye.

For Dagong, this was the moment he had been anticipating for two days since he last saw Baiyun. This nerdy, yet beautiful and complex girl, with her complicated family background had intrigued him. He wanted to know her more and understand her, and most of all, he wanted to spend time alone with her.

He needed so badly to kiss Baiyun right there under that tree, but he knew he had to control himself. He wanted to pretend not to notice the crowds of people as they passed them on the street, because she was gazing at him deeply with her full, innocent eyes.

She looked so beautiful to him, her red lips and her flushed cheeks, her smooth face with the tiny freckles and the beauty mark that enhanced her so perfectly. He needed her.

Yet, Dagong asked himself, did he deserve her? Maybe twenty-three years ago, when he was fresh out of high school and just about to enter the famous Beijing University, he would have deserved to find happiness with someone like her. But now? He was old and married with a son. How could he tell her the truth, and how would she react if she knew? He did not have any answers. All he knew was that he could not stop seeing her. It was a time of change, he reasoned; maybe his own life would soon change dramatically.

Dagong held Baiyun in his arms. She fell naturally into his chest and buried her head in it. Then she looked up at him. Their faces were so close to each other.

After what seemed like an eternity, Dagong broke away and said, "Let's catch up with the others."

He held onto Baiyun's left hand and led her as they started running; he pushed through the crowd.

Baiyun was a little disappointed that he did not give her a passionate kiss; she had been anticipating it for two days. Still, she was grateful that it did not happen in public. She would have hated to be seen in public, especially when Meiling could show up any minute and force her to go home on Lao Zheng's hideous motorcycle.

She hoped the kiss would come later, at a more appropriate time.

Baiyun was thrilled to be a part of the movement along with Dagong, and she did not want to do anything that would jeopardize her being there.

Together, they ran toward the Beijing Workers' Union banner. As they ran, a cold wind swept across Baiyun's face. She galloped, and if it were not for Dagong's tight grip on her hand, she would have leapt over the crowd and flown.

She felt as if nothing could stop her.

Finally, they decided to try to avoid the crowd. They ran into the wooded area by the road where it was not as crowded, and Baiyun began to run even faster.

"Wow. You are fast!" exclaimed Dagong. He looked at Baiyun with passion in his eyes.

"Of course." Baiyun gazed back at him with a big smile.

How heavenly this was, she thought.

It did not take long before they caught up with the Beijing Workers Union.

Dagong and Baiyun took the 'Democracy in China Now' banner and they marched in the front row.

A middle-aged worker pointed to Baiyun and said, "Good for you, Dagong. You recruited a pretty girl for our team. What boost for our morale!"

Dagong nodded happily.

The street was getting very crowded. Thousands of Beijing citizens left work and school to join in the march.

Some climbed up into trees, shouting, "We love you, students! We support you whole heartedly!"

When they were approaching the Three Ring Road, students from other universities like Qinghua University and the Beijing College of Economics and Politics joined them.

The common folks were lining the streets, cheering and beating their pots and pans.

Everyone was in high spirits when the march came to an abrupt halt.

A row of policemen in crisp green uniforms with red stars on their hats stood in front of the demonstrators, facing them. Each of them carried a club and wore a pistol in plain sight. Their faces were without emotion.

Longfe stepped forward. "Let me talk to them."

He carried his loudspeaker as he walked toward the police, followed by Big Li and Yumei.

The policeman standing at the center of the row calmly broke from the line. He walked forward to meet them.

"Should we go and back them up?" whispered Baiyun to Dagong.

She was worried about Longfe, Big Li, and especially Yumei. She knew how ruthless the policemen could be.

"Not yet," said Dagong.

Involuntarily, Dagong inched forward a few steps, ready to leap forward to aid them if necessary.

Longfe stopped walking when the policeman was about a meter away from him. The policeman took a few steps more; he saluted to Longfe, and Longfe saluted back.

"We are students marching peacefully. Would you please let us pass?"

"You must guarantee to march in an orderly fashion with no destruction of public property," said the policeman.

Longfe turned back to the crowd. Into the loudspeaker he asked, "Can we promise not to destroy any public property?"

"Yes." The crowd called back.

"Do we want to turn back?"

"No."

Longfe turned back to the policeman. The policeman nodded. He motioned to the other policemen to clear the road.

"Victory!" The crowd roared, and even more people joined the march.

When they passed the Friendship Hotel, students from Beijing Normal University and the Beijing Agricultural University joined them.

They crowd took over the entire street. The traffic was at a standstill. Cars, buses and even bicycles had been paralyzed.

Soon, another wall of policemen stopped the flow of the demonstrators.

Before Longfe could go forward to talk to the police, a few students from Beijing Normal University broke through by sneaking between gaps in the policeman's line.

"Peace. Peace," called Longfe through the loud speaker.

The policemen took Longfe at his word. They cleared the road.

"The policemen are so civilized," commented Baiyun.

Her face was red with exertion and her pink sweater was soaked with sweat, yet her spirit was high. She held the banner with Dagong and smiled at him. She was writing the best episode of her life.

"Don't be too happy yet." warned Dagong.

Being older, he was much more cautious, yet he could do nothing but follow the sea of people. He suspected that the display of tolerance by the government would only be temporary. He had seen it before.

During the 1957 anti-rightist movement, when the government encouraged people to criticize them. In the end, the people who were honest and dared to stick their necks out were thrown into jail for life.

Thirty-two years had passed; Dagong was a small child at the time, but he remembered it clearly.

The old saying was that it takes a generation to forget lessons of the past. The students were young and they would not have witnessed the anti-rightist campaign. Had their parents not told them, or did they not at least learn about it in their history lessons? What about the people who lived through it, and are now supporting the student's movement?

Dagong thought that everyone, himself included, must have gone mad. He knew things could only end badly; the older people must have realized that. He dreaded thinking of what would happen once the government had its fill of humoring the idealistic students.

Human life seemed to be worth very little in China.

As the march advanced, Baiyun realized they were approaching Tiananmen Square.

The sun hid itself behind the clouds temporarily. A cool breeze swept through the people, covering them with a thin layer of the dust that seemed to cover everything in Beijing during the springtime.

She glanced around and saw soldiers equipped with rifles were posted everywhere. There were soldiers in a row along both sides of the Chang'an Avenue, and there were more marching in the distance.

She suddenly felt a chill, as if it was winter.

People began to shout slogans enthusiastically, as if they did not notice the soldiers.

The people surrounding Dagong and Baiyun were chanting "We love the People's Liberation Army!"

Baiyun turned to Dagong. "Do you see the armed soldiers? Am I hallucinating?"

"No. They are real," said Dagong solemnly. "We should be very careful."

As they were talking, the march stopped suddenly at the intersection of the Chang'an Avenue and Xidan Avenue, less than a block from Tiananmen Square.

Looking ahead, Baiyun could see an imposing wall of armed soldiers blocking them.

Big Li ventured forward and tried to run through the imposing barrier, only to fail. Two soldiers crossed their riffles in front of him and pushed him away. The more he struggled, the more the soldiers pushed him back. Longfe and another student tried to stop Big Li.

Longfe understood the danger of the situation. "Let's turn around now. We have come far enough," he said to Big Li, who continued to struggle.

Big Li pushed forward. "We are almost there. Ten more steps and we'll be in Tiananmen Square"

A soldier struck Big Li on the head, grabbed his arms and twisted them behind him.

Longfe stood back and put his hands up. "The People's Army loves the people," he said calmly. "Please, let him go. We will turn around."

A soldier clubbed Longfe on the shoulder with the butt of his rifle.

Dagong took a step toward the soldiers. "Don't hit the students. Hit me. I'm guilty of encouraging them to go forward."

He waved his fist in front of the soldier. The soldier grabbed him and began to beat him with his rifle. Some of the workers stepped forward to fight the soldiers off as the others shielded the students.

Baiyun cried out as the soldier beat Dagong. She ran toward him and was blocked by a large worker.

She struggled to free herself from his grip, but he was too strong for her. "Crazy girl! You will be hurt."

The workers, true to their pledge to work as bodyguards, formed a shield between the soldiers and students.

"The People's Army loves the people," chanted the citizen on the street.

"Stop hurting the students. Be on the winning side!"

"Down with the corrupted government!"

"Free Press. Democracy in China!"

Once again, the sheer mass of the people's power overwhelmed the army.

The clouds moved aside as the people broke past the soldiers. The sun was shining once again and people swarmed into the vast Square.

"Dagong!" Baiyun broke loose from the worker who restrained her.

Dagong was lying on the ground surrounded by many students and workers. Blood was streaming from his forehead and one of his eyes was swollen. Baiyun knelt by him and wept.

"He tried to protect us, so he got the brunt of it," cried a young worker.

A middle-aged woman in a white coat with a stethoscope draped around her neck pushed through the crowd that had gathered around Dagong. "I'm a doctor; I can take care of him," she said.

Dagong pointed toward another worker who was lying nearby; blood was pouring from the man's mouth. "Please, take care of him first,"

"I can do both. I need to take care of you first, since you have a head wound," said the doctor.

The doctor put antiseptic on Dagong's wounds and wrapped them with bandages before going to treat the other wounded worker.

Baiyun held Dagong to her chest and gave him some water to sip.

Dagong gazed at her; she looked exceptionally beautiful at that moment. He smiled. He knew he could never find anything better than to be held and nursed by Baiyun. He wished the moment would last forever.

The sound of motorcycles approaching could be heard. It was 'The Flying Tiger Brigade' coming to assist the wounded. Lao Zheng and Meiling, followed by Broomstick and two other young men on scooters, approached as the crowd cleared the way for them.

"Baiyun, are you okay? My poor daughter..." Meiling jumped off the motorcycle before Lao Zheng had a chance to come to a complete stop; she tripped and nearly fell.

She ran to Baiyun and knelt, her hands on Baiyun's face.

"Mother, I'm fine. Look at my friend; he's the one you should be concerned about." Baiyun pushed Meiling away, embarrassed.

"Okay. We can take him home." Meiling looked to Dagong. "Do you live close by?"

"Yes." Dagong turned his face away and closed his eyes.

When Broomstick realized it was Dagong, he pushed his skinny body through the wall of people. "Dagong. What a hero! I'm proud of you."

Broomstick knelt beside Dagong. He saw that Dagong was in pain and he spoke softly. "I can take you home. Okay?"

Dagong nodded.

Dagong did not want to go home; he would have rather died there in Baiyun's arms than gone home to face Zhang Ping with Baiyun by his side; now both of them would find out the truth.

It would have been easier to die, but fate was not concerned with that.

Dagong's head ached and his body was wracked with pain. He could do nothing but oblige.

Broomstick helped the workers to carry Dagong to his scooter and they helped Dagong to climb into the seat behind Broomstick.

They rode away as the bystanders opened a narrow path, and Baiyun persuaded one of the young men with 'The Flying Tiger Brigade' to carry her on the back of his scooter.

They followed Broomstick and Dagong, with Lao Zheng and Meiling close behind.

CHAPTER 11

The vast Tiananmen Square was filled with students from many different universities, which could be identified by their flags. There were citizens of Beijing, foreign journalists and photographers from all over the world, as well as vendors who were selling a variety of food items.

Armed soldiers in green uniforms walked among the citizens, who seemed not even slightly afraid. Some even offered water to the soldiers, who politely accepted while keeping their solemn facial expressions.

The scene in the Square puzzled Baiyun as she rode past with a young man from 'The Flying Tiger Brigade'.

They followed Broomstick as he carried Dagong to his home. The image of Dagong's bloodied head was still fresh in her mind.

"Why are the citizens not afraid of the soldiers?" She asked.

"Did you hear the loud speaker earlier? They said Zhao Ziyang is on the student's side. Zhao Ziyang was the General Secretary of the Communist Party. He spoke favorably about us in an Asian Development Bank meeting. So the soldiers must have been told not to hurt the demonstrators anymore," said the young man.

"I heard that, but I wasn't sure if it was true or not. Good! It looks like we might win this time," said Baiyun.

It sounded like a breakthrough; she felt her spirits rise. The good news about Zhao Ziyang's support, the bright sunshine, the warm weather and the wind from the motorcycle made her feel intoxicated with a sense of victory.

They drove slowly and zigzagged through many small crowds.

As they rode, Baiyun saw a young woman saw standing on a wooden box with short hair and a red shirt. She waved her arms and said, "We are ready to sacrifice our young lives for a better and democratic China."

Many photographers snapped pictures of her.

The idea of sacrifice started sinking into Baiyun's mind. She no longer thought that her blood was too precious to shed after seeing Dagong shed his blood for the cause. She would always fight alongside Dagong, she told herself.

After a half hour of maneuvering through the crowds, they arrived at Dagong's Hudong.

At the entrance, there were vendors selling water, steam-buns and even umbrellas.

Pumpkin and Marshmallow sat by a pot of steam buns, smiling until they saw Broomstick approaching with a bleeding man on the back of his scooter.

Pumpkin rushed towards Broomstick. "What happened to the student?" She asked, and then she recognized the man who sat behind Broomstick.

"Oh, no. It's Dagong." She told Marshmallow to take care of the steam bun stand and she followed Broomstick past the gate.

After Broomstick parked the motorcycle, he and Pumpkin helped Dagong to walk into the courtyard, where Zhang Ping and Little Turnip sat eating lunch.

They ran to Dagong and helped him to sit in a chair.

Zhang Ping squatted by him, planting kisses all over him. "How did you hurt yourself? Did the police beat you up?" Her mind quickly turned from her husband's wounds to her concerns over herself. "Have you forgotten about us? If something happens to you, what would we do? How would we ever get to America without you?"

Zhang Ping stopped kissing Dagong. She began to wail; it was so loud that the noise from the nearby Tiananmen Square faded into the background.

"I'm fine. I just feel a little dizzy," Dagong opened his eyes and held Little Turnip under his arm.

Pumpkin brought him water.

Everyone was very quiet; even the cat sat motionless on a bench, staring at Dagong with its two big green eyes.

Then someone broke the silence from outside the yard.

"Stay outside and wait. Why do you have to come in?" Meiling told Lao Zheng. "You don't even know the man."

"I want to help. I might be able to help carry him around in the yard. Hey, you never know when they will need a big guy like me," said Lao Zheng. He wiped his face and said to Meiling, "Are you embarrassed by me?"

"Yes," answered Meiling. "Okay, come in. Just be quiet."

Meiling and Lao Zheng followed Baiyun into the yard.

Something dawned on Baiyun when she saw Zhang Ping and Little Turnip crying as they surrounded Dagong.

"Oh, my God!" Her whisper was so low that only Meiling could hear her.

Baiyun felt dizzy; she stumbled a few steps and had to hold on to Meiling's shoulder to steady herself. She looked down, trying to hide her flood of tears.

Naturally, Meiling understood the situation as quickly as lightning. She grabbed Baiyun's arm, which was already on her shoulder, and said, "Let's get out of here." Then she pushed Lao Zheng forward out of the yard.

"But we can't leave him like that; what if they need my help?" Lao Zheng was totally clueless.

Meiling suggested, "Look at Baiyun. She is fainting. How about we take Baiyun to a restaurant? She must be starving, after all that marching"

"No."

"Well, where do you want to go, Baiyun?"

Baiyun knew she could not go back to her dorm. She would have to tell Yumei that Dagong was married with a kid. Her friends would laugh their heads off at her.

She could not stand the thought of sitting in a restaurant, listening to Meiling's advice as strangers at the other tables stared. She was sure they would know her shame just from the look on her face.

She did not want to go home, to face the awkwardness of sitting with her cuckolded father as her mother and Lao Zheng frolicked loudly in the next room.

Baiyun thought of her father. His wrinkled red face and his mindless vocalizations, mewing like a cat to drown out the moans coming from the bedroom, gazing at his roses to avoid seeing his wife in the arms of another man.

Suddenly, Baiyun understood a small part of her father's pain.

Who knows what was worse, she wondered. She did not want the most comfortable solution. She just wanted to go some place where she could sort through it. Some place where she could figure it out; where she could weep openly and act like a mad woman and no one would notice.

In her state of confusion, Baiyun made the worst decision she could make. "I... I just want to go home."

Baiyun rode sandwiched between Lao Zheng and Meiling.

The numbness began to fade, and she felt so much worse. She leaned on Lao Zheng's leather jacket and pretended to sleep. She soaked his smelly jacket with her tears.

"What a sneaky guy who dares to steal my daughter's heart. I wish I could punch him in the face." Meiling could not stop cursing Dagong.

Baiyun wanted to ask her to be quiet, but she was too exhausted to say anything.

As they passed the Beijing Industrial University, life was not going on as usual.

Instead of rushing back from work and class on their bicycles, people were forming groups by the roadside. They had discussions, held heated debates and they shared gossip.

There were students who marched on the streets, holding flags and banners that displayed 'Never forget the spirit of May 4th' and 'Fight the Official Corruption'. They were on their way to join the students in Tiananmen Square.

Occasionally, people would stop them and offer them tea and homemade steamed buns.

They would tell students, "Keep up the good work."

Students would say, "Join us next time. Let's form a Great Wall of people."

The old men and women would nod and smiled whole-heartedly.

They arrived at the apartment and while Lao Zheng parked the motorcycle, Meiling and Baiyun went in first.

As soon as they opened the door, they could hear the loud, haunting strains of Mendelssohn's First Violin Concerto, which echoed within the small apartment.

"Good, the old man is partying and completely unaware of the demonstration outside," said Meiling as she and Lao Zheng walked toward Meiling's bedroom

Then she stopped and turned towards Baiyun, "We're gonna take a nap. After that, Uncle Lao Zheng will make pot-stickers for you."

"I'm not hungry," said Baiyun while leaping over the vegetables in the hallway toward the living room.

She could see her father and his friend Lee Fe sitting on her father's bed, facing each other. Lee Fe was playing the violin.

Lee Fe knew Baiyun's father from when he was known as Professor Yang. His right arm pushed up and down rhythmically, while his head moved along passionately. His black-framed glasses had slid down to the tip of his nose due to the sweat.

Father stared at him and his old eyes were twinkling. His salt and pepper hair danced as he swayed his head along with the music.

On the dining table next to the bed, there were two half-drunk glasses of red wine.

Father picked one up and had a sip. He said "Meow. Meow!"

Baiyun had seen enough; she went to her old room.

She lay down on her bed, and she could not help looking at the tall bookshelf next to her. It contained all of the textbooks she had ever used, as well as all her notebooks, her final exam papers and her report cards.

Meiling had saved everything. Yet the ones that stood out the most to Baiyun were the TOFEL books. There was 'The Official Guide to the TOFEL Exam', 'TOFEL Essentials', 'Practice Exercises for the TOFEL with Audio CDs' and '400 Must-have Words for the TOFEL'.

These reminded Baiyun of her derailed attempt to go to America. Maybe Meiling was right to encourage her to go abroad; she would soon pick up the pieces and try again, and she would not allow herself to be derailed by romantic nonsense or idealistic talk of a democratic China.

She closed her eyes.

All she could see was Dagong surrounded by his weeping wife and son. She could see Dagong's agonized face. She tried to forget about him, to forget about loving him and even to forget about hating him. Yet she failed miserably.

Suddenly, her curiosity was piqued. She wondered why Dagong never mentioned his wife or his son to her. Was he just a lousy dog trying to cheat on his wife with a naïve young student, or was there something more to it?

She decided she would confront him to find out the truth, and she wanted to do it sooner rather than later. As she resolved herself, her eyes grew heavy and she drifted into sleep.

"Hey, Baiyun, want something to eat?" A voice woke Baiyun up from her nap.

She opened her eyes and saw Lao Zheng standing by the bed with a plate of steamed meat dumplings in his hand.

She sat up immediately rubbing her eyes.

"You woke me up," she complained, yet she could not refuse such good food.

However obnoxious Lao Zheng was, Baiyun had to admit that he was a good cook. She took the plate and gobbled down the dumplings.

Lao Zheng sat down on the bed and leaned toward Baiyun. He wore a fake smile that made Baiyun want to vomit up the dumplings even as she was still eating them.

Lao Zheng's beady little eyes were aglow; he smiled, exposing his crooked teeth. "What do you say, Baiyun? Let's go out sometime on my motorcycle and have some fun."

"Oh, my God. Here he goes again," Baiyun thought.

Normally, she would get up and rush out of the house to get away from him. But after all that she had been through, she was very tired and confused.

"Okay." Baiyun kept eating.

"When should we go? Maybe I can take you back to school." Lao Zheng inched toward Baiyun a little more.

"If you would excuse me, I need to run to the bathroom." Baiyun stood up, pushed Lao Zheng away and squeezed through the gap between the bed and the bookshelf to get to the bathroom.

She slammed the door. In a second, she could hear Meiling yelling at Lao Zheng, "What are you doing in there by yourself? Where is Baiyun? Did you scare her away?"

"No. She went to the bathroom."

Baiyun held her head between her hands trying to think straight.

The troops had moved in. Soldiers had been posted everywhere in Tiananmen Square. Regardless of what had happened between her and Dagong, she knew she needed to get back to school so she could help. She would not be a coward. She decided she would not see Dagong again. Still, she had many friends and classmates at Beida and she could not abandon them. Life would still be interesting, she told herself.

After she flushed the toilet and got out of the bathroom, she decided to go to sleep and leave early in the morning.

She stuck her head into the living room and saw that her father and his friend Lee Fe were so engrossed in their music that they did not notice her.

They were playing Tchaikovsky's First Violin Concerto.

It reminded her of what she had learned of the platonic love affair between Tchaikovsky and his patron and lover Nadezhda von Meck. They never even met each other, yet Tchaikovsky could write such romantic music for her.

She thought of Dagong and sighed. She cared about him very much. She wished he had kissed her that last time in front of her dormitory. Maybe she would see him again; perhaps if he came to see her at Beida she would speak to him.

With that thought, she went to bed accompanied by the beautiful music.

In the morning at 8:00 am, Baiyun got up and ventured to her father's room.

Lee Fe was gone, and Father's head lay sideways on the dining room table; he was sound asleep and Baiyun could hear him snoring.

His wine glass had tipped over and wine soaked through the papers on the table.

Under the dim lamplight that burnt through the night, the flushing of his face made him look like a roasted animal.

She gathered up a few things from her room and left without saying farewell to anyone.

CHAPTER 12

Baiyun returned to her dorm and found Yumei in bed among many blankets, eating lunch.

"Hi, Yumei. Are you sick?"

"No. I'm tired of staying at Longfe's home. His parents invited me to stay with them last night. They are hard to deal with. They are typical Pekingese; they look down upon small town people like me." Yumei yawned and pulled her thick, long hair to the back of her head.

Her eyelids were slightly swollen. Her high cheek-boned face had a few new pimples, which were shining under the rays of sunshine from the window. Her naturally oily face was the culprit and the thick lotion she put on sometimes made it worse.

"Where is Longfe?" Baiyun sat on the bed across the table from Yumei.

"His parents want him stay at home for a while and I am not going to wait for him. I am going to do something exciting!" Yumei smiled while putting a dumpling into her mouth.

"What are you going to do?"

"I'm going to try to be one of the representatives from the Chemistry department in the dialogue delegation. I know the head of the organization. He's also from my home town." Yumei sounded very confident.

"Is he that student from the Political Science department?"

"Yes."

"That's great. He is really one of the top student leaders."

"That's right. What have you been doing?"

"I have been working for the News Center as a reporter," said Baiyun modestly.

"I know. I thought you had followed Dagong home after the police beat him."

"Yes. Then my mother and her boyfriend took me home."

Baiyun stood up and wanted to leave before she had to tell Yumei the truth about Dagong.

"Oh, I'm sorry to hear that. So, why didn't you stay with Dagong and take care of him?" Yumei probed further.

"There was plenty of help there. What, do you think that we're husband and wife or something? You think I have to take care of him?" Baiyun snapped before stomping out of the room.

She slammed the door behind her.

As soon as she got back on the street, she heard that a major news conference was being held in the conference hall. She decided to go there first.

By the time she arrived on foot the conference just started.

Students crowded the conference hall; all of the seats were filled and more students stood in the back, sat on the stairs and filled the entryway outside of the hall. The hall was extremely quiet, except for the speaker on the stage and thousands of beating hearts.

"It is time for us to launch a mass Hunger Strike!" A deep, strong voice came through the speaker in the hallway where Baiyun stood.

The crowd stood mute, as though they were hit by a blow and were slow to respond.

Then Baiyun heard several voices announcing their support.

Baiyun looked around. Most people were quiet. They stretched their necks and stood on their tiptoes. It seemed that they believed that if they were a little taller they would actually be able to see the stage from the hallway.

The speaker continued. "Our conditions for ending such a Hunger Strike are that first, the government should officially declare the movement a patriotic action. Second, the government should conduct a dialogue with the students. Our movement has been successful up to now. But we have to strive hard to convince the government that we are determined so that we can force them to accept our conditions fully and bring the Pro-Democracy movement to a complete victory!"

Applause and cheers followed the first speaker.

Students in the stairways were stirred too. Everyone tried to push forward to witness the extraordinary event.

Baiyun tried to move up a few steps because too many people were packed tightly into the humid hallway and they were pushing forward from behind.

The people around Baiyun were drenched in sweat, and her own armpits and chest were soaked. The smell of perspiration around her was suffocating. She thought she might collapse but she stood there firmly like a flagpole.

"I have an idea." A fresh young voice came through the microphone. The crowd suddenly calmed down again. "I have been practicing Qigong since I was a child. I have gone on many hunger strikes in order to fight my father. You must master Qiqong if you want to survive a prolonged hunger strike. It is the secret to victory. I want to be a hunger striker." He said to the cheering crowd, "I want you to join me in the Hunger Strike and I want all of us to practice Qiqong!"

The crowd laughed aloud.

"Practice Qiqong? Maybe we all should go to the Tiananmen Square and practice Qiqong there. Then the government would be happy about us because we would feel so peaceful we'd forget about the movement." Somebody in the crowd near Baiyun joked.

Some people chuckled, but Baiyun was not amused. She did not think the Hunger Strike should be decided on yet. It was a serious matter that would put people's lives at risk.

Baiyun thought the student leaders should at least consult with doctors and experts before they made the final decision.

"I, Longfe Huang, and the rest of the Beida Student Federation have decided that the Hunger Strike will begin tomorrow. Everyone should feel free to join us." Baiyun was not surprised to hear that Longfe returned from his parents' home that morning.

He had grown into a confident student leader; he would not let his mother and father keep him from the Pro-Democracy movement.

Baiyun asked herself, would I be willing to be a hunger striker? She was not ready to die yet. She was a girl with dreams. She had worked hard and had high expectations for the future. She has not had a chance to experience life yet. She wanted to graduate from college and to go to America, to become a scientist and a writer, to meet a nice young man and fall in love with him. She wanted to experience real love.

With Dagong, she thought she had found true love, but it was short-lived. Now, she was deeply hurt and confused about their relationship. Would that make her want to die? No.

Baiyun remembered a debate she once had with her roommates. She told them that she had a strong will to live, and she would try to stay alive even if she had lost all of her limbs.

"I would commit suicide if that happened to me," said Wenjing. The world always looked grayer to this hard-working and intelligent girl.

"Yeck, I couldn't imagine living that way," said Yumei with a smirk. She could even be a pragmatist sometimes.

After that argument, the words 'weird' and 'crazy' were often used to describe Baiyun, and she didn't mind at all.

In Beijing University, one could be proud to be crazy, but in this moment, Baiyun was not crazy. She knew she did not want to die and she was not going to risk her life either.

Her own calmness surprised her. She was an adventurous girl now and she was easily tempted by new challenges, but in the case of a Hunger Strike, she felt more comfortable to remain as an observer, or else she would join in the Hunger Strike later in a quieter, less visible fashion. Nevertheless, she disagreed with the urgency to start a hunger strike. She had a feeling that the organizers of the Hunger Strike had some unknown reason to announce it today.

At that moment, a tall and muscular man pushed and shoved forward. In a while, a deep and rather hoarse voice came through the speaker.

Baiyun knew that was Big Li. "I'm here to tell everyone that I want to participate in the Hunger Strike. Why am I doing this? It is because I want to see the true face of the government. We are fortunate enough to have parents who raised us to become college students, but it is time for us to stop living in comfort, and to do this we must stop eating. The government has again lied to us and ignored us. They even sent troops to Tiananmen Square to scare us and beat us. We only wanted the government to acknowledge us and to say that we are not traitors. We, the children, are ready to die. We are ready to use our lives to pursue the truth, and we are willing to sacrifice ourselves for our country's future."

Baiyun could imagine Big Li's swarthy face and his eyes, framed by his thick eyebrows. Those eyes were full of sincerity. They said; Believe me, I am telling the truth.

Baiyun was ashamed of her own selfish thoughts. Big Li's behavior after the start of the prodemocracy movement was a total surprise. She was happy to see that a hard-working nerd like Big Li could become a courageous student leader. She was also surprised how much she had changed herself.

Two weeks ago, she was still studying hard on TOEFL exam in the library and now she was at the center of the Pro-Democracy movement.

Big Li's impassioned speech had swayed her to believe it was worthwhile to make such a sacrifice. They were asking the government for dialogue and recognition. Were these two things worth dying for? She did not think so, but Big Li's speech made her realize that the Hunger Strike was about much more than those two demands. It was about seeing the government's true face.

The meeting hall was in chaos. More and more students struggled forward to join the hunger strike team.

As a member of the News Center, Baiyun decided to volunteer to be a correspondent to the hunger strikers, which would be an important role as well as a good challenge. She was beginning to thrive on witnessing and recording important historical events.

When Baiyun was finally pushed out of the conference hall, she met Li Yan from the News Center. They both had to go back to the main campus on foot; since the streets were so crowded it would be impossible to ride through the crowds.

Li Yan agreed that Baiyun should follow the hunger strikers to Tiananmen Square the following day.

Baiyun was deep in thought as she pushed her bicycle through the crowded campus. The mood was somber on the streets; students were urgently rushing around, and many wore white headbands on their heads.

She guessed that some parents either had already brought their sons or daughters home or had gone home themselves after fruitless effort of persuasion. She could see clusters of students and workers on street corners, looking more intense.

As she was approaching the Triangle, she spotted a tall middle-aged man with a white bandage wrapped around his head wearing a pair of green sunglasses.

It was Dagong; he wore a faded gray shirt and blue jeans and he was talking to a group of students. "The movement has reached a crucial point. The government has refused to talk to the Beida Student Federation after the students have appealed to them repeatedly. Now Russia's president Gorbachev is coming. When the news reached us that the students were going to start a hunger strike, the Beijing Workers' Union immediately organized a support team. We, the Beijing Workers' Union, will support the students and jointly stage a Hunger Strike in the Tiananmen Square to show the government that we are serious about our demands of Free Speech and Democracy in China. We will provide the moral and material support. We want the government to stop calling us instigators of illegal activities. We want the government to have dialogue with the students and broadcast it to the whole world."

Baiyun thought Dagong somehow looked thinner, almost gaunt, yet his voice was loud and full of confidence.

Baiyun was utterly moved by his appearance. A part of her wanted to slap him, walk away and never see him again, but a part of her wondered if maybe he had a good reason for not telling her about his family. Maybe he had not had time to tell her yet. Maybe he was planning to, but never had opportunity. A part of her was still very curious about the man who wooed her without telling her he was married.

Did he take advantage of her innocence, and if so, was she supposed to be mad? She did not know what to think. Maybe she would have an opportunity to clear it up. She waited for Dagong to finish his speech and she pushed her way to the front of the crowd.

"Dagong."

"Baiyun." Surprised, Dagong quickly resumed his composure. "Nice to see you here. What a coincidence!"

"What? You are here in the center of my college and think it is impossible to run into me?" Baiyun said and tried to tease him a little.

"You are right. I was hoping to see you."

Baiyun stared into his eyes behind the green sunglasses in order to get a clue of his intentions, but it was too hard to see through them.

"We can take a walk here around the campus. I'd like to show you around," suggested Baiyun.

It was an awkward situation, but Baiyun was quite good at dealing with them after years of training at home.

"Sure, I have some time. Do you want me to take you on my bicycle again? This time you can sit on the front handle bar and lean against my chest like a lover. The back seat is reserved for my wife and son," Dagong joked.

Baiyun laughed in spite of herself. She could not believe he had made her laugh when the day before she could not keep herself from weeping.

"Let's just walk," said Baiyun. "I'll take you to see the 'Nameless Lake'."

After Dagong parked his bicycle, they started walking. By 5:00 pm, the sun had gradually disappeared behind the buildings and trees.

The air turned a little cooler, but the amount of activities on campus had not decreased at all. It would go on until midnight. Nothing normal was happening on campus anymore. Everyone seemed to be enjoying the class boycott with no homework to worry about or tests to prepare for.

It was no longer necessary to sit in the library all day long to grow calluses on their bottoms. This new student culture was like a dream coming true and they were enjoying it intensely while organizing their unprecedented prodemocracy movement.

They spent their days meeting and talking with people, organizing meetings, having news conferences, writing posters and riding bicycles to Tiananmen Square.

Because of the traffic on the street, Baiyun decided to take Dagong through an old, almost abandoned residential area on campus.

It was located near Baiyun's dorm but across the street and was encircled by an old brick wall. The enormous encircled area mainly consisted of trees and stones. Occasionally a reddish colored brick house appeared. If the house were occupied, clothes hanging on the rope under the roof on the front porch and heads of bok choy and celery lying against the wall would be an indication.

Baiyun and Dagong were walking on the dirt road over many layers of dry leaves. They were silent for a while. They both realized that they were in an ideal place for lovers, since it was not officially a part of the present-day campus, very few students ventured into the area.

Baiyun was nervous. When she first ran into Dagong, she thought she would slap him on the face and walk away from him. She could not believe she not only took him for a walk but also lured him to a lover's haven.

For many years, she wished she could find a nice young man to rely on and to bare her heart to. Dagong almost became one, and then the complication happened. She discovered the truth, and she knew she should never see him again. Yet he showed up again in her life and she took him back for reasons she could not understand. She was confused and excited. She did not know which emotion was stronger.

She was a heroine in a forbidden love, about to plunge into a dead-end relationship. She hoped that she would come out unscathed. It is too late to back out and say, let's see what happens.

She was naturally curious, so this would be a chance to understand Dagong better.

Baiyun was too nervous to touch him, but Dagong was an experienced man. He wrapped his arm around Baiyun's shoulders and looked into her eyes. Their faces gradually moved toward each other; Baiyun saw that Dagong's eyes were full of love and anticipation. He was going to kiss her.

Just before their lips were about to touch, Baiyun suddenly turned her head away. In recent years, she had always imagined kissing a boy, and wondering how it would feel.

Would this be the same as I imagined? she asked herself.

"Are you afraid?" asked Dagong.

Baiyun nodded silently, trying not to appear frightened.

She was suddenly crippled by shyness, and at the same time, the excitement inside of her was overwhelming.

"How about we find a place and sit down for a while?"

Baiyun nodded again, both eager and somewhat afraid. She could feel her heart beating like a drum. She could sense what was going to happen, and she felt fear but also curiosity. How could she refuse him? How could she refuse to get closer to such a charming and attractive man? She almost forgot he was married, but she knew she had to ask him about it.

They sat down on a bench under a tree.

"Woo. Summer started early this year," said Dagong.

He unbuttoned his white polyester shirt and sat on the bench. "Even the stone bench is warm," he added. "I saw a pair of lovers just left."

Baiyun and Dagong could feel that the bench was still warm where the couple sat.

Baiyun sat next to Dagong. She wanted to ask him about his family but she decided to wait, not wanting to disturb such a pleasant atmosphere.

Dagong chuckled. Even in the shade, Baiyun's face was radiant. Her straight black hair was glowing under the sunlight that filtered through the trees.

She put her hands on her bare legs, stretched out and she said, "I'm so excited! This democracy movement is fun."

"You kids just want to have fun," said Dagong teasingly.

"Stop lecturing me! I know your generation!"

"What do you know? Have you ever worked in the countryside?" questioned Dagong.

"Yes."

"How long?"

"Two months."

"Okay. That's nothing. I am talking about 10 or 20 years. Have you ever worked on a hog farm?" Dagong raised his voice.

"No. So what?"

Dagong stood up to face her.

"So you don't know what hardship is. Have you washed your body with icy water? Have you slept in a place where eggs cracked due to the cold?"

Wanting to argue on an equal level, Baiyun stood up to face him directly.

"No. No and no! Your generation is passive and letting others turn and twist your fate. You don't have guts any more. You have lost all your edge through years of bad fortune." Baiyun was so surprised by her own assertiveness.

She stared at him. He gazed at her. Her face was pink down to her neck and his neck was red up to his ears.

"Hey, you kids are getting damn serious," said Dagong, breaking the momentary silence.

Baiyun giggled and then said, "Don't just laugh it off. Where is your answer?"

"Do you want a kiss?" Dagong looked at Baiyun with affection.

Baiyun stood there quietly and dreamingly. She sensed people walking past them like in a show.

"No answer. Does that mean Yes?" He put his arms on top of her shoulders. She moved forward. Their lips reached out for each other. Baiyun had hundreds of reasons not to kiss Dagong, yet she allowed the one reason she had to kiss him rule her. She loved him after all. The bandage on his head made her love him even more. He was a hero of the movement. Who would not want to kiss a hero? Whether he was married or not, she did not want to care about it now. She was indeed her mother's daughter and her family genes were certainly at work.

"Hello. Baiyun, Baiyun!" A voice took them out of their fantasy.

Baiyun raised her head. Like a strange nightmare, her mother, Meiling appeared in front of them. Only it was real.

She sat on the back seat of her boyfriend Lao Zheng's motorcycle. They both wore leather jackets and blue jeans. There was a guitar on Meiling's shoulder.

"Hi, Mother." Meeting Meiling so unexpectedly, and with Dagong after witnessing his family together with Meiling not long ago, Baiyun felt totally embarrassed and even guilty.

"I don't mean to disturb," Meiling winked at them, but mostly at Dagong, who was dead silent. Then she pulled

Baiyun to the side and said, "You are seeing him again. I want you to explain that to me. Why are you seeing a married man?"

"Mother," this was the first time Baiyun was caught red-handed by her mother for doing something wrong. It was usually other way around. "I will talk to you later. Okay?" She stared at her mother innocently, trying hard to get her approval.

"Baiyun is a big girl. She can take care of herself," said Lao Zheng. Then he turned to Baiyun and gave her a sleazy smile, which did not make Baiyun feel like throwing up this time, but only because she was still thinking of Dagong and she refused to let Lao Zheng ruin the moment.

"Okay, maybe I will see you soon. Take care of yourself." Meiling handed Baiyun a bag of food and a jacket.

Then, Meiling and her boyfriend disappeared in a cloud of smoke and noise.

"So now you've met my mother," said Baiyun uneasily. "Sorry it had to be like this."

"No. I have met her a few times. She seems like quite an exciting person."

Something bothered Dagong; he suppressed the urge to tell Baiyun that he thought Meiling looked familiar.

"Thank you."

"I take it that man is not your father."

"No. He is too young to be my father."

"Where is your father?"

"He died a long time ago during the Cultural Revolution." She lied.

"I see," Dagong moved closer to Baiyun, "I guess your mother stole our kisses," Dagong beamed at Baiyun.

Baiyun turned her head toward him and said, "That's a good thing." Baiyun teased.

"Why?" Dagong was surprised.

"Because I don't know you yet. And..." Baiyun lowered her head looking at her fingers. "You are married."

"Do you want to know why? I would love to tell you and I'm sorry that I didn't tell you earlier. I didn't want it to spoil our relationship because I love you so much," Dagong leaned toward Baiyun and touched Baiyun's long black hair.

"Sure," said Baiyun. She took his green sunglasses off. The top of his right eye still showed purple and was swollen from the beating. "You look handsome in spite of this."

"My parents died when I was five years old. My aunt Rose raised me and she passed away when I was twenty. I was doing hard labor in Inner Mongolia. She left me alone in this world. I was a straight A student but I was not allowed to go to any universities due to my family background. I worked so hard on the farm that a miracle happened. I was assigned a job in Beijing working as a janitor at the Beijing Zoo. The head of the Beijing Automobile Parts factory discovered me there and he assigned me to work for him. He gave me a good position and his daughter fell in love with me. We got married and had a son. So that's it," said Dagong. "That's the short version. The long version might take a thousand and one nights. I'm not sure that you want to hear it." Dagong stood up and walked away.

Baiyun stood up and chased him down. "I understand, and I don't care. I still love you."

Dagon turned around and they kissed passionately. They held each either tightly as though they would never let each other go. After a few minutes, their lips separated.

"Don't you feel guilty that we are kissing while others are planning the revolution?" Baiyun asked.

"No," said Dagong firmly.

"Why?" Baiyun was surprised by his conviction.

"Because this is revolution too."

"What? You mean this?" She pointed her finger to her lips, "You mean the kiss?"

"Yes." Dagong looked at the bewildered Baiyun and smiled, "Because we were not allowed to kiss before."

"Have you ever kissed anyone before?" asked Baiyun.

"Of course. How about you?"

"Yes," said Baiyun, feeling that point it was better to lie. She glanced at him to see his reaction.

"I know you are experienced when it comes to love. When was your first love experience?"

"I fell in love with my violin teacher when I was fifteen. Then I fell for my mother's lover," said Baiyun.

"Oh. You are more experienced than any Chinese girl around."

"We didn't do anything besides kisses and hugs. How about you? Tell me something about your love experiences."

Baiyun really lied. Her so-called love experiences were actually unrequited love and she did not even have the courage to convey her message of love to these men.

"No. I'm an old man, compared to you. You know my life is too complicated to tell. Do you want to walk a little further?" Dagong changed the subject.

"Sure," said Baiyun.

She wished they would find a more private place so she would not feel so nervous.

Finally, they reached the corner of an abandoned building. They sat side by side against a wall, hidden behind two tall pine trees. From the garbage littered around, they could tell this was a popular place for lovers.

They kissed slowly and passionately for what seemed to Baiyun like hours. It was a lot like her dreams about Dagong, only stronger. She could feel the gentle softness of his lips, but his passion almost took her breath away.

After a while, Dagong slowly unbuttoned Baiyun's shirt. He reached behind her and unsnapped her bra. The sudden freeness of her breasts caused her to inhale quickly, but softly.

He turned her slightly toward him, and cupped her small but now eager breasts in his large, firm hands.

She had never been touched that way before, and she was surprised by the waves of pleasure that surged through her body and caused a wonderful tingling sensation between her legs. She felt her nipples harden under his touch.

Dagong unzipped his pants, and slowly guided Baiyun's hand down to touch him. She felt guilty, but at the same time, being there with Dagong, it felt so right, so comforting.

She gently probed inside his pants, feeling the throbbing and the increasing hardness. She had only seen a penis once, in a medical school specimen jar, and now she held one in her hand.

Baiyun suddenly felt guilty; she thought about how after she got admitted to Beijing University, she went to visit a high school classmate who was going to attend the Beijing Medical University. Her friend showed her around campus and she took her into some classrooms. She told her about the fact that the bodies used for anatomy classes were kept underground in caves. She asked Baiyun if she wanted to see them. She told her classmate no, all she wanted to see was some specimens. As they walked along the hallway where the specimen jars were kept in glass cabinets, she noticed a black, wrinkly tubular thing floating in a medium sized jar.

"What is this?" she asked.

"That's called a penis, the male sexual organ," her classmate said matter-of-factly without a trace of embarrassment.

Baiyun did not dare to ask any more questions after that.

Some of the guilt Baiyun felt came from a discussion she had with her roommates a couple of years earlier.

Wenjing opened her small eyes behind her thick glasses and began the discussion. "I don't understand why people would ever want to kiss each other. It is very unhygienic behavior. Do you know how much bacteria our mouths contain? How many germs and diseases can be transmitted through our saliva?"

Li Yan laughed.

"Yes, but why do people do it?" mumbled Baiyun. Her voice was so quiet that nobody even noticed that she spoke.

"You'd better give it a try yourself and then you will find out why people kiss. Like Chemistry, you have to do experiments to determine whether your theory is correct or not," argued Yumei.

She sounded like she already knew why people kiss, and her sly smile confirmed their suspicion.

"You don't always have to use experiments to decide whether a theory is correct. You can use assumptions and calculations to predict the answer. Besides I don't think I would want to risk my health just for a kiss," said Wenjing.

So much was happening. Baiyun's whole life had changed in the last two weeks since the movement had begun that day in the crowded Square. She had never felt so busy and yet so happy, so involved.

The unhappy loner has turned into an organizer and an activist. She no longer had to worry about her weight problem. The many sleepless days and irregular meals had shrunk her puffy waistline in spite of her recent dining with her mother. She liked it. She had never made so many friends before and on top of all of that, she met Dagong.

Dagong reminded her of Meiling's old boyfriend Weiming, with whom Meiling had a relationship for seven years. For the longest time Baiyun felt that her Uncle Weiming was more like her real father. After Meiling broke up with Weiming, Baiyun had a hard time. It was like losing a close relative. She always wished to find a replacement '"father," but she didn't know how.

She felt that finding a boyfriend of her own would not be a solution, since most of the young men her age were far too immature. Since she realized Dagong could now be the one, the replacement she had been looking for, she did not know how to describe her joy. Of course, she could never have predicted the relationship would progress so far, so fast.

Dagong slowly massaged her nipples while kissing her. Baiyun hesitantly touched his totally erect penis; it was reaching out from his jeans, and she was unsure of exactly what to do with it.

She could tell from his deep sighs when they paused for air between long kisses that she was at least doing something right. They paused and looked intently at each other. His shirt buttons were open and exposed a white tank top tucked tightly under his belt.

Dagong moved his hand to the inside of her thigh, kissing her intently as he slowly moved it up between her outstretched legs. As he reached the seam at the top of her legs, she pulled away.

"So this is your first time?" asked Dagong.

"Yes," murmured Baiyun and nodded hesitantly.

She felt a little embarrassed, like a teenager drinking alcohol behind her parents back.

Dagong had become a different person in front of her. She now looked directly at him, or to say it more precisely, she looked at his totally erect penis, which was much more attractive than the one in the medical school specimen jar.

She had been blindly touching it earlier while they were kissing and caressing, but when Baiyun finally saw it for the first time, Meiling's warning appeared in her mind.

"You could learn something from your mother. Stay away from the boys. They will only make trouble for you. Study. Study hard!"

Her head dropped and she pulled her hands away from Dagong and rested them on the grass.

"I'm making you uncomfortable. I will stop. I would never force you into anything," Dagong, now becoming flaccid, closed the zipper on his pants. "You're still a virgin, aren't you?"

"Yes," answered Baiyun quietly. Her voice was so low that it was almost inaudible.

She could not predict what Dagong was going to do. Would he ridicule her? Would he leave in anger? Baiyun did not want to stop the kissing and touching, but at the same time was afraid to continue.

"I'm surprised, I didn't think that you Beijing University students were that old fashioned. Not many people think of virginity as being a big deal anymore." Dagong looked at Baiyun with curiosity, and maybe little sadness. He did not want to hurt this lovely girl's feelings.

"But for me it is important to be a virgin," she said as she re-buttoned her bra, but left her shirt undone. "Mother told me that if I found out things about boys, I would never be able to be a good student anymore," said Baiyun seriously with a slightly louder voice, as she became more confident.

"Why do you have to believe her?"

"It's because my mother had a lot of experience. I grew up with Mother's many secret love affairs."

"So did she enjoy her little affairs?"

"Sure, but she has wasted all her life with men. It's not worth it."

"Is it not worthwhile to have some fun in life?"

"No. The pain involved makes it not worthwhile. Mother always says that life consists of endless pain and a few moments of joy. It is especially true between men and women."

"Woo. Do you believe that?"

"Yes, because my life has been just like that, too much pain, very little joy."

"Oh, my poor girl," Dagong stroked Baiyun's head as he spoke to her. "Why didn't your mother just marry one of her boyfriends?"

"My father... My father isn't dead..." said Baiyun slowly, word by word. Each word was like a bullet penetrating her heart.

"He is still alive? I thought you said he had died a few years ago."

"No, he is not alive. He is just not dead. He spends his whole day in the green house tending his flowers and the whole evening playing violin. When he is in the apartment, he makes cat like noises as though he were an animal. Except for occasional yelling and cursing, it's hard to tell if he's alive."

"Woo. You mean that your mother, her boyfriend and your father actually live together?" Dagong stared at Baiyun. He felt sad for her, and a bit angry. "You should get out of there."

"I did move out. I live in the dorm, but they're still too close. I need to go to a place far away. Only then can I forget about the whole situation. But how do I do it?"

Dagong did not answer. He did not have an answer for her.

In China, a person is not free to live anywhere they wish. The government determines where the citizens live.

"So my only choice is to study hard and pass the exams to go to America."

"I think you should," said Dagong.

Baiyun's words reminded him of his own desire to go to America. He did not have as clear an objective as Baiyun did. Although Dagong's life was not perfect, he had long gotten used to it after having finally lost any thoughts of going away.

"That's why I don't go out with boys. I believe that any mistake can spoil my chances to go to America," said Baiyun. She sounded like an adult.

"Why are you here and not studying now?" asked Dagong.

"I can't. My mind is filled with other things lately. I can't study anymore. I'm afraid I would never get out of here. I'm stuck here, but I'm here with you." Baiyun leaned toward Dagong.

They hugged each other.

He slowly buttoned Baiyun's shirt for her and straightened her hair. "Let's go to the lake," he said as he helped Baiyun to stand up.

Her legs had fallen asleep.

"Oh. My legs." Baiyun cried aloud as she stretched out her cramped legs. She leaned down and rubbed her thighs and calves before she walked along with Dagong.

The sky turned pink, while the wind swept through the dried dust on the ground around them. The almost full moon had silently risen in the sky. They walked quietly toward the lake, holding hands like lovers.

Dagong was surprised to hear Baiyun's complicated life story and to learn of her tragic and confused family life. He was also glad to know Baiyun. It was first time in his life he found a girl with the depth to truly understand him. He, too, had an unfortunate life story. He felt like maybe he could tell Baiyun everything about himself.

They caught the last glimpse of the sunset after they found a bench by the lake. The sun was half of a cold and sanguine ball falling into the horizon. The wind had stopped and the air became still.

The lake was like a mirror hiding a bottomless hole, which had swallowed everything around it; the island, the bushes on the island, the willow tree by the shore and the sun as it set. The sun and the sky had become a symmetrical object in this endless and bottomless world. For a while, it was hard for Dagong tell the sky from the lake, the top from the bottom and the heavens from the earth.

"It's a beautiful sunset." He whispered excitedly to Baiyun.

"Yes, except for the sun. It looks like a heart soaked in blood." Baiyun was suddenly in a bad mood.

"Don't just dwell on your painful past. You will feel better in a while. Nature has the power to heal."

"Really?"

"Yes. Let me tell you my story." He told her about how twenty years earlier, because of his family background, the Beijing University and all the other universities rejected him in spite of his excellent academic record and his high test-scores in the college entrance exams. "I rode my bicycle here, and I found a bench like this one. I sat and stared into the lake for an entire day. I thought about committing suicide. Then the magic happened. Gradually the lake in front of me turned into an underworld, which was full of life and nature, where birds were singing and people were dancing. I began to communicate with the trees and the earth around me. They all seemed to whisper one sentence to me, 'There is hope! There is hope!'" The last sentence slipped out of Dagong's mouth unconsciously, like a stream running down a mountain.

He stared at the lake as though that magic was happening again, but this time for the two of them.

It was completely dark. The lights and stars had become candles on the calm lake. It looked like a ceremony was going on in the underworld.

They both heard singing; it came from a distance, but to them it seemed to float up from the lake, solemn and graceful;

On a bright and sunny day in May,
We are going on a Hunger Strike.
We are young but we are ready to give up our lives.
We don't want to die so in our youth,
But our country suffers from so many wrongs.

Baiyun cried out, suddenly filled with joy. "I see the students, my friends. Can you hear them singing?"

"Yes," Dagong whispered.

Together they leaned forward and gazed under the surface of the lake.

Baiyun held her arms out to them, ready to join in their song.

CHAPTER 13

It was after eight o'clock by the time Dagong made it home on his bicycle. Everyone was having dinner and the smell of food was pungent.

The first family he saw was Lao Liu's family who were sitting around a little table in the yard eating stir-fried pork with cabbage and rice.

They all nodded to Dagong.

"Wow. You're back. You know Zhang Ping has been looking for you the whole day." Lao Liu put down his chopsticks and turned toward him. "I think you are in for a punishment." He made a face.

"Don't scare him," said his wife, Wu Zheng. "She understands you need to organize the workers and support the students. Look at your head. You are still bleeding. I can see blood seeping through the bandage. Let me find a new one for you."

Wu Zheng ran into her apartment.

"How is the Square?" asked Lili. She wore a polka dot summer dress and looked beautiful.

"It's getting crowded. Students from many colleges and universities have moved here and pitched tents in Tiananmen Square. It is like a county fair over there. Farmers have brought their trick-performing pigs, goats, cats and dogs. I saw an amazing Qigong display the other day."

Dagong sat down so Wu Zheng could replace his bandage.

"It's not a country fair. You guys are crazy!" Lao Liu yelled.

"Calm down, Lao Liu," said Wu Zheng. "It looks like the people will win this time."

"Soldiers are not doing anything. They just stand there to make sure everything goes smoothly. It looks like they've been told not to do anything. People are not afraid. It is really different this time. It is as though someone has sprayed laughing gas all over the Square to intoxicate the people, or they are just intoxicated by the winds of democracy," said Dagong.

Lao Liu noticed Dagong had become much more confidant.

Lao Liu was aggravated; he waved his hands while talking. "Yes. The soldiers are told not to do anything because the political leaders are conflicted. Currently the General Secretary Zhao Ziyang is ahead. He can speak positively about the student unrest in the Asia Development Bank. He can openly support the students. But how long will that last?" Lao Liu lowered his voice, sending a chill through everyone who heard his words. "They'll let the students party for a while and let them have their fun. But when they decide enough is enough, they'll be able to clean up very quickly. The soldiers are there with guns, and the tanks are not far away. You will see." He stood up. "Let me show you something."

He dropped the cat who had been sitting in his lap. The cat hissed, arched his back and jumped on the stone railing of the fishpond.

Lao Liu stuck his head out of the door and yelled, "Dagong, come in and I will show you a video."

Dagong obeyed.

Lili jumped up and asked, "Mom, can I go and find my friends in the Square? I will be back soon. Please. Let me go before Father gets out and locks me up again." Her big and beautiful eyes were so sincere that they almost melt Wu Zheng's heart.

"Okay. I will go with you."

Wu Zheng quickly cleaned the dishes and was ready to go.

"Why? I'm old enough to go alone. I'm seventeen. Or have you forgotten?"

"I know, but if I don't go with you, your father will be shouting at me and asking me to find you. Where do I find you in that vast place? This way, at least I know where you are. Do you want to go or not?" Wu Zhang started walking toward the gate.

"Okay." Realizing this was her only choice, Lili followed.

In the apartment, Lao Liu showed Dagong the surveillance videos he had found.

Dagong watched in disbelief as Lao Liu spoke. "You see. They have videos of everyone there. They have videos of you, of your student friends, of Pumpkin and Broomstick, even videos of Potatofeet." Then he lowered his voice. "The only person I don't see is Mr. Wang."

"I thought he had been going there a lot," said Dagong.

"Yes. I think he works for the government. He has installed many cameras for them so he knows where the cameras are and where not to show up. You see, in the end, these would be used as evidence to arrest whomever they want."

They stepped out, and Dagong followed Lao Liu as he walked down the steps.

Lao Liu stopped suddenly, putting his hand on his chest as though he was having a heart attack. "Where is Lili? Where is Wu Zheng?" He yelled so loud that even the cat was woken up from its nap.

"They went to the Square. Lili was stir-crazy. Wu Zheng decided to follow her." Little Pea walked over with a plate of food in her hands as she told him the news about his wife and daughter.

"Crazy. Everyone is crazy. I guess I have to show my old face there." Lao Liu raced out of the gate.

When Dagong was just about to go into his apartment to see where Zhang Ping and Little Turnip were hiding, he heard the door slam and Zhang Ping rushed out, looking disheveled and insane. A hair clip randomly bunched up her permed hair, it looking like a bird's nest. A half-buttoned white shirt loosely hung over a pair of faded baggy jeans and revealed her shallow cleavage. Makeup was smudged all over her face, along with sweat and the day's soil.

"My dear Dagong. It's so good that you came back." She came down the steps and fell on his shoulder. "I have been waiting for you the whole day and I just fell asleep before you got here."

Dagong helped her walk to the bench and they both sat down.

She leaned toward Dagong and cupped his head in her hands. "Oh. Look at your black eye and the fresh scars. You look like a Pirate!" Then she started to unbutton his shirt.

"Maybe we should go inside," said Dagong.

"No. I want everyone to see what a handsome man you are!" Zhang Ping ripped his shirt off him. She leaped up and stood in the center of the yard. "You are out there participating in the Pro-Democracy movement. You nearly sacrificed your life for it. You forget about your wife and son. I will forgive you for that because it is hard not to be swept into this exciting movement when you have a chance to be a leader." Her speech slurred slightly; spittle flew from her protruding front-teeth. Zhang Ping continued, her voice increasing in volume. "But how can you forget about the past, and the suffering you have gone through in the previous political movements because of your family's background? Do you remember when we first met, when you were working as a janitor in the Beijing Zoo?" She was always throwing it in Dagong's face that he was only a janitor when she found him, but that was usually in the privacy of their small apartment. Now, she was shouting it in the yard where anyone could hear.

Dagong's cheeks began to flush as he listened to the words spewing from her mouth. "When we found you outside of the bathroom you were cleaning, you looked so thin and your face was yellow. We thought you had Hepatitis or something. Dad and I took you to the clinic. It turned out that you were just malnourished. When Dad told you he would get you out of there and assign you a job in his factory, you cried."

Dagong could not stop her from rambling; he listened helplessly as she spoke. "I still remember the teardrops on your handsome, tan face. Come on. We don't need a revolution. We have suffered too much already. We need food and housing! So people like Little Pea and Yu Gang can get married and have their own apartment."

She went to Dagong; he was relieved at first, thinking she was finished and ready to sit down, but instead she started to beat his chest. "Why don't you understand?" Tears streamed down on her red, distorted face.

"Mom!" Little Turnip rushed out of their apartment and fell into Zhang Ping's arms.

She stopped beating Dagong and held Little Turnip. He seemed not to recognize Dagong.

Dagong looked into the yard, feeling touched by his wife. He was not surprised that his son did not recognize him, since he had not been home much lately. Kids forget things very quickly.

What would this revolution bring to Little Turnip? Dagong did not know, but all he knew was that it had gathered up so much momentum that no one could stop it. Maybe they are onto something this time, he said to himself.

Dagong knew that Zhang Ping still lived in the past. She did not understand why he joined this pro-democracy movement. She wanted him to stay home and study for the TOFEL exam so they could go to America.

He did not have a clear vision why he got involved in the movement. All he knew was that he had never felt so free and so happy. He decided he could go to America later, after the movement had ended successfully. He hoped he would have freedom then. Perhaps he would be free to go to America, get a divorce and do whatever else he needed to do. Zhang Ping was fragile, but he believed she would be better in America, and then he could ask her for a divorce and she would let him go.

Broomstick stepped into the yard with Potatofeet. They both carried helmets in their hands.

Pumpkin sauntered over to them and shouted, "You can come home to eat when your bellies grumble. I have food for you. I'm not yelling at you. You two are heroes."

She went into the kitchen and brought out some pork steamed buns, stir-fried cabbage and Tofu soup.

"What is new, my heroes?" asked Pumpkin.

"We zoomed around the Square passing messages. It was fun. Even Potatofeet enjoyed it. Right?" said Broomstick after swallowing two steamed buns quickly.

"It was f-f-f-fun. I got to sit on the back of the muh-muh-muh-motorcycle while B-B-B-Broomstick g-goes around to p-p-pass the muh-muh-messages."

"So you can watch the bike, you dummy." Broomstick was so proud of himself to make use of his brother.

"That's wuh-wuh-what... what I thought, sm-sm-smart b-brother," said Potatofeet.

He finally wobbled to a chair by the Square wooden table and sat down. He took the last two steamed-pork buns, one in each hand and swallowed them down.

"What's the news?" asked Pumpkin after sitting down herself.

"The Government is still unwilling to have dialogue with the student leaders. So they've decided to stage a full scale hunger strike."

In order to demonstrate what a hunger striker was like, he jumped up and knelt on the concrete ground with two hands clasping in front of his nose looking solemn.

"Hunger strike! That's dangerous." She wiped her face with a towel and said, "Well, I was going to make more steamed pork buns for the students, but it looks I don't have to now."

"Ya. But I would still be eating! So please still make some for us messengers." Pumpkin frowned, and Broomstick sat down realizing the Hunger Strike was not something to joke about.

"Pretty soon, no one will be eating. Everyone will want to be a hunger striker," said Pumpkin.

"What? A hunger strike? You are all crazy." Marshmallows came out of the apartment door and joined in.

"Not us. The students." said Pumpkin.

"Yes. They are insane. In the end, they will all be rolled over by the tanks and die." Then he turned to Pumpkin, "What do you think the odds are that'll happen?"

"This is revolution, not gambling." Pumpkin stood up and went inside, leaving the rest of family seated around the table silent.

"How about playing a game of 'Catching Black Seven'?" Marshmallow suggested looking at his sons with a forced grin.

"Sure," answered Broomstick and Potatofeet unenthusiastically.

As Marshmallow dealt the cards, Mr. Wang scurried in. He walked fast and avoided eye contact with everyone. As soon as he walked through the beaded curtains to get into his apartment, he was in trouble.

"Why are you back so late?" Marshmallow heard Mrs. Wang yell angrily at Mr. Wang.

Marshmallow looked at his sons as they listened.

"I have a lot of work to do," Mr. Wang answered her timidly.

"Working? Nobody works now! You're lying!" Mrs. Wang yelled. Her shout was followed by the sound of a loud crash, and the sound of a flat hand beating against bare skin came from the doorway.

Marshmallow and his sons ignored the noise as they played their card game.

CHAPTER 14

Baiyun was awakened at 7 am by the alarm. She sat right up.

Today is a big day for the hunger strikers, she told herself. Even though she would merely be reporting on the hunger strike, her friends Yumei, Longfe and Big Li all had made the commitment.

Yumei and Li Yan leapt out of their beds. The three of them quickly got ready. Wenjing woke up, too, but as usual, she did not get up with others.

"I may join you later. I need to lose some weight," said Wenjing. She hid her head under the blanket.

Yumei put on a white T-shirt and a pair of black pants, the official hunger strike uniform. Baiyun decided to put on blue jeans and a red shirt for good luck, since red meant 'good luck' in Chinese culture. Li Yan wore a white T-shirt and blues jeans in order to be casual.

"Let's bring our radios. If the Government finally agrees to have a dialogue with the student leaders as demanded by the Student Dialogue Committee and the United Student Federation and they broadcast it through the official radio station, we would hear about it," said Yumei. "Let's go to the Last Supper, except this time it is the Last Breakfast for some of us,"

"Are you sure that you can eat enough?" Baiyun was deeply concerned about Yumei volunteering to be a hunger striker. "You usually eat so little and your body is too small to store a lot of food. I will bring some snacks just in case you faint so I can feed you."

"What? You can't do that! This is an official Hunger Strike!" said Yumei.

Yumei was very tense and serious. Baiyun nodded. "Okay. Whatever you say. Just be careful."

"Thank you. Being careful is not our priority now. We have committed, haven't we?" Yumei raised her fist forcefully. "This is our last chance to force the government to have a dialogue with us. Gorbachev is coming in two days. If the students and the government don't reach an agreement before that, we will stay in the Tiananmen Square. The government will have to send the troops in to disperse us."

"Yes," cut in Li Yan, "I see danger written all over this." She straightened her shirt, "But we are committed and we can't back out now."

She marched out. Yumei and Baiyun followed.

Once they were outside, Baiyun realized how big a deal it was. After they mingled with groups of people walking toward Cafeteria number 1, people came to shake Yumei's hands and gave her hugs.

"Yumei, you are a brave soul. We admire you. Take care." Yumei, who was used to having a lot of attention, was wordless at that moment.

Baiyun could see tears lingering in her eyes but she held them back. She looked determined.

Forty hunger strikers sat in the middle of the cafeteria, and many reporters and camera men from CNN, The London Times, The China Daily, Hong Kong News and World Report were snapping pictures of them. The flashbulbs were like lightening flashes in the normally dark cafeteria, which cast an ominous shadow over the event.

Yet, Longfe easily illuminated the shadow as he gave a speech. "We want to tell our parents not to pity us when we are hungry and thirsty. We want to tell our aunts and uncles not to feel sad when we have gone. We only have one wish; that those whom we leave behind will have a better life. And we have only one request; that you remember us as young men and women who pursued life, not death."

The forty hunger strikers boarded a nearby bus after their last meal.

Using reporter's badges, Baiyun and Li Yan were able to enter the crowded bus that was full of reporters, camera crews and hunger strikers.

As the big coach bus moved slowly through the streets towards the Monument of the People's Heroes, a group of students on bicycles from Beida, Qinghua and Beijing Normal University followed it waving flags and shouting slogans.

"Long Live Democracy!"

"Students are Patriots, not Instigators!"

"Long Live the Chinese People!"

When Baiyun got off the bus at the Monument of the People's Heroes, she saw the flag of the 'Beijing Workers' Union' billowing in the air and a group of fifty workers in white shirts and black pants were sitting on the top tier of the Monument steps looking solemn. Along with them were students from a few other universities.

Baiyun stood on her tiptoes trying hard to look for Dagong, and finally she saw him under the flag. She could see his sharp but fierce eyes and his swarthy face under his slightly curly black hair.

An idea hit Baiyun. Dagong was up there sacrificing his life. Why couldn't she? Maybe Dagong could not marry her, or even date her, but they could sit next to each other in this Hunger Strike and fight alongside each other in the Pro-Democracy movement.

At that moment, she was standing under the Monument of People's Heroes, which gave her more courage.

The Monument was located in the south side of the Tiananmen Square and was built in memory of the martyrs who gave up their lives for the revolutionary struggles of the Chinese people during the 19th and 20th centuries.

As depicted by the marble sculptures along the sides of the Monument, over the course of Chinese history, millions of people had lost their lives during the First Opium War, The Jintian Village uprising, The Wuchang Uprising, The

May 4th Movement, The May 30th Movement, The Nanchang Uprising and The War of Resistance Against Japan.

Standing at this majestic monument, she could sense the magic seeping through the marble sculptures and flowing into her heart. She felt bold and free.

She waited for the student hunger strikers to walk up the stairs and sit down before making her announcement. She also waited for Li Yan to finish snapping pictures.

"Li Yan, I would like to join the hunger strikers." Baiyun poked Li Yan. "I can do my report writing up there." She pointed her finger toward where the 'Beijing Workers' Union' hunger strikers were.

"What? You are getting crazier and crazier. If I told people you used to spend the whole day and night in the library studying, nobody would believe me. I will join in later, but now, I would like to take some good photos before going up there and sitting down. I can't just let the foreign journalists take all the good photos," said Li Yan.

"Can you lend me your white shirt?" Baiyun realized that she would be the only person in red among the hunger strikers.

"You can stand by the red flag and no one would notice. Besides, where would we exchange?" Li Yan was always the practical one. "Very soon, all kinds of people will join the Hunger Strike. So you wouldn't have to be in white and black."

"You are right. This monument is magical and will attract all kinds of people to join the Hunger Strike." Baiyun could not wait to join Dagong.

"Make sure that you turn on your radio while you are there. If the dialogue between the Student Dialogue Delegation and the government Propaganda department is successful, we are supposed to clear out of the Square. I know you don't want this to end. You are having too much fun here," said Li Yan before going back to snapping pictures.

"You rascal!" Baiyun hit Li Yan's shoulder with one of her fists. Li Yan did not react, because the attempt was so weak. "Of course, I want it to end."

Baiyun's voice trailed off. She had not considered what would happen in terms of her relationship with Dagong. Could he get a divorce? If not, should she still see him secretly or openly like her mother Meiling? She had not yet talked it over with Dagong.

In her mind, she was telling herself, I would not want to be like Meiling. Yet right now, all she wanted was to run up the steps and give Dagong a big hug and sit with him as long as she could.

"Bye, Li Yan." Baiyun ran up the steps two at a time towards Dagong.

As she was getting closer to the top where Dagong sat, Baiyun slowed down.

She noticed the solemn tone of the atmosphere. She squeezed through a sea of people before she reached Dagong. She sat down and looked at Dagong, who beamed at her briefly and then grabbed her hand.

Baiyun could feel the warmth of his body passing through her. They were together in that crucial moment of the movement. This was a beginning for Baiyun, and with him, she was ready to fight any obstacles. Maybe she even could die with Dagong.

She thought about 'Romeo and Juliet,' the play she read the month before.

"Why are you a hunger striker? I thought your will to live is stronger than the will to die?" asked Dagong without looking at Baiyun.

Deep inside him, he knew why Baiyun was there but he liked to hear it in her own words.

"It is because I want to die with you." Baiyun turned her head toward Dagong, looking at him affectionately. "We can be the Chinese Romeo and Juliet," Baiyun whispered into his ears.

Dagong nodded and wrapped his arm around her tightly.

"The Government cheated us again. Instead of broadcasting the Dialogue between the Student Dialogue Delegation and the Head of Propaganda department on CCTV (Central China TV), they broadcast the Asian Soccer game," said Longfe through a load speaker. "This Hunger Strike must go on!"

He threw his fisted hand into the air. Everyone followed.

After five hours, a few people fainted due to the early summer heat.

"I worry about Yumei," said Baiyun breaking a long silence between her and Dagong. In order to conserve energy, they had their mouths sealed most of time.

"I agree," said Dagong. "I think in order to preserve our manpower; we should have a second shift come here tomorrow - if we are still here tomorrow."

"What do you think is going to happen?"

"If the students and the government don't reach an agreement tonight at midnight, the government might send the troops in to clear us out. They will need at least one day to clean up the blood before Gorbachev comes. On the other hand, it might be embarrassing for the government if they do a massive killing just before Gorbachev's arrival. The situation is very dicey now and the domino could fall either way."

"No matter what happens, I will be with you," said Baiyun. Her head fell on Dagong's shoulder as she spoke.

She was growing tired as the day progressed. The flag provided a nice shield for her, so no one could see they were in such an intimate position.

"Sure, I will try to carry you if you can't walk anymore. You can become a part of me."

"Won't your wife be jealous?"

"I don't know. You are a sick student hunger striker. I have to help. What can she do?" Dagong sighed. "She wants me to take her to places she has no ability to reach by herself like the United States. Now I have lost interests in going. I don't know if she still loves me. Look, 'The Flying Tiger Brigade' is here to rescue fainted hunger strikers." Dagong touched Baiyun's head lightly.

"Oh, no! My mother." Baiyun ducked her head, trying to hide behind Dagong.

At that moment, more people joined the Hunger Strike as medical personnel and motorcycles carried the sick people away. It was no longer quiet. People turned on their radios and even battery-powered portable TVs to find out whether the dialogue had been broadcasted live.

It was obviously not the case. Only the voice of a soccer game announcer could be heard all around.

Dusk had fallen upon them with a beautiful sky that consisted of red, black and blue.

"Silly, I don't think your mother would find you in this chaos and darkness," said Dagong. "Look at the moon. It is almost full." Dagong pointed to the sky.

"I hoped it would be full, just in time to commensurate the people who would die after midnight tonight."

"We don't know what is going to happen yet." Dagong tried to comfort Baiyun, yet his voice was not too convincing.

"I never expected life to be perfect. I could be happy with a moon that's almost full." She turned to Dagong looking a little sad. "If I could spend tonight with you, I would be very happy. If I could spend tomorrow night with you, I would be happier, but I'm not asking that much."

At that moment, a few policemen approached them, and like a gust of wind gave Baiyun a chill down to the bone.

"Who is Dagong Liang? Can you step out? We have some questions for you," asked the tall, thin policeman.

"I'm Dagong Liang." Dagong stood up.

The policeman turned to a bald man with a solid built who had accompanied them.

Although Baiyun did not know the man, Dagong recognized him immediately.

The policeman asked, "Mr. Wang, is he the right person?"

"Yes." Mr. Wang nodded, avoiding eye contact with Dagong.

"I am arresting you for instigating illegal activities in Tiananmen Square," said the Policeman.

"Okay." Dagong stood up and held his wrists out to allow the policeman to put handcuff on his wrists.

"Dagong!" Baiyun stood up and yelled.

The policeman pushed her, and she fell back down onto the steps.

Baiyun could hear loud noises down below and Yumei asking for help for Longfe.

Then she saw Longfe and a few other student leaders being escorted away by the police.

She went down the steps and saw Yumei in tears. Baiyun and Yumei held each other as they watched them disappear from sight.

CHAPTER 15

Six days later when Zhang Ping came home from work around 6 pm, she found the students had invaded her home.

About fifty students were bundled in thick blankets and lying all over the yard. Some of them were sleeping, while some were unconscious. Their eyes behind their white-rimmed glasses were closed.

Six days into the Hunger Strike, their faces were dark and sunken. Their hair was gummy.

Little Pea was trying to feed them with hot porridge. Her boyfriend was cooking more in the kitchen.

A woman doctor dressed in a white coat was walking around with a stethoscope over her shoulders. She was checking on the sickest of the students. An occasional cry or scream could be heard.

Zhang Ping looked around and saw that hundreds of towels, shirts, pants, pairs of underwear, tank tops and even women's period strips were hanging on ropes between the trees.

The various items obscured the sky from the yard and dripped water as though it was raining.

Since the yard was so crowded, Zhang Ping had to maneuver around the bodies to serve the hot porridge.

Then she noticed that the corn, the sunflower plants and the vegetables she had planted during the spring were all trod upon. So were the neighbors' plants. The student movement had turned everybody's life into chaos.

Maybe for some people it was a joyful chaos, because chaos could bring changes to one's life, but for Zhang Ping, that was not the case.

Her husband Dagong had not been home very much. She knew where he was. She had gone to the Square and tried to persuade him to come back. He told her that he was busy, and he had become the Hunger Strike leader for the workers.

She threw herself onto the ground and begged him not to do such a dangerous thing. She told him that she did not want him to die.

He told her not to worry. Out of desperation, she and Little Turnip went back to her parent's home to hide out for a day.

Today she came back herself to check what was going on, and of course, there was a lot of chaos.

Zhang Ping opened the squeaky wooden kitchen door. The door was so old and shaky that it could break away at any minute. It was obvious that the door needed new hinges, but the wood was so rotten that it could no longer hold its hinges.

Zhang Ping remembered when she and Dagong built that kitchen ten years ago, when they were first married. They built it by laying bricks and tiles one by one. Dagong nailed together a few strips of wood onto the outside of this door for reinforcement.

Now, everything had fallen apart. Even the glass window was broken two years before and was now covered with several layers of newspaper. The wind blew through the paper and made the room very cold in the winter.

Zhang Ping lit a match trying to start the gas stove. Nothing happened.

"Shit." She realized that the stove had run out of the gas. It was impossible for her to hook the gas can onto the back of her bike and ride to the gas station to exchange it; she was not strong enough. Dagong usually did that.

Not knowing what to do, she sat on the steps in front of her door. Looking at those students made her think of Little Turnip, and she worried about where he might be. Her head was in a big mess. She was trying to remember where she was when she last saw Little Turnip.

At that moment, Mr. Wang stepped out of his home, yawning after a nap. "The weather will soon change. The weather will change." He said mysteriously, somewhat like a prophet.

Zhang Ping looked into the sky. It was clear blue without even a trace of cloud.

"The thunder is coming!" Mr. Wang exclaimed.

Zhang Ping did not answer. She knew Mr. Wang could be crazy sometimes.

"Hurry! Hurry!" Pumpkin and Marshmallow each carried a hunger striker into the yard.

Zhang Ping soon found out that they were Lao Li's daughter, Lili and her student boyfriend. She did not know that Lili had joined the Hunger Strike. She was shocked.

Little Pea helped to put these two people down, feeding them hot water and wrapping them with warm blankets.

Marshmallow dragged Lili's father, Lao Liu out of the bed, where he had been lying for more than two days. He figured that as a policeman, the best support he could give students was to call in sick.

"My daughter!" Lao Liu rushed toward Lili with only a T-shirt and underwear on. He held Lili in his arms.

"Lili. Lili. This is your father." Tears rolled out of his small eyes onto his unshaven face.

There was no response from Lili except for occasional moaning.

"We should take her to the hospital. They will take in some of the very sick students," announced the doctor.

Looking at the chaos and listening to the non-stop sirens, Zhang Ping's mind drifted away.

It was 20 years ago when Zhang Ping was a high school junior. The situation was worse then. The continuous gunfire was hurting her eardrums, much like the New Year fireworks.

She was manning a machine gun in a dormitory window in Beijing University after joining her father's 'United Workers' Union'. They tried to occupy the chaotic campus.

When they arrived at the University gate, their good intentions to forge a peaceful solution soon disappeared. Two student groups were fighting fiercely to gain control of the university since they were responding to Chairman Mao's slogan to send all of the 'corrupted' top university officials and intellectuals to a detention center.

'The United Workers' Union' was forced into self-defense.

She remembered that students came toward them one by one to prevent them from going in. The students were shooting and they were shooting back. The students were falling down one after another. She could still remember their radiant and sweaty yet naïve faces.

After the shooting was finished, the main street in the university campus was full of bodies. For days, the street was soaked with blood. It was the first time that she had seen so many dead bodies.

After that day, Zhang Ping changed. She felt ill and stayed in bed for two weeks without eating anything. She started having nightmares. Everyone she had shot down had come back to life again in her dreams. They cursed her, spilled their blood on her and promised to torture her after she descended into their world.

Zhang Ping had lost all her revolutionary enthusiasm. She became so empathetic that she had to resign as the captain of the Red Guard in her high school.

After that, she did not go to school very much. She did not have to anyway. The school stopped operating because of the Cultural Revolution. She stayed home and learned knitting and sewing. She got her high school certificate soon after she returned to school and found a job at the Beijing Automobile Parts Factory where her father was the president.

She worked in the assembly lines, personnel department and the food service. Finally, she was appointed the head of the food service.

After three years, Zhang Ping met Dagong. Her father Lao Zhang discovered Dagong in a park where he worked as a janitor. When Lao Zhang took Dagong to a restaurant, he got deadly drunk and told him his life story; it was the sort of story that people usually avoided telling.

In the bar, Dagong passionately expressed his dream of going to college. Lao Zhang liked his honesty and fought to get him a job in the Beijing Automobile Parts Factory.

In 1975, he went to the Beijing Normal University when the universities only accepted students on the basis of their political background instead of their academic achievements, but Dagong appreciated the opportunity and made the most of it.

After he returned to the factory, he became a technician. The same year, Zhang Ping married Dagong, following her father's wishes.

Zhang Ping really fell in love with Dagong when she first met him. He was the most gentle and beautiful human being she had ever met. She liked his six-foot frame, his confident and charismatic manner. She admired his intellect.

Their fifteen-year marriage was peaceful, until just recently, but Zhang Ping had never known what Dagong thought of their marriage. He seemed to sit high above her and she could never quite reach him.

The ambulance finally arrived. About ten students were herded into the van one after another. Looking at their fragile features and listening to their moaning, Zhang Ping felt like crying.

In order to conceal her sudden burst of emotion, she ran into her room. Tears poured out of her eyes after she collapsed on the bed. It was the first time she wept that hard since she had drained out all of her tears during the Cultural Revolution.

The doorknob turned and Zhang Ping could not believe that the person who just stepped in was Dagong. His long hair and his face unshaven; his beard had not diminished his features. His skin was tan and rough. He looked dirty. His white polyester shirt had turned gray and smelled sour. His blue jeans were shiny with grease. His shoelaces were missing.

With her face still buried in her arms, she pretended not to see him.

Then she heard him open the dresser drawer, ransacking through the clothes. She could not stay silent anymore.

"Why... Why are you coming back?" She mumbled through her hoarse voice.

"Looking for some warm clothes," he said and kept looking.

"So you think this is a hotel where you can come and go anytime you want." She sat up and held herself against the back of the bed.

"Zhang Ping, they need me there!" He finally turned his head around and stared at her directly. "Students are dying there. They are going without food or water in order to do something for our country. Police arrested a few student leaders including a dear friend of mine. The police detained me for a week but released me because they didn't know what to do with me. Don't you feel guilty for just sitting and complaining?"

Oh, she loved that face of his. She wanted to hug him, to bury her face in his chest. His swarthy face and messy clothes made him look like a street-smart outlaw, but his mind was elsewhere. She could not warm up to him until he became her nice and easy-going husband again.

"I have used up all my revolution energy in the past." She sighed and continued, "All I know is that a person needs to eat and have clothes on their body. Do you still remember the Cultural Revolution and all the suffering you have gone through? Without my father's help, you would be still sweeping the park and cleaning public bathrooms."

"Yes, of course. I remember. That's why we need to make changes." Dagong's voice sounded much more confident after serving as the president of the Beijing Workers' Union.

"But you know the change is not up to us." Zhang Ping was on the verge of crying again.

"I understand what you are talking about. In fact, maybe you are right, but I hope you are wrong. If we all think we are powerless, we are never going to have a good life. It doesn't matter whether you are right or not. It is too late to pull me out of there. Go to the Square and you will understand. The students have moved me. They are brave, bright and fearless. Our generation has been too cynical, like the rocks on the beach, which have been washed thousands of times and have lost all their edges. It's not a sign of maturity but a sign of death. We should be ashamed of it."

Dagong was so excited that the blood vessels on his neck were bulging. He did not realize he was giving a lecture.

"Okay, it's not my business to tell you what to do, but you have to care about our Little Turnip." Zhang Ping's voice turned hoarse and choked with tears. She was now sitting on the edge of the bed with her legs dangling like a child. Her face was red and her hair was messy.

"What. What about our son?" Dagong shifted his attention from the dresser to Zhang Ping. His two big eyes with black circles under them, stared at her.

"He is lost in the Square." She fell onto the bed again.

"Where is Little Turnip? Where is Little Turnip?" Dagong grabbed Zhang Ping from the bed and shook her so violently by the shoulders that Zhang Ping hit her head on his chest.

Tears mixed with the dirt from Dagong's shirt soiled her face.

"It's my fault. It's all my fault. I should not have let him go."

Her face touched his chest, her husband Dagong's chest. All of a sudden the numbness she had experienced since the movement had started, since Dagong stopped coming home, disappeared. She felt the hurt. Her heart felt hurt.

It was that morning when she and Little Turnip were wandering through the Square, desperately looking for Dagong, squeezing through the crowds of people that were packed in there.

The chaos in the Square that morning was all too familiar to her. She suddenly felt like a sleepwalker walking in her dreams. The people in the Square suddenly became thousands of dead bodies lying on the ground. She saw herself wearing the green uniform and a red armband with yellow letters saying 'Red Guards' on it.

She carried a gun under her arms. She was forced to fight. She stepped forward reluctantly and then she ran all the way home. It was not until she got home that she realized that she left Little Turnip at the Square.

Dagong stared at the table and at Little Turnip's smiling face in the picture frame. He felt like someone had chopped a piece of his heart away. Although Little Turnip was much closer to his mother, Dagong always considered Little Turnip as a precious gift from God. As a son, Little Turnip would be able to carry on Liang's family tree.

Dagong carried Zhang Ping on his back and walked out of the room, into the yard and onto the street.

"D-D-Dagong. Ge, wuh-wuh-want a p-p-p-popsicle?" Potatofeet was sitting behind a white wooden Popsicle cart with his crippled legs invisible. He had a big grin on his face as he always did, with drool dripping from the edge of his mouth. In his hand, there was a piece of baked sweet potato.

Dagong bought a red-bean paste Popsicle. Then he patted Potatofeet's head and said, "You are doing a great job helping the revolution!"

Potatofeet answered with the same old smile but today with a newly added joy. That was because he was doing something useful.

Tiananmen Square, after many days of occupation by the students, looked like a refugee camp.

No buses were running on their normal routes. No regular policemen were posted at the intersections directing traffic. People went around on their bicycles and scooters. Armed police and soldiers could be seen everywhere. The smell of rotten food, human feces and sweat lingered in the air.

People had to climb trees in order to see what was happening. Moving around was difficult. People were tightly packed in there; they would not allow themselves to be pushed past passively.

Only the ambulances, with their deafening sirens, could maneuver freely through the sea of people.

There were hundreds of banners on the Square. They were not only banners from different universities around the country, but also from factory workers, schoolteachers, high schools students, peasants, journalists, hospitals and surprisingly even state employees.

Dagong and Zhang Ping were washed into the sea of the people before they realized it. Then it was too late to get out. Just being in the Square made them feel better. They felt closer to Little Turnip.

From the distance, Dagong could spot Beijing University's flag. He imagined Baiyun sitting there, shivering with the rest of the hunger strikers beneath the wind, with her porcelain white face turning into a dark oval sunflower seed.

Through the loudspeakers, they heard that the student leaders were waiting in the People's Congress Meeting Hall to talk to the government. It said that the meeting would be broadcast live when it started. The meeting was the result of the students' Hunger Strike and the impending visit from the Russian president Gorbachev.

The Square suddenly became quieter. Two hundred thousand people were waiting anxiously for this last thread of hope.

"Why don't you move forward and talk to the man with the microphone about our Little Turnip?" Zhang Ping suggested.

Dagong tried to push through the crowd, but failed.

"Why don't you shout? He might hear you."

Dagong's lips trembled. He shook his head. Tears were lingering around his eyes. Although the loss of Little Turnip was still stirring in his heart, he was like everyone else on the

Square, waiting quietly for the news that would end this chaos.

"The Government broke their promise. They didn't want to broadcast the meeting," someone was yelling in the crowd.

Dagong's heart sunk, but he secretly wished that it might only be a rumor. It would soon be proven that the fellow protester was right and that the government had broken its promise.

"Comrades, how are you?" Premier Zhao Ziyang's voice came through the loud speaker, "Although our country has arrived at a crucial intersection, please stay calm and restrained. I would like to persuade the hunger strikers to go home. You are our country's future, you should stay alive and healthy. I promise you, there will not be retribution for the citizens and students who participated in the movement." His oratory was getting lower and weaker. It sounded like he was frustrated and hopeless.

"No mention of the dialogue between the government and the students. This must be a hoax," shouted someone in the crowd.

Dagong could sense an obvious hopelessness in the speech too. He turned to Zhang Ping and said, "Zhang Ping, why don't you keep looking for Little Turnip? I'll have to go to work."

Dagong suddenly remembered that as the head of the Beijing United Worker's Union, he had responsibilities.

Zhang Ping stared at him. She stared at his face so intently, and with such hatred, that she felt her eyeballs would fall out.

After Dagong squeezed through the crowd and disappeared, she still stood there frozen.

In her mind Zhang Ping drifted back to 1966; she was in the midst of the Cultural Revolution.

Tiananmen Square was filled with people wearing green army uniforms, with a red star on their hats and a red armband on their left arms. Everyone was waving a little red book.

"Long live Chairman Mao! Long live Chairman Mao!" They were chanting as if they were in trance.

She had tears in her eyes, she remembered. Like everyone else, she was standing so far from the Forbidden City and she could only imagine Chairman Mao's large figure on the balcony, waving at them. It was so strange that she cried.

Maybe it was because everyone else in the crowd cried. A sense of unity and camaraderie moved her. Besides, what was the best way to show her loyalty to Chairman Mao and to the Communist Party? That same day, she also shook hands with a comrade who had shaken hands with Chairman Mao. They all tried to smell his hands in order to catch the scent of Chairman Mao's skin. They clenched his hands hard in order to feel the warmth he obtained from Chairman Mao.

Of course, that was the past, which was considered foolish nowadays. No one could get her to do that anymore. Deep inside her, she knew that she was still sincere. She could turn her heart inside out to prove that.

Their innocence was just being used by a few power seekers in the government, but it hurt whenever she thought of it. It was like being cheated once and never believing in anything ever again.

Suddenly the crowd behind her moved. A young worker wearing a red badge came over to push the crowd away.

"Please back off. There are more organized demonstrators coming."

Zhang Ping flowed with the crowd. Then she saw Little Turnip in the distance. She saw him standing on the balcony of the Forbidden City, waving at her.

"Come here, Mommy. Come here!"

"Little Turnip!" she ran toward the Forbidden City while squeezing herself through the crowd.

Her loud voice did help her to open a path to her goal. Nobody wanted to stop a crazy woman shouting to nobody.

She wailed and shouted at the empty balcony, as if some ghost was standing there waving back at her.

CHAPTER 16

The student dialogue with the government's Propaganda department in the United Front Office failed since the official media decided not to broadcast it. They also refused to honor student's demands.

"What's next?" Baiyun asked herself as she walked out of the building with the rest of News Center students. She left the hunger strikers to file a report at the News Center. People who had been waiting outside for three hours immediately surrounded them.

"Did the government agree with our demands?"

"Why didn't they broadcast the meeting live?"

Baiyun was exhausted due to lack of sleep and food. Without eating anything for nearly seven days, the Hunger Strike had taken a toll on her.

She also did not know what to say. She did not want to be the one to announce that the dialogue had failed, and if the students failed to leave the Square before Russian president Gorbachev's visit the next day, the government's troops would move in and clean up the Square.

Personally, she did not want to see it happen, but it was too late now. To move students out of the Square at that point would be like trying to empty the ocean. She was no longer afraid. She was proud to be a part of this historical event, able to witness and report on such an exciting movement.

If she had to die, she only had one wish. She wanted to be with Dagong, Yumei, Longfe, Big Li and Li Yan. Where were Dagong and Longfe? Last time she saw them was when the police put handcuffs on them and dragged them away. The scene had been sitting on her stomach like a rock. She wanted to be with them. Maybe she should try to get herself arrested. It was worthwhile to die alongside so many important and dedicated people.

She and Li Yan exchanged glances as they walked back to the Square.

They returned to the Monument after walking around many piles of garbage, students who were sleeping and tents, which had occupied every inch of the Square.

They passed a group of student leaders who were arguing about whether they should withdraw from the Square or not. "We have already gained a great deal of momentum in the movement. We should press forward to achieve our goal of asking the government to agree with our demands," said Big Li who was vehemently against the idea of withdrawing. Stubble had grown on his previously shaved head and his round face had shrunk a little.

"Gorbachev is coming. We have to keep our oath not to disturb the normal functions of the public and the government. So we have to leave the Square soon," said Yumei, who was leaning against Longfe's chest.

"What? Longfe is back?" Baiyun jumped.

Then Li Yan poked her and pointed to the left, where to her surprise she saw Dagong. He wore a clean shirt and jeans. He was growing a mustache and beard.

Dagong stepped forward and threw his fist into the sky. "I represent all the workers here in support of keeping the movement alive!"

"Dagong!" Baiyun ran toward him and gave him a big hug right in front of everyone.

She was no longer shy.

Dagong went further. He held her head in his hands and started kissing her passionately. Their lips touched and were melted by their love toward each other.

Then they sat down on the step holding each other tightly.

"Dagong, I thought you were arrested. Did you escape? Should I hide you?" Baiyun looked at Dagong puzzled.

"That would be nice if we could hide somewhere for a while," smiled Dagong. "I guess I don't have such luck. They

let us go because the top hasn't decided what to do with us."
He turned and started kissing Baiyun again.

Baiyun did not stand up to argue. She was very satisfied to
be with Dagong. She somehow agreed with Yumei's logical
argument, although she wished the movement would go on.

She could not imagine how she could go back to her
normal school life if the movement suddenly ended. It was as
if she had opened a mystery book and could not wait to read
all the way to the end.

The argument ended with no conclusion and the leaders sat
down from physical weakness.

Feeling exhausted, Baiyun, started to doze off.

Dagong's voice came from a seemingly remote planet.
"My little angel, can you stay awake?"

"No. My eyelids have been fighting with each other for a
while until they both went dead."

"Oh, no. I hope they're not dead. You can sleep on my
lap," said Dagong while letting Baiyun fall into his lap.

He stroked her shining, but messy black hair slowly.

"Do you feel warmer now?" Dagong was holding Baiyun,
who was nearly asleep.

After an hour, she sat up but soon fell into Dagong's chest.

"What a beautiful night! It is so strange that it is night
while we are waiting to die. Who knows? Maybe we are in
heaven already." She smiled and felt safe in the embrace of
Dagong.

"How do you know it is a nice night with your eyes
closed?" asked Dagong.

"I can smell the steamed buns in the air. I can hear the
breeze blowing by my ears. I can also feel the stars in the
clear sky staring at me."

"Big Li. Big Li." A woman's sharp scream broke the
momentary silence.

Baiyun and Dagong bolted toward the scream.

After seven days into the hunger strike, the usually-strong
Big Li finally collapsed.

Longfe was holding his body and trying to feed him water, but his mouth clenched tightly, his body shivering.

Yumei and others piled blankets on top of his body.

"Maybe we should send him to the hospital," suggested Longfe.

Xia Nan came over and added, "See, people are dying here. Why don't we withdraw? We have already done enough."

Since the movement began, he had disappeared for a while. His sudden appearance did not surprise anyone who knew him, and did not make him any more persuasive than before. No matter how much sense he made, people just disagreed with him. They booed him instead.

A worker walked by who did not know what was going on and joined the conversation.

"Are you a student leader? Shame on you!" He spit on the ground. "You shouldn't tell people to surrender. You should lead us to fight until the end. Some leader!"

While this was happening, Li Yan did find a motorcycle to take Big Li away.

Although even with a high fever, he seemed to know one very important fact - he wanted to stay.

He held onto the tent as they carried him away. The tent tore away and then he tried to hold onto the cement ground. Blood oozed out of his dark and grease covered fingers.

"Don't take me away. Let tanks roll over my body. There are two hundred thousand people here. Our blood will drown the troops. Our iron bones will ruin their vehicles." After these words, which sounded like they could be his last words, Big Li collapsed again.

Baiyun came over and held onto his hands tightly.

"Let him stay. We are going to die together, aren't we?"

Suddenly there was silence. The word 'death' finally registered in everyone's mind. It seemed that they needed a moment to comprehend.

The loud music was still playing in the distance. Crickets began chirping.

"Look at the stars in the sky." Dagong had more experience dealing with a crisis.

"Yes. See The Hunter? Orion is right over my head." Baiyun replied.

"It's so clear tonight that I can see his sword," said Li Yan.

"Really? Where is it?" Longfe soon realized there really was a constellation named 'The Hunter,' which was over his head in the sky.

Yumei showed him once, but he could not see it. He did not know about the constellations because he grew up in the city, which sometimes drowned out the light of the stars.

"Oh. I see. There are arms, head, legs and his belt. I get it." Longfe was pleased with himself. At this moment, a small victory meant a great deal.

"I have heard we all become stars after we die," said Yumei. "Maybe we should form a constellation." Her voice was low but clear.

"Yes. Let's form a sword that can penetrate the sky. So whenever the Government leaders look into the sky, they will shiver from our mighty strength," said a young, baby-faced student.

"Let's turn into thunder and shake this regime into extinction!" Longfe's sudden poetic skill had surprised everyone.

"Let's turn into lightening and electrocute those conservative leaders." Even Li Yan spilled out poetic lines.

"Dagong, I hope we still know each other after we die," said Baiyun, resting comfortably in Dagong's chest.

"We will become spirits and will not know the difference," said Dagong.

"That's too bad. We haven't done anything together yet," said Baiyun, regretting that she stopped Dagong the last time.

"It is too late, girl. You haven't enjoyed the greatest joy in the world and now you are going to die, my poor Baiyun."

Dagong tickled Baiyun's small nose with his pinky, teasing her. He understood what Baiyun meant. In fact, at this moment, he wished to press his lips against Baiyun's, and kiss and hug her passionately. Then he would bring them into the highest peak of joy. He knew this was not the time for it.

When? He asked himself sadly.

Dagong had lived through most of his live as a dog by tolerating every kind of insult and suffering. The only driving force in his life was to hope that someday a miracle would happen and his fate would turn around. Here, when the happiness finally arrived, he was about to die. This was a fact that was hard for him to swallow.

"What are you thinking?" asked Baiyun. She was too tired to open her eyes.

"I'm thinking about what our life is going to be like after we both go to heaven."

"Let me tell you. We are going to have a house among the evergreen trees. We will manage a farm and have half a dozen kids."

The corners of Baiyun's mouth lifted slightly. Her two big eyes opened and stared at Dagong like mirrors.

"Yes, Baiyun." Dagong kissed her.

They were roused from their waking dream by the sound of a motorcycle. It came to a stop near them. Both the driver and a rider on the back seat were well equipped with helmets, shining leather jackets and thick quilted pants as if they were impenetrable.

"This is the message from the headquarters of the United Student Union."

After putting on a pair of glasses, the middle aged woman in the motorcycle passenger seat started reading, "We have no intention to withdraw tonight. Our negotiation with the government has failed. We want to force them to the negotiating table again by staying here. With Gorbachev's visit tomorrow, our movement is going to attract international attention. Up to now, there are no sign of

Government troops coming into the Square. Rest well and be prepared for tomorrow."

From the voice, strong and masculine for a woman, Baiyun realized that the lady who just read the message was her mother, Meiling.

She was stunned. Meiling was among the brave students and ready to sacrifice her life. She was no longer ashamed of seeing Meiling sitting on a motorcycle with a younger man.

She ran toward her mother. "Mother."

"Baiyun, I'm so glad that I found you here. I have been looking for you," she held Baiyun's small face, "Let Mother look at you."

"Mother. I'm Okay."

No wanting to be treated like a child, she pushed Meiling's hands away.

"Okay. Stay here and be strong. Mother is proud of you." Meiling reached over and hugged her. Then she took out a bag of hard-boiled eggs and handed them over to her.

"I'm a hunger striker, mother," said Baiyun while trying to push away the eggs.

"You can save it for later."

Lao Zheng took off his helmet and shook hands with Baiyun. He winked at her and Baiyun looked away immediately. She did not like the way Lao Zheng looked at her.

"Mother. I'm proud of you too."

Then she ran away because she could feel tears swelling in her eyes.

"This is your mom? Woo!" After Baiyun's mother had left, Longfe and others cheered for Baiyun.

"So what? Where is your mother," shouted Baiyun proudly.

"Our mothers are at home and praying for us. Your mother is the brave one. Hooray!" More cheers came from the crowd.

Baiyun felt proud. Meiling was no longer a mother she was ashamed of - a dirty woman, and a whore like neighbors called her behind her back. Now she had a brave and patriotic woman as a mother. What more could she ask for?

She was also surprised that Meiling hugged her. She had been waiting for this hug. During the last ten years, Baiyun and Meiling were not very close. She disagreed and disliked Meiling's life style. Meiling's endless love affairs had caused embarrassment for Baiyun and her crazy old father. For years, she and Meiling's relationship was business-like. They were business partners who ran their household. Or rather Meiling was like a sick sister, who had screwed up her life and could not get back on track; a psychiatric patient who needed Baiyun to consistently confess her problems to. Now she had Meiling back.

"Baiyun, you are crying. What happened to you?" asked Dagong.

Baiyun did not answer. She started dozing off again. She felt peaceful here at the Square in the middle of the chaos, especially with Dagong. After several hours, Baiyun opened her eyes. Dagong was still cradling her head, but his eyes were closed.

She saw the sunrise. The sun emitted rays of lights into the eastern sky like streaks of red dye. She suddenly felt as if she was sitting on top of a mountain. The Forbidden City and the Monument to the People's Heroes had turned into golden palaces in the distance. Thousands of sleeping people in the Square became like rocks. The wind blew her matted hair and it felt fresh.

"Dagong. Dagong. Where are we? Are we still alive?" Baiyun tried to wake Dagong up.

"What?" Dagong opened his sleepy eyes, "What are you asking?"

"Do you know where we are? Are we still alive?"

"We're in Tiananmen Square. We are still alive!" Dagong exclaimed.

"Oh. We are not in paradise? I'm so disappointed," pretended Baiyun.

Then they both jumped up and hugged each other. Then Longfe and Yumei came over.

"We are still alive! We are still alive!" Students, one after another rose up from under their thick blankets, and cheered. They were so happy that the government troops did not come in to clear up the Square and cause bloodshed.

The new day started with such enthusiasm. It was like a big victory, a huge triumph for simply being alive.

Soon an order came from the United Student Federation leaders that everyone, and especially the hunger strikers, should move to the east side of the Square.

In order to show the government that they were negotiating in good faith and did not mean to disrupt the first Sino-Soviet summit in thirty years, the student federation was still trying to clear the Square, or at least a part of it.

Of course, it was too late. It was just too chaotic in the Square. People asked all sort of questions. "Which side is the eastside? "Why do we have to move?"

When someone began to move, others soon filled up the vacancy. Somehow, they moved the hunger strikers to join the students from other colleges.

After eating and drinking something, Big Li recovered and was strong enough to join the Hunger Strike again.

The radio station moved, too.

Baiyun decided to follow the hunger strikers because they were the biggest news. She switched to being a reporter again from a hunger striker - just temporarily.

Yumei and Longfe were still holding the fort as hunger strikers despite Yumei's poor health.

The number of hunger strikers had drastically increased since the night before. The number jumped from three hundred to near one thousand just among Beijing University students alone.

Yumei hugged Baiyun and said, "Well, I guess our big journalist needs to stay strong and well fed."

"Yumei, I admire you. Be careful," said Baiyun, finding tears around her eyes, "Dagong went home to get some blankets. Maybe I will return to the Beida Hunger Strike group tonight."

Then Baiyun pulled Yumei to the side and whispered into her ears, "Dagong is married, his seven-year old son was lost in the Square and his wife has gone crazy."

Baiyun looked straight into Yumei's eyes, waiting for her reaction.

"My God, your life is soooo complicated. I guess misery always looks for company," said Yumei sympathetically. "You are a big girl and you can deal with it." Yumei bumped her shoulder to Baiyun's.

"But how should I deal with it?" yelled Baiyun. She could not believe Yumei's reaction. This was her happiness they were talking about.

In the last few days, she had been so happy thinking her prince had finally arrived. Yet the happiness was so short-lived and it was going to slip away soon. Maybe Meiling was right. It was not worth the effort to suffer through the pain.

"All my life I just wanted peace and you see what I end up getting?" Baiyun started sobbing.

"It is because you are crazy and weird," Yumei's voice was getting louder.

"I agree with you one hundred percent!" sobbed Baiyun.

"Baiyun, don't worry. You should enjoy it while you can. Who knows how long we are going to be alive," said Yumei while looking deeply into Baiyun's eyes.

She gave Baiyun one more hug and walked away to join the other hunger strikers.

The first thing Baiyun decided to do after she went back to the News Center was to do a 'Missing Child' announcement for Little Turnip.

She understood how important Little Turnip was to Dagong.

After that, Baiyun would concentrate on the work at the news center dealing with the current crisis. Since so many people joined the Hunger Strike, she felt that the News Center needed her even more to cover such an important historical event.

For a while, she enjoyed being an individual again. Besides, she liked being a journalist.

Dagong started serving as the sole radio repairman at the News Center, as well as being the head of the 'Beijing Workers' Union' and the leader of hunger strikers among the workers. He also had to deal with his own family crisis.

By the time the News Center was set up, it was already 11:00 am.

There was still no sign of Gorbachev.

Baiyun quickly made an announcement about Little Turnip.

Then the news came in through the radio broadcast. The welcoming ceremony had taken place at the airport instead of Tiananmen Square.

Then she heard reports that Dagong organized the Workers' Union to bring water quickly to a group of students who poured gasoline over their bodies and were ready to set themselves on fire. They were protesting Government's refusal to conduct a direct dialogue with the students.

"Where are Dagong and his water fast group?" Baiyun asked Broomstick, a messenger on the motorcycle.

"They are in front of the Zhongnanhai compound, right in the center of the power."

Baiyun nodded. Zhongnanhai was the top Chinese official's residence. Protesting in front of it meant visibility and danger, which, of course, was no longer an issue. Most people here on the Square were either thinking about death or ready to die.

Broomstick, moving closer, asked Baiyun "Are you Dagong's girlfriend?"

"Yes," said Baiyun. Baiyun felt proud even though Dagong was married. At this time of life and death, details like that did not seem to matter.

"You'd better get there soon. They have been there for almost two hours. They refuse to eat or drink anything. People were pouring water onto their faces but they refused it. And some of those students could set themselves on fire anytime," said Broomstick anxiously.

Baiyun jumped onto the back of Broomstick's scooter and raced to the Zhongnanhai compound as fast as she could.

The idea of Self Immolation - of burning oneself to death - was a thought that appalled Baiyun.

Baiyun's aunt had died in that manner by pouring gasoline all over herself in her bathtub. The family believed it was due to a psychological condition, which likely originated during the Cultural Revolution. Although Baiyun was not there when it happened, the event had given her many nightmares.

Baiyun had to jump off the scooter a half mile from the Zhongnanhai compound because of the crowds. With the number of people surrounding the compound, it was impossible to go forward. Fortunately, for Baiyun, with her special radio station pass, she was able to go through the crowd to get to the front.

Sitting in a row behind a white line were five young men with shaved heads. They wore monks' gray cotton robs and sat cross-legged. They held their palms together right in front of their noses. Their gasoline-coved heads were shining under the sun like huge pearls. Their robes had been drenched with gasoline. A cigarette lighter was located in front of them. Behind them was a row of water fast workers who wore white shirts and black pants. They sat in the same gesture as the front row protesters with their backs erect and heads slightly bowed.

Dagong was arguing with a soldier whose bayonet was pointed directly at Dagong's neck. There were a dozen soldiers with rifles in their hands guarding the gate to the Zhongnanhai compound.

"What do you want?" said the soldier.

"I want to go inside." Dagong's voice sounded hoarse.

"What for?"

"Do you see people are dying? Do... Do you have eyes to see that?" At his emotional peak, Dagong was stuttering, These...These precious students are preparing to burn themselves to death!" He shouted and his neck even touched the tip of the bayonet a few more times, "I want to talk to a government official!"

"Who are you?" An officer came out of the gate.

"I'm the head of the 'Beijing Workers' Union'."

"Okay. Come here."

Dagong followed him closer to the gate. The soldiers stepped aside.

"Dagong! Dagong!" Restrained by several people holding her arms, Zhang Ping screamed at the top of her lungs.

"Who is that? Is that woman calling you?" asked the officer.

"Yes," Dagong looked at the direction where the voice came from, "That's my wife. Our child is missing."

"Oh. I'm very sorry," said the officer with a smirk.

"You don't have to feel sorry for me. You should feel sorry for these students." Dagong raised his voice again.

"But you know the central committee members are busy now," said the officer with a fake smile. He looked calm. One could tell that he had been through this kind of situation many times.

"What can be more urgent than this?" Dagong walked closer to him and cornered him against the wall. "Look at these students. Do you know that they are suffering?" Dagong pointed towards the demonstrators.

"Two water fast demonstrators just fainted." Someone yelled in the crowd.

"Can you hear this? Do you have ears?"

The official nodded, but did not say anything.

Suddenly the crowd moved away from Dagong toward the demonstrators. "Stop the fire! Oh, my God!"

Dagong darted towards the crowd. It was obvious that someone had started burning himself.

Baiyun was stunned. Always proud of herself as a tough girl, the scene in front of her was a little too much. Her head was expanding. She felt dizzy after several days of deprivation. All she could do was to try hard to memorize every detail of what was happening. Her brain was like a rusty machine cranking along.

First, she saw Dagong facing the soldier's bayonet by the gate of the Zhongnanhai compound. Before she could join him, she heard his wife Zhang Ping screaming. Then she saw the fire rising in front of her face. She had to admit that she covered her eyes for a moment to avoid seeing the burning demonstrator, but she could still hear the demonstrator's warning and people shouting

The figure in the fire was glowing. The yellowish fire surrounded him like a ring, and gradually it engulfed him. His baldhead was smooth and his gray robe was rapidly disappearing. His hands were folding together, praying with his eyes closed. Like a Buddha toward the incarnation, his ashes were rising toward the heaven.

"Baiyun. Baiyun." Baiyun opened her eyes and found herself held tightly by Dagong.

He was holding a water cup in his hand. His face had narrowed even more. The stubble on his face made him look wild. She liked it. Her hands touched his prickly beard.

"Baiyun. Welcome to the world. You scared us," said Dagong.

"Where are we?"

"We are back to the Beida station again."

"What happened to the student who burnt himself?"

"We put out the fire by throwing blankets over him and pouring water on him. He was sent to a hospital. He suffered third degree burns, but they said he'll recover. The Government agreed to hold another talk with the students. Right now the dialogue delegation is having a meeting with the government at the United Front office," said Dagong at a rapid pace.

"I see." Then Baiyun looked around, "What is happening there?" Baiyun saw a few people sit around in a circle, talking.

"They are talking about Big Li. He's in a serious condition."

"Really?" Baiyun stood up. She was dizzy; she waivered.

"Baiyun. Are you alright?" asked Dagong.

"I'm fine now." She walked toward the crowd.

"Big Li. Big Li!" She ran towards him.

"Be careful!" said someone.

Bundled up in a thick blanket, Big Li was lying there calmly. His head was covered with a thin layer of hair. He had grown a thin mustache and the start of a beard. His face was as gray as dust.

"He has calmed down a lot after I gave him the injection," said a middle-aged woman doctor sitting next to him. "He has been in and out of consciousness."

"What are you going to do with him?" asked Baiyun.

"I called the ambulance two hours ago. I hope it will come soon," said a young doctor.

Baiyun stared at Big Li and really felt sorry for him. Holding his hands, which were hot from fever, she leaned forward to took a good look at him.

"Big Li. This is Baiyun," her tears fell onto his face.

"Baiyun." Big Li opened his eyes. "Where are you?" He looked around and tried to locate Baiyun.

"I'm here," she forced herself to smile for him.

"Baiyun. Thank you for...c-c-coming to see me."

"I'm so sorry." Baiyun held his hand and cried.

"If you...Survive this...Would you go to my home and... Tell my Dad... Tell my Dad what happened?"

"Yes."

"Keep up the good work... Don't. Don't give up..." His head rolled to the side. He lost consciousness again.

Baiyun leaned forward and hugged him. Then the ambulance came and took him away.

The bad news came soon after that. "The dialogue failed again. The government rejected our demands for a Free Press and a Multi-Party government. They also refused to acknowledge us for being patriotic," said a motorcycle messenger.

Everyone around suddenly became quiet. People stopped arguing about the food. Some stopped playing cards. The volunteers stopped distributing the blankets for the evening. They were all simply petrified.

Someone started singing 'The Internationale,' a song for the international workers and the socialists. More joined and soon it spread over the whole Tiananmen Square.

"Arise, the damned of the earth,
Arise, prisoners of hunger,
Reason thunders in its crater,
It is the eruption of the end!
Let's make a blank slate of the past,
Crowds, slaves, arise, arise!
The world is going to change from its base,
We are nothing, let's be everything!
This is the final struggle
Let us gather, and tomorrow
The Internationale
Will be mankind!"

Leaning against Dagong's chest, Baiyun could feel his heart beating.

The fact that he had a wife and a son seemed so trivial now. She felt so fortunate to have met him. She was very much in love with him. She wished she could hug him and kiss him now, but she knew this was not the time.

Through the song 'The Internationale', she felt the solidarity with thousands of people on the Square.

She said to herself, Yes, we're determined. We were determined to sacrifice our youth for a new China.

Then she turned her head and kissed Dagong, perhaps for the last time.

CHAPTER 17

"I don't believe that those bastards will fail us! Down with Marshall Law!" Pumpkin's voice could be heard even before she entered the gate to the yard.

She stopped at the gate. She rolled her bicycle's front wheel over the edge of the wooden door and she lifted the back of the bicycle over it, which was weighed down by two sacks of wheat flour.

On the handle bar, there were two nylon bags full of noodles, bok choy, potatoes and a dead chicken.

"I almost lost my old life in order to get this food. Marshall Law has been declared, stores have closed and many people have gone home to hide. There are still plenty brave ones on the Square," said Pumpkin.

She sat down on a stool to catch her breath.

"Hey, you'd better be careful. You could be thrown into jail if you say something wrong," said Marshmallow, who was sitting on the step by their apartment door, smoking.

"You can't wait to get rid of me," Pumpkin snapped back.

"Hi, Mother." Little Pea came out to welcome her mother.

Wearing an apron around her waist, Little Pea was chopping vegetables in the yard on a table by the sink. Their kitchen was only big enough to hold their stove. She put down what she was doing and walked over to help Pumpkin unload the groceries.

"Be careful, don't let the flour get wet," said Pumpkin to Marshmallow, who lifted the two sacks of flour from the bicycle. The yard floor was full of laundry water.

"Okay. I know, old woman," said Marshmallow while walking back to their room.

"Where is Yu Gong," asked Pumpkin, referring to her son Broomstick by his given name.

"He is still in the Square and working for 'The Flying Tiger Brigade' by zooming around on motorcycles. He sent me back to cook more food so he can distribute it. Just before I left, they were doing something really crazy." She resumed her vegetable chopping; "They were puncturing the buses' tires, so nobody could use them to transport the demonstrators back home."

"That's great," said Pumpkin while wiping her forehead with her sleeve.

"Look at that crazy woman," said Marshmallow as he came back out of his apartment.

"Mother, why don't you get some rest? I'll get the dinner ready in just a few minutes." Little Pea dropped the chopped bok choy into a frying pan, and then mixed it with some ground pork and scallions.

"No, I want to make some snacks quickly and go to the Square." Pumpkin ran toward their room.

"What can I say?" He sighed. "She just wants to leave me," said Marshmallow.

"Hey. Old man. We have been married for thirty years. You have never cared about me so much before. What has happened?" said Pumpkin with one of her feet already stepping into their room.

Marshmallow stood up and walked over towards Pumpkin. He suddenly pulled at her shirt collar.

"Old woman, it is dangerous there. Don't you know that?" His voice was low but firm. One could tell that it directly came from his heart.

Pumpkin was stunned. She was silent for a while. "Okay. I will be careful. But I have to go and take a look."

"Let me go with you," Marshmallow followed her.

"Don't follow me like a shadow. If you really want to go with me, you'd better be prepared to do something." She stood arms akimbo like a woman warrior. "I don't want to go and just watch which direction the wind blows." She waved her arms.

"You want to poke holes in bus tires like those kids? Don't you care about your own life? Let me tell you that it is against the law to damage public property. There are video cameras everywhere on the Square. It will haunt you after the fact." Marshmallow's voice was unusually high. Unlike his usual easy going self, his face was livid. His head tilted to one side as though he was trying to make a point. Occasionally saliva sprayed out of his mouths as he spoke.

"Let her go. They may well be successful," said Lao Liu, the policeman while looking at the plant in his hands. He was holding a small branch freshly cut from a rose bush. He put the branch into a pot and started pouring sand into it. He was pouring so slowly as though he was counting the sand grains as they fell into the pot.

Since the movement had started, he became a full time gardener. He moved all his roses from pots to the ground in the yard. The red, yellow, purple, pink and even green roses bloomed better than ever. He even built a wooden fence for them.

"Really, do you have any insider knowledge?" asked Marshmallow. He immediately turned back from the gate.

"No. I haven't been at work for three weeks. I don't know what is going on. I have been sick, which was the best way I could help the students." He raised his head, a pair of small-framed reading glassed hanging on his nose. "Now I have a feeling that the situation might be dicey, hard to predict. The scale of the movement has surprised me."

Marshmallow nodded and then turned around. He found his wife was gone. "That woman!" He quickly went out of the gate.

Lao Liu resumed his work.

Then Mr. Wang's black cat sauntered over and sniffed at the flowerpot.

"The weather will be changing!" Mr. Wang strolled out of the door with a pipe in his hand.

Lao Liu smiled and did not respond.

Mr. Wang stepped down one step and sat down without looking. He stared straight ahead, his face was serious and his eyes unlinked. He seemed to be meditating.

Mrs. Wang came out of the door with a chamber pot in one hand, pushing the door closed with the other. Her four boys were pushing behind the door and trying hard to get out. They were like birds eager to get out of the cage.

"God damn. Don't try to sneak out," said Mrs. Wang. She stood against the door firmly. Then with an extra push, she locked it.

"Don't keep telling people about the changing weather. It just rained and it is not raining now. So what's new?" Mrs. Wang asked. Still sitting, Mr. Wang did not say a word.

Mrs. Wang walked to the water tap in the middle of the yard and poured the urine into the drain. She turned on the tap and let water run for a while. The water splashed onto her folded-up pants despite her efforts to stay as far as she could from the drain. The water was dripping from the roof where it collected after the rain. It sounded very crisp.

"My roof leaked during the rain. I hope there is no more heavy rain before I can get my roof fixed. How about your roof, Lao Liu?"

"Mine is getting better. It leaks at the corner. I managed to glue a piece of plastic onto the roof since the repairman never showed up," said Lao Liu while concentrating on trimming more rosebush cutoffs.

"I see that you are lucky. My leak was pretty big. I have to put a pail under it to collect the water. I guess this rain may be good for your roses. But for me it's trouble." Mrs. Wang started rubbing clothes on a washboard in a basin. The bubbles jumped out of the basin like snowflakes.

"This previous one was okay, but a heavy one could be very damaging. Before, when these roses were still in pots, I could move them in when it rained heavily. Now I can do nothing since I planted them permanently in the ground, so they can grow more freely, but freedom always involves risk. I hope the students understand that."

"Is that what they want? Freedom." asked Mrs. Wang while still beating the laundry.

"Yes. Young people want to be free to do things and say things."

"That sounds ridiculous. A country is like a family. Without rules and laws, even a family can't run smoothly," said Mrs. Wang seriously.

"The storm is coming. The seagulls are still fighting in the sky!" Mr. Wang shouted passionately as though he was acting in a play.

"You old man. Stop. Don't disturb our normal conversation," said Mrs. Wang.

As if he was suddenly shocked with electricity, Mr. Wang jumped up. Slapping his knees with one hand, he raised the other, pointing to the door with the pipe. "You goddamn woman. Get out of here. Don't stay so close to me. Go!"

"Okay. I go. You can take care of the kids. You can cook. You can do these too."

She pushed the basin full of soapy clothes toward him. Because of the wet floor, the basin slid toward him with such great speed, that it almost spilled all over him.

As Mrs. Wang walked away, the boys suddenly broke the door open and dashed into different directions.

"For heaven's sake!" Mrs. Wang turned around and started chasing them along the corridor like chasing escaped chickens.

Little Pea and Yu Gang sat in front of a table by their door, rolling out the dough, kneading it into a long rope, cutting them into small round disks, rolling them into small round skins, putting the meat in the center and closing them by gathering up all the edges to the center to make steam bread.

"It's finally quiet here. I can't believe that it was completely different just minutes ago. Without mom and dad, don't you feel strange?" asked Little Pea.

"No. I don't think so. This is the way we ought to live," said Yu Gang quietly.

"Don't be dreaming. Look outside. Troops are coming to town. Who knows what the outcome will be. Maybe we will go back to the 'Cultural Revolution'. We may never be able to own our apartment."

"Maybe you are right, if this movement drags on, I'm beginning to miss my job and I really want to go back to work."

Little Pea did not answer. Although she was not a slogan shouter by nature, she sort of liked the movement.

Firstly, her mother Pumpkin became much nicer and generous. She turned into an excitable and happy mom from a loud complainer. Life for her had turned into a joy and adventure instead of tedious and routine.

She and Yu Gang had a chance to run from one side of the Tiananmen Square to the other, shouting and singing along with others. She learned how to dance Disco and sing modern songs.

After standing behind the food stand for days, for the first time in her life she realized that she could not only feed people but also make them laugh. She had changed from a shy and quiet girl to a mature and outgoing lady.

She could even argue with Yu Gang loudly, no longer a submissive little girlfriend. Actually, she thought Yu Gang liked her better this way. This had never happened before, even during the peak of their relationship.

Through her education and upbringing, she believed that steady hard work brought happiness at the end. In the last few weeks, she had more fun than she ever had in her life.

Besides distributing the steamed pork buns to the demonstrators, she also sang and danced. What would all this bring her? In the past, if she worked hard at work, she would be elected as a worker's hero. Now she would be rewarded with a bonus.

What would the demonstration bring her? Freedom? All she knew was that people still needed to eat and to stay in a shelter, even in a free world. She was not even sure if all the students understood what they were doing. Some of them seemed to enjoy being there, staying away from their school and families. They were still kids.

"Yu Gang, I don't think we can make any difference," said Little Pea while putting the last pork bun into the steamer.

She was making dinner for her family, and she wished that her parents would come back soon.

"Since so many people have participated in the movement, I don't think we will be punished for being involved," she continued.

"Well, we can't control that either." Yu Gang stood up and pulled Little Pea toward him. He gave her a forceful kiss. "Let's go in."

Little Pea pulled her head back, gazed at him for a second and gave him a beautiful smile. They walked into Little Pea's apartment, shoulder to shoulder.

This was the biggest benefit coming out of the student's movement. They could use Little Pea's empty apartment to enjoy the greatest joy - making love on Little Pea's bed instead of outside in the bushes.

Zhang Ping was helped into the yard by Pumpkin and Marshmallow. She was shouting in some Cultural Revolution slogans.

"Red Guards, Red Guards,
Stand Up.
Sweep, sweep
The capitalist's running dog,
Into the historical garbage!
Long live Chairmen Mao!
Long live the Cultural Revolution!"

Potatofeet trailed behind them with a cup in hand. The water was swooshed around due to his unsteady hands and bouncing steps.

"Okay, Zhang Ping. Be quiet. Here we are. We are home now." Pumpkin patted Zhang Ping while trying to restrain her from waving her arms.

Zhang Ping struggled forward, stamping her feet hard on the concrete yard floor, glad to have the platform to perform on.

"Poor girl. What can we do?" asked Pumpkin.

Then she turned toward her husband Marshmallow, who was trying to calm Zhang Ping down by holding her arms.

"Hi, old man, why don't you say something?" asked Pumpkin.

As soon as they stopped in the yard, Zhang Ping started struggling even harder.

She kicked Pumpkin and Marshmallow on the legs and hit their faces with clenched fists. "You arrested the revolutionary Red Guard. You are the capitalist's running dog."

"See. What can I do? She is a wild animal. We can't stop her. Nobody can stop her. Besides the whole town is crazy," said Marshmallow.

"You're useless!" said Pumpkin. "Let's bring her into our apartment and tie her down on the bed."

"No. Don't. Please let her go. She will be tired in a while," said Mrs. Wang.

As soon as they released her, she leaped onto the corridor in front of Mrs. Wang's apartment. She was jumping while singing. She waved her fists forcefully into the air while shouting "Long Live Chairman Mao! Long Live the Cultural Revolution!"

Pushing her sleeves high and arms akimbo, she was marching forward on the corridor that was all along the apartment. As she was marching along, the flowerpots and the washbasins on the corridor railing fell down one by one along the way. "Planting flowers is a stinky capitalist's idea. We should dig them out of their roots."

Mr. Wang, his four boys and the cat looked out of their window nervously. Their eyes flinched as Zhang Ping passed by.

Lao Liu rushed out of his door and threw his arms into the sky. "Help! Help! Help to stop this crazy woman."

Before Lao Liu could get a hold of her, she jumped onto the top of the railing where the flowerpots used to be. She danced and sang in rhythm. Her style was between a marching band and an acrobat. She showed an incredible ability to balance on this narrow strip of the platform.

Not knowing what to do, Lao Liu along with the rest of the neighbors watched her.

Little Pea and Yu Gang had come out of their apartment and joined the crowd.

It was as if a mad woman finally conquered the world. The people were worshipping their newly crowned queen even though their queen was in a rage.

In their hearts, they actually agreed with Zhang Ping. They were all crazy during the last few weeks. Nobody was working. They were throwing a tantrum over their government.

Zhang Ping was a performer who was demonstrating what was in each of their minds, a mirror in which they could see themselves. Was this an outpouring of her insanity or her pent-up energy accumulated after years of living under an oppressive regime?

They were watching her as they were questioning themselves.

"Mom and Dad!" Broomstick, Little Pea's brother broke the silence.

He came into the yard accompanied by the noise of a scooter.

"Mom and Dad, what are you doing here? There are tanks, even missiles moving toward Beijing. I just saw four yellow jacket airplanes above my head. Truckloads with more soldiers have already started moving into the Square."

Pumpkin, Marshmallow and Mrs. Wang turned around and stared at Broomstick as though they could not comprehend what he was saying.

Zhang Ping hypnotized them all into such a trance that reality did not matter anymore.

This scared Broomstick, who did not know what had happened to them. Looking numb and lost, he joined the crowd.

"Aaeh...... Comrade, let's march forward!" In a fraction of a second, she jumped off the corridor railing and galloped toward the gate. At the same time, she threw her fists into the sky and shouted, "Long Live Chairman Mao! Long Live the Cultural Revolution!"

The spectators followed, but nobody could go as fast as she could.

As they passed the alley, Little Pea's brother Potatofeet found his water stand where he used to sell tea. "Muh-muh-mother, someone t-t-tipped over muh-my water c-c-can!" He cried. Tears and snot covered his face. He tried to walk faster but his deformed feet did not help. He was in no way going to catch up with everyone.

Pumpkin stopped and wiped his face with the corner of her sleeve. "Wait here, okay? I'll be back in a few minutes."

Then she ran away towards the street where the crowd gathered.

Zhang Ping just reached the end of the alley where the wide Changan Street began.

It was full of people confronting a column of army vehicles. Hundreds of people including citizens and students locked their arms and tried to stop the armed trucks loaded with soldiers going forward.

As soon as Zhang Ping arrived, they gradually opened a pathway for her. Her loud voice and hysteria had an unspeakable command over them.

"Hey, this is a real brave one."

"Let her go forward."

"I think she must have just come out of the psychiatric ward."

"So what is wrong with that? Even the mental patients know what justice is."

Zhang Ping rushed in front of the first truck that was packed with soldiers in green uniforms with rifles in hand. Her permed hair was dry and sticking up, which made her head resemble a male lion. She locked her arms against her waist like an angry animal. Her excited face was like an eggplant, long and purple.

"Hey, soldier, you want to harvest the revolutionary fruit? No way!"

Then she was doing the revolutionary dance again. This time she was doing Yong Ge, a harvest street dance in which one had to swing their arms and hips while walking.

Soldiers were dumbfounded. They stared at Zhang Ping and did not know what to do. It was not that they felt helpless in front of one mentally ill woman. They were confronted with a whole Square full of crazy people. They were worried about their own sanity. They asked themselves why they did not join the crowd.

"The People's friends are my friends!
The People's enemies are my enemies!"

After reciting that saying of Chairman Mao's, Zhang Ping turned around and faced the crowd. She sat down cross-legged. Then she started conducting with her arms.

"The east is red.
The Sun is rising.
China had gotten a Mao Zedong..."

She was singing one of the oldest Communist songs and China's most popular song. Like magic, the crowd started singing too, then the troops.

Dagong, who tried to go home but got stuck in the crowd on the Square, had been watching Zhang Ping for a while. It was clear in his mind that his wife was crazy.

He fought hard to get through the heavily packed crowd in order to get closer to her until the crowd started singing along with her. The crowd's patriotic attitude had moved him. He stopped moving forward and joined the singing. Like many people around him, he could feel tears rolling down from the corners of his eyes. He shared others' passion and frustration.

During their desperate move - using their bodies to stop government's army trucks and tanks, they still tried to worship their dying god - Mao Zedong. They did not ridicule him. They just wanted government officials to hear their voices and understand that they still loved China just as much as they did. They just wanted to voice their demands more openly.

Now they wished that Chairman Mao had been there to hear it. Maybe he would have reacted differently.

CHAPTER 18

When Baiyun heard that Martial Law was going to be imposed, she did not react at all.

It seemed she already knew. That was what Dagong said. Actually, that was not the reason. The real reason was that she had become fearless.

Then she heard a girl from the Federation Headquarters coming to the broadcast station to announce that the Hunger Strike was over. Since the surrounding area was so noisy, it turned out that her speech was not effective at all.

"Why don't we go to the Square to be messengers ourselves?" Someone suggested.

"Okay, I would like to do it." Baiyun jumped up immediately.

She felt bored. Since Martial Law was declared, everyone had a feeling that the movement was going to be over.

Students began eating the reserved food and signing paraphernalia for each other.

Baiyun offered her white broad brimmed hat for others to sign. Very soon, her hat was full of reddish signatures and comments like 'A hard working girl,' 'A good writer' and 'Baiyun, you are wicked.'

Baiyun folded her hat and put it in her jeans pocket carefully.

Yumei came over. "Baiyun, do you want to walk around the Square?"

"Yes. You have read my mind."

Baiyun looked at Dagong, who was sitting and staring at the students. They were fighting to get an autograph from the woman student leader who made the announcement to suspend the 'Hunger Strike'

Dagong did not join the autograph crowd. Baiyun thought that maybe he was too shy or maybe just deep in thought.

"Hey. What are you thinking about?" Baiyun tapped him on the shoulder. "Do you want to walk with us on the Square?"

Dagong looked at her and nodded. Then he stood up slowly and wiped off the dust on his bottom with his hand.

"I'll walk with you for a while. But I need to stop at home soon while I still can," he said slowly, trying not to make Baiyun jealous over his wife.

"Oh. That's what you are thinking about. You are different, a man with a family. You have to think twice before facing death," said Yumei teasingly.

"You kids don't understand!" Dagong walked away from them, and the two girls followed.

"His son is lost." Baiyun whispered to Yumei. "I really feel sorry for him, but I don't know how to comfort him. I'm so inept at such things. What do you think?"

Yumei smiled. "I don't know," she said, pretending not to pay attention to Baiyun.

"Come on, Yumei. Even though you're younger, you are much more experienced in such matters. I'm a bookworm and you are not." Baiyun nudged Yumei.

"What experience? What are you girls whispering about?" asked Dagong.

He suddenly stopped walking and turned around towards them.

"We are talking about you." Both girls answered in unison.

"Okay. You can talk about me all you want. I have to go."

Dagong resumed walking toward his home, while Baiyun and Yumei walked towards the center of the Square.

"Do you love him?" asked Yumei.

"Yes."

"That's the best comfort you can offer," said Yumei.

A short man wearing a red armband and a white headband spoke with a heavy southern accent. "I'm a Marshal here. Who are you? Everyone has to show a pass in order to pass through here."

He tried to block Baiyun and Yumei.

"Okay. Here it is." Yumei showed him her pass.

"No. This is yesterday's pass. We just issued new ones," said the Marshal seriously.

"This is absurd. We've just come from the Broadcast station." Yumei pointed her hand towards the Monument of the People's Heroes. "We have an important message for the hunger strikers."

"Okay. There is a tent full of 'Dare to Die' hunger strikers over there," he waved his arm toward his back. "You can talk to them, but don't go any further."

"How come they suddenly changed the passes and even the Marshals are brand new," said Baiyun as she and Yumei were walking away.

"Power struggle. The Hunger Strike leaders have been fighting with the Federation leaders for control of the Square for a long time. I work for the Federation, so I know. It's terrible that people are fighting for their own jealous needs while everyone is facing life and death decisions. They even fought over who was going to announce the ending of the Hunger Strike. If we fail the movement, I think they are to blame." Yumei sounded much more mature.

Since the movement had started, she had lost some weight, especially after she recovered from her illness. Her original dancer's slender figure had been trimmed down to almost a child's body.

"Don't talk about failure. It sounds like a bad omen."

Baiyun hated to see the movement over. In a period of a month, she had gotten used to this lifestyle, sleeping under the sky, and running around the Square all day long and sharing the company of like-minded friends.

She could no longer be satisfied with a life consisting of the library, dorm and cafeteria anymore. She wished that this lifestyle could go on forever. If not, she was ready to die.

She thought about death a lot recently. The more she thought about it, the less frightening it became. She should have been dead a few times already, she was telling herself. She was living on borrowed time, which would not run forever.

Now the 'Martial Law' had been declared. The government had tightened its grip. She could almost envision tanks moving in and soldiers opening fire on students and citizens.

She was no longer afraid. Before she wished that if she could die with Dagong, she would be fine. Now as long as she could sacrifice her life with some of her friends, like Longfe or Yumei, she would also be very happy.

Tiananmen Square had been cleared somewhat since 'Marshal Law' was declared.

It was a bright sunny day, which reminded everyone that summer had arrived. Students were running around in shorts and skirts.

It was strange that the atmosphere on the Square was so relaxed. It was almost like a festival and a celebration. Students were walking around the Square, congratulating each other and signing memorabilia.

In the background, students' stereos were playing popular music once more. Although the trash, including sunflower seed shells, peanut shells and apple peels became more visible due to the withdrawing of the people, the newly pitched tents of the students from Hong Kong had added color to the Square.

Under a large red tent in front of the People's Congress Meeting Hall, Baiyun and Yumei discovered ten brave hunger strikers. It was hard to believe that ten people could fit into such a small tent.

Their small size made it possible. Most of them crowded together under a very large floral blanket, sleeping or simply lying there with their eyes shut. Some of them listened to music with headphones over their ears.

There was one lonely girl sitting in the corner reading a book. Like everyone else, she wore a white headband. Her face was pale but full. Among the cluster of dried-up, skinny and grotesque faces, it was amazing how good she looked. Maybe she was a new hunger striker, Baiyun thought.

After they crawled into the tent, both Baiyun and Yumei shouted, "Aaeh. Wenjing, is that you?"

Slowly raising her smooth face, Wenjing looked at them over the top of her glasses - like a scholar.

"Hi, Yumei and Baiyun."

"You. Scholar! How did you suddenly become a hero?" Yumei went over and hit her on the shoulder lightly.

"I'm not," she sounded a little weak, "Don't tell anyone but I was sneaking in chocolate bars for the first few days. I'm used to it now though and it should be good for my weight loss program."

Yumei and Baiyun laughed. Wenjing still had a good sense of humor.

"So you decided to become an activist?" Baiyun asked.

"Nope," said Wenjing while waving a TOEFL review book. "I can still study for the TOEFL exam here."

"You, rascal!" Yumei hit her again on the shoulder. "As long as you have books to read, you'll never die a hungry scholar."

"And I can be a hunger striker at the same time!" Wenjing smiled. Her small eyes formed into a thin line behind her thick white glasses.

"Now, I represent the Federation to declare that the Martial Law has been declared by the government," said Yumei. "In order to preserve our strength and save lives, the Federation decided to stop the Hunger Strike and ask everyone to get ready to withdraw."

Yumei sat with her legs crossed and her back erect, she conveyed her message with authority.

"What Martial Law?" Some of the students started to wake up, rubbing their eyes with the back of their hands.

Yumei repeated the message. Afterwards there were hardly any reactions. Some of the hunger strikers even went back to sleep.

"Did you hear me?" Yumei asked desperately. "Are you still alive? Am I talking to a group of dead people?"

"We have already decided to die several weeks ago," murmured someone.

"I'd rather die than give into the government," another one mumbled.

"This is an order. Do you know? We, as an organization, have to work together."

"Who are you?"

"Okay. I should have introduced myself earlier. My name is Huang Yumei. I'm the Secretary General of the Beijing branch of the Student Federation. I used to work for the dialogue delegation." Yumei's voice sounded a little angry.

"I have never heard of the dialogue delegation," someone snapped back.

This was like plug that was stuck into Yumei's mouth, which made it impossible for Yumei to speak.

"Martial Law has been declared today!" The president of China, Yang Shangkun's voice could be heard over the radio. "Troops are moving into the city. Any organizations, any groups and anyone who still remain in the Square will suffer severe consequences."

The radio finally convinced some of the students, and they struggled to get up.

"Okay. If you have food, please eat something. We will get the federation's buses to come and pick you up," Yumei said urgently.

"Do you have any food," asked Baiyun.

"No, We haven't stored food here for a while. We are HUNGER STRIKING here!"

"Okay. We'll try to get some for you," said Yumei.

When Yumei and Baiyun got out of the tent, the whole Square was stirred up again. "New! New Hunger Strike organized by Professor Chen Ninyuan! We need 200,000 people, the largest in the history to protest the government's outrageous decision!"

Someone ran over and poked his head into the tent, yelling, "Comrades, keep up the good work!"

Students in the tent flopped back onto their blankets.

Yumei and Baiyun stared at each other.

"Okay. At least we will tell the Federation to transfer you into a bus," said Yumei before leaving the 'Dare to Death' hunger strikers.

Yumei and Baiyun could feel the newly heated atmosphere in the Square through the cool breeze around them.

Although the number of people on the Square had decreased, every one of them (mostly students) was as energetic as before.

They followed the crowd to the Monument of People's Heroes, where the main Hunger Strike stage was still centered.

There were twenty to fifty vehicles around the Monument of People's Heroes, most of which were buses filled with student hunger strikers.

It was an unusual situation. The monument, which was a sacred place and used to be a place where people came to pay tribute to People's heroes, had become a Rock & Roll concert stage.

People ran around, wearing white headbands and armbands which said, 'Long Live Democracy,' 'Rather Die than Give Up' and 'Fighting to the Last Drop of Blood'.

People were not fixing the buses; instead, they were taking them apart. Tires were punctured, and the steering wheels were pulled out. The place looked like a junkyard.

On the other side of the monument, there was a Rock & Roll concert with the famous singer Cui Jian on stage. People were cheering and roaring.

Immersed in this moving atmosphere, Yumei and Baiyun strolled around the monument and absorbed everything. Yumei, a good singer and dancer, was humming the current song along with the crowd, while Baiyun could not help but write a news article about the spectacle in her head.

"Yumei, have you noticed this?" Baiyun pulled Yumei's arm to go through a narrow avenue between the buses.

They approached the neatly trimmed pine trees around the monument. Instead of green, the trees were white, because they were covered with white cloth.

This very much resembled the time when Premier Zhou died fifteen years ago and the same trees were covered with white paper flowers decorated by millions of Beijing citizens to mourn the death of Premier Zhou.

"It looks so sad," said Baiyun.

"These were some of the hunger strikers' death wills." Yumei stopped humming and started examining the white strips of cloth carefully.

"Look at this one." Yumei pulled Baiyun closer. The words were neatly hand-lettered in what appeared to be a brown ink:

Dear Mom,

When you see this message, I probably will not exist anymore. Please do not feel sad. Your son doesn't have time to pay back your love, because his motherland needs him for an even more important mission.

Mother, stop crying. Look around you. You can see your son smiling among hundreds of smiling faces.

Mother, stop weeping. You should be proud of your son who contributes to the happiness of millions.

"It was written in blood," said Baiyun.

They were moved by the sincerity of the words.

"Don't you think we should join the Hunger Strike again?"

"I have been thinking about it," said Yumei while looking at the hundreds of white strips on the square-cut pine shrubs around the monument.

"I don't think the News Center needs me now. I used to think that I'm a writer, so my job is to observe life and record it. Now I want more. I want to experience life fully using my blood or even my life," said Baiyun. Her voice was getting louder. "Besides, this may be our last chance to join the Hunger Strike."

"You really think so?" Yumei could not believe her ears. She would never have imagined Baiyun going this far.

It was such a big change for Baiyun to go from being a bookish and selfish intellectual to a committed activist and hunger striker, but who could understand any of the events that happened recently? Disaster or danger could often bring the best out of people. Maybe this side of Baiyun just had been hidden until the right moment.

"I don't really know. I tried not to think about it too much. Sometimes I wish this movement would go on forever. It is very hard for me to imagine going back to school and sitting in the library all day long or going back to my strange family. Now even Dagong has gone back to his wife. What do I have left?" Baiyun's confession surprised Yumei because she had never talked so much about herself to others."

"Dagong will come back to you," Yumei tried to comfort Baiyun.

"I'm so happy that you are my friend," said Baiyun. She gave Yumei a hug.

"Hi, girls. What are you doing here?" A well-dressed man walked towards them with his hand touching the white cloth on the pine shrubs. "Which school are you from?"

"Beida." Yumei found him strange.

"Oh. Great. You are local. I'm from Shanghai." He attempted to shake hands with them; they refused.

"You don't sound like Shanghainese," said Baiyun. Her mother Meiling was originally from Shanghai, so she would recognize the accent.

"I grew up in the Shandong province," he said leisurely. He looked as though he had the whole day to chat.

"Do you enjoy staying in Beijing?" Yumei asked, but her eyes were looking elsewhere.

"Yes. I wish that I could spend the summer here. The summer in Shanghai is like hell," he said, as though he was living in a hotel in Beijing with air conditioning twenty-four hours a day. "Do you know who I really am?" His eyes formed a thin line. He moved closer towards Yumei. His crew cut hair glimmered under the streetlight.

"No." Yumei and Baiyun backed away from him. They were waiting for him to say that he was the Devil from Hell.

"Ha-ha. I know you can't figure me out. Let me tell you. I'm a plainclothes police officer. There are a lot of us around here. You'd better get out of here as soon as possible. Otherwise, it will be too late. I know exactly what is going to happen tonight. You can't even imagine how fast the troops are moving in."

Approaching the girls, he boasted the secret, "You'd better run if you can!" He waved as though trying to chase the chickens away.

Yumei and Baiyun turned around and ran away as fast as they could.

It was not that they were afraid of the policeman. It was because they felt the information was urgent and they wanted to find someone in charge. They wanted to go back to the headquarters to find Longfe and Xia Nan.

Xia Nan, the head of the student organization in the Economic department, had switched from an anti-movement advocate to one of the Beijing Student Hunger Strike leaders. When the hunger strikers took control of the Tiananmen Square, he became even more powerful.

He was in many news conferences with the foreign press, and formed new alliances with some of the most powerful student leaders around. He seemed to always be at the right place at the right time.

Yumei and Baiyun hoped to find him in the new Hunger Strike Headquarters in one of the buses around the monument.

People were still enjoyed the frenzy of destroying the buses. Now they were jabbing holes on the already flattened tires. Their actions were merely for show, since the tires had been destroyed to such a degree that they were impossible to repair. The Rock & Roll concert still went on and the cheering was louder than ever.

As they checked from bus to bus for Longfe and Xia Nan, Baiyun suddenly noticed two familiar people standing next to a motorcycle under a streetlight.

It was her mother Meiling and boyfriend Lao Zheng. They were unashamedly holding each other in an intimate position while talking to a third person.

Too embarrassed to tell Yumei, she kept quiet. Actually, she wished she could dig a hole that was deep enough to hide in.

This has not been the first time she was so embarrassed by one of her parents that she pretended she didn't see them.

In 1975, in the midst of the Cultural Revolution, she was nine years old. One day when she was playing jump rope with her friends outside of their apartment, one of the girls pointed to an old man walking towards the apartment.

"Look. Who is that?" asked the girl.

He wore old faded pants and a wrinkled shirt. His hair and stubby beard were gray. There was a rolled-up quilted blanket hanging on his back, weighing him down yet his head was only slightly bent. In his hand, there was a beaten up duffle bag.

It took a moment before Baiyun realized that it was her father, Professor Yang and how could Baiyun admit that he was her father?

He had just come back from the labor camp and he still looked like a prisoner. He had caused her enough trouble at school already and because of his political problems, she never had any friends at school.

She was not allowed to perform in any plays or musicals because of him. Kids chased her and threw stones at her because of him. Now, finally she had a couple of neighborhood girls to play with and she was fearful that he would once again ruin it. She was determined not to admit that he was her dad.

"I don't know him," Baiyun said, and the girls kept playing.

Fortunately Professor Yang did not notice her when he walked past them. Since he was busy looking down, he seemed not to notice anyone or else he, too, was ashamed.

When he finally went inside the apartment, Baiyun was so relieved that she almost fell.

So Baiyun had ignored a parent before, and she knew she could do it again. Unfortunately, as they got closer, it became obvious to Baiyun that they would encounter Meiling and Lao Zheng, because as they embraced each other they were speaking with Xia Nan.

Baiyun saw Xia Nan nodding his big head with shoulder length hair and shaking hands with Meiling.

Lao Zheng, who now had grown a mustache, was standing next to his shiny new motorcycle under the streetlight next to a red bus.

"That's Xia Nan! That's Xia Nan!" Yumei exclaimed.

Of course, Baiyun did not remind her that her mother Meiling and her new boyfriend were standing next to Xia Nan.

"Let's go, Baiyun," commanded Yumei, as bossy as ever.

Baiyun could not understand why Yumei got so excited to see Xia Nan. Baiyun obediently followed Yumei as if she were a dog following her master.

"Okay. I will tell headquarters about your information. Don't worry. We will find a way to deal with it." Xia Nan was still nodding.

"Hey. Baiyun. Do you know who Xia Nan is talking to?" Yumei turned around, pulling Baiyun's sleeves. "That old lady and her young boyfriend look like people who belong to 'The Flying Tiger Brigade'. They're just common workers. I could not imagine that our comrade Xia Nan could deal with people like that."

"I don't know." Baiyun cast her eyes down and kept walking forward. She wished she could disappear.

"Hi, Baiyun!" Through her tinted glasses, Meiling was the first one to notice her.

"Mother. It is nice to see you," said Baiyun quietly, her fingers crossing and her face burning. She did not want to admit that she was proud to see her mother here.

"Hi," she also nodded to Lao Zheng, who smiled at her.

Leaning against the motorcycle, dressed in a leather jacket and gloves, Lao Zheng looked quite handsome. With a white headband on his slightly baldhead, he looked like the perfect member of 'The Flying Tiger Brigade'.

Yumei, of course, was stunned to see this. Having heard a lot about Baiyun's mother, this was actually the first time she had ever met her. Staring at them, she did not even notice Xia Nan reaching his hand out to her.

"Hi. You crazy girls, still here?" Xia Nan sounded like an old man.

"So what?" Yumei said firmly as she stomped her foot and tilted her head toward one side.

"Longfe has been looking for you." Behind his big thick glasses sitting on top of his hollow cheeks, Xia Nan looked sympathetic.

"Tell him that I can take care of myself," said Yumei. She was determined to sound tough.

"Okay. I don't care what is going on between you two, but do you know how serious the situation is here?" Xia Nan moved closer to Yumei, his mouth wide open.

"Who says we don't know?" murmured Baiyun.

"Do you think you girls can run around like this forever?" Xia Nan continued.

"We are not just running around. We are working!" Yumei's voice was still firm. Yet the sense of doubt started showing on her face. She looked concerned.

"Okay. Okay. Okay. You girls are iron women. No missiles or tanks can stop you. At some point, I have to give the order for everyone to leave. The situation is just getting too dangerous."

"Yes. It's very dangerous. So why don't you order everyone else to leave?" Yumei yelled. Her face was red and her eyes were moist. "Do you know that soldiers are coming tonight to the Square through the subway? I just heard that from a plainclothes policeman."

"Really? An honest soldier. I'm surprised, but don't worry. Meiling from 'The Flying Tiger Brigade' just told us that our Beijing citizens have already disconnected the electricity in the subway, so the soldiers are stuck there now. Although the situation is getting tense and the government will figure out a way to send the troops over. You really should seriously consider leaving here soon."

"No. As long as we are here, the victory will be ours." Yumei said firmly.

"Hi, Yumei. I have been looking for you." Longfe rushed over and quickly nodded to everyone.

"Longfe!" Yumei ran towards him and held his tall frame. His hair had grown longer than the last time she saw him. In the front, his hair covered his eyebrows and ears while in the back it covered his neck, which made his small face even smaller. Like many people on the Square, he wore a white headband

"Okay. I will let you take care of these ladies." Xia Nan seized an opportunity to get out of the torment.

"Mother, aren't you afraid?" asked Baiyun. She was still in Meiling's embrace. She felt very close to Meiling.

"No. This is exciting. I have never had so much fun in my life. I feel young! I feel proud!" Meiling's face was radiant. She did look young for her age.

"What about the threat of death?" asked Baiyun. Then she regretted it; she was afraid that talking about it might be a bad omen.

Under the light, even Lao Zheng, standing tall in his newly oiled leather jacket and gloves, looked heroic. He smirked.

Meiling patted Baiyun's shoulder. "Baiyun, your mother is not afraid of death." Meiling made death sound like a trip to Shanghai.

Sure, Baiyun remembered the countless times Meiling talked about death frankly.

There was the time during the 1984 earthquake when Meiling chose to stay inside of their fragile home instead of following the orders to move out. Her father had raised a cleaver and threatened to kill Meiling during one of their many fights. Meiling faced the cleaver and her eyes did not even flinch. Baiyun knew her mother and she knew her well. The situation back then was different though and Meiling acted out of desperation.

Now Meiling finally found her role in society and found a way to contribute to her country. Why would she want to die? Unless, of course, she thought death itself was a contribution to society.

"Longfe. Let's forget about your mother's offer for us to hide in your home," Looking at Longfe's pale face and fragile body, Yumei regretted telling him that, but under such an urgent moment, who could care more than Longfe?

Longfe nodded, but did not say a word.

"Should we join the hunger strikers? Maybe this is our last chance," asked Yumei.

He nodded; she buried her head in Longfe's chest and let herself shed a few tears.

Then she turned to Baiyun. "Baiyun, does it sound like a good idea to join the final hunger strike?"

"Yes." Without hesitation, Baiyun agreed. "I'll join you."

Then she ran toward Meiling and gave her another hug. She could see tears welling up around Meiling's eyes.

"Take care, Mother!"

"You too, Baiyun!"

Baiyun joined Longfe and Yumei and departed.

The idea of losing her mother after their brief reconciliation bothered Baiyun for a while. For a moment, she wished that she had rather gotten on Lao Zheng's motorcycle and joined them.

'The Goddess of Democracy and Freedom has arrived!' Someone yelled in the crowd.

'The Goddess of Democracy and Freedom'? Where?" Another person in the crowd questioned.

The Square was stirred up by this new excitement, and people formed groups and started flowing towards it.

The Square was completely lit up.

The Goddess was a thirty-three inch high white statue made of foam and papier-mâché. The students, passing the monument, moved towards the Forbidden City, while carrying her.

They stopped in front of the hunger strikers' buses.

Students from the Central Academy of Fine Arts were still adding the last bits of touch-up to the statue.

"Long Live Democracy!"
"Long Live the Chinese People!"
"Premier Li Peng, step down!"

The slogans were deafening, especially when everyone on the Square were shouting at once.

Then someone started singing "A Piece of Red Cloth."

That day you used a piece of red cloth
to blindfold my eyes and cover up the sky
You asked me what I had seen
I said I saw happiness

This feeling really made me comfortable
made me forget I had no place to live
You asked where I wanted to go
I said I want to walk your road

I couldn't see you, and I couldn't see the road
You grabbed both me hands and wouldn't let go
You asked what I was thinking
I said I want to let you be my master

I have a feeling that you aren't made of iron
but you seem to be as forceful as iron
I felt that you had blood on your body
because your hands were so warm

This feeling really made me comfortable
made me forget I had no place to live
You asked where I wanted to go
I said I want to walk your road

I had a feeling this wasn't a wilderness
though I couldn't see it was already dry and cracked
I felt that I wanted to drink some water
but you used a kiss to block off my mouth

I don't want to leave and I don't want to cry
Because my body is already withered and dry
I want to always accompany you this way
Because I know your suffering best

That day you used a piece of red cloth
to blindfold my eyes and cover up the sky
You asked me what I could see
I said I could see happiness"

Baiyun stood on her tiptoes and could only see the top section of the Goddess through the space between people's heads. The Goddess had a Chinese woman's figure with straight hair blown toward one side by the wind. She had broad shoulders and strong, almost manly body. She was holding the torch with both of her arms. Pointing the torch toward the sky, she was facing the Forbidden City and staring at the Chinese people's formal God, the portrait of Chairman Mao.

The crowd shouted slogans in waves and rhythms, as if it were a sporting event, or as the people did during the Cultural Revolution rallies.

Along with the rhythm, Baiyun held Yumei's shoulders and jumped up and down so she could see what was going on.

Suddenly someone held her waist behind and lifted her up. She became a head taller than everyone else around her.

She turned around and shouted, "Dagong, you rascal!"

They hugged for a long time and Baiyun's face was full of tears.

"How about sitting on my shoulders?" Dagong asked.

"Is that all right?" She looked at Dagong's newly shaved face and was still trying to get used to his new look.

"Of course. Don't you want to be a Goddess for a change?" Dagong teased her.

"Can I?"

"Sure, I know you would like it."

Dagong squatted and Baiyun climbed onto his shoulders. Dagong stood up slowly so Baiyun would not fall.

A song started to play in Baiyun's mind.

She heard 'You are my Goddess! You are my Goddess!' The voice was resonating in her head but she couldn't figure out what song it was and where she had heard before.

Then she remembered it was a modified version of an old folk song called, 'You are My Sunshine.'

CHAPTER 19

On Saturday morning, just before noon, Pumpkin woke up and found that her husband was not next to her, snoring as he usually would be at that time on a Saturday.

It struck her as a bad omen. Something must have happened, she thought.

She looked around the room. Little Pea and her boyfriend Yu Gang and Potatofeet were still in bed, sleeping.

Broomstick, of course, was not there. He had not come back since he joined 'The Flying Tiger Brigade'; and he was busy riding motorcycles around the city.

Pumpkin stepped outside. Besides the noise coming from the Square, the yard was peaceful, although it looked a bit unusual. Mrs. Wang replaced her husband Mr. Wang sitting in front of their apartment. She was knitting. Lao Liu's wife Wu Zheng was watering the plants instead of Lao Liu.

"Where are the men?" Pumpkin shouted.

"They went out to see the city," said Mrs. Wang carelessly.

"They are tired of being inside." Wu Zheng added.

"They must be insane," said Pumpkin.

"Yes. Lao Liu has not been outside of the yard for a week. He would like to see what is going on. They snuck out early. I didn't even notice. Besides who could stop them?" said Wu Zheng.

"I would have," said Pumpkin.

She looked into the sky. The sky was gray; Pumpkin thought it looked like a concrete doom where no sunlight could penetrate.

The air was hot and moist, like in a shower. She felt suffocated and sick.

She had never felt so worried before. She had heard the warning about the troops moving into Tiananmen Square on the radio the day before. She had a feeling that the government was serious this time.

She thought, Gee! How could these men be so irresponsible?

Pumpkin's heart was like a tangled web; messy and confused. Without her husband around, it was as if she had lost her backbone. Then she heard Wu Zheng talking to her daughter Lili, "Lili, where are you going?"

"I'm going to see Xiao Liu. He just got out of the hospital and he rejoined the Hunger Strike right away. I'm worried about him. I'll try to find him and be his moral support," murmured Lili.

Wu Zheng grabbed Lili.

Lili pulled to get away from her; she knew her mother would stop her from going out. She lowered her head and started crying. She was in love with Xiao Liu. How could her Mom be so cruel?

"Lili, it is not me who wants to stop your enthusiasm. It's just too dangerous outside. I heard through the grapevine at work that the Chairman of the Central Military Commission, Dong Xiaoping is ready to see some blood this time. You are my only daughter. I don't want to lose you." She started pulling Lili back.

"Dad is out there, Dad is out there! I'm worried for him, too." Lili shouted and tried to get out of her mom's grip.

"Nonsense! You don't need to worry about your father. He is a policeman. He knows how to protect himself." Wu Zheng spoke with such authority that Lili knew she would be foolish not to listen to her.

Lili unwillingly followed her mother into their apartment, sobbing uncontrollably.

As Pumpkin listened to this exchange, she imagined tanks rolling into the Square; she could see her overweight husband Marshmallow falling behind the others as they ran to escape from the tanks. She saw them getting closer and closer to him. She began walking toward the gate.

"Mom, where are you going?" asked Little Pea, who just woke up and was washing her face with the cold water in the washbasin.

"I'm going to find your father and your brother. Make sure to keep Potatofeet at home."

"Be careful, Mom. Yu Gang and I may go out later to see whether we could help with anything," said Little Pea.

A loud explosion in the distance could be heard in the yard.

"It's not safe outside. You'd better stay at home. It's totally out of control there," said Pumpkin worriedly.

Pumpkin stepped outside of the gate and she saw three motorcycles arriving at the alley.

She saw her son Broomstick riding on the first motorcycle. Then she spotted Marshmallow sitting on the back seat and moaning, with his handkerchief covering his eyes. Lao Liu and Mr. Wang were sitting on the other two motorcycles with bandages on their heads.

"Dad was hit by a tear-gas canister," said Broomstick.

"Oh. My old man. That's your self-imposed suffering. Why didn't you take him to the hospital?" asked Pumpkin while helping Marshmallow get off the motorcycle.

"The road is blocked. It would take much longer to get to the hospital. We just have to wash his eyes very quickly," said Broomstick.

Pumpkin helped Marshmallow to the sink in the yard and began splashing water into his eyes.

His moaning turned into yelling and soon he lost his strength.

Wu Zheng brought her medicine box out to him.

"I would never have predicted that my nursing training would become useful again," said Wu Zheng. She squeezed some eye drops into his eyes and wrapped a bandage around them. "He will feel better soon," she said to Pumpkin, and then they both helped Marshmallow walk back to his apartment.

After they returned, Broomstick introduced the other motorcyclists. "This is Meiling. She is our group mother and our moral support."

Meiling took off her helmet, opened her leather jacket and said, "This is an interesting experience for me and made me feel twenty years younger. See, I'm just a shameless old lady." She laughed loudly.

Then everyone's attention shifted toward a young man who just entered the yard. He was a tall young man wearing a black mask over his face, which only showed his small eyes. He wore a black cape and two small ears stuck out from his tight black hat.

"Batman!" Broomstick advanced in a fencing step toward him and lunged at him with a stick.

'Batman' swiftly avoided the stick.

"B-B-Batman! You...You're muh-muh-my favorite superhero!" Potatofeet bounced toward the young man.

Just before he could reach him, his legs suddenly lost their strength, and he fell on his knees in front of the young man as though he was worshipping him.

"This is Zhuzhu. He's our 'Batman', our 'Flying Tiger Brigade' captain and our warrior!" Broomstick continued his introduction.

"Oh, my God. It's Batman!" Pumpkin came over and touched Zhuzhu's body. "Are you real? Are you really that magical?" Her big round eyes were widely open. Her fat double-chinned jaw dropped a little.

"No. I just like to dress up like one," said the Zhuzhu.

"He can leap over tall walls," said Meiling. She was standing next to Zhuzhu and looking very proud.

"Ya. A five-meter high wall," said Zhuzhu.

"Yes. You sound human to me. Do you drink tea? I can make some for you," said Pumpkin.

"No. Thank you. We have to leave now. We have to pass the news to the students as soon as possible. The soldiers have already started firing at the protesters over at Muxiudi. Right Meiling?" Zhuzhu asked.

The crowd in the yard suddenly turned quiet. Everyone's face turned solemn. It was so quiet that the water dripping from the leaking tap became loud and annoying.

Pumpkin was staring at everyone while tears rolled down her face, which she did not even bother to wipe.

Zhang Ping suddenly appeared in the middle of the courtyard. "Let's go, comrades! Let's kick some ass." She wore a faded green uniform with a red armband on her right arm and a green hat atop her disheveled hair. Her face was red, swollen and full of scratch marks.

"Stop her!" said Pumpkin.

Lao Liu and Mr. Wang went forward, trying to pull her towards her apartment.

Zhang Ping fought back by kicking. "Don't stop me! You are against the revolution. You are proletarian's enemy!"

Pumpkin joined the effort by lifting her legs. They carried her back to her apartment, still kicking and screaming.

"How did she get out?" asked Wu Zheng.

"Dagong locked her in her room before he left yesterday," said Little Pea, "She probably got out through the window."

After locking Zhang Ping back in her apartment, Pumpkin, Lao Liu and Mr. Wang came back to the yard.

Mr. Wang sat in front of their door and took out the pipe from his pocket, while his wife went to prepare dinner. Lao Liu sat down on the steps, looking at his garden.

Pumpkin walked to the center of the yard and crossed her arms on the top of her fat belly, as if she was going to give a speech to Marshmallow and the others.

"So what happened this morning?" asked Pumpkin.

Lao Liu spoke first. "I heard troops had driven into the downtown area last night and had left five trucks of weapons on Changan Avenue, just outside of Tiananmen Square. We decided to go and look. I hadn't been out for weeks." Even though Lao Liu had a bandage on his head, he did not look particularly injured. "When we first got there this morning, it was quite nice. There was an early summer breeze in the air. The few people on the street looked happy and relaxed, or maybe they were just simply fearless.

"No. It was gloomy. I could sense it." Mr. Wang cut in.

"Yes. You probably know more than we do. Have you been working for the government, Mr. Wang?" Lao Liu confronted him.

"I guess you know everything. I can't lie to you. Yes. I was. I figured it was a chance for me to get ahead." Mr. Wang found a chair and sat down. "Then I realized not a single person was willing to help the government in the Pro-Democracy movement. I felt isolated and simply was tired of lying. It looked like the people might win. I wanted to be on the winning side. I told them I quit. They told me that I couldn't, so I just ran away. It has been so chaotic and nobody knows who was in charge. So I'm Scott-Free."

"What? You coward!" Lao Liu spat his words at Mr. Wang and then turned away, ignoring him.

He continued telling the others what happened. "As we approached the Square, I could see more people around us. They either wore armbands or headbands, which were made of white cloth and made them look like Japanese warriors. Then a truck full of demonstrators pulled up. I asked them why they didn't go and pick up the weapons in the abandoned trucks. They said that they didn't want to play into the officials' tricks; they knew it was a trap and besides, they want to be peaceful demonstrators. As we went further into the Square, it became more crowded. When we were just about to arrive at the LiuBuKou (Six-steps entrance), we suddenly saw flames rising in front of us, then a loud explosion. We were so curious that we just kept walking. As a policeman, I was trained not to be afraid of this kind of violence. I pushed forward but it was impossible. There were people all around us. Then Mr. Wang suggested that we should go home, before it was too late. Marshmallow agreed.

But it WAS too late. Police cars zoomed around the crowd, throwing tear gas canisters at us. Marshmallow's eyes were scorched. Mr. Wang and I were standing a little further back so we didn't get hurt. Then Broomstick and 'The Flying Tiger Brigade' came along and brought us home on their motorcycles. What a stupid adventure!" Lao Liu sighed and started smoking a cigarette.

He also helped Mr. Wang to light his pipe.

"I saw a tear gas bomb burn a small boy's leg with my own eyes," added Mr. Wang.

"Let me tell you. This is just a warning. Something much worse is going to happen soon," said Lao Liu, eyelids widening.

Little Pea leaned against Yu Gang's shoulder and covered her mouth with one of her hands.

Pumpkin's face was purple red. Her eyes full of anger. "Those bastards!" Pumpkin stumped the ground.

"Muh-Mother, could I g-g-go and sell some…Some tea?" Potatofeet sauntered over with a teapot in one hand and a couple of teacups in the other.

"Just in the alley. Okay?" said Pumpkin without a second thought.

Potatofeet swerved toward the gate.

"You'd better come back in an hour and have some dinner," said Pumpkin.

"Shh-she-sure!"

Silence. The yard went into a temporary brooding mood again.

Someone turned on the radio. All the stations had the same program. The message chilled everyone down to his bones.

A cold female voice said: "The situation is becoming grave. A small number of thugs have spread rumors and incited the people to insult, beat and kidnap some of the soldiers. They also have seized weapons. For these reasons, all the civilians should heighten their vigilance. From now on, please do not go out onto the streets and do not go to Tiananmen Square. All workers and staff numbers should stay at their places of work and all residents should remain at their homes to ensure their safety and avoid unnecessary losses."

Marshmallow came out with a bandage on his left eye. "What did they say on the radio?"

Pumpkin ran out of the kitchen and tried to push him back. Little Pea went over to help.

"This government has really disappointed everyone. Let's go and fight. If everyone fights, we can win!" said Marshmallow while waving his fist in the air.

"Fight? You almost lost an eye and next time you will lose your head," said Pumpkin.

She was surprised that these cowardly words could come out of her mouth. She had not been feeling good lately, since she saw Zhang Ping go crazy. Dagong disappeared for a few days and her husband Marshmallow was wounded by a teargas canister. Maybe she just simply got tired. She felt as if she was facing a huge mountain in front of her.

In the last few weeks, the students and citizens of Beijing had shaken the mountain and caused a few stones to come crumbling down, some of which had wounded some people. Gestures were not enough to get rid of the mountain. They had to start digging from the bottom.

In order for Pumpkin to calm her husband down, she compromised. "Okay, let's have dinner first and then I will go over there with you."

"Goddamn it. I can't take this anymore! This government is lying. I saw it with my own eyes. These students didn't start the fight. It was the police who fought first." Mr. Wang threw his pipe into Lao Liu's garden and walked toward the gate.

Everyone was stunned to see him behave this way, but no one tried to stop him.

Even Lao Liu did not worry about Mr. Wang's pipe hurting his roses. He stared at the back of Mr. Wang with his mouth wide open.

Mrs. Wang came out of the kitchen, holding a bowl of porridge. She sat down on the same chair Mr. Wang was sitting on before he left, eating silently.

They all knew Mr. Wang was a stubborn man.

"Where is Yu Gang?" Pumpkin asked while Little Pea, Marshmallow and Pumpkin sat around a little table in the yard, eating steamed bread and porridge.

"He is with Broomstick's 'Flying Tiger Brigade'," said Little Pea. "He didn't want me to go with him, because he thought it was too dangerous."

As they ate, a loud popping sound startled them.

"Were those gun shots outside?" Marshmallow put the chopsticks down and stood up.

"It sounds like fireworks," said Pumpkin, though she knew better.

"I'm sure that it's not fireworks out there," said Marshmallow.

"Oh. God. Potatofeet and Yu Gang are still there!" Throwing the chopsticks on the table, Pumpkin ran towards the alley. "Little Pea, watch your father. Don't let him go outside again," she added.

The alley was full of people rushing back and forth. The wounded were being carried in as more people ran out of the alley into the street.

She could see that the sky was lit up and rounds of gunshots deafened her ears. It was real and those were real bullets, she kept telling herself, but she was so dumbfounded that she could not even comprehend what she was saying.

Then she saw Potatofeet's smashed tea stand and there was no sign of Potatofeet.

She started running and yelling, "Potatofeet! Potatofeet!"

People in the alley were yelling as well, "They started shooting. They are real bullets." "Those bastards! Let's go and fight." "Don't you care about your life? They are real bullets!"

Pumpkin could hear the voices. She understood what they were talking about, but she just kept running.

She saw tanks everywhere. No wonder it felt like an earthquake, she told herself.

Suddenly she felt someone nudging her on the back.

She turned around and found Yu Gang behind her. His eyes were red and swollen and his clothes were stained with blood.

"Auntie, please come with me now. Potatofeet got shot in the leg."

"What!" Her reaction was slow. It took a few seconds for her to comprehend what he meant. It was as if she was caught in a tornado. She was thrown into the air and traveling with the vortex. Then she was suddenly dropped back onto her feet. The world started spinning in front of her. Her sense of reality had been distorted.

It seemed to take Pumpkin and Yu Gang a long time to get Potatofeet home, because the alley was full of wounded people.

As soon as they entered the gate, the others heard the desperate moaning from Potatofeet.

He laid on his father Marshmallow's chest, and his round face was full of tears.

Under the dim light, his thigh was covered with bandages, which were soaked with blood.

Wu Zheng kept applying new bandages around his thin leg.

Pumpkin rushed towards them and knelt down.

"I'm afraid he got shot in the femoral artery," said Wu Zheng, "I tried to call an ambulance but all the roads are blocked by barricades and tanks. There is no way they can get here. I asked Lao Liu to try and get Broomstick and his motorcycle back."

Pumpkin pressed Potatofeet to her chest.

"Mom!" He buried his face into her soft chest like a newborn.

Mrs. Wang bought out more used sheets for Pumpkin to use as bandages. She quickly slammed the door behind her before her four boys could get out. "Stay inside! Don't you see that it is dangerous here?" Then she went to the window where her boys were looking out and pounded on it with their fists.

At the same time, Zhang Ping's shrieking voice and the noise Mrs. Wang generated by shaking the door were, muffled by the popcorn-like sound of gunshots outside.

"What a crazy woman!" Mr. Wang said as he walked toward Potatofeet and the people around him.

Potatofeet had stopped moaning. The glow of life was fading from him. His head drooped down. His hand, which once held his mother's waist tightly, had loosened its grip. His arm slid down to the ground.

"Potatofeet!" Pumpkin cried.

Wu Zheng stopped wrapping his wound.

Little Pea wiped her eyes with a handkerchief.

Marshmallow stood, grinding his teeth. His eyes were full of fire, enough to ignite the bandage around Potatofeet's leg.

"I can't take this anymore! Instead of dying of anger, I would rather die in a battle!" Lao Liu threw away the cigarette butt in his hand, stood up and walked toward the door.

"Let's go!" Pumpkin and Marshmallow followed him.

Mr. Wang stood up, glanced at his wife and followed.

Zhang Ping broke open her door and reciting the communist slogan during the Cultural Revolution, "Hey, forward, forward!" she came out.

She had covered her disheveled hair with a hat and put on a few dabs of make-up on her swollen face without the lipstick. Zhang Ping swept across the yard before anyone else realized that she was free.

She ran in front of four angry people, dancing and singing. She ran over toward the wounded people along the alley and gave them big hugs. "Be tough, comrade! Don't moan! Power comes from the barrels of guns!"

Zhang Ping ran towards the end of the alley, shouting, "Chairman Mao said that 'Power comes from the barrels of guns'. Let's go and fight!"

Zhang Ping walked toward the crowd on the street.

People in the crowd were throwing stones and pebbles towards a slow moving tank.

A soldier wearing a green uniform with a red star on his cap climbed out of the tank looking dazed but he quickly went back into the turret.

The tank began to fire, spraying gunfire at people's feet.

"Don't beat up the soldiers, they are our friends!" Zhang Ping's voice rang out through the crowd. "Our hero Lei Feng said, 'Treat your friends like summer's heat. Treat your enemies like winter's cold!'"

A row of bodies fell in front of Zhang Ping.

She stared at the bloody bodies in front of her and gasped.

Then she saw a flash of bright light ahead of the tanks. Two buses barricading the road were set on fire by people on the street. The beautiful orange light against the night sky suddenly excited her. She jumped, clapping her hands.

The tanks pushed away the wreckage, moving forward slowly one after another.

Besides the tanks, there were military vehicles carrying loudspeakers. They were blaring slogans like, "The people's liberation army loves the capital! We love the people of Beijing." "Soldiers and people are one!"

These lies were emitted into the air, over the bloody bodies on the street and into the crowd.

Angry citizens began throwing stones towards the tanks again.

Suddenly Zhang Ping remembered the bloody fight more than twenty years ago during the Cultural Revolution. She was protected by the gunfire, and she followed her father, stepping over bloody bodies and seizing an enemy vehicle on the street.

"Forward!" She ran toward the tank. She stepped on the dead bodies as though she did not see them. Soon she fell under the gunfire. She joined the rest of the bodies without even knowing.

Lao Liu went over and pulled Zhang Ping's body back to the alley. She was shot three times. Her blood spilled out like running water.

"Zhang Ping." Pumpkin threw herself onto Zhang Ping's body, crying. "Why did you have to die so soon? Why did you have to die so miserably? God, where is the justice?"

Lao Liu pushed Pumpkin away and carried Zhang Ping's body on his shoulders. Blood dripped all over his body and face. He soon looked like a butcher, covered in blood. He squeezed his eyes hard and then tried to open them.

With Zhang Ping's weight on his shoulder, Lao Liu walked slowly toward the moving tanks. The dripping blood created a red trail behind him.

Pumpkin and Marshmallow followed him as though Lao Liu had magic power. Gunshots could be heard nearby.

They marched toward the tanks fearlessly.

As they nearly reached them, one of the military vehicles stopped. A baby-faced soldier, about seventeen years old, crawled out of the tank. His eyes were red and swollen like a mad animal.

"I just... I just want to show this to you!" said Lao Liu. He tried to lift Zhang Ping's body up to the soldier's face.

Tears rolled down Lao Liu's face, dripping down red like blood.

Silence.

"Do you know that you are in Tiananmen Square?"

The soldier shook his head. Lao Liu knew that the soldier was just a boy; he must have been from some small village and he probably did not even know what city he was in.

The soldier was too young to know that in 1949 the People's Liberation Army freed the city from the Guomingdang, the Chinese Nationalist Party, and not a single shot was fired on Tiananmen Square.

The boy soldier did not understand history. Surely, Lao Liu thought, the boy must have understood what he was doing by following the orders he was given.

Lao Liu screamed at him one last time, "Do you know you are shooting your own people?"

The boy soldier stared at Lao Liu blankly.

An angry voice from inside the tank shouted, "Stop arguing with them!"

Like a robot reacting without emotion, the boy crawled back into the tank turret.

A moment later, the tank fired; and in one blast, Lao Liu's head blew apart. His skull broke into pieces. A piece of it landed as far as the railing along the street.

As the frightened Pumpkin and Marshmallow tried to move away from Lao Liu's body, they saw a middle-aged lady suddenly appear in front of the slow-moving tank. Her short hair was tangled and half-covered her face. She wore a white polyester shirt and brown pants. Her fragile body stood there firmly, which showed her determination. While the tank gradually moved toward her, Pumpkin suddenly recognized that she was Lao Liu's wife, Wu Zheng.

"What is she doing there? Let's go and save her. Hey. Wu Zheng, don't be dumb! Come back!" Pumpkin ran toward her, realizing that she might have seen what had happened to her husband.

The tank stopped for a moment, and fired a few shots over her head. She stood there as though she had taken root there.

A soldier jumped off a truck next to the tank, carrying a pack of rope-like things.

As a short stout man, he approached her slowly as though he was afraid of her. When he was two feet away from her, he released the black rope in his hands. It was a two-meter long black leather whip.

The whip was like a snake dancing in the air and hit Wu Zheng's body. She did not move and did not even look at her torturer. Instead, she ran towards him.

"Give me back my husband!" Wu Zheng cried like a wild animal.

The whipping continued. Her white blouse was broken into shreds and was full of bloodstains. Then she caught the whip in her hand. She started pulling at it. With God's power in her hands, she got the whip away from the soldier and started whipping him.

While this was happening, Pumpkin struggled in her husband's embrace. "Let me go! Let me save her!"

"Are you crazy? You are going to be killed. I'm not going to let you go!" His face touched her face, and their tears mixed. This was the most intimate act they had ever shared.

Wu Zheng tightened the whip around the soldier's neck and began strangling him.

Cheers came from the crowd. "Kill him! Kill the bastard!"

The tank started rolling and crushed them both.

The angry people moved over towards the tank.

They threw fire torches and gasoline; the tank caught fire. It blazed in the dark and moonless night.

Everyone cheered as if they were the ghosts in Dante's Inferno as the two soldiers were forced out of the tank.

The soldiers stumbled towards the angry people. As soon as they were away from the blazing tank, they were in the hands of the mob.

They beat them with sticks and metal bars. They spit on them. "Shall we kill them?"

"Of course. Why do you speak for the enemy?"

"They are not our enemies. They don't even know what they are doing."

"What do you mean? They have already killed innocent people. They are criminals." A middle-aged man went over, pulling at the collar of a young man as though he wanted to start a fight.

The soldiers disappeared in the crowd as their bodies were torn to pieces, and they quickly disintegrated through hundreds of angry hands.

Red-eyed people threw body parts back at the burning tank.

They held up their hands in a 'V' sign, until a spray of bullets from another vehicle gunned some of them down.

Others in the crowd dropped down to avoid the gunfire. Marshmallow and Pumpkin fell to the ground, searching for cover.

Pressing his wife to the ground with his own body, Marshmallow protected Pumpkin from the dense gunfire.

The tank stopped firing and ran over the wreckage of the burning barricades.

They kept moving forward.

Some people rose up from the ground, throwing stones and pebbles at the tanks. The insignificant rocks did nothing to stop the tanks.

Pumpkin and Marshmallow got up slowly once the tanks had passed.

"Let's go home," said Marshmallow.

Pumpkin stared at him as though she did not understand. Her round face was covered with blood and her eyes were bulging out. Under different circumstances, she might have been mistaken for a cannibal.

"It's dangerous here. Don't you understand?" Shaking, Marshmallow tried to pull Pumpkin to his chest.

Pumpkin bent down and held onto a dead girl's body, trying to pick it up.

"What do you want to do? She is dead!" Marshmallow realized that Pumpkin was convinced she could help the girl and she could not be swayed.

He helped to lift the body onto his wife's back, hoping she would allow him to lead her back to the safety of their Hudong.

Pumpkin carried the body, and she walked towards the crowd.

"Hey. This way!" yelled Marshmallow. "That's the wrong way!"

Pumpkin did not respond. She passed through the bystanders along the street and walked directly toward the moving tank.

"Hey. Please stop her!" Marshmallow ran towards her and grabbed her blouse from behind, but Pumpkin's will was so strong that she started pulling him forward.

Several people came over to stop them.

Pumpkin heaved, allowing the girl's body to fall to the ground. She vomited and turned towards her husband; crying. She fell into his arms and Marshmallow kissed her vomit-covered face as though he would never let her go.

"Let's go!" He caught her hand and ran toward the alley.

The alley was full of death. Most of the people there were either dead or wounded. Occasionally, one could hear the yelling and moaning of their friends or relatives nearby.

When Pumpkin and Marshmallow walked into the yard, they found it was full of people busily tending to the wounded.

They looked at each other as though saying, "Can we still deal with this? Have we not had enough?"

The yard had temporarily been turned into a hospital. People in urgent need of treatment were being treated without any anesthetic. Their agonized cries made the place seem more like a torture chamber than a hospital. Still, the makeshift clinic seemed to be working efficiently.

A dozen wounded protesters were lying on the concrete floor under blood soaked blankets. A doctor and a nurse, wearing white coats and hats, walked bristly from one patient to another.

As Pumpkin walked towards her door, she noticed that a table stood among the wounded and the dead.

On top of the table was a bowl of steamed buns, a bowl of soup and three plates of half-eaten food, abandoned by the people who dined on them.

Those people were gone though; whether they were dead or alive, Pumpkin was not sure of.

CHAPTER 20

Baiyun and Dagong were surprised to find Yumei sitting alone in one of the tents by the monument, singing along with guitar music from a nearby tent.

She wore a red sweater, black rayon skirt and red lipstick. She looked beautiful and clean, except for the dirty athletic shoes on her feet.

She was lying on a pile of blankets like a sleeping beauty.

"Hey. Yumei. Why are you alone? Where is Longfe?"

"He went home. He promised his family," said Yumei, still lying there. Then she rubbed her eyes and sat up. "I'm waiting here to die!" She pointed at her skirt and said, "See. I have already chosen my death clothes."

"Come one. You look like you are trying to get a new boyfriend," said Baiyun.

Yumei jumped up and squeezed Baiyun's neck. "Baiyun, what happened to you? You have really become a mean girl!" Then she looked at Dagong and said, "You must be teaching her."

"Me? Don't you know that I'm a nice man?" said Dagong. Then he suddenly jumped onto Yumei's back and got her arms off Baiyun's neck.

He started twisting Yumei's arms behind her back.

Baiyun was stunned to see Dagong and Yumei play fighting each other.

"Comrades, anyone who wants to stay until the last moment can come and pledge with us at the monument," Longfe said, coming over to gather people.

"Longfe. Why are you here?" Yumei was surprised to see Longfe. "I thought that you were at home with your parents."

"I escaped. I couldn't just let you stay here and hold the fort."

Looking at Yumei's fragile frame, Longfe could not help hugging her.

"Let's go!" Longfe waved at Baiyun and Dagong.

Thousands of students were gathered in front of the monument and had pledged to die for the cause of greater freedom and democracy. They stood by the makeshift tents and raised their right hands.

Longfe spoke the pledge. "I swear, for the democratic movement and the prosperity of the country, for our motherland not to be overturned by a few conspirators, for our one billion people not to be killed in the white terror, that I am willing to defend Tiananmen, and defend the republic with my young life. Our hands can be broken, our blood can be shed, but we will not lose the People's Square. We will fight to the end with the last person."

During the movement, Longfe became a confident leader.

Baiyun's eyes were wet. She turned her head toward Dagong. His face was somber, but peaceful.

Baiyun could not understand why, even during such a crucial moment, Dagong could not show any emotion. Either he did not care, or he was incapable of showing it.

"Hey. It's your last chance to have your picture taken." Li Yan came over with a camera in her hands. She never seemed to run out of energy.

"I'm here." Yumei stood next to Baiyun and crossed her arms in front of her chest as though she was a warrior.

Baiyun tried her best to follow her.

"Hey. You guys have to pay beforehand," said Li Yan, like a businesswoman.

"What? I can't believe you! Is money more important than your life?" argued Yumei.

"Well, not necessarily. But if I survive this week, maybe I will become a famous photographer by selling all these valuable photos I took here." Li Yan shook her big head and smiled.

"There is still one optimist here," said Dagong. "Why not?" He gave her a five-yen bill.

Then he grabbed Yumei and Baiyun, one on each side of him. He wrapped his arms around the girls tightly, with his head slightly tilted toward Baiyun.

"Ready and ... smile." Li Yan raised the camera.

"Why do we have to smile today? Why do we have to pretend to smile?" said Yumei.

"Okay." Li Yan gave in. "Do whatever you want, but you'd better think it over. These could be historical events. Think about the influence your pictures might have."

"I'm happy. I will smile," said Baiyun.

"I know you will. You have turned into a teenager since the movement started." Yumei stared at Baiyun in disbelief.

Then she turned to Dagong. "Dagong? How about you? I know you will go home soon and chicken out. I know what your generation experienced - but cowardly."

"Hey. I'm a tall man, I can stay calm under any circumstances."

As they were arguing, Li Yan clicked the camera.

"Do it again. I wasn't ready yet," shouted Yumei.

"I assure you that you will look good in my pictures. You are very photogenic," said Li Yan.

"How about a photo of just Baiyun and me?" asked Dagong.

While he and Baiyun snuggled together, Li Yan clicked the shutter.

"How about a kissing one?" Li Yan asked.

Dagong turn his head and first kissed Baiyun on her cheek and then on her lips.

"Wow. If you go any further, I will have to close my eyes. Stop it there." The shutter clicked, and Li Yan took this intimate picture.

It even surprised Baiyun that she had gotten used to displaying intimacy in public.

She thought that she would be more embarrassed, but she wasn't somehow.

At this moment of life and death, she had bigger issues to worry about or she just simply didn't care anymore.

Yumei fell back down onto the blankets on the ground, crawled over to turn on the tape player.

Baiyun and Dagong sat next to her, and started singing along to the music.

There is a river in the Far East.
It is called the Yangtze River.
There is a river in the Far East.
It is called the yellow river.
Although I haven't seen the beauty of Yangtze,
I often explore the river in my dreams.
Although I have not heard the roar of the Yellow River,
I hear it in my dreams.

"You guys are competing with Hou Degong!" Wenjing strolled over and she was limping.

She hunched her shoulders over with her hands in her pockets, even in this warm weather. She still wore a pair of glasses. Her round face narrowed a little after several days of the hunger strike.

"Hey. Professor, you are still here?" asked Yumei.

"I'm leaving. I'm not crazy like you guys, staying here forever," said Wenjing.

"Yes. You should be at the American embassy by now," said Yumei, teasing her little. "You should go there and kiss their feet to let you out of the country."

"I'm not going to join the crowd now. I'm going in the next few days, when it is not so crowded."

"You go! You go! I'm ready to die." Yumei rolled over and buried her face in the blanket, weeping, "I wish my mother knew I was here and that I died as a hero."

"Yumei. Think of it this way. You are a top student in a top university. If you survive, you'll be able to contribute more to your country than by being dead."

"No. I feel I belong to here. I can't leave because I have already planted my roots here in the last few weeks," said Yumei as she calmed down a little.

"I'm not sure I agree with Wenjing," Dagong joined in and he was still as calm as a stone. "I used to think that way. I used to value myself more than our country, but if everyone were like me, we wouldn't have a movement like this. Now we are on the verge of victory, so why not stay until the end?"

"Victory? The government has weapons. They're coming to wipe us out like ants. I don't think it's very wise to sacrifice so many brilliant students," yelled Wenjing as though nobody was listening to her. Her usual pale face was as red as an apple.

"Really, they're coming to kill us?" Baiyun finally said something.

Her mind was in a state of confusion. On one hand, she wished this demonstration would go on forever so she would not have to go back to school, back to studying, or to go back home to face her mother's boyfriend Lao Zheng, who always seemed to desire her, or to see her father, who was turning more into an animal each day.

That world seemed so cold and far and far away. She had started to consider the vast Tiananmen Square as her home, the best home she ever had.

On the other hand, if staying meant death, she thought she was ready. She wanted to be with her friends, especially Dagong, even if it meant being run over by tanks.

"Don't listen to me. I'm always the pessimist. Death has never frightened me. I'm always ready for it. But the issue is whether it is worthwhile to die," said Wenjing seriously.

"I think there are two possibilities." Another student joined in. "One is that the citizens will prevent the troops from coming in, and secondly, if troops do come into the Square, they would simply send us back to our schools. Maybe they will just push us and shoot us with some rubber bullets to scare us away."

"What do you think, Dagong?" asked Yumei.

Dagong stared into the distance and did not answer.

Baiyun nudged him. "What happened to you?"

He buried his head between his knees, and still did not say anything.

Then he raised his head and said, "I don't know. Anything could happen."

"Let's not worry about it. It is useless to be worried now."

Everyone became silent.

Then someone started humming the 'Internationale' along with the loud speaker in the distance. Others joined in.

After so many days of malnutrition they lost some of their youthful enthusiasm and sense of invincibility; their voices sounded somber, almost suicidal, especially Yumei's voice.

The Square was very noisy. Besides the many student-controlled PA systems, which were broadcasting the 'Internationale' or Rock & Roll music constantly, there were government-controlled loudspeakers, which were repeatedly broadcasting the same warning message: "Now the situation is grave. A small number of thugs are spreading rumors..."

"The government is farting again," said Yumei.

"I hope it won't blow everything away with its smell."

Rather than blowing everything away, the opposite happened.

Changan Street had emptied since the enactment of Martial Law, but it was suddenly full of people again.

The people, mostly citizens of Beijing, had left their homes and streamed into the street on bicycles and on foot to help protect the students.

"What do you want to do?" Dagong looked into Baiyun's eyes.

"Stay here. Right, Yumei?" She pushed Yumei, who fell back under the blanket again.

"I don't know." Yumei murmured.

Li Yan came over, who was still very energetic and was followed to the tents by the loud sound of motorcycles." Baiyun, your mother is here!"

As Meiling jumped off her motorcycle, she called to Baiyun.

Baiyun ran towards her and held her pair of hands in leather gloves.

Now wearing a hat on her permed black hair, Meiling seemed to have lost some weight. Her freckled face was thin; and her belly had disappeared. Although there were some wrinkles on her face, her trimmed body made her look younger. "Baiyun. My brave girl, still holding onto the Square."

Lao Zheng came over and gave Baiyun a handshake, which almost made her cry.

Lao-Zheng said, "Yes. It seems safe. No one believes the Government's warning. People are getting out again." Baiyun looked straight at Lao Zheng; she no longer felt embarrassed by him.

"That's why we are here." Lao Zheng said seriously. "Why don't you tell her?" He nudged Meiling.

"The shooting has already started"

Baiyun was startled by the news. She looked at Meiling first and then she turned towards Dagong and Yumei, and back to Meiling again.

"You can tell the students about this news later," said Meiling as though she had read her daughter's mind.

Baiyun signaled for Dagong to come over. "Mom, this is my...."

She looked at Dagong who was approaching them, for an answer, but Dagong was silent, while staring at Meiling as though trying to retrieve a memory from long ago.

Meiling looked startled too.

After shaking hands, they backed away from each other.

"Meiling, you still look the same," said Dagong.

"You. Dagong. Is that you?" Meiling edged toward him slowly. "Ha-ha. You rascal!" She jumped at him and gave him a hug.

"What? You know each other?" Baiyun's eyelids were wide open.

"How have you been?" Without listening to her daughter, Meiling said to Dagong. "I hardly can tell it's you. Maybe it's just your beard." She touched his brushy beard. "But it looks good on you. You used to have mustache, correct? But this looks better."

"Oh. Thank you. You know, I haven't spoken with you since I left my position at the Zoo... I couldn't..."

"But at least you should've written to me."

"I got married and had a son. You know, it's a long story," he sighed.

"I see." She looked at Baiyun, turned back to Dagong and gave him a questioning look.

Dagong answered Meiling's unspoken concern. "Don't worry. I will take care of Baiyun."

"Okay. I will have to go. Nice to see you all."

Then Meiling turned to Baiyun, "Baiyun."

"Mother."

"I have to go to some other places to spread the news. You can decide whether to stay or to go. Just be careful."

"How about you?" Baiyun looked at her mother, her eyes full of tears.

Meiling turned to the rest of 'The Flying Tiger Brigade'. "Aren't you having fun yet? Let's rock & roll!"

Meiling waved her arms and drove away on her loud, thumping motorcycle.

Looking in the direction where Meiling disappeared, Baiyun's heart sunk. She felt like she had lost something.

Dagong came over and put his hand on her shoulder.

Baiyun gazed up at him, and he in turn stared down at her. There was a wall between them now, but it was not a good time to talk about it.

Baiyun yelled to the others, "The shooting has started at Mushidi!"

"Oh. Really? Goddamn those bastards."

Dagong suddenly jumped up. "Okay, Baiyun. Tell me, what do you want to do? If you want to stay here, let's stay here and fight to the end!"

Baiyun smiled. She was happy to see Dagong had gone back to his old toughness. She liked it.

"Okay. Let's stay," said Baiyun firmly.

With possible death approaching, she felt fearless. She was startled to feel this way and it could have been the camaraderie between everybody around her, that made her feel tough-minded.

"Let's go to the headquarters to see what is going on," said Dagong.

As they passed by the tent, they saw Yumei was still lying there, looking depressed.

"Yumei. We are going to see what is going on at headquarters. Do you want to come along?

"That's fine. You two can go. I will just stay here and die alone."

"Come on. We are going to have some adventure." Baiyun could not believe that she said that.

"Adventure? You must be crazy like your mom." Then she sat up. "I'm waiting for Longfe. Where is he?" She opened her arms to the sky.

"I don't know. Maybe he is busy organizing," said Baiyun.

The headquarters near the monument was very noisy. The student broadcast was blaring, telling the story of brave Beijing citizens blocking the troops from coming to the Square all over the city, building barricades, exhorting the troops, and some dying under the gunfire. People were jammed in a circle.

Dagong went on to find out what was going on.

"Fighting has already started at Mushidi. They are going there to help," said a middle-aged woman.

The crowd gradually opened a passageway. A row of hefty students, all wearing white headbands, marched out.

They were armed with iron bars, wrenches and wooden clubs. Some of them carried sharpened wooden sticks.

They were joined by hundreds of bicyclers, shouting "Down with Li Peng! Long Live the People!"

An open truck, packed with young men and women, also wheeled past. They chanted, "One, two, three, stop the army!"

"It looks like everything is still alive," said Dagong, sounding energetic and excited.

He felt relieved that he finally realized who Meiling was and that Baiyun finally knew about his association with her.

Baiyun, on the other hand, felt uneasy. Knowing Dagong's past relationship with Meiling had added an additional complication to their relationship. Dagong suddenly became much older in her eyes and the feeling of possibly becoming her mother's rival made her a little nervous.

"Let's go. Let's see what's going on!"

Holding hands, they joined the crowd on Changan Avenue.

Tens of thousands of bicyclers filled the six traffic lanes.

Random shouts of "Down with Li Peng!" and "Long live the people!" mingled with the continuing ringing of bicycle bells.

The further they went, the more roadblocks they encountered. The barricades were heavy concrete bars, steel guardrails and garbage cans.

Many bicyclers had to lift their bicycles up to pass the barricades. Hurdling over the barricades, Baiyun and Dagong looked at each other and smiled.

"Mother used to be a hurdler in college," said Baiyun.

"Yes. She told me about it before. I guess you must be very good at it too."

"Good at what?" Baiyun challenged.

"Good at everything." Dagong surrendered.

"Do you mean better?" Baiyun marched further.

"Um...Yes. Look." Dagong held onto her shoulder, "What happened between your mother and me is over. It was a short relationship more than twenty years ago. That's in the past. Don't burden yourself with it anymore."

"Okay. What else should I worry about then?"

Dagong frowned. Obviously, Baiyun meant his wife Zhang Ping.

"We can talk about it later. Let's survive this first."

"Let's survive this first!" Baiyun reciprocated.

They ran ferociously past the slow moving crowd.

As they approached Xidan, people stood by the side of the road and stopped moving completely.

"Stop, Baiyun. Be careful!"

Dagong pulled Baiyun to a side street where people pushed as though they were trying to hide behind each other. Baiyun could feel a sense of panic floating in the air. It was getting dark and people were unusually quiet.

"Look. There are tanks."

The bright headlights of the army carriers were blinding. Tanks ran over or broke through the barricades and were approaching slowly.

People began throwing stones, bricks and broken pieces of steel railing at the tanks. Obviously, it did not stop the tanks, but people were not deterred.

They threw more things at the tanks, including burning torches and bottles stuffed with flaming rags. Some of the tanks caught fire.

People cheered as the flames burned.

"What are they throwing at the tanks?" Baiyun was just as happy as everyone else was, but she was puzzled.

"Molotov cocktails."

A tall slender young man with long hair showed Baiyun a brown tall bottle with a greasy rag sticking out of it. "We just fill these beer bottles with gasoline and kerosene and light them. We made them in our factory." He smiled proudly and leapt forward. "Get out, butcher." He shouted toward a stopped, blazing tank.

The fire mixed with the smoke shot towards the sky, which made the Square look like a battleground or a New Year's Eve party with too many fireworks.

The soldier climbed from the burning tank; his uniform was in flames. He jumped to the ground and rolled.

People ran towards him and screamed as though they were going to eat him alive.

"He is dead. He is dead three times over," said an old man next to Baiyun.

Then more people ran towards a tank that was trapped by a concrete barricade.

The tank lurched back and forth and then stopped. The grounding of the tank's treads against concrete generated a shower of sparks like welding. A young man in shorts and a tank top jumped onto the top of the tank, hammering the turret with a steel bar, and others followed.

They first used a Molotov cocktail to set the tank on fire. The young man on top of the tank laid a blanket soaked with gasoline over the turret. The crowd was pounding the tank to force the driver to get out.

Looking at Baiyun's radiant face near the blazing fire, Dagong asked, "Are you afraid?"

"No. It's exciting!" Baiyun jumped against Dagong and hugged him.

"Let's join them," said Dagong.

Just when they were about to dive into the crowd, beams of light leaped through the sky, followed by several whistling sounds.

"They've started shooting." Dagong jumped on top of Baiyun and pushed her down.

"What?" Baiyun was bending down and lying against the wall of a building along the street. She was shivering violently. It was the first time in her life she ever heard real bullets flying in the sky.

People swarmed back to the side streets. Their yelling and screaming mixed with the sound of gunfire. Some struggled in the crowd to find their loved ones; some tried to get out, as some helped to save others.

"They're real bullets...They're shooting people... I saw a boy shot in the head, he's dead...," said an old woman, tears smeared her face.

"Baiyun. Are you okay?" Dagong tried to get her up.

She buried her head into Dagong's chest, crying. "It's terrible. It's terrible."

"Okay. Okay. It looks like they haven't shot people on the sidewalks yet." Dagong patted Baiyun. "I think we should run back to the Square to tell them what's going on. Are you ready? We have to run fast."

Baiyun nodded.

They began running hand in hand down the side streets.

It was a moonless night. The Square was dark and frightening. Fire from the burning vehicles and buses flickered in the distance. The smoke in the sky had further decreased the visibility. Bullets whistled through the sky intermittently. Tanks stopped people. People ran back and forth around the center of Tiananmen Square, shouting and cheering each time a tank caught fire.

Baiyun and Dagong ran along the trees on the sidewalk. Some trees were burning while the spectators occupied some of the other trees.

Frightened people escaped from the streets, trying to find a hiding place, but most of the larger buildings along the streets were closed. They held onto each other tightly.

"Ah. My shoes! Dagong," yelled Baiyun as her shoes were kicked away by the crowd and she was left with bare feet.

"What happened?"

They stopped and soon were being pushed off the sidewalk by the crowd.

"Put mine on," said Dagong.

"No, they are too big. Let's just take a break."

They sat under a tree, a safe distance away from the fighting. They could still see people cheering, clanking metal pots and pans. In the distance, the tanks inched forward.

Baiyun was so tired that she instantly fell on Dagong's lap. Dagong started kissing her hair, and then her ears.

Baiyun turned her head around so his lips could reach hers.

Without thinking about it, he unbuttoned her floral cotton shirt and touched her braless chest.

Baiyun felt her body dissolve under Dagong's embrace as the chaos of the battle in the distance melted away. She wished so much that the moment would last a little longer, but Dagong stopped.

"Maybe we should go and see whether we could help with something," said Dagong.

"It seems that they are holding up the tanks." Still breathing heavily with the excitement, Baiyun said.

"But the tanks are not backing off. I don't know how long they can be held off. Let's go. At least we would be with our fellow students and I would like to offer my apartment as a hiding place if we decide to withdraw."

"I couldn't go to your apartment," said Baiyun with uncertainty.

"Of course, you must come. Hurry, we are almost there."

When they were across the intersection to the Square, the gunfire suddenly became more intense and continuous.

Tanks seemed to be coming from all directions. People were running wild like animals being chased by hunters.

The Square was half-empty. Besides some makeshift tents scattered around and garbage, very few people were left.

Dagong ran into a tent and woke the person inside who were sleeping.

"Where is everyone?" asked Dagong.

The student rubbed his eyes as though he was awakening from a dream. He pointed his finger to the monument. "They are over there."

As they approached the monument, it was very quiet. Hundreds of people surrounded the monument, their heads lowered.

They were mourning someone. They were so quiet that even the gradually approaching gunshots did not disturb them.

Then the strains of Mozart's 'Requiem' filled the air. It played from the speakers of the student-run radio station. Many in the crowd hummed along unconsciously.

"Who are you mourning?" asked Baiyun of a young man next to her.

"Oh. You don't know them. They are 'The Flying Tiger Brigade'." He stretched his arms and held his hands down with two fists. "They rode motorcycles. You know, that woman who is fifty years old, although she looks thirty."

"Oh. What happened to her?" Baiyun's eyes widened.

"She got shot on her way here from Mushidi." The student sighed.

"Mother!" Baiyun screamed and pushed people away violently.

"Baiyun. Baiyun." Dagong followed her.

As shocked as she was, he did not know what to say.

They finally reached the front of the crowd. Meiling's body lay on the top of the steps. Lao Zheng sat next to her, holding her head and crying.

Still in her leather jacket that was now ragged and stained, Meiling looked peaceful. Her eyes were closed, her cheeks sunk down, her head-full of thick black hair still gleaming, even her thick energetic eyebrows curled down as though she was having a nice dream.

Baiyun rushed over and threw herself onto Meiling's body, wailing.

She held Meiling's neck, which was wrapped with bloody bandages. She cried, "Mother, why did you leave me so soon? I have a lot to tell you."

The crowd was suddenly quiet again.

A student leader came in front of the microphone, "As we are mourning the dead, we should ask ourselves what we should do to continue the work she had not completed. Now I would like to share a story with everyone…There are a group of ants, one point one billion of them and one day there was a huge fire at the foot of their anthill. The ants knew that their family could only be saved if they went down the hill, so they held on to each other and rolled down the hill together. Some of ants were killed, but many more were saved. The committee has decided that we will all walk out of here together. Soldiers may fire at us; tanks may roll over us, but as long as we are together, we are strong."

The light went off suddenly and then the students formed a line. They marched across the Square in the dark with their arms locked together. They were singing the 'Internationale'.

Lao Zheng carried Meiling's body on his back, leading the march.

Dagong and Baiyun locked their arms marching along. Baiyun was no longer afraid, because dying with so many students and friends would be heroic.

Meiling lived without a fear of death, and in that, Baiyun took after her. Even in Baiyun's deep grief, there was excitement.

The sky turned light as they walked towards the east and through the passageway, the army had opened up for them to evacuate.

As they left the Square behind them, the east side of the sky turned red.

It was not just around the edges. The entire eastern sky was red. The place was soaked in blood.

EPILOGUE

It was an unusually gloomy day in June.

Dagong and Baiyun strolled through Tiananmen Square. They left their bicycles behind at the Xidan Market, about half a mile away.

With her hands in the pockets of her red windbreaker, Baiyun walked one meter behind Dagong. Her long straight black hair gleamed under the dim sunlight. Her face was solemn, yet her occasional sighs showed that she was holding back her emotions.

The Square was still heavily guarded, especially near the Forbidden City.

Armed soldiers wearing green uniforms stood in front of the maroon walls of the Forbidden City as though they were rows of evergreen trees.

Since tourists were very few, the Square was still scrubbed clean. Burned buses and shattered military vehicles were towed away soon after the Massacre.

The flags along the reviewing balcony of the Forbidden City flapped in the wind; they generated hollow, alien sounds, like hundreds of suffering souls murmuring in the distance.

Baiyun followed Dagong. She appeared to be a traditional subservient Chinese woman, walking several steps behind him, but that was not the case.

'Martial Law' prevented them from strolling shoulder to shoulder.

Dagong complained to her for the third time: "I have to turn my head around every five seconds, literally every five seconds to see if you are all right. Just in case you might be kidnapped or seduced by one of those good looking soldiers!"

He kept walking; if he stopped to talk to Baiyun, it could be seen as evidence of assembly.

"Soldiers, air-headed scare-crows. Who needs them?" Baiyun snapped back.

Then she looked toward the Forbidden City and the Golden Water Bridge in front of Chairman Mao's portrait.

Her steps got shorter; she stopped momentarily and stared at the bridge.

It was the first time she visited the Square since the morning of June 4, 1989.

"Who knows? You always go for the handsome ones." Expecting a playful blow to his back from Baiyun, Dagong walked faster.

He was wrong; Baiyun did not react at all.

She stared at the Forbidden City and the Golden Water Bridge, her mind full of images.

Oh, where was that head? During the Massacre, she saw a smashed head on top of the middle pillar of the bridge's right railing. Poor head, it seemed like many bullets had pierced it. It sat on the top of the pillar as though it wanted to reclaim its dignity. There was nothing left in the skull; it was just a black hole.

She imagined hundreds of skulls approaching from the far side of the arched bridge. Tears poured out of their eye sockets as they were swept forward in a river of blood.

She squeezed her eyes shut and turned around, then stared back at the immense empty Square.

Her eyes rested on the place where her mother's body lay fallen. The thought made her recoil.

During the night of the Massacre, with the Square full of people, they all locked arms to form a human barricade. They thought they could deflect the bullets and stop the tanks.

Then came the bullets and the tanks, and the blood and the skulls.

They had to retreat and narrowly escaped the final 'Death Ring' where hundreds, even thousands of people had lost their lives.

As Baiyun ran away from Tiananmen Square, from the place she had made her home during the previous month, she felt a sense of loss. It was not just the loss of her mother, the failure of the movement. It was the loss of focus, the loss of her sense of purpose in life. After all of that, where would her life begin?

After Meiling's memorial service, Lao Zheng came to talk to Baiyun.

"It's so sad that your mother died. I'm very sorry, Baiyun." Lao Zheng had said, wrapping his arm around Baiyun and squeezing her. "Since your mother has died, who else can take care of you?"

Lao Zheng held Baiyun against him. She was too weak to resist, although his manner, his cigarette and the alcohol smell of his leather jacket annoyed her. "Are you going to marry me?" He asked and touched his lips to her forehead.

"No. No!" Baiyun broke away.

He grinned and moved towards her. "There's no hurry. It just takes a little time."

"Oh..." Remembering, Baiyun moaned.

She covered her face with her hands and ran toward the Golden Water Bridge. She stretched her arms, as though she wanted to hold her mother and all of those who lost their lives during the Massacre.

Baiyun's bizarre behavior puzzled Dagong; she was already too far away before he realized that she was heading in a different direction from him.

He hurried towards Baiyun and saw her resting her head against the marble pillar of the bridge railing.

"Baiyun. Let's go."

Then he caught a glimpse of a soldier striding towards them. "Hey, what's going on?"

Dagong was on alert.

"Stay away from the bridge! It's closed during Martial Law." The soldier shouted at them.

Dagong ran towards Baiyun. He tried to pull her away from the bridge.

"No assembly allowed under Martial law." The soldier put his hand on his rifle.

"Let's go." Dagong grabbed Baiyun's arm. "Come on. This has gone too far. For god's sake, don't you give a damn about your life?"

Baiyun locked her arms around the pillar. Looking down to the moat, she saw her face reflected in it; a blurred, distorted image in the rippling water. Her eyes were swollen, her hair tousled.

She had not slept much lately and had not been successful in keeping Lao Zheng away from her. Something in him made her like him, which frightened her.

Then her mother's face appeared, excruciatingly twisted. "Baiyun, how can you do this to me? He's mine! He's mine!" Baiyun saw her struggling in boiling water and a shot of steam swallowed her.

Lao Zheng's leering face emerged in the stream. He grinned, winked and waved at her.

Then there was the face of Dagong, his old, pale and frozen face, his eyes emitting a cold light. That was the face of Dagong when she first met him, the face which had been bitten, punched and had become hard as stone. Baiyun had melted his face with love but it was not enough; it hardened again in spite of her.

The moat was filled with blood from the people who fell into the water during the Massacre. The officials fished the bodies out, but they could not remove the blood from the water. The moat was the witness.

"Comrade, you have two choices. You either leave here or die. It's Martial Law. Anyone who disobeys will be executed."

Dagong leapt forward. He pulled Baiyun to his chest. "Let's go, please."

"Did you hear me?" The soldier shouted.

"Yes. Please. We will go in a second."

"No. Let her leave by herself."

"Comrade, please. She's crazy."

"I'm not crazy." Baiyun said firmly.

What was the meaning of living in a cold grave, a dead volcano? She wanted to go to a place where birds sang, angels danced and she could breathe freely.

After giving the Forbidden City a farewell gaze, she made up her mind.

"Okay, you have five seconds to get off this bridge. Five, four, three..."

Dagong struggled to free Baiyun from the pillar as the soldier counted back to one.

He opened fire. They fell onto the marble bridge as they clung tightly onto each other. Their blood ran together and soaked the marble. It created a stain, which resembled an angel.

ABOUT THE AUTHOR

Born and raised in Beijing, China, Lisa Zhang Wharton is a graduate of Peking University and University of Minnesota.

She is an engineer by education and an author by avocation.

She has previously published several short stories about life in China and the United States in various literary magazines.

Her short story "My Uncle" won a second prize in a WICE sponsored Paris Writer's Workshop.

"Last Kiss in Tiananmen Square" is her first full-length novel.

She lives in St. Paul, Minnesota with her husband and son.

Don't miss Lisa Zhang Whartons' new novel,

CHINESE LOLITA

Available 2012 in paperback from Fantasy Island Book Publishing.

Turn the page to read the opening chapter...

CHINESE LOLITA

Coming 2012

It was a Sunday morning. Mother said she was leaving for work. Father hollered "You goddamn woman, get out of here. Go, stay with your fucking boyfriend. You all get out of here, get out of my house!"

Father had just awakened. His eyes were still fogged. He sat on the bed, meditated for a while, and then stood up. He stumbled a few steps toward the door and poked his head out of his room.

"Meihua, come back. Who said you could go?" He caught me before I slipped out the door. "Go to the kitchen and see if the garbage needs to be emptied. Goddamn shit! Why do you always have to be reminded?" Waving a filthy athletic shoe in his hand, he stared at me with his half-open, beady eyes. It seemed he might throw the shoe at my head if I did not obey him. I went to the kitchen and did as I was told.

"Where are you going?" Father saw me put on my tight nylon sweater, which showed my two small breasts, and a few dabs of blush on my round face.

"I'm going to work!" I said, and I slammed the door behind me.

It was a cold winter day. The sun moved slowly from behind the white clouds, like a shy girl. Water from melting ice was dripping from the roof. "Dita, dita." It sounded so crisp. With slightly softening soil under my feet, I opened the metal buttons on my grey down-coat and untied the blue wool scarf from my face. I breathed deeply and let the clean air enter my nostrils and flow into my lungs. What a beautiful day! I wanted to cry out. Everything was going exactly as I had planned. Father was right about mother meeting her boyfriend. But he did not know my secret. I was going to see one of mother's boyfriends too, of course a different one. I used to call him "Uncle".

It was eight years since I had last seen Uncle Weiming. I had lost track of him completely, but I was quite sure that he was still working at the same place. People in China do not move until they scuff a hole deep enough to bury themselves in. Therefore, what should I do if I wanted to visit him? Just go to the factory? Like the old saying says: if you want to go north, just follow the North Star. In this case I followed my instinct.

Sitting on the bus, I gazed at the trees that passed by so fast that I wished the bus would slow down. Questions kept going through my mind. What was I doing here? Visiting mother's old lover who had disappeared eight years ago? Begging a thirty-five year old married man to be my father while I was old enough to be his lover? Asking him to be my sister Mingming's father again when Mingming did not even know he existed? It was like I was trying to pick up an old rotten melon. My only accomplishment could be to soil my hands.

But in the last couple of weeks, a memory kept haunting me.

It was in 1976, a few weeks after Chairman Mao died. At an early afternoon, Uncle wandered into our one-story red brick apartment without knocking and sat down on a chair by the dining table. Father, who had used to mother's varieties of friends, nodded stiffly and walked out of the door.

"Uncle!" Having not seen him in two weeks, I was excited. Uncle looked at me and did not respond. "I'll get Mom for you!" I went in front of Mom's bedroom where door was shut closed. "Mom, Uncle is here." I knocked.

"Yes, just a minute." In a while mother strolled out with a cigarette in her mouth. She closed the bedroom door (where she had a visitor) and sat next to Uncle. They both kept silent for a while.

"Got someone new?" Uncle directed his chin toward mother's closed bedroom.

"It's none of your business."

"You pick up fast. Let me say this, if I may. I know who he is. He is a notorious asshole."

"OKAY!" Mother stood up, ran into her bedroom and rushed back with a paper box in her hand. She opened the box and smacked the whole box of photos of her and Uncle onto Uncle's face. "Get out of here, I don't need you anymore! You'd better go back to your pretty young girlfriend!"

Uncle rose up and strode out of the door.

"Uncle, don't go! Uncle, come back!" I chased him and burst into tears.

From then on, laughter and happiness had disappeared from my life. My heart along with those memories had become frozen until now. There had been enough chaos at home. My quiet, hard-working nature had pleased mother and father. I had become such a useful child for them. Gradually I had taken over the household. I cooked, I shopped and I even managed the money. When mother had a problem, she would complain to me; when father was hungry, he would ask me to make something for him to eat. I had been used to the life and felt proud for the responsibilities until I went to college. My vision for life suddenly changed. I realized people did laugh and joke in life; life did not just consist of constant working. I felt incompetent. I needed help. But who could help me? Uncle, the long disappearing Uncle suddenly came back into my memory. "Go to see him. Go to see him." A voice was telling me.

The sun hid behind a cloud for a moment after I got off the bus. Bicyclists, wearing tight blue jeans and red or green down-coats, mingled with the slow moving trolleybuses on the street. The riders shrugged their shoulders. They tried to shrink into their jackets as much as possible to be sheltered from the cold wind. Bags of groceries on both sides of the bicycle handle bars bounced against the wheels. A gust of wind blew into my clothes. I shivered. I snapped closed all the buttons on my down coat, pulled up the zipper as well, and wrapped my scarf around my face.

While walking toward the factory, I felt my heart beating faster. What was I going to say? Uncle's involvement with my mother had not brought him good luck. Seven years ago he had been sentenced to two years community service, while mother served two years in prison for reading Western books and having an extramarital affair. Maybe he was sweeping the floor, or cleaning bathrooms now. The Deng Xiaoping government could not immediately resolve millions of cases like that. Besides, it was not even a political case. My visit could cause him more trouble.

The dull-colored factory building gradually appeared in front of me. Although it was just a one-story, flat-roofed warehouse, it seemed as big as a mountain. A white board painted with the words "Beijing Automobile Parts Factory" was hung on the one of the pillars of the gate, glowing under the sun. I took out a piece of toilet paper in my pocket and wrote down the address. Yes, I had arrived, I said to myself, as cold sweat icily ran down my back.

"Hey, girl, do you need any help?" Like a ghost, a little old man suddenly materialized in front of me.

"I want to ... want to see Wang Meiling." I stuttered. In the panic, I told him my mother's name.

"Who?" After returning to his little station next to the factory gate, the guard glanced at me over the top of his glasses and blinked his raisin eyes.

I did not answer him instead I stared.

"Oh, I know who you are talking about. She's not here anymore. She...she...was arrested years ago." Then he leaned closer to me across the windowsill, widening his lids. "Hey, girl, do you know what kind of crime she has committed? If it were a political crime, the new government by now probably would have pardoned her. But she committed both political and sexual crimes." Suddenly he extended his neck out of the window and spit onto the ground. "To tell the truth,

I hate to dirty my mouth. I doubt if she's ever going to be pardoned. Stay away from her!"

I could feel my face burning down over my neck. I wanted to dig a hole on the ground to duck into. When I was just about to escape, I caught a glimpse of some uniformed workers passing the gate. One of them might have been Uncle.

"Uncle!" I ran toward them.

"Stop! Where is your visitor's pass?" The guard jumped out of the station, arms akimbo. His eyes searched through my body. "Oh, I know who you are. You're that dirty woman's kid. I can tell from your face. Get out of here, shit!"

I turned around, and ran away as fast as I could. When I got home, my heart was still pounding like a drum. The next day I wrote a letter to Uncle at the factory.

Dear Uncle,

It has been so many years since you last saw me. I do not know whether you still remember me or not; or if you do, whether you would still recognize me on the street. I am a college student now. I passed the college entrance exam and entered Beijing University. I was the number one student in my high school class and I think you would be proud of me.

Things have hardly changed since you left. Do you still remember my sister Mingming? She is a very intelligent girl. If given a little push, she could become an outstanding student. But that has not happened. My parents are unwilling to give her any attention.

Recently, mother has revealed to me that you are actually Mingming's father. I am not surprised, but I wish you were kind enough to take her away.

I am approaching adulthood. There are things I do not understand when I look back on my life. Maybe you could help me.

Meihua

While enjoying the excitement of this bold adventure, I could not guess if I would receive an answer to my letter. Somehow, deep in my sixth sense, I felt confident. I was quietly, secretly waiting for a reply.

The following Monday, there was a letter on my bed at home.

Dear Meihua,

I was so glad to receive your letter. I have not forgotten you. I still remember your big beautiful eyes staring at me, trying to get me to tell you stories. I can also recall vividly our long evenings together, talking about China's future. You are one of the most beautiful memories of those turbulent years.

Concerning Mingming, the issue is much more complicated than you can imagine. Societal pressures are too great. She could suddenly become the center of attention at school, be trashed as an evil, illegitimate child.

I think maybe we should meet sometime and talk. How about next Thursday, five O'clock at the Lidou Subway Station? You can write me to say whether that suits you or not.

Fondly, Weiming

I picked him out easily from the crowd around the subway station. His face had not changed much, high cheekbones, long straight nose and sharp eyes. His unusual curly hair made him stand out among Chinese. Age had turned him from a pale young man into a stout man with a slightly bulging belly and weathered skin. I ran toward him. When I had nearly reached him, I stopped, and said, "Uncle?" He was smiling at me, his swarthy face glowing in the dusk. I did not want to shake hands, the gesture seemed awkward to me. A hug was even more out of the question.

Finally I uttered, "It's nice...nice to see you." I cast down my eyes shyly.

"It's nice to see you! Just like your mother, what a big girl!" He came forward and shook hands with me. "Oh!" I nearly cried out. His big hands almost crushed my fingers. Then he threw his arm around my shoulders. We walked into the subway.

"How are you?" Turned, he looked into my eyes, and sounded so sweet.

"I'm okay."

"How is your mother?"

"As usual."

"What's new with your father, your brother and sister?"

"As usual."

"How is the family situation in general?"

"As usual."

"What is it about all these 'as usual's?"

"Don't you remember? Don't you remember anything about them? Don't you remember how horrible it is? You walked away scott-free. You walked away!" I snapped at him. Before he could react, I bolted toward the train. He followed me. We sat next to each other on a bench as the train rattled down the track. He was quietly looking at the window on the opposite side. In the reflection I could see his solemn face. No longer able to hold them back, my tears streamed down.

Uncle passed me a handkerchief. "I know life has not been easy for you. But I want you to know how lucky you are. You are in college. You should appreciate what you've got." He paused, embracing my shoulders with his arm. "I used to dream of going to college. But I never got the chance to."

Uncle's father was a banker before the Communists took over. He was in high school when the Cultural Revolution came along. After wandering for a few years without a job or home, he was assigned to work in the Beijing Automobile Parts Factory, which was a good luck compared with thousands of high school graduates who were forced to spend their lives working in the countryside.

He sighed and continued. "Now it's too late for me to go to college. I'm old and have forgotten most of the things I learned in school." He gazed out the subway window. His tone implied some kind of grief and repentance that I had never heard from him before. In my memories, he had always been a young and happy person.

By the time we left the subway station, it was already dark downtown. In the lighted streets, people rushed back and forth, bicycle bells ringing around us, stores closing.

Uncle walked me to the bus stop. As we were waiting, the question finally burst out. "Are you going to take Mingming away?"

A gust of wind blew my question past his ears. He did not respond.

"I know I shouldn't get into this. Please take her away, please!" I snatched his coat, pulling and shaking violently. "She's twelve years old and has already got into drinking and smoking." I cried.

"Meihua, your bus is here." He pushed me through the door. "Goodbye, college student! Write to me!"

The bus lunged. I did not answer him and cried all the way home.

I went back to school after winter vacation was over. My college life had been very quiet. Nothing went on except for studying. Students had become very diligent after ten years wasted during the "Cultural Revolution". We did not have a choice anyway. No dates or parties were permitted on campus except for special occasions. We had to be in our dormitories before eleven O'clock at night. Therefore, I had plenty of time to satisfy Uncle's expectations --- studying hard. But things did not progress wholly that way. It was impossible to keep my mind working on Physics and mathematics 12 hours a day. Although I made myself sit in the library after classes, my mind was often miles away, fantasizing romantic relationships.

I kept writing to Uncle from time to time. His answers were usually short and matter of fact, mostly about his work and his new job in the purchasing department. He rarely mentioned his family. I was not eager to see him again. He had acquired a different image after I had met him. It was hard connecting the Uncle of reality with the Uncle of my memories. First of all, he seemed not as handsome as earlier. After many years of cultivation, he had changed into an ordinary workingman from a rich playboy. Somehow, I had felt responsible for finding Mingming's real father, although his disinterest toward her had surprised me. In the back of my mind, I probably needed him too. But I had not figured out how. I did not confide in mother until I received a letter from Uncle one day.

It was Sunday afternoon. After taking the mail out the mailbox, I found Uncle's letter and tore it open.

Dear Meihua,

I have not heard from you in a while. My new job in the purchasing department is very challenging. I realize how much I have to learn. Last Sunday, I visited the area where your family lived. I rode my bicycle down the street, hoping to encounter you. But I was disappointed. Then I went to the apartment building. I saw your shadow, outlined on the curtain. I tried to imagine you laughing, joking. I stood there for two hours until my hands were frozen, my legs numb......

Fondly, Weiming

The letter made me realize that he was still the old romantic of eight years ago. Since I was so lonely and unhappy, I thought he was the one who truly liked me and needed me. I folded his letter, went to the bathroom, and read it over and over, until mother knocked on the door, to see whether I was all right. I came out, red-eyed and face full of tears.

"What happened?" Mother asked. "Are you all right?" Then she spotted the letter in my hand and snatched it away. After reading the letter, mother sighed and took me into her bedroom. "What's all this about?"

"I went to see Uncle Weiming, and then..." I told mother the whole story.

"Jesus, why do you do that for? He is history. He is gone!"

"Mother, I'm sorry."

"No, I just don't want you to make the same mistake your mother have made. He is very good at flattering girls. If you believe it, you are in trouble." Taking a deep drag of the cigarette, mother sank into deep thought. The cigarette almost burned to the end. Ashes fell on the floor.

"He was always interested in you, you know? He didn't want to be stuck with an old married lady like me. But you were still too young." She blew out smoke slowly, as though she wanted to breath out a painful memory. Then she stubbed the cigarette butt into the ashtray, twisting it hard as if to kill it.

"Stop writing to him! Stop the whole thing! Ok? I beg you. I beg youuuuu..."She grabbed my hands, bursting into tears.

"Look at your mother. Look at your mother. Am I beautiful? Am I smart? Yes. But I was much prettier, and I was smart. Please don't waste your time on someone like him. You have much more important things to do. Study, study hard!"

"Damn it! What are you guys yelling about?" Father sauntered over and pounded his fists on mother's half opened bedroom door.

"We're not talking about you."

"Then stop screaming and shouting. You're going to wake up the whole neighborhood! You don't care about your face. I do." He turned and added, "I know you guys are always plotting about murdering me. Hey, I'm going to live longer than any of you!" He wobbled away.

Mother had never revealed to me that Uncle actually had been interested in me many years ago. I was shocked. I also felt sorry for myself. If only I had known, if only I had known...... It was too late now. He was married. But still he could be my friend, maybe boyfriend. Why not, mother had done it. Having a boyfriend might solve my problems. Lately I often dreamed to be hugged and kissed by someone. I longed for someone who would care about me and listen to my complaints. But I did not like those young men in college. They might be good looking and good students. But they were too simple minded. Could they understand I had acted like a mother for my brother and sister when I was fifteen? Could they understand my mother's boyfriend and my father had lived under the same roof for many years? I was not normal. It was not easy to find someone to understand me.

Without telling mother, I had accepted an invitation from Uncle to visit his home.

On Saturday morning, I took the bus according to the directions he gave me in his letter.

It was a newly developed area. Several grey concrete apartment buildings lined the road. Others were under construction, and their naked skeletons and innards were exposed, bare and ugly.

I walked into a side street, which was the only old-fashioned alley left in the area. The third door on the left was Uncle's. I went through the squeaky wooden gate between two stone-lion sentinels. It was a traditional Chinese house, with a Square "four-corner" courtyard in the middle and rooms surrounding it on all sides. An old gray-haired man with darting eyes brushed his teeth in front of the shared outdoor sink. He smiled at me while letting the toothpaste drip from his mouth. I gave him a smirk.

I knocked at the door I thought was Uncle's. A middle-aged lady appeared.

"I am Meihua. I have come to visit Uncle Weiming."

"I am Wuhua, Weiming's wife." She took my hands, "Come on in." I followed her.

"It's nice to see you. I remember you when you were a little girl." Wuhua glanced at me, and smiled.

Good! I thought. She did not mention my mother.

Their daughter Qinmei was just getting up. Uncle was braiding her pigtail, which reminded me of the past.

"Could you fix your own pigtails now? Oh!" Uncle looked at my freshly trimmed short haircut, shook his head. "Do you still remember what I told you? Girls should have pigtails, boys have short hair."

I smiled quietly. Wuhua handed me a basket full of delicious "Big Rabbit" candies from Shanghai. After dressing Qinmei, we left for the subway station. We were going to take a ride around the new subway system.

Uncle's wife, Wuhua, was a typical working woman. She had short straight hair and dark skin. She wore an old semi-transparent polyester blouse, a pair of faded pants, and a pair of not-so-clean, soft walking shoes. Uncle carried Qinmei on his shoulders. She spun her head.

"See, Mommy, I am taller than you are!" She shouted proudly.

Wuhua and I followed quietly. I stared at the ground, counting my steps. I did not know what to say to her. She also worked in the same factory and knew a lot about mother and Uncle. To my surprise, she was very nice to me. I asked myself, "Okay, what am I doing here?" Uncle had finally given up his crazy oath to "never marry in his life". He had found a wife, had a daughter, and lived like everyone else. Why should I not leave him alone?

A gust of cool air swept my face as we walked down the stairs in the subway station. The guards, wearing winter down-coats in the late spring, with their hands in the coat pockets, walked back and forth. Their faces were shadowed, backs slightly hunched.

"Dad, tell me a story." Qinmei whispered into his ear, while we all sat together in the train.

"Which story do you want to hear?"

"I want to know what happened after the 'little cloth boy' got lost from Linlin's pocket." She stared at Uncle with two wistful eyes.

"Ok. After the 'little cloth boy' slipped out of Linlin's pocket during her primary school graduation party..."

While Uncle was talking, the window on the other side of the train turned into a mirror against the dark. The mirror reflected Uncle with his child, and his wife watching them.

Then the scene changed to one that had happened fifteen years earlier when I was seven years old. Sitting on Uncle's lap, I listened to him tell the same story. Mother sat next to us, holding a cigarette. The clanging of drums outside the window during those noisy "Cultural Revolution" demonstrations still rang in my ears.

Gradually, the scene shifted to my home when I was fourteen. Mother and I sat around the pot-bellied coal stove, listening to Uncle narrating a banned story about Mrs. Mao's illegal activities right before the fall of the "Gang of Four".

Then the scene switched to another that had occurred in the same room.

After staring at me for quite a while, Uncle said, "Meihua, do you know you have a pair of very beautiful eyes?"

"Thank you, Uncle." I put down my head and nodded shyly. Mother sat next to me, smiling. "Just like mother's." I added. I honestly thought mother was prettier than me.

"No, your mother's eyes are round like peanuts while yours are long like almonds." Uncle squinted as though he was measuring the size of my eyes.

From then on, I would look at myself in the mirror every day, trying to comprehend Uncle's comments: you have a pair of very beautiful eyes. Although I always thought my nose was too flat, my mouth too big and my face too wide, Uncle's comments were certainly encouraging. After all, my eyes were beautiful, even more beautiful than mother's. After Uncle had left, I became so unhappy that I messed up my eyesight and put on a pair of ugly glasses.

With the sad memory still floating in my mind, the scenes faded. Our trip finally came to an end. I jumped out of the train and walked forward quietly.

"I hope you didn't feel too cold in the train," said Wuhua.

"No. It's the darkness that bothers me." I answered.

She nodded. I was not sure that she understood what I was talking about. No one could imagine life with a mother who had both a husband and a boyfriend. It was a slow torture of the heart. It was like the subway system, an existence without sunlight.

It was noon. The sun struck my face. I had difficulty opening my eyes. They kept blinking for a while.

In his house, Uncle tied an apron around his waist and became the cook. Back in the past, one of the biggest joys of Uncle's visits was his cooking. I still remembered vividly how much I had liked his deep fried pork, chicken and meatballs, varieties of stir-fried dishes, and steamed fish. He sat in front of our coal stove, waiting hours for the oil to get hot. Fortunately, the gas stove he had now was much faster. As I hoped, everything arrived on the little table in the courtyard in about an hour. We sat around it on little stools. Uncle served everyone a bowl of rice. In five minutes, three pairs of chopsticks swam in the dishes of sweet and sour pork, stir-fried green beans, hot and spicy bean curd, and chicken turnip soup.

Wuhua fed Qinmei. Busy with eating, Qinmei was unusually quiet, except when she asked for what she wanted.

"No, I don't want pork, I want bean curd." She pointed her fat little finger toward the table, while trying to spit out the pork in her mouth. She had a hard time doing so because the meat had stuck between her teeth.

The neighbors were cooking and doing laundry in the yard. The stir-fry smoke and the melodies of the Peking Opera on the radio lingered in the air, like an invisible roof over the courtyard.

Uncle sat quietly through dinnertime. Unlike the others, he did not have any rice. Instead, he drank white wine. Under the shade of trees around the house, his face was like a bronze statue, solemn and motionless. Along with eating roasted peanuts, he drank slowly.

"You are at Beijing University. It must be an exciting place." Wuhua started a conversation.

"Not really. It's a very boring place." I answered.

"Boring? Why? I thought Beijing University was the number-one university in the whole country."

"Yes. But it's also very boring. Nothing happens. We spend our days in the library, studying, studying and studying."

"Is that right?" She looked lost.

"But recently it has been fun. Local free elections had turned the campus up-side-down." I thought I should tell her about another aspect of my school. "Big-letter posters about reforming our country had covered the campus like a snow storm. Candidates gave public speeches on the street corners and in the cafeterias, from morning till night. I had been to public debates every night. Sometimes the meeting hall was so crowded that we had to stand outside to listen. We discussed everything from the pros and cons of Communism and Capitalism to the Feminist movement. For the first time in three years, I discovered friendly, interesting students at my university. Finally, the citizens of Beijing West District elected one of our brightest graduate students to represent them."

Uncle and Wuhua listened quietly. Maybe it was hard for those who had wasted their youth in political movements to share my enthusiasm for the demonstrations, and to comment on the college life they had never experienced.

In a while, Uncle stood up, the shade of nearby trees scattered on his face. His eyelids glistened under the spots of sunlight. He put his hand on my shoulder, looked into my eyes and said to me, "I am going to lie down for a while. I'm tired. You and Wuhua can talk. Ok?"

He left quickly. Wuhua was about to help him into the bedroom. He pushed her back and said, "I can take care of myself."

Wuhua came back and sighed, "I am sorry. He is like that once in a while."

Seeing Uncle in such a bad mood, I began to ask myself again what I was doing here.

"Do you have to clean dishes?" Wuhua asked me, trying to put aside her worries.

"Only during weekends at home." I said, beginning to admire her.

"How lucky you are! But you'd better be prepared for it. After you get married and have children, you have to do it every day."

"I'm not sure I want to get married." I said uncertainly. In my mind the idea of "marriage" still seemed far, far away. Love was yet to come, let alone marriage.

"Why? It's nice to be married and have children." She was really surprised.

As I washed dishes at the sink, the old man I met earlier came up to me and asked, "Are you Wuhua's......"

"No, Weiming's niece."

"Oh, his brother's daughter?"

Nodding my head, I lied. During the years I grew up while mother enjoyed her modern life style, I had learned how terrible gossip could be. Gossips could chop you into pieces. Wuhua handed me more dishes and turned around, facing down the old man.

"Hey, what are you doing here? Does she bother you? Let me tell you it's none of your business who she is! You'd better piss on the ground, and admire yourself in it!" Then she grabbed the dishpan from my hands, and walked back into her home.

Wuhua hung some winter jackets and blankets outside to make use of the bright summer sunshine.

Walking through the house alone, I noticed two books lying on top of the dresser. One was high school algebra; the other was a book about international trade. I opened the second one, started reading. The clock struck 3. I wondered about my being there. It had been an hour and half since Uncle had gone to sleep.

I tiptoed into the bedroom. Uncle snored heavily. With his eyes half open, his rough, freckled face was red and twisted. His chest bulged. His hands were clenched into fists. It seemed he was ready to fight someone in his dream. The longer I stayed, the louder his snoring became. It resonated in my head like the humming of a primitive song, like a desperate cry, like the rumbling of thunder. Then it stopped. Uncle was awake.

He stared at me with red, sleepy eyes. I rushed toward him. He grabbed my arms and murmured, "Meihua, Meihua, is that you?" His dry cracked lips trembled.

"Yes, Uncle." I moved closer to him. He opened his mouth again, and struggled to say something. But he sighed and dropped his head instead. "Meihua, would you leave here, please?" My heart, which had risen up in my throat, now plunged down like an anchor deep into the sea. I quietly stood up and walked toward the door.

"Meihua, wait a minute." Uncle got up quickly, opened the bottom draw of the dresser and pulled out a beautiful pair of stone washed blue jeans. "Please give these to Mingming." Then he turned around and never looked back.

The sun glared in the sky like an iron sphere, the air hot and still. Summer had arrived. Young women, wearing bright colored skirts and broad brim hats, rode their bikes slowly and beautifully. Young men, dressed in tight blue jeans and fashionable sunglasses, comfortably wrapped their arms around the young ladies' bare smooth shoulders.

I adjusted my sight, and everything became much clearer. I walked faster, trying to catch up with everyone.

CHINESE LOLITA WILL BE AVAILABLE FOR PURCHASE IN 2012

VISIT FANTASY ISLAND BOOK PUBLISHING

www.fantasyislandbookpublishing.com

FOR UPDATES ON ALL OUR EXCITING

PRINT BOOK AND DIGITAL RELEASES

Also by Fantasy Island Book Publishing

A Way About – Roxanne Barbour

After Ilium - Stephen Swartz

Binary – Jennifer Coons

Black Numbers - Dean Frank Lappi

Brother, Betrayed - Danielle Raver

Children of the Elementi - Ceri Clark

City of Champions - Daniel Stanton

Darkness Rising - Ross M. Kitson

Devil's Kitchen - Alison DeLuca

Ednor Scardens - Kathleen Barker

Emeline and the Mutants - Rachel Tsoumbakos

Enchanted Heart - Brianna Lee McKenzie

Land of Nod, The Artifact - Gary Hoover

Losing Beauty - Johanna Garth

Sakuri - Jacob Henzel

Sax and the Suburb - Marilyn Rucker Norrod

Silent No More - Krista K. Hatch

Sin - Shaun Allan

Sons of Roland: Back Story - Nicole Antonia Carson

Terps - Elaine Gannon

Tower of Bones - Connie J Jasperson

The Last Good Knight - Connie J Jasperson

The Last Guardian - Joan Hazel

The Lollipop Club - J. Darroll Hall

The Night Watchman Express - Alison DeLuca

Sand - Lili Tufel

Made in the USA
Lexington, KY
02 April 2012